THE KNOWLAND RETRIBUTION

FORTHCOMING BY RICHARD GREENER

The Lacey Confession

THE KNOWLAND RETRIBUTION

RICHARD GREENER

MIDNIGHT INK
WOODBURY, MINNESOTA

First Edition
First Printing, 2006

Book design by Donna Burch
Cover design by Lisa Novak
Cover photo © 2005 by Nicholas Hughes / Getty Images
Edited by Karin Simoneau

Midnight Ink, an imprint of Llewellyn Publications

Library of Congress Cataloging-in-Publication Data
Greener, Richard, 1941–
The Knowland retribution: a novel / by Richard Greener.
p. cm.
ISBN-13: 978-0-7387-0862-1
ISBN-10: 0-7387-0862-3
1. Escherichia coli infections—Fiction. 2. Revenge—Fiction. I. Title.

PS3607.R4535K59 2006
813'.6—dc22 2005052251

Any Internet references contained in this work are current at publication time, but the publisher cannot guarantee that a specific location will continue to be maintained. Please refer to the publisher's website for links to authors' websites and other sources.

This is a work of fiction. Names, characters, places, and incidents are either the product of the author's imagination or are used fictitiously, and any resemblance to actual persons, living or dead, business establishments, events, or locales is entirely coincidental.

Midnight Ink
Llewellyn Publications
2143 Wooddale Drive, Dept. 0-7387-0862-3
Woodbury, MN 55125-2989, U.S.A.
www.midnightinkbooks.com

Printed in the United States of America

To Phil,
who asked, while choking on a pastrami sandwich,
"You're writing a novel?"

". . . while the future's there for anyone to change,
still you know it seems,
it could be easier sometimes to change the past."

—Jackson Browne

PROLOGUE

New York

THE HUDSON RIVER BEGAN with a single drop of water in the wilderness. It fell from a leaf or blade of grass into Lake Tear of the Clouds, no more than a pond on the shoulders of Mt. Marcy, the highest peak in the Adirondacks. It flowed downhill, gathered speed, increased its number. Each drop joined others of its kind, first one, then another, and another, until there were many billions—trillions—a number so immense it could not be imagined.

That's how this began, unseen and unnoticed, with something microscopic, so small no one could see it, marshalling the wicked force of nature as its ally, eager to pour down devastation upon all who touched it. Many things start long after they've actually begun. This was such a thing.

It started on June 25 with Pat Grath's phone call to Wesley Pitts. Pitts was, as always, the first one awake. Grath called at five thirty in the morning New York time knowing full well Wesley Pitts had been in his office at least fifteen minutes and was already settled in for the day. From his office window, looking out into the morning darkness, Pitts could see the Hudson River three hundred miles from its obscure beginning, expanding through New York Harbor, pushing out to open sea. What he couldn't see were the cows.

Caller ID told Pitts it was Pat Grath in Houston on the other end of the line.

"Hi, Pat," he said cheerfully. "How you doing? Four-thirty. You're up a little early this morning."

"Yeah," Grath said, exhibiting none of his trademark jovial nature. "Ain't that the truth." The concern and worry in his voice plus the early hour in Texas gave Pitts an uneasy feeling. An urge deep inside him cried out, *"Run!"*

Grath said, "Look Wes, I've got Billy Mac with me here. We've got a little problem."

"Oh, Christ," thought Wesley Pitts. Nobody, certainly not Pat Grath, calls him with a "little" problem at this time of day. For the tiniest fraction of a second Pitts thought the unthinkable. He wondered if the problem, whatever it was, would disappear if he simply told his biggest clients to fuck off and hung up the phone. Instead, in his most charming and confident voice, he said, "Tell me about it."

ONE

St. John

Cruz Bay is a dumpy little town. It sits alongside the largest harbor of St. John Island under a broiling sun, cooled only slightly by intermittent breezes. St. John is part of the United States, but only because they say so.

The people are Caribbean. The island is neglected. The roads are narrow, bent, and curved, in terrible condition—nearly undrivable here and there. They paint orange circles around potholes but never fill them in. All buildings except the posh hillside and hilltop homes appear to be in some state of disrepair. The island is littered with old and broken cars. When a car stops running they push it off to the side and carry on.

Except in Cruz Bay, the capital, there's no way garbage can be collected at the source because large trucks cannot manage these single-lane, hilly roads winding their way through and around the narrow, nine-mile island. Instead, St. John makes do with frequent drop-off points where the locals, and the visitors too, pile up large bins of loose garbage, brightly colored plastic bags—large and small, stuffed to bursting—empty beer cases, anything else they no longer need. Most will concede, with varying degrees of interest in the subject, that this detracts from the beauty of the place, from its natural charm.

The island does have remarkable good points. Nearly two-thirds form a national park, splendid and untouched. St. John has some of the most beautiful beaches anywhere in the world. And, best of all, there's no way to reach St. John except by boat. The much larger St. Thomas looms nearby, twenty minutes by ferry. Still, St. John is not a busy spot. When you rent a car they tell you there's a thousand dollar charge, a fine really, for taking your car on the ferry to St. Thomas. How will they know? You ask yourself this only until, and it does not take long, you realize that they know everything. It's a small place. The permanent population comes to less than four thousand, including the exiles: the twenty-two-year-old girls from Seattle and Boston and Sioux City who've run away for however long it takes them to go island nuts waiting tables in Cruz Bay. St. John's four hundred or so vacation homes and villas accommodate a couple of thousand owners, renters, and guests at high season. A few campers come for the park. Most people shop at the island's two supermarkets and there's nothing super about either. It's a great place for scuba diving and looking at fish, if that's the kind of thing you like, but there's no golf course on St. John and that keeps the riffraff out. It lacks the Old World allure of Curacao, the mystery of Grand Cayman, or the sexy extravagance of St. Barts, but St. John is the perfect place to be if you're looking to be alone.

Walter Sherman often found himself contemplating one or another of these points. The old habit never ceased to give him satisfaction. He felt good now, comfortable in his regular seat in Billy's, second from last at the end of the bar, away from the street and near the standing fan next to the kitchen door. Cruz Bay is a bar town. Walter liked Billy's best. It nestled securely on the west edge of the square, directly across from the slip where the St. Thomas ferry docked. Like most island bars, Billy's is an open-air establishment, dependent on rare cool winds off the water and a few large fans for comfort. It admits more than enough natural light to require sunglasses for some, and to welcome the affectation of hip shades by others. Billy's wide open front is guarded by a low, white picket fence separating it from the sidewalk. The white tables, some nearest the front with colored umbrellas, lead to a rosewood bar that runs the whole length of the building at the far end. Behind the bar, with a full view of his kitchen, Billy holds court. When he was on the island, Walter breakfasted at Billy's most mornings, took an occasional lunch there, and every so often, dinner too. But no one could remember Walter being in Billy's later than that. This morning he sipped his routine Diet Coke and quietly ate scrambled eggs with toast. He was trying hard to forget about a newly painted pothole, forty feet down the road from his hillside home, and was reading the obit page of the *New York Times* when heavy steps broke the silence around him. He glanced quickly toward the wide doorway.

Walter Sherman was in his mid-fifties, of average height, and, like most men his age, at least twenty pounds heavier than he wanted to be. He wore his hair long in the back, but carefully combed and not so long as to attract attention. He hadn't lost much of it, but over time the color had changed from dark brown. It looked washed out, and it was streaked with gray, especially around the ears. Women commented favorably on his leathery tan and pale-blue eyes. He thought he looked good, even in Billy's scratchy bar mirror, but he also looked a good fifty plus. He was clean-shaven and dressed in his usual faded jeans and oversized pastel T-shirt. It gave him a casual appearance that some mistook for messiness. He was no tourist, and it didn't take much to spot that.

It was late September and this time Walter had been gone almost a week—Boston, Pittsburgh, and, finally, of all places to find someone, Beckley, West Virginia. All three were disappointingly wet and cold for this time of year. The whole east coast had been an unpleasant mess. The island's morning heat felt glorious. The back of his neck at the top of his shirt under his hair was damp with sweat. He loved working up a sweat, especially when all it took was eating breakfast. Walter spotted the three newcomers right off the bat. How could he miss them? One large black man, two white men. They wore suits, shirts, and ties, and dark socks and shoes with laces—the kind you never see around here. They were not renters, or owners, or guests. They might have been FBI, or some other law enforcement wasting their time worrying about cigarette boats smuggling crack from Tortola, but the suits were custom-made and the haircuts too expensive. They looked well rested. Walter gently crunched another piece of toast. These guys, he decided, flew into St. Thomas late yesterday, took the afternoon ferry, and ended up at Caneel Bay or the Westin, probably the latter because it's closer to town. They awoke this morning and, hard as it might be for some to believe, got dressed like they were going to work in New York City. They were traveling light—one very slightly wrinkled suit each.

He swigged his Diet Coke and turned to the *Times* business section because nothing else there interested him. His focus on the three was now complete. He was not at all surprised when, after two minutes of guarded grunts and glances, one of them approached.

Before the man had a chance to say anything at all, Walter said, in his loosely strung, neighborly voice, "Sit down." He motioned to the seat beside him, the last one before the fan and the kitchen door. "Who are *you*?" he asked amiably, as the big man's broad bottom hit the high wooden seat.

"My name is Tom Maloney," the visitor spoke pleasantly, through a slight, formal grin. Pretty calm too, thought Walter, who tended to make quick and lasting judgments about people. Every woman he'd ever loved, he'd loved at first sight. He'd been told many times, mostly by ex-lovers, that this was a serious character flaw. Walter saw it as a mixed blessing but a definite net plus, a self-protective reflex he was sure had saved him more than once in the rush of the past thirty years. Maloney was Walter's age, give or take a few either way—round-featured, smooth-skinned, and pink. He had thin, once-blond, once-wavy hair, heavy shoulders, and a big, Irish beer belly just about hidden by a skillfully cut chocolate silk suit. Rich, no doubt, and smart too. But still a messenger for one of the other two. "Which?" flitted across Walter's mind.

He liked this one.

"What can I do for you, Tom?"

"You are Walter Sherman, aren't you?"

"Yeah." Walter lifted his sparse eyebrows and took a longer sip. "You want one of these?"

"No. No thanks," Maloney grinned a little more easily. "Too early for me."

"You know who I am. You wouldn't be sitting here if you didn't."

"Right," Maloney's cherubic face broke into the full, friendly smile Walter knew it would. "That's why we're here," he said. "Is there some place we can talk?"

Walter took another forkful of eggs, folded his paper, and put it down on the bar. He looked back at Maloney's companions—giant and micro-man—whispering by the door, and his voice rose half an octave, acquiring an edge. "The way you guys are dressed it better be someplace air conditioned." Then he spoke softly again, demonstrating his regard for Tom. "Meet me here." He handed Maloney a bar napkin with an address he'd scribbled. "Five o'clock. You can introduce us then, not now."

"Excellent," Maloney said. "Excellent."

"Take a cab," Walter called after them as Tom urged his party into the sunlight, "You'll never find it on your own. And dress comfortably, for God's sake."

He had no idea who these guys were, but he knew what they wanted, why they needed to see him. The coming scene had played out many times before, not necessarily here on St. John, but always along predictable lines.

An unhappy high school counselor once told Walter that few people know much in advance what their life's work will be. Some doctors perhaps, because their parents make the decision for them when they are born. Some sons of business owners who must prepare to become *& Sons*, often to their lifelong chagrin. Conceivably, a handful of precociously pious pastors get the call in the cradle. But how many children tell their friends, "I want to sell office equipment"? How many college students look in the mirror and practice asking, "You want fries with that?" And few, if any, Walter learned, ever intended to wind up teaching high school physics to the underequipped, let alone advising profoundly limited youngsters on their career options.

Walter Sherman was called neither to God nor to medicine. He had no father, not even an uncle who owned a business. He sold his share of french fries, but never considered teaching physics or anything else. He joined the Army at eighteen, on his birthday, in 1970. He had nothing better to do. As he still sometimes said when thinking it was appropriate—it seemed like a good idea at the time. At the time he was a high school graduate working as a car washer and gofer-boy at a local Ford dealership. He was living in his mother's house just outside of Rhinebeck, New York. Before he could say "I made a mistake!" he was in Vietnam. He could not remember why he re-upped, but he did. When he left the Army at twenty-five he had no better idea of how to make a living than he'd had seven years before. The army had trained him with guns and knives and handheld explosives. If Dutchess County New York had that kind of work available, he didn't know where it was. Nor did he know anyone who needed to be found.

Colonel DeScortovachino called Mrs. Sherman's house on a rainy Sunday in the spring of 1977. The call gave Walter's life direction.

"Walter!" the Colonel began in a false-hearty tone.

"Who is this?"

He introduced himself as "Colonel D" and explained that Walter's Vietnam CO was now attached to the Colonel's unit, hence Colonel D's "fortuitous awareness" of Walter.

"Son," he intoned, "I need your help." The Colonel was assigned to The School of the Americas and lived near Fort Benning just outside Columbus, Georgia. His sixteen-year-old daughter, Jessie, was nowhere to be found.

"She's not really missing," the Colonel said, "She just ran away. Her mother says we . . . shit, that's not important. My point is that Jessie's gone." His voice changed just then. Its theatrical flourish fell away and a strange, melancholy pleading rose to soften the Colonel's military twang. Walter didn't recognize it then, but over the years he came to know that sound well. It signaled a desperation only someone who's *lost* someone feels. It was all about *lost* and *missing*. *Dead* may or may not kill you, but, Walter learned, *lost* and *missing* rip the insides with hot knives. *Lost* and *missing* produce a perpetual frenzy of mind that makes many people think they are close to insane every minute of every day. Such people always had, when their energy flagged, that sorrowful sound in their voice.

Walter didn't need to ask why a colonel a thousand miles away, a man who didn't know him from Adam's uncle, would make such a call.

In the absurd jungle that was Saigon in the early 1970s, Walter was often called by the descriptive nickname *Locator*. It wasn't a funny nickname like Bonehead or Lardass, or chummy, like Chip or Chief. It wasn't the kind of nickname you used to bum smokes. Nobody said, "Locator, got a butt?" This was a nickname of the highest order. It was earned. The earning of it started with a member of Walter's platoon who'd gone AWOL.

There were, as Walter recalled, two reasons most soldiers ran away, which was all that AWOL really was—running away, escaping jail, dashing to imagined safety somewhere. Either they went temporarily nuts—from the combat, from the drugs, from the simple unrelenting madness of what was going on—or they went over; defected. American MPs in Saigon took little joy in finding the nutcases. They followed the drugs; followed the girls. They usually found their AWOL soon enough. But after a week, if the missing soldier wasn't found, he became a "motherfucker," a political deserter. MPs got off on them because the reward for becoming political could be death. The order of the day was no longer "find and return," but "dispatch." More AWOLs turned up as combat deaths than anyone talked about.

When Freddy Russo—a hard drinking, drug using, pussy-chasing Chicago hitter—took off, the MPs searched for a week but couldn't find him. Walter knew they'd kill him when they did. Walter and Russo had hardly spoken, but an odd, insistent impulse moved him to see his CO and request permission to find the man before headquarters issued its next order. On the spur of the moment Walter lied. He told the CO that Russo had saved his life one night in a very notorious bar. In truth, no such thing had ever happened. Freddy was no friend of his, but Walter knew they would kill him and he knew he could prevent it. He asked for two days, certain he wouldn't need that much time. Walter did not think of himself as especially well organized. His mother, however, always marveled that her son, so unlike most children, never lost anything. And if something—a pair of socks, a jacket, a book, or a toy—was missing, Walter always found it. Should his mother misplace her purse she called for Walter. As a teenager he never "forgot" where he parked the car or lost his keys or his wallet, and his knack of finding other people's lost belongings became a mysterious aspect of his personality. Walter thought too much was made of it.

He found Russo the next morning—never said how—happily lounging in a ditch behind the whorehouse where Russo had never saved anyone, where in fact, he once watched coolly, smirking, while Walter talked his way past two drunk Navy Seals bent on mayhem. Russo was covered in God knows what, still drunk, and narrowing his eyes to work the last quarter inch of a joint that smelled like buffalo dung. Walter returned the ungrateful Freddy to his platoon. The CO covered his ass by sending the MPs a report saying there had been a mistake, that Specialist 4th Class F. Russo had been injured while off duty and had thus been unable to contact his unit until that morning. The written report credited Pfc. Walter Sherman with the "rescue."

Walter's Vietnam was an evil funhouse with no sense of proportion and few secrets. Everyone soon had a version of the event—and the Locator tag was born. Two weeks after, Walter's CO received an order assigning Walter to Headquarters Company. Now he was to find someone else—not an AWOL, not a political. This one was a bona fide POW. They airdropped Walter in the middle of fucking nowhere and he cursed himself all the way down. Still cursing, he trudged alone into the buggy jungle to find a captured American helicopter pilot. The officers who sent him on this mission and the helicopter crew that delivered him never expected to see Walter Sherman again. He turned up three weeks later with a gangrenous toe and identifiable fragments of the pilot's body. Walter was soon a sergeant and his only job after that was finding people. Sometimes he looked for Americans, other times Vietnamese. He found them more often than not, mildly bemused that others could not. Then Walter went home to civilian life, too old and too wise for college.

When the Colonel called, Walter was working whatever hours he could for a food distribution warehouse. He pushed boxes of fruit juice from here to there and loaded cases of canned vegetables onto trucks. Some weeks he worked seven days and overtime. Other weeks he had no work at all.

"What do you want me to do?" he asked the Colonel.

"Find her. Bring her home."

"Well, I got a job now, and I have to work—"

"I'm not asking favors, son. I have money and I'll pay you whatever it is." That sound again.

"Okay, sir," said Walter. And so saying he stumbled onto the path that brought him a better life.

He found the Colonel's daughter four days later in Panama City, Florida. She was over her head in sex, drugs, and rock 'n roll, and not always rock 'n roll. He didn't clean her up. He just took her home. The Colonel paid Walter a thousand dollars. During much of the flight to New York he kept his hand in his pocket, on the money.

Locator.

Reputations grow most quickly in sensitive lines of work. Walter had a talent made for an apparently insatiable market. The sons and daughters of notable people—rich ones, celebrities, public figures; mostly, in fact, the daughters—were opting for the AWOL life in very impressive numbers. Almost all of the younger ones, the kids in their early teens, were into sex and drugs. Once they had some of either they couldn't get enough. For the older ones, the college kids, it was parents driving them over the edge, and they just had to get away. Rarely did any have any idea of how to avoid being captured. Their survival skills amounted to a credit card and a Holiday Inn. They were easy for Walter, if not others, to catch.

He found wives who'd slammed the door and peeled off in the Mercedes and forgotten the way back. There were endless embarrassing family members, the boozy, brawling brother-in-law, the loving husband gone deep underground, the off-kilter auntie who thought the better of coming home from the club one day. It might be the CEO taking a breather from heterosexual pretense, so much in love that he failed to notice the passing of the time. It might be his horsehide-happy spouse. The kinkier the sex, the more anxious the contracting party; the more the client was more than willing to pay.

Famous, wealthy, and public people, Walter quickly discovered, can be embarrassed by almost anyone close to them. When those close disappeared, when they went *missing* or *lost*, and especially when they seriously intended to stay that way, Walter was the man their protectors found to find them. He much preferred the droll situations, the high-priced peccadilloes. It was the melancholy Walter could do without, the hard-core human interest.

He made it his business to offer his clients the commodity they held most precious: privacy. He didn't start a firm. He didn't promote himself. He did not become *Walter Sherman, P.I.* He didn't print cards, open an office, have a secretary, or even a phone. He worked only by referral. You couldn't get to him unless you knew someone who knew someone who knew someone else. Consequently, he did not do this work often, and for another year continued his shifts at the warehouse. But that, his mother pointed out, was how to really advertise discretion.

Back then, if you did your due diligence and actually managed to talk to Walter Sherman, you did so on his mother's line. And before he stepped foot out of her house, you'd had someone hand-deliver a box full of fifties and hundreds.

TWO

St. John

"OFF THE RACK?" ASKED the old black man sitting at one of Billy's tables, the square, chronically creaky one nearest the front. "I don't think so!"

He was short and thin like an old broom handle. He wore a close-cut white beard and had almost no hair under a pink baseball cap sporting the red bulldozer logo of a construction company on St. Thomas. His small, delicate, deeply creased face always seemed to be smiling, and maybe it was. The smile showed a full set of wonderfully large and strong-looking yellow teeth. Ike had to sit near the front because he smoked cigarettes one after another and Billy hated smoke. That particular dislike struck Walter as a singular disadvantage for a man who owned a bar. But there it was.

"Tailor made," said Walter.

Ike nodded contentedly. "New York or Hong Kong? I'll say Hong Kong. They make a lot of suits over there in Asia." Ike nodded again, this time definitively.

"Italy." Walter told him.

"Italy?" Ike half-whispered, half in agreement, half not. "What you think, Billy?"

Billy Smith wasn't his real name—William Mantkowski was—but the locals laughed at that jumble of sounds and divided it into five parts, with witty pauses between each and prolonged laughter at the end. After a month on St. John, William Mantkowski rechristened himself Billy Smith. He bought a bar called Frogman's and, once in charge, changed absolutely nothing except the name on the sign out front. No one on St. John asks a white man where his money comes from. That was eleven years ago. Walter had been a regular at Frogman's, and, like the furniture, stayed.

"New York," said Billy, leaning back on the other side of the bar opposite Walter at the far end. His skinny, ostrich-skinned elbows rested on the faded gray formica liquor shelf behind him. He stood there, tall and bone-white, almost as white, it seemed to Walter, as his ugly rugby shirt, shaking his head like he had some great wisdom he was about to impart. "Italian tailor, maybe, but the suits are from New York. Where exactly, who knows. But New York." He meant that he couldn't specify where in Manhattan this New York tailor tailored. He jutted his thick, black-stubbled jaw.

"They all from New York?" Ike squinted as he pursued the investigation, absently blowing smoke from his mouth into his nose.

"Ike, that shit will kill you," Billy growled. "Yeah, they're all from New York, and the suits too. Right Walter?"

Walter shook his head. "Made in Italy."

"Hong Kong," mumbled Ike.

"Write it up, Billy," said Walter, confirming closure.

Billy shambled to the center of the bar, grabbed a blue chalk stub from beside the fifty-year-old cash register, and carefully printed several more words onto the four-foot-square rimless blackboard propped against the streaked and pitted mirror. They were: "New York/Hong Kong/Italy." He was confident New York would garner the most votes.

"Walter, you know the problem with New York?"

"No, Ike, what's the problem with New York?"

"Too big," the old man said gravely. "Too damn big."

In that instant Walter's thoughts alighted again on Tom Maloney and the substantial possibility that by bedtime he'd have in hand just the type of assignment he liked best—one involving excellent money and minimal human interest—which caused him to surprise his friends with a sweetly incongruous smile. "And too fucking cold in the winter," he said.

THREE

Atlanta

"SORRY, NO TIME," SAID Leonard Martin.

Nina turned to him, disappointed.

"Harvey just called. He wants me there. You know he wouldn't bother me if he didn't have a reason."

Nina's frown stayed put. He knew what she was thinking and took her unspoken point. "He's not imagining things. It's a difficult deal. He spoke with the client last night. The old man's in a mood."

She gave him the smirk that never changed, narrowing her left eye—clear and hazel-bright as ever—bunching up the smooth, curved lips that still held their exquisite shape. Through it all, he'd loved her skepticism.

"Did Harvey tell you that?"

"Not in so many words. He hates to admit he can't handle it. But he said he'd like me there. And I bet that's what it is. But you make the decision. I can have breakfast with you and the kids, and I'd really love to do it. But if something goes wrong with this big ol' deal, and something or other falls through the cracks, and it's all 'cause an old client's gout is making him act difficult . . ."

She turned to the bowl of batter she'd been fixing. They'd had a good night, the first in a while. She was feeling happy and too unsure to risk his eyes going distant. "Then get your big ass to wherever you're going." She turned her head back for a kiss and said, "I'll tell the boys you're making millions to build a basketball court behind their house."

"I'll do it, too," said Leonard Martin, "and don't you think I won't."

His daughter pulled into the drive as he closed the front door behind him. The boys poured out of the van.

"Where you going, Grandpa? Ain't you having breakfast?" Mark, the eight-year-old, grabbed him around the waist. Mark's younger brother Scott hung back. Scott was thinner, quiet as an infant, reserved and grave as a child—very much his father's child, and far more deeply affected when his father moved out. Leonard told his grandson he had to skip breakfast and added, loud enough for Ellie to hear, "Tell your mom not to pay much attention to anything your nana might say about basketball courts."

"See you later, Daddy. We're going to go shopping. Why don't you come home for lunch?" She kissed his cheek and gave his belly a pat. He stood in the driveway, listening as the three of them bustled inside.

It was eight forty-five on a beautiful Thursday morning in June. From the driveway he could see bright sunlight pouring into the high kitchen windows. The still, cool air shifted gently. The doors to the back deck were open and he imagined the air slipping through the house and into the kitchen, bringing with it the sounds around him, the early morning bird calls, the voices of golfers already on the second fairway not thirty yards from the house.

And they had a fine breakfast without him. Nina and Ellie threw apple chunks into the scratch batter in the bowl, and they heaped each plate with Georgia's Own pork sausage, honey-sweet and dripping with country flavor, grilled on an open skillet, filling the house with the scent of heaven itself. The boys gulped milk and the women sipped cappuccino from the coffee machine Leonard forced his wife to buy on the last day of their last trip to Milan. Harvey Daniels had been right. This client was in a mood. It wasn't that the deal would go bad. They were all too committed for that. But when any client starts picking at legal language, delay was in the cards. He did it to satisfy some inner need, very likely to make whatever his ailment behave, and nine times out of ten it was mistaken for conscientious representation.

The firm of Stevenson, Daniels, Martin, had long ago learned that client whims meant time lost sprinting in circles. They'd also discovered the remedy: Leonard's patented, "Fuck with us Jim or John or Joan and it all goes down the crapper" speech, delivered in a corner, in a serious, menacing tone, but always accompanied by a semi-friendly poke or elbow-squeeze.

Harvey had tried it once. The client took offense and nit-picked all the more fiercely. None of them ever considered Nick Stevenson for the role. This time the ploy worked especially well; Jim allowed that Honest to God he had no *serious* problems. The papers got signed and another developer staked his claim to fifty more acres of doomed Georgia pine.

Leonard Martin, Harvey Daniels, and Nicholas Stevenson partnered in 1973. Lenny and Harvey, novice attorneys, were part of Atlanta's late sixties population explosion. They'd come for jobs at the same big downtown firm. Every time it snowed in New York or Chicago, two dozen lawyers applied for a job in Atlanta. That was the office joke. There were kernels of truth in the gag and they didn't try to deny it; Atlanta was warm and wonderful.

Lenny and Harvey bought pricey new homes in the growing northern suburbs. They were among the first to join an exclusive North Fulton golf club. A partner joked that the club was so far north that they should have done it right, found one in Tennessee. They were also among the first to see the riches that real estate law had to offer down the road. Atlanta was growing so fast, so many people were moving in, so many homes were being built—and so few lawyers were even half awake—that they took one good look and made the leap. They approached Nicholas Stevenson, a laid-back Southern gent with a one-man real estate practice out in Dunwoody. Stevenson was a few years older and the butt of collegial humor concerning his ethics. He was considered obsessively honest. He agreed that the boom was only beginning. They formed Stevenson, Daniels, Martin, Attorneys at Law, and set their sights on closing more real estate deals than any firm in Atlanta.

Five years later they were in six locations. By 1983 they had eleven—in Fulton, Cobb, and Gwinnett counties. The next ten years took them farther north—into Cherokee county, Forsyth, and Hall. Now they had sixteen offices, all doing upscale residential work—from sleek, modern condos in Buckhead, to million dollar retreats up on Lake Lanier, to old-boy mansions down in the wool hat country around West Paces Ferry. But their focus remained on Atlanta's astounding northern sprawl. They soon got into commercial transactions, helping to turn north metro into a land of office towers, convention hotels, and mall developments everywhere. When they celebrated their twentieth year, each of the three was earning eight hundred thousand dollars plus.

Leonard and Nina vacationed in Europe and week-ended at their beachfront condo on Hilton Head Island off South Carolina. They educated Ellie in Atlanta's top private schools, then sent her off to Duke, the school everyone in their circle called the Princeton of the South. When Ellie came home she married a systems analyst, Carter Lawrence. Leonard and Nina helped them buy a house in nearby Roswell. When, after Scotty was born, Ellie lost interest in her marriage, they tried to turn her around. But she'd done nothing very exciting at Duke and wildness took hold of her ten years late. While they could not keep Ellie and Carter together, they did keep Carter close. Now that she was quieting down, Leonard hoped they might try again, but Nina had her doubts. Carter never found anyone else, *and* the boys were his only real interest, *and* he'd set himself up as some kind of consultant, *and* seemed to be making a go of it . . . *and* Leonard had his hopes.

Leonard had two hobbies. He played golf, badly. Unlike most men, however, he really enjoyed it. He cared nothing about the score. "You're the only one I ever play with," Harvey told him, "who doesn't cheat." Why should he? Four, five, six, whatever—it didn't matter. Leonard liked getting up early and going out to the course while the grass was still wet and you could see the steam and haze all the way down the fairway. He liked riding in those silly golf carts, racing up hills, taking the turns too fast, always scaring Harvey, who seemed in constant fear that they were about to crash. Most of all he liked hitting the ball. Where it went was secondary. He was thrilled by the feel of the metal clubhead against the cover of the ball. The tension in his arms and legs. The sound—the hoped-for sharp click. The divot. The flight of the ball even when it went into the woods. Leonard had a wonderful time playing golf. Aside from his family, his business, and golf, Leonard's great passion was reserved for acting. He joined the North Georgia Community Players soon after he and Nina moved to Alpharetta. "Go on," she'd urged him when he mentioned it one day. He did some acting in college. He was in a few plays and Nina knew he loved it. In his thirties he often played the male lead, the romantic lead if lucky, or the featured male role, the best friend, partner, sidekick, even villain. In his forties his frame got heavier and his parts got smaller, but his years of experience seemed to bring a deeper understanding to all his roles than they usually received in community theater productions. His biggest success was as Lenny in *Of Mice and*

Men. The play was such a hit that the company brought it back, by popular demand, every two or three years. No matter who played the other roles, Leonard Martin was always the slow-witted, vulnerable Lenny. His friends kidded him about it, pretending to be a little retarded themselves, and Leonard's real name didn't hurt his association with the role. "You really are Lenny," was something he heard many times. He considered it a compliment.

Barbara Coffino joined the company when Leonard was at the height of his *Mice and Men* popularity. She was an artist, a jewelry designer with her own studio in Dahlonaga, a thriving arts and crafts village complete with a town square surrounded by antique shops, art galleries, and a scattering of coffeehouses and restaurants. Originally the town had been the site of the great gold rush that hit the Georgia Mountains years before anyone thought there might be gold in the west. Although many Californians would hate to know it, the famous call "there's gold in them thar hills" referred to Dahlonaga, Georgia. The dome of the Georgia State Capitol on Martin Luther King, Jr. Boulevard in downtown Atlanta shines brightly in the southern sun coated with pure Georgia gold. Every ounce of it came from Dahlonaga. Barbara Coffino used some of that gold to make her jewelry.

She was a little older and just a little heavier, but she was often told she looked like Debra Winger. She certainly had some of the actress's sexy, self-confident attitude. Leonard did a Chekhov play with her during her first season with the Players. She played a Russian woman of high nobility, and her costume was a flowing gown with a high waist, plunging neckline, and significant cleavage. One night she came off stage and whispered in his ear, "You have to stop looking at me like that—or ask me out."

Their affair began that night. He and Nina had been together for so long, since college. It's not that they had grown apart, but the spark was not much more than an ember and the heat was on low flame. He couldn't help himself. He wanted Barbara and she wanted him. Barbara was divorced. Leonard, of course, had a wife and family. That fact seemed to bother him more than her. Barbara was content to spend time with Leonard as the opportunity arose. She led a busy, independent life. She made no demands on him that he was unable to fulfill. She had no intention of breaking up his family or of ever marrying Leonard Martin or anyone. They didn't sneak around. Leonard never told Nina he had to meet someone for dinner or go out of town on business. He was always home for dinner. He was his own boss, answerable only to his partners. He made his own schedule. He would drive the forty-five minutes to Dahlonaga, spend a morning or an afternoon with Barbara, then drive back. Sure, he told the small lies. He'd say to Nina he had to get going early for a morning meeting. Sometimes, when Nina would call to see if Leonard could meet her for lunch, he would beg off, using the excuse he had to be somewhere else or that he just couldn't get away. Most of the time Nina thought he was looking at a piece of real estate for a client or for some other purpose. At least Leonard believed that was what she thought and she never gave him reason to believe otherwise. So he told the little lies, nothing big, nothing specific. He had no trouble telling them. If she didn't know, she couldn't be hurt. He almost convinced himself he was doing the noble thing. When he refused breakfast this morning it was not because he was driving to Dahlonaga. At least not until later. He hadn't seen Barbara in more than a week. He looked forward to spending the morning in bed with her.

As Ellie and others were fond of observing, middle age brought unwanted physical change. Leonard's waistline had grown apace with his escalating net worth. Throughout the Reagan boom and into the Clinton years his stock investments and property interests thrived. Each year brought larger bonuses and shame-faced trips to the tailor.

All in all, Leonard and Nina Martin thought they had a bit more than most—certainly more than folks who didn't like work, or had no get-up-and-go. They enjoyed their church, and loved their friends, and though neither was ignorant, or dense, or callous, both considered themselves the most average of Americans.

Leonard's cell phone rang just before noon. He would not have taken it, but the phone was nearby and he saw that the call came from Ellie's cell. She rarely called him, and Leonard felt a sharp concern that something was wrong with the boys. The voice was Mark's.

"We're having a cookout, Grandpa. Mamma and Nana said they want you to come here right now and eat some burgers with us by the pool. Okay?"

It was then that Nina took the phone from Mark. She said, "How about it? You want some?"

"How come the boys are still there?"

"They've been here all morning, in the pool mostly. They look like a couple of prunes. Ellie went shopping, but she's back and we're going to have a cookout—delicious, juicy, rare burgers. I know how much you like that."

The invitation was more than appealing—grilling outdoors with the boys running around making noise, Ellie talking sensibly as she had now for several months, and Nina looking hopeful and young. Just then he would have preferred to be home, but he couldn't leave Dahlonaga.

"Sorry dear," he said. "I can't. See you tonight."

By one thirty Mark and Scott had stomach pain. By two they were throwing up. As the afternoon wore on their rising fever frightened Ellie and Nina. They put the boys in Ellie's van and headed for North Fulton Regional Hospital, less than fifteen minutes away. "Mom," said Ellie as she turned the car north on Alpharetta Highway, "I don't feel well either." Nina Martin didn't say anything. She didn't want to worry her daughter. But Nina's effort to stay calm failed minutes later, when she fell to her knees in the hospital parking lot and vomited all over herself.

Leonard was still in Dahlonaga when Nick called, asked him where he was, and then, without waiting to be answered, told Leonard to get to the hospital as fast as he possibly could. When he arrived, police from the City of Alpharetta, and Fulton County cops, were crawling all over the North Fulton grounds. State Troopers too. Leonard parked and made his way to the main reception desk. He gave his name and two women quickly approached. They identified themselves as employees of the Centers for Disease Control in Atlanta.

The first—dark, dumpy, and sweet-voiced—said, "Mr. Martin, do you know what your wife and family ate this morning? What they had for lunch? Did you eat the same food yourself?"

"We'll need to examine you too," said the other, slimmer, pale, and gruff. "Make sure you check with us before you leave."

"What's going on here?" he said.

A tall man in a white coat appeared. "What's your name?" he asked, and when Leonard told him, he took Leonard firmly by the arm, saying, "Please come with me." They walked down a noisy, crowded hallway, chaos gaining a foothold around them. It was almost four o'clock. The man in the coat told Leonard that both boys had died an hour before. Then he dropped him off in a bad-smelling room where Nina lay beside two other women, all slack, pallid, unconscious. He sat there for twenty minutes and then found Ellie four rooms down. She was in and out of consciousness, sometimes moaning, sometimes saying, "Daddy, where are the boys?"

Nina died at four thirty, her moist hand limp in Leonard's. Ellie finally went at five seventeen.

At six, Leonard attempted to leave. Police still surrounded the building. Official-looking people rushed through the halls. One of them seemed to know who he was and led him to an examination room. A doctor showed up minutes later and worked him over, asking questions he did not hear, or did not understand. And then he was outside, sitting in his car, staring at glints of the late afternoon southern sun in the hospital's dark reflective glass.

He remembered talk of a virus, bacteria, something—people may have mentioned meat. It had no particular meaning. He'd been sitting in the car for an hour before a Georgia State Trooper asked if he was feeling all right.

He did not know how he got home, but Carter was in the driveway when he did—skinny frame more insubstantial than ever, all too likely, it seemed to Leonard, to blow away in the slightest breeze, reddened eyes sunk impossibly deep in colorless hollows. They'd missed each other, somehow, at North Fulton. Carter followed him into the house, into the darkening living room, neither speaking nor moving where they sat. And then the phone started ringing.

People said Harvey Daniels took it the worst. From the moment they met he'd mistaken Lenny for his older brother—the one his parents neglected to provide; the strong, good-natured gentleman brute who'd be there when little Harvey cried for protection. Harvey knew from the instant he got the news that Leonard Martin was lost to him. He wept so inconsolably that Ginny, his wife, had him put on medication. And she kept him from daily haunting the Martin house, sensibly aware that Leonard had enough to carry.

Nick Stevenson was another matter. Now silver-haired, he'd long ago assumed the pose of a good grandee—a sometime southern progressive, a symbol of lawyerly elegance. He avoided the really taxing work, the mind-numbing legal cogitating that Harvey seemed to enjoy, the hard-boiled wrangling Leonard always seemed made for. He mobilized good looks, good golf, and good manners to constantly expand a roster of platinum-plated clients. He did his share of the thinking too, but mostly on a strategic level—who needed what from whom. His honesty no longer set off jokes; it was no longer quite so obsessive. But his handshake was absolutely firm and everyone in Atlanta knew it. There was a vault-full of equity in that.

He wept at the news, as did his wife, their kids, and their eldest grandchild—all of whom held the Martins closer than most of their larger family. But grief did not disable Nick. It turned him into a battle wagon. He thrust normal business into the hands of younger men and women. He spent the next weeks, when not with Leonard, in front of his own TV that he rigged to carry four channels at once, roaming the Internet, reading statute, calling around. He didn't learn much that the public did not learn, or recover legal precedents an intern could not have found. But he had it all by heart.

As time went on he came to favor the BBC, NPR, and a campus radio station that carried a radical network he'd never heard of. The anchors on the major American networks and cable were paralyzed by reluctance to think; once they'd done the headlines Nick found them useless.

On day two, it became settled fact that the deaths occurring throughout the south were caused by ground beef sold in five supermarket chains. The anchors and their expert guests speculated on what other chains might be involved. Before long consensus developed on this: all the ground beef and pre-packaged hamburgers, all marketed under store brand labels, came from one or more of six packing plants in the southeast. As a BBC reader observed, appalled, "Despite what shoppers seem to have thought, it all appears to have been the same meat—its origin, thus far, impossible to pinpoint."

Throughout the week people sickened and died from Kentucky to the Florida Keys, from western Louisiana across the south to the coastal Carolinas. By the time all the bad meat had been recalled, more than 17,000 people were stricken and 864 had died—disproportionately children. Because families often ate together, many suffered multiple illness. Some children were left without a parent. Many parents lost a child. But Nick never heard of anything quite so bad as what happened to Leonard Martin and Carter Lawrence.

Nick was not always entirely pleased with the way some media seemed to celebrate death in the U.S.A. He once told his wife, "These morons are happy as pigs in shit." In America—the on-air personalities repeatedly told Nicholas Stevenson—food is everywhere. Fresh meat and fish, fresh fruit and fresh vegetables, every conceivable type of baked, fried, roasted, and cooked meal—available to millions of people in hundreds of thousands of close-by locations twenty-four hours a day.

One Republican state chairman, rotating from one cable network to the next, reminded Nick and all Americans that the genius of America "is the art of distribution, and no nation on earth gives a finer example to the peoples of the world than the closely coordinated efforts of the various industries supplying 275 million Americans, wherever they might be, with whatever they want to eat, whenever they want to eat it."

There were, of course, sad and serious moments when anchors and guests confronted the fact that sometimes mistakes were made, but smiles and notes of fortitude always returned to their faces and voices in unison cried out in affirmation that America's God-given food supply was safe. Lest there be any doubt on that subject, experts strongly agreed with each other that the safety and security, and, yes, the credibility, of this vast distribution system was seen, in official circles, as essential to public well-being.

Many made the point that safe food was necessary to national security. Nick was amazed by the few who anxiously cried that the hand of Satan had made its way from the fires of hell to the supermarkets of the Southeast. But those voices came and went in a couple of days.

The public needed to know that their supermarkets were fine. They needed to know the restaurants were safe. McDonald's was clean. You could eat there. Enormous amounts of money were spent on TV ads and public relations pleading with Americans to continue buying and eating ground beef as well as all other food.

Within several days, intellectuals, athletes and entertainers, artists and physicians were talking about the virtues of dining out, and cooking in. Movie stars ate burgers flipped live on *Good Morning America.* A former American President filmed a public service announcement grilling steaks in his kitchen, his wife looking on approvingly, daintily taking a bite.

Eventually, those sickened recovered. After the summer, with holidays on the horizon, the cable news networks, the talk show producers, the magazine and newspaper editors turned their attention to other, newer matters. And only the survivors of the dead cared very much. Them and their lawyers . . . especially those few who were personally involved.

Nicholas Stevenson ran the wrongful death lawsuit. He listed Leonard Martin and Carter Lawrence as plaintiffs. Nick felt that years of handling deals worth hundreds of millions of dollars—and harrowing weeks imbibing facts through his pores, and the eager support of Atlanta's leading liability attorneys—might offset his inexperience as a plaintiff's attorney. That, and the facts of the case, which arrayed themselves like Xerxes' Persian army at his back. Not knowing which of the six offending plants was responsible, he filed against each of them, and, if they had one, their parent company as well. Five of the six responded with an answer of complete denial. Their filings were not accompanied by even a phone call to Nicholas Stevenson.

It was surprising when Knowland & Sons and its owner, Second Houston Holding, retained a Boston law firm. A young associate called Nick, and after delivering the mandatory denials—given the lie by the call itself—he made an offer of settlement. It wasn't as if his client had done anything wrong, the young man told Nick. It's just that the nuisance of it all, coupled with the deep regret that any misfortune had befallen anyone, motivated Knowland and Second Houston to offer fifty thousand dollars to be split any way they like by Leonard Martin and Carter Lawrence.

The offer was a foolish and miserly mistake. But that was fine with Nick. "Young man," he said, meaning full well the contempt intended, "go back and tell the fella you work for that fifty thousand dollars won't pay the deposit on the expert testimony we'll be introducing." Stevenson's studied southern accent and polished ease worked well with folks from up there. Northerners, he'd long ago discovered, were often thrown by the gentle self-assertion of the civilized southern white man—and the older he happened to be, the stronger the spell he was able to cast. The next day the same associate called back asking for a person-to-person meeting. "I've got some time tomorrow afternoon at three," Nick said. "C'mon down." Why, Nick wondered, would five of the six meat companies file court papers asserting zero liability, while one, Knowland & Sons, hires a bigshot law firm in Boston and immediately tries to settle? Although authorities continued to maintain that they could not trace the exact origin of the tainted beef, was it possible that Knowland & Sons itself knew it was responsible? It sure seemed that way to Nick Stevenson.

On behalf of the other worthies sent by Boston's Porter, Scudd, Porter—a full partner and two senior associates—junior partner Harkin Smith, a plump, self-possessed, forty-year-old Boston native, expressed his personal sorrow. He showed special sensitivity in framing PSP's awareness that Leonard Martin was Mr. Stevenson's partner and friend, as well as his client. Smith implied that the offer would be significantly larger for that; he all but said that it might be seen, although certainly never named, as a lawyer-to-lawyer bonus. He expressed a professional apology if Nick had been insulted by their assumption that he was a plaintiff's attorney accumulating E. coli cases, looking eagerly if not greedily for settlements. Until that little speech, Nick was unaware of such assumption. Nevertheless, he nodded his appreciation. They were certainly pleased that Leonard Martin and Carter Lawrence were Nick's only clients. Again, Mr. Smith rehashed the horror of it all, and the soul-wrenching pain they faced together, as brothers at the bar. All this in Nicholas Stevenson's comfortable fifteenth floor office conference room, overlooking the junction of I-285 (East-West) and Georgia 400 (North-South), with seven lawyers and twelve more staff sitting statue-still at their desks outside, their minds alive with prayers and curses and tears and recollections.

Then Porter, Scudd, Porter presented its offer of $1.2 million dollars—along with the usual clause requiring silence on anything having to do with the case. The female senior associate, a frail-looking, long-nosed Ms. Wittlesy, handed Nicholas Stevenson a magnificent leather folder enclosing two cashier's checks. One was for Leonard Martin, the other for Carter Lawrence. That, and a fully drawn-up agreement ready for both to sign.

None of the folks from Porter, Scudd, Porter began to imagine the anger behind their opponent's gentle smile. He spoke ever-so-slowly, quietly and confidently, in a deftly exaggerated drawl.

"My clients have lost everything." He said the last word again, "everything," with a sigh. "Mr. Martin's wife, a woman who had been by his side, his soul mate since they attended college together. His only child. And his little grandsons too. And Mr. Carter Lawrence has seen his former wife, a beautiful young woman with whom he was in the midst of reconciliation, ripped from him, together with his two sons—sweet little boys hardly old enough to know what life's all about. Two boys, I might add, who have napped on the couch right behind you there, on which your young Ms. Wittlesy took her ease a few moments ago, before we began." Ms. Wittlesy stole a furtive glance at the couch. "I know you will all agree that no young man on God's green earth should be made to suffer as Mr. Carter Lawrence has."

Nicholas Stevenson moved his head slowly from side to side. He breathed deeply, quite nearly sighing again. "Mr. Leonard Martin's entire existence has now been called into question, if not destroyed. As you say, I am his friend and his partner. From that unhappy vantage I have looked into a soul as charred and blackened with grief as the fires of hell could themselves arrange. And now I must remind you that it is *only* your client, your client *alone*, who stands before the world as the author of this unspeakable tragedy."

He paused again, allowing his turn at cornpone theatrics to have its effect—looking for an eye or two to roll.

"And I must also tell you in total candor that it's gonna take a lot more money than you or the little pricks you work for have even thought about to begin to dissipate Leonard Martin's sadness and put Carter Lawrence on the road to blessed recovery."

"You know, $1.2 million dollars is a large amount of money, Mr. Stevenson." The Boston lawyer, to Nick's practiced ear, spoke uneasily. Nick watched his eyes, thinking that his gently flickering pupils signaled discomfort. "We're not talking chump change here," he said.

Nicholas Stevenson leaned back in his swivel armchair, clasping his hands behind his head. "Actually, $1.2 million dollars is less than the advance on an HBO movie," he said. "It's far, far less than what could be in the works from someone like Steven Spielberg or that fella Oliver Stone, about whom I do have my doubts in the ordinary context of things. I urge you to remember that Mr. Leonard Martin, and Mr. Carter Lawrence too, have suffered a greater loss than most any other survivor of this. Do you know what? I will tell you what. This does all sound like a movie. In the interest of a speedy and appropriate solution, we have kept the whole horrid business off the television, away from the press. Lord, everybody wants to talk. We've got newspapers from all over the United States, Europe, Japan, and all points east and west on our neck.

"We've got news magazines and TV programs—*60 Minutes* and *20/20*—and all those folks at HBO who would make a movie out of God knows what if they had a way to, because they have no sense of shame in pursuing the almighty dollar—and, of course, the book publishers too. They call here all day long. Shall I get Ms. Betty Lee Washington in here to tell you how many calls she gets in a single day? How many agents and hangers-on would exploit my clients' grief? Shall I call Ms. Betty in here this very minute?"

He paused again, now leaning forward, glaring at each by turn; focusing last on the junior partner's light, uncertain eyes.

"Why, I could take a lunchtime break any day of the week and drive right down the highway here to visit with Mr. Larry King, or Mr. Ted Turner, as far as that goes. Or would you prefer Geraldo Rivera? And should my clients go public, your assumptions about eager, greedy lawyers might be a self-fulfilling nightmare. Would it please the misbegotten corporate criminals who pay for the gas in your Mercedes to see my clients sitting next to Oprah? I beg you now to think carefully; what *is* it you and your clients *really* want."

"What exactly did you have in mind?" That came with a cough from the senior partner, a barrel-chested older man with a deep bass voice at the far end of the table—who'd been silent after initial words of condolence.

Agreements were signed the next morning. Six million dollars was wired into an account established for Leonard Martin, and the same was done for Carter Lawrence. Stevenson, Daniels, Martin took no fees.

None of it meant anything to Leonard. His parents had passed years ago. His sister was little more than a telephone call on holidays. His unspoken contract with Harvey was broken. They commiserated often, but that took more out of Leonard than he could give. Nicholas had done what he could. He remained a rock and offered himself for whatever service he might perform. But he faded into the background after settling the case—not because he wanted to, but only because it happened.

Leonard avoided his many other friends, and none of them seemed to mind. He and they knew that he carried the plague of grief. Only Carter Lawrence meant anything to him now.

Carter had youth on his side, and a large, supportive family. His life was not over, they told him, not by a long shot. But Carter dreaded the future, and he fled from it to the Martin house. The two of them sat together for scores of hours watching ballgames and movies in foreign languages they didn't understand. Like Leonard, Carter stopped working regularly. He had very little appetite. He watched his father-in-law eat heavily, day and night, and drink. He watched him let himself go, stop shaving and bathing regularly. Carter told his mother he felt like the walking dead, and only Leonard Martin could walk by his side. He did not want to kill himself, and often wondered why. He took it for granted that Leonard also fought the demon, and Carter wondered which of them would prevail.

FOUR

Boston

Most members will tell you that the sixth hole on the west course at Holcomb Woods County Club outside Boston is tougher than it looks. The green is only 387 yards from the members' tees, but the hole runs straight uphill into the prevailing wind to a severely elevated plateau made all the more treacherous by a downright sadistic design that slopes the green sharply from back to front. Two bunkers bracket the entrance. You cannot hold back on your tee shot. No matter how well you hit your drive it's a rare second shot that doesn't call for a long iron, sometimes even a fairway wood to get you up that hill, over the traps, and safely home.

If you hit the front of the green your ball may roll whence it came, down and off the putting surface. Overshoot the green and you'll probably wind up out-of-bounds, on the wrong side of a low fence that marks the western edge of the club's property. Your ball will lose itself in the dense, fifteen-foot deep thicket of old oaks that separate the fence from a narrow outside road curving gently away from the course at just that point.

Christopher Hopman, Chairman of the Board of Alliance Inc., inhaled the sharp, early morning fragrance, bent from the waist, and pushed his wooden tee into soft grass still wet with miniature worlds of dew. On its tiny platform he placed a brand new Titlest ProVI high compression ball. He'd been playing golf forty years and still felt the adrenaline whenever he opened a sleeve of new golf balls to put one in play. The son of a New England Catholic banker, Hopman proudly typified the upper reaches of American management. After a parochial school and undergraduate education he went to Wharton for his MBA and continued on at the Law School of the University of Pennsylvania. He was nearly twenty-eight before taking his first real job. His business career was blessed by swift, untroubled advances.

Four years before, he'd replaced the CEO who brought him into the company a few years earlier. He promptly turned a medium-sized, cash-rich manufacturing outfit into a voracious, often hostile buyer of companies. He hunted in many fields, from textiles to auto parts, hard-money lending to publishing, processed foods to minor professional sports, even timber and windmills. And he succeeded dramatically most of the time. A childless widower, Christopher Hopman worked long hours day after day, for months on end. When he did relax it was with a new friend in a Ritz Carlton suite, or an old friend on the golf course.

He once stood six-four and played college hoops with his shoulders and elbows. At fifty-seven, he prided himself on being able to see his dick without bending forward. Hopman had his clothes custom made and did not check the prices. Today he wore dark gray slacks with a red pullover. His four-hundred-dollar golf shoes matched the sweater. He looked and felt impressive.

Hovering over his golf ball he dug both feet into the ground, swaying from his hips, moving his lower body side to side for maximum traction. His fingers gripped the Calloway Big Bertha driver. Its oversized titanium head barely touched the close-cut grass behind the ball.

He breathed deeply through his nose to clear his mind of all thoughts. He glanced toward the distant green. His teeth touched as he centered his energy on the swing. "Smoooth," he whispered to himself. His hands and arms took the club back in an easy motion. His shoulders turned to shift weight to his right side. He kept his left arm as straight as possible, locking the club at its zenith, pointing straight ahead nearly perpendicular to the ground.

At that instant his body jerked backward and both feet left the ground. He had, in fact, been cut almost in half at the waist. Bloody pieces splattered his playing partners, who were behind him and off to the side. Two froze. One sprinted. Later, none could recall seeing anything or hearing anything unusual. Perhaps, one told the police, there might have been a popping sound, like the noise of a beer can being squashed far away.

Christopher Hopman didn't hear that sound or feel the bullet that entered the left side of his body to explode his upper chest and most of his back. He died instantly, torso flung backward and sideways, as if a very large, strong person had smacked him with two hands at once, on both shoulders. His lower body seemed to have died a death of its own, the pelvis and legs impossibly twisted, one foot turned into the ground, the other toward the fairway. Hopman's ball still rested on its tee, now impertinently bright in a darkening scarlet sea. Moments later, the silky whisper of a car engine could have been heard from beyond the fence and the oak trees, in the distance, beyond the green.

FIVE

St. John

A SUBTLE HAZE HAD settled into the air by late afternoon. The visitors hired a car and driver at the Westin. Tom handed the driver Billy's bar napkin. He suspected it wasn't necessary, but had no way of knowing. It is a small island, he'd reminded the others as they waited in the lobby, suited up again after hours of being shoeless and tieless, on phones, in chilly, air-conditioned rooms, unable and unwilling to surrender themselves to the view of the ocean calling them beyond the window across the balcony of their suite. A trio of strange men in three-thousand-dollar suits and three-hundred-dollar sunglasses ordering up a car and driver couldn't be much of a mystery here, not after walking in and out of Billy's Bar, not after chatting up Walter Sherman—not after most of the day had passed since then. The way the driver glanced at the napkin showed Tom that he knew where Walter lived. When Wesley repeated the street and the number, the driver said "Thank you" tonelessly, without a hint of interest.

They drove out of Cruz Bay on the road leading to the beaches, up into the hills, and then made three turns, only the last of which was marked. Tom reckoned that a careful driver would have needed about twenty minutes for the trip. A driver who didn't know where he was going would take at least forever. This tropical automaton delivered his fare in twelve minutes flat, maneuvering impassively, maniacally, all the way. Wesley took the turns and lurches with rigid stoicism.

It never occurred to Tom to complain. He used calculations and observations to distract himself. He noted that the houses on that part of St. John were built below an often steep road tucked into the side of a mountain. Most properties must have had sharply descending driveways because Tom saw bits of roof from the road, but hardly any houses. The road afforded a view of the sea, St. Thomas, and several much smaller islands. As the car slowed for the first time, Tom was surprised to find himself wondering whether, on a perfectly clear day, he might see all the way to St. Croix. It would not have pleased him to know he was looking in the wrong direction.

The taxi rolled up to a massive wrought-iron gate. The driver lowered his window slowly and pushed the single unmarked button on a pole next to the mailbox. The gate swung open. They drove down a narrow driveway winding to a concrete pad barely large enough to let the car turn around.

The house looked very tropical and, Tom thought, more-or-less Asian. The grounds were landscaped with crushed rock and brightly-colored flowers, which he liked. A vaguely Japanese fountain gushed into a gutter that ran under wide wooden steps leading to large double doors made of dark, heavy wood. White shuttered windows faced the driveway. Maloney got out of the car first. The other two followed. "Wait here," Maloney said to the driver, who certainly did not need to be told.

A sturdily built, sharp-boned black woman answered the door in a dark blue dress hanging down to her toes. Her age made her look hunched over, although she was not. The phrase "Wicked Witch of the West" danced stupidly through Tom's mind.

"Follow, please," she said slowly and very softly, in the familiar Caribbean rhythm. "Mr. Sherman's expecting you. He's out on the patio. If you will follow me, please." They walked behind her from the small, wood-paneled foyer into a room that must have been forty feet long and nearly that wide, with dark hardwood floors and a vaulted ceiling upwards of twenty feet high. There was a small stone fireplace on the left and an open kitchen with a long, massive island counter on the right. Above the kitchen counter, copper-colored pots and pans and gleaming utensils dangled from a bright silver grid.

Set into the wall next to the kitchen, Tom spotted the highest and widest TV screen he had ever seen. "Radio Goddamn City," he heard himself thinking. Near the fireplace, a long, polished dinner table stood surrounded by eight matching chairs. Four fat, leather easychairs congregated haphazardly around a big glass coffee table in the middle of the room. Beside each of these chairs stood a stainless steel lamp plugged into an outlet set in the floor. Twin brass and glass chandeliers hung from the ceiling at the same level as four rattan fans. All the fans rotated slowly, silently, seemingly in synch. The far wall, opening out to the sea, was entirely glass and extended the full length of the vaulted roofline. Above three double sliding doors the glass was fitted with wooden blinds. The view was westerly, the sun high in the afternoon sky. The room—and Maloney was far from sure that such a space could even be called just a room—was awash, aglow, with soon-to-ripen yellow sunlight.

A deck patio made of pale, shiny wood, perhaps fifteen feet deep, ran the whole length of the house. Part of it was covered by a roof. A round black-marble table with six bamboo chairs occupied that protected space. A fan and lamp descended from a chain above it. A covered hot tub and high-tech grill kept each other company at the other end of the porch. Tom's wide eyes lingered there. Stepping outside, he imagined himself at ease, with the first or second of his wives laughing beside him—at his comical apron, or at the cautious way he turned a crimson lobster on the grill. That's what he wanted to worry about; how to turn the lobster on the grill.

The old woman had shown them to where Walter waited. He rose from one of the bamboo chairs with a fixed, businesslike smile. He suggested they take off their jackets, roll up their sleeves, and loosen their ties. "Dress comfortably," Walter had said, and left to his own devices Tom would have. Now, he lost no time. The other two followed reluctantly, as though the suits were slyly fashioned Italian armor.

The house perched near the top of the mountain looked down and out to a glittering vastness. Scattered clouds drifted across St. Thomas, a speck in the world but a continent next to its tiny brother; on St. John they called their larger neighbor "the rock." Sunlight filtered downward, like pillars plunging toward the sea, and fragmented beams of dusty sunlight bounced back up off the dark water to throw mysterious shadow patterns onto the small hilly islands to the right, where no one lived. Walter watched them absorb it, jackets in hand, motionless for a moment.

"Tom, will you introduce your friends?"

Tom took his sunglasses off and put them in his shirt pocket. "Walter Sherman, I'd like you to meet Nathan Stein and Wesley Pitts." The formality startled Walter; these two might be Tom's parents, and Walter his brand new girl. Nathan Stein was a small man, five feet six inches, lean and fit, already sweating profusely under his arms, agitated, eager to commence whatever business had brought him to this place. Walter made him a starving rat of a man, all purpose and fury, a fortune builder. He'd seen this kind before. Walter knew a man like this in the war, an admiral's son who hated his father, a talented liar and full-time taker. He wound up drafted and partied with colonels who knew what he could do for them in the real world. A promoter, Walter called him then, shorter even than this one, a wolverine in shrimp's clothing. Nathan Stein was the boss, and Walter did not like him.

Pitts was a big man: six-three, 260 pounds at least. He once ran the forty in four and a half seconds. Some time ago. Now he must be thirty-eight or -nine. For a moment that astonished Walter. And it hurt him that he'd not spotted Wes in Billy's. He soothed his pain with the rationalization that the man was at least twenty-five pounds over his playing weight, and his red-brown face had gone from long and dangerous to cheerful and round as a plate. He carried a large black attaché case as if it were a cracker-jack box with a handle.

"Mr. Pitts, I'm sure you are recognized more often than not," Walter said. "It was always a pleasure to watch you. I've long considered tight end an underappreciated position, and especially the way you played it."

"Thank you very much, Mr. Sherman. It's always nice to be remembered, and please call me Wes." Pitts kept a bright smile alive at the center of his moonlike face. He projected an earnest manner and shook hands firmly, but with care. He had what Walter knew must be widely celebrated as a winning personality, no particle of which did Walter suppose to be authentic. Wes let go of Walter's hand. "That's some gate you've got there. Security?"

"Keeps the goats out," Walter told him. "The island's full of them. Cows too. The damn goats ate my flowers so I had to put up the gate."

They sat at the marble table: Walter, Nathan, Maloney, Wes. Comfortable and shaded. Wes set his case under the table. The old woman had brought cold drinks and food on a square silver platter. Walter nodded appreciatively at the artfully arranged meat, cheese, fruit, and crackers. "Mr. Stein," he said, "what can I do for you?"

"I need to find somebody."

"Yes, I see. Who?"

"I'm not sure. How the hell am I supposed to know?" Stein turned angrily, awkwardly on Tom, jabbing a finger toward Walter, barking like a Chihuahua, "Goddamnit, Tom. That's supposed to be his end."

Tom leaned forward to settle a gentle hand on Stein's child-size shoulder. It seemed a practiced gesture. Walter took it to fall within the job description. Wesley plainly regarded it as routine. Tom kept his hand in place as he spoke. "What Nathan means to say is that we need to find someone and we're not absolutely sure of his identity. We need to find out who he is. Then we need to find him, and then come to a resolution of our problem. We've got a problem here, Mr. Sherman, and we're all a bit stressed. Given your experience with difficult matters I'm sure you'll agree that that is normal enough."

"The stress I can see," said Walter sternly, "but I know nothing about your situation. I can't agree or disagree until I know what you're talking about. Why don't you describe your problem."

"He's trying to fucking kill us!" yelled Stein in a voice like troubled gears, his mouth a ragged thing beneath his sharp, vein-crossed nose. "Is that enough of a fucking problem?"

If it was a performance, it was a good one. Walter was inclined to think otherwise, to believe that the little sac of testosterone was genuinely off-stride. Walter let his eyebrows jump and cocked his head to show interest. Then he tried an ironic note, mimicking discovery. "And you're not sure who this person is? Have I got that right, Mr. Stein?" A muttering sneer came back.

"You got it," said Pitts unexpectedly, from another county, mouth full of ham and cracker. "But he damn sure knows who we are and the murderous cocksucker's already—"

Tom cut him short with a twitch of his head, then said, "Maybe we're getting ahead of ourselves, maybe just a little."

At least twenty painfully prolonged seconds followed. Nathan Stein turned peevishly toward the water, wrestling no doubt with whatever tiny demons labored to unglue him. Wesley Pitts nodded aimlessly, removed his glasses, wiped his eyes with the backs of his powerful hands, and backpedaled to his appropriate place in the order of things. Walter felt for Tom. As point man he was supposed to keep things together, especially at moments like this. Now, he needed help. Walter reached for a chunk of apple. He chewed it, released a sigh, and applied a mild, mournful tone to his next observation. "Guys," he said, "This doesn't really sound like my kind of work."

SIX

Atlanta

AFTER THEIR SECOND OR third closing, all these decades ago, Harvey decided to have a photo taken. He had a secretary use a camera he had brought from home. The buyer and seller each got an 8x10 glossy, suitable for framing. It showed happy folks shaking hands on a life-changing deal. This became an extremely popular perk, and soon they had so many closings that Nicholas suggested they hire his gifted nephew for the work. Young Harold cut school when needed and did a fine job for three years, until he left for college. Then they worked out a deal with a large Atlanta studio. The relationship was still in force.

The story of Leonard's life played out in those thousands of pictures. Over the years they told a graceful tale. The years had transformed this vigorous, handsome, fit young lawyer into a broader, more imposing figure, paunchier to be sure, but never more commanding, never projecting more life and assurance.

Now everything in his life belonged to *before* or *after*.

And there were only a handful of *after* shots, because Leonard soon gave up going to closings. The few pictures that were there were hard to look at. They showed a fat and slovenly man; an unfortunate man who belonged in some other picture. His inner disturbance transformed, disfigured his face. And his weight had ballooned to the point where his suits no longer fit and he could not button his shirts at the top.

Once, trying to make the button work, trying to put himself together for a closing, Leonard thought he heard Scott whisper that grandpa's belly was fat. He looked around the room and then trembled for several minutes, sitting on the edge of his bed and holding his stomach.

He came by the office once a week, not to work, or socialize—not, it seemed, for any reason that anyone could see. Otherwise, he stayed home and kept the blinds closed. On some hot Georgia days he left the air conditioning off. He told the cleaning people not to come back, and handed each of them three one-hundred-dollar bills. Leonard ate and drank and fell asleep on the couch in the den in front of the TV. Carter came by two or three times a week to reassure himself that Lenny was sane. He'd stay for an hour, tell Lenny to hang in there, go home, and call Nick Stevenson with his report.

The partners were profoundly distressed, as were the associates, paralegals, and office staff whose affection Leonard's consistent kindness had earned over the years. One afternoon, Nicholas Stevenson, with Harvey Daniels in tow, strode into Leonard's office overlooking I-285. He had been there for over an hour, quietly stinking of alcohol.

"Time's up, Lenny." Nicholas said. "Get yourself professional help. Go every day of the week if that's what it takes. Take a leave of absence. Take as much time as you need. Harvey and I talked it over. Your share goes in the bank every month, whatever you decide. Spend some time in Paris or Rome. Hilton Head maybe, or Mississippi. Go sit in a cafe in Amsterdam. Fuck your brains out. But don't keep doing what you're doing. It's killing you and it's killing us, my friend."

Leonard Martin took his leave of absence.

But he didn't go to Biloxi, to the beach, or to Europe. And he didn't go for help. He stayed in his house and kept drinking and eating. He screened his calls and returned very few. Barbara called him. She left messages. As quickly as he recognized her voice, he stopped the tape. He erased them all without listening. If not for her where would he be? The answer made him sick. Still, she called. And after the last few messages from Dahlonaga, he got Carter to buy him a phone without an answering machine. Eventually it stopped ringing.

One weekday morning in February, eight months after the death of his family, Leonard awoke on the couch in the den after a fitful night of sleep. He turned off the TV and stumbled into the kitchen to find there was nothing there. No soda or beer, no coffee, no crumbs or even sour milk. Eating was now his vocation, and Leonard favored junk: doughnuts, cookies, chocolate cake, greasy take-out chicken, ribs, cheeseburgers, fries, blizzard shakes, pizza. He'd been strikingly fat when he made his last closing. Now he was seriously obese. He got into his car and drove to a shabby diner on Alpharetta Highway. He hated eating in public but this place was almost always empty—for excellent good reason. Along the way he bought a *New York Times* from a vending box.

"Could you bring me some coffee please?" he asked, "and eggs and bacon, and ham, and toast . . . whatever you've got is fine." He glanced at the headlines, skimmed the first section, turned to the sports, checked the hockey and basketball scores, didn't recognize some of the teams: Wizards, Avalanche, Thrashers.

When he got his hands on a paper now, he always read the obituaries. *Before* he never looked at that page. But *after*, it seemed to matter.

He started with McKinley James Houston, seventy-eight. After lengthy illness. Architect of some renown in England. Pronounced *How*-ston. Lester Shapiro, fifty-three. Heart attack last night at a charity dinner. Owned office buildings in New York City. Survived by his wife Sylvia, five children, three grandkids. Dr. Ganga Roy, forty-one. Noted research scientist/teacher. No survivors. Apparent suicide. *Suicide*. The word stopped his eye. He read the piece twice. Found by cleaning woman. Died by taking poison. Born in India. Colleagues praised her work at the Rockefeller Institute. Well-regarded at Albert Einstein College of Medicine. Victim of unsolved hate crime seven months earlier. Apartment burglarized and burned. Anti-terrorist slogans painted on walls. Leonard stirred his coffee till it was cold. *Suicide*.

Two days later Leonard squinted into the bright Georgia morning, and set a course for the end of his driveway. He picked up a batch of local papers lying there and opened his overstuffed mailbox. He hadn't done that since . . . sometime last week? He brought the mail inside and tossed it all, unopened, onto a kitchen counter, knocking several other envelopes onto the floor. One of these caught his attention: a brown six-by-nine with a Postal Express label on it. In the upper left-hand corner, gracefully scripted in blue ink above a New York address, was a name he thought he recognized.

The envelope contained a single computer disc. A paisley-patterned notepad page fluttered out of it, to the floor. He picked it up. Across it were written the words "Forgive me," and at the top Leonard read: "From the desk of Dr. Ganga Roy."

SEVEN

St. John

Nathan's outburst and the tension it uncorked had distracted all but Walter from the single dark cloud approaching them out of a bright sky at an altitude not much above the house. Conversation stopped abruptly as a very local, very surprising tropical downpour threw warm sheets of water onto the deck. The roof was so constructed that Walter had stayed put in precisely that spot during three hurricanes. He looked forward to rain in the closing moments of a hot Virgin Islands afternoon. It was a perfectly wonderful thing. Tom, Nathan, and Wesley apparently disagreed. The three of them maneuvered their legs prissily under the table to keep their silk trousers safe from water bouncing off the glistening planks.

"Won't last long," smiled Walter, mightily amused.

Tom checked his companions, as though to be sure that neither was going under. He resumed in his calm, rehearsed tone:

"This *is* your kind of work and we need your help. I know many of your clients are celebrity types, show business people. I've heard about some politicians. Maybe our needs are somewhat different from the ordinary run . . ."

Walter raised his hand, palm out. Tom stopped.

Walter's hard look took them all in and he spoke with calibrated impatience that sharpened as he continued, "The first thing most people give me is a name. The *first* thing. Then I get a photograph and a description. They give me a story. Usually, they tell me a lot more than I want to know. They parade their hopes and dreams and the names of their pets. I see love and hate they keep from their shrinks. Sometimes I get the feeling I'm the only person they ever leveled with. And you know the people I'm talking about. If you think this is my kind of work, the first thing you better do is tell me is what the work is."

"Fair enough," Maloney said. Now he reached to cover much of Nathan Stein's short forearm with a thick, rosy hand, anchoring that bird-faced bundle of nerves, hoping, no doubt, to keep him seated during whatever was to come. Then Tom spoke, uninterrupted, for forty-five minutes. When he was done he looked at the others, his suddenly forceful expression telling them, "If you have anything to say, say it now." Neither uttered a sound. Nathan Stein's face had gone from deranged to pathetic. He seemed to have aged and weakened during the speech, as though—forced to hear them all—the endless, disturbing details had worn him down. His narrow chest heaved silently. Wesley's big, shrewd eyes had stayed with Maloney throughout. Now they returned to the glories of nature.

The rain had ended twenty minutes before, and the air was a good deal cooler. A breeze blew in off the water and the small boats had returned to the open sea. The sunlight was now a richer yellow, anticipating the reddening sun and the advent of the evening sky. Walter rose, walked around the table, and then, slowly, toward the grill and the tub. He stretched, took a deep breath, turned quickly, returned to the table, and resumed his seat. Tom had concluded by stating, and repeating forcefully, that they had no way to know what might happen. They had, he insisted again, done their due diligence. Dr. Roy had given them a green light, and now their lives were in danger because of "a terrible, a grossly unfortunate misunderstanding" that they sought desperately to correct. To do so they had to find someone only Walter could locate. When Tom used the word "locate," the look in his eyes told Walter the depth of their research.

Walter looked at them all, more kindly now, and tilted his head. The gesture conceded that possibilities might exist. Then he said, "This will take much more of my time than I'm used to giving. We're talking about weeks, possibly months. That's a long time to devote to a single client."

"Money is not a factor," said Maloney.

"There's more to it than money," Walter replied. "It's also about how I prefer to work."

Tom's eyes sparkled almost merrily, giving his angelic face a surprisingly racy cast. "We know you take eight or ten clients a year and rarely spend more than a few weeks on any one of them—sometimes a few days. We know of one client who didn't come to you till a full month after his wife disappeared. You handled that in twenty-four hours, which was more than he expected, and much more than he hoped. We're not expecting miracles, Walter. But we have a problem and we need fast action."

Walter shook his head, preparing another objection.

Maloney went on, "Please let me finish. You didn't file a tax return last year. It looks like you haven't filed one since you were twenty-five. You're independent. You're a free man. Not easy to find. We heard someone call you a phantom. You've been in this line of work for a long time and you've done especially well in the last ten years. You took good care of your mother before she passed. We like that. It shows character. You have an ex-wife in Chicago who's never remarried, although she could have. You're very generous to her. You have a daughter in Kansas City with a less-than-successful husband and you're helping them. You have trusts for three grandchildren. There has never been a mortgage on this house. You rent a desirable apartment on the Near North Side of Chicago. You don't owe anyone anything and you spend as you wish. But you are by no means a wealthy man. Your checking account pays your bills. Your special account in the Caymans contains $774,526." Maloney stopped to savor and punctuate the moment. He took a sip of iced tea and said, "You are earning slightly more than three hundred thousand dollars a year. There are cops and teachers and building inspectors with more equity in their pensions. Walter, we get what we want because we know what other people want. We think we know what you want. We're not looking for drunken sailors or doped-up sixteen-year-olds. We face a challenge and we're confident that you will help us deal with it."

"Really," Walter said, because, for once, nothing else came to mind.

Tom leaned across the table and grabbed a large handful of grapes from the silver platter. His eyes were sparkling furiously now. "A few years ago my mom had to go into a nursing home. She was a churchgoer, a devout Catholic, a member of St. Ann's parish for many years. She wanted to go to the Catholic Home near where we lived. The home is connected to St. Ann's church. For many years she did volunteer work there. She told me if she ever needed to go to a home, that was the only one for her. I went there. The nun in charge of admitting new residents told me there was an eighteen month wait. Walter, my Mom didn't have eighteen months. I asked this nun what sort of contribution I could make to speed things up. I asked flat out how much money it would take. She said to me, 'Mr. Maloney, if your dear mother was already on our list and we passed her over because a man, like yourself, gave the church fifty thousand dollars or a hundred thousand dollars you would be extremely upset, wouldn't you?' Then she stopped. Just stopped talking. And Walter, you know what she did next? She looked into her soul and had a wrestling match with Satan. It took five seconds, maybe six. When it was over she said to me, 'But Mr. Maloney, if the contribution was of a certain amount, whatever that amount might be, I imagine that you and even your dear mother might very well understand.' Then this nun looks me in the eye and says, 'One million dollars, Mr. Maloney.'"

Tom paused for another, smaller drink of his iced tea. "You know what I said, Walter? You know what I said? I said, 'How do I make the check out, Sister?' "

Maloney motioned to Wesley Pitts, who produced his attaché case from under the table. It was a big one, the kind that opens with a double flap at the top. He gave it to Maloney, whose body registered the weight. "If you work for us," he said, "you'll get four hundred and fifty thousand dollars. Add another fifty for expenses and you've got half a million." He opened the case to let Walter see. "You are looking at half a million dollars right here. And underneath it, another half million. It's yours."

Walter knew you don't get through an airport carrying a bag with a million dollars in it—not these days. "You've got friends here in the banking business," he said.

"Yes, we do," Tom said. "We have friends everywhere."

EIGHT

St. John

"FIVE HITS BY THE Harptones," Ike crowed as Walter walked into Billy's. "Billy don't know no more than three." He laughed through his big lemon teeth. Smoke came out of his nostrils.

"'Sunday Kind of Love,' 'My Memories of You,' 'The Masquerade Is Over.' I can't remember no more," said Billy.

"Walter?" asked Ike.

"The Harptones are okay," said Billy, eager to put the subject behind them. "But they ain't the best. Not even close."

"I agree with that,'" said Walter.

"Five of 'em. Can you?" Ike persisted, now apparently blowing smoke through every bodily orifice. Walter admitted his bankruptcy with a shrug. Ike took on Billy, "Who you think's better?"

"The Paragons," Billy said. "I'll take them on 'Florence' alone."

"I heard that," said Ike. "You may have got me there." He threw his head back and launched a mangled falsetto, "*Fah-lah-ho-rance—hoooo weeee . . .*"

Billy turned to Walter at the end of the bar. "What beats 'Florence'? Nothing does. Even Ike knows that."

He put Walter's usual beverage on a new Billy's coaster. But he kept his thin, white fingers around the bottle. Walter had to speak up for his drink.

"'Gloria,'" Walter said.

"The Cadillacs," Ike nodded his approval, and his tortured falsetto took off again, *"Glaw-haw-ree-ha oh oh—it's not Mah-ree-hee-hee—Glaw-haw-ree-ha—it's not Sher-ee-hee."*

"The best," said Walter. "You ever have a girlfriend named Gloria?"

Billy shook his head.

"Me neither," said Ike in a very soft, strained voice. He knew the name of Walter's ex-wife.

"I did once," Walter said. "I think of her when I hear that song. It's been a long time. But even that brought it back." He raised his bottle to Ike in salute.

Ike said, "You know Enchantment?"

Billy said, "I know the word, but you mean something else?"

Ike lit another cigarette. "The group Enchantment. One of them one-hit groups. They did a cover of 'Gloria' in, I don't know, mid-eighties. Damn good too."

"Enchantment," said Billy. "You want me to write it down?"

Walter said, "Write down Cadillacs and also Paragons. Ike, you still need to give us one. Just one." The old man mulled it over. Walter sipped contentedly. Ike chuckled and dragged on the evil stick he was smoking. "Close as you boys are to me, I feel better the closer you are. Gentlemen, I offer you The Channels." Billy picked up the chalk and wrote it all down: Cadillacs/Paragons/Channels. All three of them took special pleasure watching Billy's regulars, as well as the tourists, mull over their choices and cast their votes. The delight was all the greater since nobody had any idea why they were voting at all. Someone would yell out their selection and Billy dutifully lifted his chalk and made a slash mark beneath it.

"The Channels," said Ike. "That's nice. Very, very nice."

NINE

Atlanta

LEONARD SHOWERED, SHAVED, AND found clean clothes. He raised the blinds and opened all the windows. The kitchen doors leading to the deck were thrown wide open for the first time since . . . since that terrible day in June. The winter air blew through the house and out again, taking with it the stink of Leonard's isolation that had settled in over eight months. He cleaned everything. He rubbed and scrubbed and vacuumed, washed the dirty toilets, and wiped the dust from the furniture. It took him all day and most of the evening. It made him feel good again. The next morning he got a haircut, and before he returned home he shopped for fruits and vegetables and fresh-baked bread. He tossed out all the liquor still in the house. That night he couldn't sleep, so instead he began taking inventory of his belongings.

Leonard Martin sold everything. Everything.

His contacts in the real estate community connected him with the right agent to sell his house in Alpharetta, for which he got top dollar. The same agent was able to refer Leonard to a realtor on Hilton Head.

He did better with the Hilton Head condo than he thought he would. Before he closed on his house he disposed of his personal property—furniture, art, and Nina's jewelry—for which he sought help from a diamond dealer with whom he had worked on a series of rental property purchases.

"You want to sell everything?" the diamond dealer asked him. "You might want to keep something. This was your wife's."

Leonard replied, "All of it."

"I can help you. I know someone who can handle the jewelry. I will take the diamonds myself, if that's alright with you. The art work too?"

"Yes."

"And the books, the music, the furniture?"

"All of it."

"Okay," he said.

"Sell it all," Leonard said.

"I understand. I'm sorry Mr. Martin. I'm so sorry."

Leonard nodded, but said nothing more.

He went to cash with his portfolio and then moved the cash and closed his brokerage account. He called Nick Stevenson and told him he wished to exercise his option to sell his interest in the firm. He insisted on accepting only twice his best year's salary.

"Lenny, your share is worth much more. Much more. You must know that."

"It's okay Nick. That's what I want."

"What do you say we just keep you as a partner—inactive—but still a partner? You don't have to sell."

"I know, Nick. Thanks, but this is what I want." Arrangements were made. The money was transferred to Leonard's bank.

It all came to just about twelve million dollars, including the money from the Knowland settlement. He told Nick and Harvey that he was moving to the Bahamas, that he planned to buy a boat, that he would write when he settled himself. He said goodbye to Carter and Carter's family, telling them the same story. He didn't bother calling his sister. And then, he was gone.

He bought a house in Jamaica that was little more than a hut. He bought a boat not much bigger than a dinghy. He also bought a vacant lot in Raleigh, North Carolina, and 270 acres in the high desert north of Santa Fe, New Mexico. These properties were titled in the name of a corporation he set up in North Dakota. After the closing, each was quitclaimed twice until the property belonged to Evangelical Missions Inc., a North Carolina entity with an address that was the empty lot. Leonard bought an SUV in North Carolina. He drove to New Mexico, and as soon as he arrived there, the vehicle was titled to Evangelical Missions Inc. In New Mexico, his nearest neighbor was eight miles away, an Indian ninety years old and half blind. He never went near the Bahamas.

By mid-April he had settled into his new home, a renovated hillside hunting cabin hunched into a thicket of brush, at the end of a winding dirt road miles off the main road into his own property. The cabin had electricity, but no phone. The front porch stood above a clearing that marked the end of the dirt road. Inside, made entirely of logs, he had a living room with a vaulted ceiling and a large fireplace, a small kitchen area, and, down a short hall, a small bedroom and a toilet and shower. He had a radio, plus the one in his SUV, but no television. His laptop computer connected to the Internet via the cell phone belonging to Evangelical Missions Inc. In nearby Taos, he bought simple, wooden furniture, a table and some chairs, a small couch, a couple of lamps. He did not buy a bed. For months Leonard had been having nightmares, awful dreams where strange creatures reached out for him only to grab Nina, Ellie, and the boys instead. The monsters savaged them while Leonard watched helplessly. One night, while still in

Alpharetta, he awoke suddenly, disoriented, shaking, and tearful, and tumbled out of bed onto the floor. He didn't get up. He stayed on the floor and fell back to sleep. He slept the rest of that night without further attack by the demons. He hadn't slept in a bed since. Each night he climbed into a sleeping bag on the hard wooden floor of his small bedroom, zipped himself in, and waited for the bad dreams. They came, but not every night, and he credited this partial success to his new sleeping arrangement.

Leonard had a single goal in mind, a simple objective, but one he knew would take time. It didn't matter. Time had no meaning. He had infinite patience. He established a vigorous program of physical exercise—rehabilitation for his abused and obese body. He limited his diet to a thousand calories a day, mainly eating vegetables, fruit, and soups. He drank enormous amounts of water. He stopped eating meat altogether. Once a week he allowed himself the small joy of a can of tuna fish. Although just an hour from Taos, after buying his furniture and initial supplies he never went back to town. For new supplies he drove all the way to Albuquerque, three hours each way, and he bought in bulk.

During the first year Leonard dropped eighty pounds, scaling back to 210. He cut his hair stubble-short, grew a full beard, then cut it short and guessed that the cold winter turned it gray. He pretty much ignored the natural beauty around him. He spent his early days in relentless exertion. He awoke at first light each morning through the spring and summer. When the colder months brought shorter days, Leonard was always awake and starting his day before the sun. He chopped wood and ran up and down the hills comprising his land. He bought gym equipment in Albuquerque, trucked it back in his SUV, and assembled it in the living room of his cabin. Each morning while his coffee brewed, Leonard did thirty minutes on the treadmill and thirty more on the complicated calisthenics apparatus. He believed, and it seemed to be true, that the constant effort helped him control his dreams. They had elements in common and were always extremely unpleasant; some tore him from sleep, some tortured him within it. Those that did not involve his family had Dahlonaga in them, Barbara, and others he left behind.

After the first four months, Leonard began collecting and learning to use an assortment of guns. In time, this occupied most of his time. Many days he rose with the early light, worked out, ate a simple breakfast, and fired his rifles until dark. At night, with a small fire going and the sounds of classical music coming from his radio, he disassembled, cleaned, and polished his weapons. He took enormous pride in this. Each piece of each weapon was cleaned and shined and laid out on the table in front of him. When the rifle had been completely stripped, he patiently put it back together again. He bought all of his rifles on the Internet. He spent hours researching sniper rifles and shotguns, scopes and ammunition. He liked it. He began to see these weapons as his tools, and he studied them with something akin to parental sensitivity. He had his favorites. He became a fan of firearms designers like Dr. Nehemiah Sirkis, with his Israeli conversions of the US M-14. Sirkis's models became known as the M89s, with the M89SR one of the world's outstanding long-range rifles, complete with a sound suppressor. Leonard envisioned the day when he could hold one to his shoulder and hit a target no bigger than a baseball at a thousand yards. He knew that day would be his. For the shorter-range targets he leaned toward the Yugoslavian Zastava M76, a challenging weapon because of its reduced ammunition loadout. It demanded a first-shot strike.

Every weapon he found could be bought somewhere on the Internet. Many were very expensive. A Holland and Holland double rifle can be had, but only for twenty-five thousand dollars or more. Some of the extremely rare guns brought prices well above that—when they were available at all. Leonard spent months seeking a Walther WA2000, a semiautomatic rifle made in Germany. For accuracy, power, handling, and recoil, Leonard considered the Walther to be the finest gun ever built. Like the Sirkis M89SR, the Walther had only a six-shot load, but with its exceptional accuracy, Leonard did not see that as a drawback. Only a few of them had been built. He badly wanted to own one. When one of them became available, Leonard rushed to buy it. The Internet was his schoolroom; just the place for a single-minded student. He had no interest in price. Money meant nothing to him. Everything he bought was eventually shipped to Evangelical Missions Inc. at a private mailbox drop in Las Vegas, New Mexico, where he picked them up.

Leonard had always heard that shooting comes naturally to some. When he first moved south he was not surprised to learn that so many sons of Dixie found it so. At Nina's suggestion he found excuses to leave the room when talk turned to shooting doves. Of course, he never accepted an invitation to go hunting. He would say, "The only hunting I do is for lost golf balls."

But he found that he too had a knack for guns, and from the start he had a deeply comfortable sense that they belonged together. He liked the feel of the stock against his shoulder, the touch of the cold, metal barrel in his hand. His finger felt good gripping the trigger. He quickly mastered the pulling, smooth and even. He liked the smell of guns when they fired, and when they had to be taken apart and cleaned with oil and rags, and when he held them reassembled, ready for use.

He started slowly, took his time, mastered each phase before moving on. He spent months shooting simple and basic rifles, without scopes, at short distances. Ten yards at first, then thirty, then fifty. From August through Thanksgiving he fired thousands of rounds. Always, he studied and evaluated his efforts, learned about windage and elevation, the effects of temperature, humidity, distance. "Imagine the path of the bullet," he told himself, "calculate the factors; at a thousand yards in a twenty mile-per-hour wind a bullet can veer ten inches off course. Even the round makes a difference; some ammunition is more accurate than others; some more powerful. Make choices. Make allowances." When he could put enough shots into a twelve-inch target at fifty yards to disintegrate it, he moved on. Then he installed the scopes that allowed him to hit targets up to fifteen hundred yards away. He spent many weeks utilizing the scopes at shorter distances—two hundred yards; three hundred yards; five hundred yards. Finally, he set himself up and began firing at targets as distant as a thousand and fifteen hundred yards. He took aim slowly, adjusted his scope, corrected for the wind, elevation, all the conditions subject to change, and then squeezed the trigger and watched the bullet strike the target so far away. Time after time after time.

As his skill increased, he swapped bulls-eye paper targets for life-sized cardboard humans. A year's work and tens of thousands of rounds took him from hitting the center of a man's chest at fifty feet to doing it from a half mile or more. By then he could take apart and reassemble every rifle he owned in less than sixty seconds. He learned the specs on every type of round: who manufactured it, what it could do; what kind of weapon and which particular ammunition was best for every possible circumstance.

During the second year, Leonard's weight leveled off at 170 pounds. The stubble-short hair on his head now matched his beard, steel gray with patchy reminders of darker days. At fifty-six years old he'd never felt nearly so powerful. He was also certain that few individuals had ever attained comparable accuracy with so varied a group of long guns. He'd put thousands of hours into his shotguns and rifles. He'd perfected his skills in the heat of the desert's summer sun, in the driving rain, the cold and snow, and all this at morning light, high noon, and twilight. He had total confidence he could hit any target in any circumstance. He'd even achieved a high degree of mastery while practicing by standing on a small trampoline. The target and the shooter move, and then the moment arrives, the trigger is pulled, the bullet flies, and the target is hit.

Two years alone can do strange things to a man, even a man so resolved in his purpose as Leonard Martin. He had stretches of time as long as a month or more when he didn't speak a single word to another human being, not to anyone. He began speaking to himself, not out loud, but still they were conversations with himself. He had long talks about the weather—how to spot the movement of a storm, what the changing shapes of the clouds meant for the next day—and about the creatures he shared the New Mexico wilderness with. "The rabbits," he'd say to himself, "they run four or five jumps and then change direction. Why do they do that?" He studied them closely, sometimes sitting on a chair in front of his cabin for many hours without moving. There was a method to their movement, he realized. At least three-quarters of the time when a rabbit jumped in another direction it was to his right. "If I were a coyote," he said, "I'd chase to the right and I'd have rabbit for dinner." Leonard watched all the living things around him: the birds, the deer, and the prairie dogs; even the insects, the beetles, the spiders and butterflies. They all had a purpose, and they all had a pattern to their lives. He'd never given a thought to any of them before. Now he felt he knew them, knew them in a way other men did not. Some of the larger animals he came to recognize by sight. One rabbit in particular became his favorite. He was scruffy like all the others, but he had a dark spot on his hindquarters and a piece missing from one ear that made him easy to identify. Leonard named him Henry, after Frogman Henry. There were no frogs around, so the rabbit would do. He often sang, out loud, "Ain't Got No Home" in his best Frogman Henry voice. One day Henry didn't show up. Leonard never saw him again. "It's a cruel world," he said to himself. Leonard could not hurt any of the animals that lived around him. In fact, he couldn't even stomp on a pesky insect. They all had complicated lives, he told himself, and he had no business disturbing them. They respected him. He respected them. Many times he could have shot any one of a multitude of living creatures racing, jumping, or crawling about his personal firing range. In truth, it would have been very helpful to do so, but he never fired a bullet in anger at any living thing in New Mexico.

After two years in the mountains of the southwest, Leonard Martin packed everything he needed into the evangelical SUV and began his journey to Boston.

TEN

New York

IN THE GRAND SCHEME of the newspaper business, the common run of those who write obituaries comprises youngsters on an anxious path to better things, and played-out pros with more past than future. There are, of course, exceptions. For many years, the *New York Times's* obituary page framed the work of Robert McG. Thomas, considered by many to be the newspaper's finest writer. After he died, others searched vainly for his magic, Isobel Gitlin among them.

She stood out in the paper's notorious garden of strivers—aggressive, obsessive, persistent young weeds growing with graceless gusto to the light. She'd been hired out of graduate school, where she studied Western Classics, not journalism, pretty much at her leisure, and wrote a column in the campus paper, popularly referred to as *3S* but officially called "Sex and the Serious Scholar." When she first heard of Christopher Hopman, Isobel had put four uneventful years into the *Times* and acquired a faint reputation for cheerful detachment.

Isobel seemed genuinely pleased with every assignment. She never badgered her editors for work on better stories. The ones she did get, while varied, were always local and rarely involved significant news. Whatever she worked on—Brooklyn sewer problems, Manhattan zoning battles, crack run amok in the Jersey suburbs—didn't really have to be published. If it struck someone as interesting and fit the space plan for the day, it might pop up in the back somewhere, to Isobel's delight. Most of the time she gladly researched stories for fellow reporters. Her self-regard was not tethered to the byline, and this was what set her dramatically, eerily, apart. She often wondered, if only for a moment, if it was her evident self-confidence or easygoing style that made certain editors feel uncomfortable. She was "sent to Siberia" after the firing of an aged, embittered elephant, Phil Ross, a reporter who had enjoyed decades of high status before his banishment to the bowels of the obit page. Sent there by editors not even born when he filed his first byline story in the *Times,* Ross, in his anger, apparently bet a colleague fifty bucks he could populate the obituary page, time after time, with feature items on the deaths of mediocre, second-rate athletes: a shortstop who, in an otherwise undistinguished career, drove in the tie run in the eighth inning of a World Series game in the 1940s; an Irish lightweight, little more than a club fighter, who fought thirty-eight times, winning thirty-two without ever boxing for the championship. A month after praising the Irishman, he snuck in a small obit for a woman he claimed was "the finest athlete" ever to attend the all-female Vassar College. Shortly after that, he got caught when, in a fit of reckless exuberance, he tried to lead one edition with an obituary for someone he dubbed "Mr. Shuffleboard."

When permanently assigned to obits, Isobel understood that someone had succeeded in getting her out of sight, or out of hearing. That did not diminish her sense that this lateral demotion was a fine thing:

a chance to do serious, worthwhile work, the work of Robert McG. Thomas.

The *New York Times* is the world's newspaper of record and also a key asset in a very large media conglomerate of nearly twenty newspapers, more than a half-dozen television stations, and a couple of radio stations; it is a publicly-owned company sensitive to all the demands and requirements attendant upon high profile corporate identity. Of those at the paper who knew Isobel, some claimed that she was hired and retained only because she was Fijian—a white girl, but nevertheless a real honest-to-goodness Fijian. Her mother was a porcelain-skinned French nurse who struck that island's fabled shores on a long-awaited vacation and never went back to Mother France. She soon met Isobel's father, an Oxford-accented British Jew with South Pacific business interests that had moved him, some time before, to become a local citizen. Thus was Isobel born on Fiji's soil, beneath its hopeful, sky-blue flag, soon to speak its three great tongues, plus English and Parisian French besides.

Her father named her Isabel. Her mother pronounced it Eee-so-bel, and so they spelled it Isobel. She was five foot four in stocking feet, and although unable to ignore a half-dozen unwelcome pounds, on a good day Isobel could admit that she probably looked as good as a thirty-year-old woman should. She did not confuse herself with the flat-bellied, hard-assed, high-titted beauties infesting the *Times*. But after a drink and a glimpse in a flattering mirror she could be confident any man worth coming across might think her attractive. Isobel's jet-black hair was cut to the shoulders. It complemented her creamy skin and small, hazel eyes. Her nose was thin but good, her cheekbones high like her mother's, and her chin very much English. Isobel dressed less carefully than most. She liked loose woolen suits in bright, clear colors. She wore rimless drugstore glasses for reading, which meant that she looked through them most of the time. She once heard a sympathetic colleague describe her appearance as "studious." Isobel did not know if that was to the good.

Diversity, an ongoing enterprise and a major cultural force at the *Times*, is not an inordinately difficult pursuit for that institution. Droves of Latinos, African Americans, Euros, Asians, and diverse others, representing the wide world's groups and classes, constantly besiege the paper for jobs. Yet some at the *Times* contend that management is never satisfied. They hold that its Human Resources barons (hardly newspaper people themselves) hunger unreasonably for the still-under-represented. Pacific Islanders were always at a premium. Thus, a female Fijian (white or not) crossing the HR horizon appeared as glory incarnate, a pearl very much above price. That Isobel suffered, on frequent occasion, from a vexing stutter added to her luster. The *Times* chose to classify it as a disability. After her first long interview, Isobel Gitlin e-mailed her parents that she had much to be cheerful about. The following day the *Times* offered her employment.

Isobel Gitlin wrote Christopher Hopman's obituary. Although the news section of the paper carried a prominent story about the killing, her obit's high point was the cause and manner of death: great man gunned down on golf course by high-powered rifle, no trace of physical evidence, no suspect, no hint of motive. She researched his life as a captain of industry, arts patron, and philanthropist. It was well documented and easily discovered through standard sources. Amid a generation of senior corporate executives that blossomed in the Reagan years, Hopman excelled as a driver of corporate expansion wielding leveraged debt as his weapon of choice. He didn't *run* companies. He bought and sold them. His business was rerigging, repainting, rewrapping them for sale. As Isobel studied Hopman's history she identified only one exposed mistake: his acquisition of controlling interest in a Houston-based holding company that included among its assets Knowland & Sons—the company most thought had precipitated the great southeastern E. coli disaster three years earlier. She highlighted that point in her notes and included it as a subordinate clause in a lengthy sentence somewhere in the middle of the piece.

"There are only two places in the paper," an editor told her once, "where you'll find absolute certainty: Sports and Obituaries. You make sure you get the score right." She took that more seriously than he could have hoped.

ELEVEN

New York

Nathan Stein was angry. He hated whatever he did not understand, and now he felt that a good deal of gobbledy-gook had been shoved in his face, possibly to make him feel small, trapped, mocked, morose.

"Agar? What the hell's 'agar'?" he demanded, "and this 'sorba whatever, something MacConkey'? And what the fuck is 'smack'? I thought it was some kind of heroin. What the hell kind of equipment is that?" He'd liked this Hindu woman, or whatever the hell she was, at first glance. She was pretty as a picture: dark and sharp featured, with little green stones in her ears and a nice yellow, silky thing hanging off her shoulder. He thought she was supposed to have a dot in the middle of her forehead, but no matter. She looked like a lovely doll and stood a good six inches shorter than him, a difference he enjoyed infrequently. She'd been standing there for half an hour before she had a chance to say a word.

"Sorbitol, Mr. Stein," she replied in a lilting, chimelike voice. "It's called a sorbitol-MacConkey agar. That is S-M-A-C, or smack, if you will. As noted in the report before you, the agar itself is made up of agar-agar. It's—"

"Agar-agar?" he exploded. "Give me a break! And smack is a goddamn illegal drug. Christ, Tom!" he whined, exasperated, appealing to the man on his left. "This sounds like Abbott and fucking Costello. Agar's on first and agar's on second."

Big Irish Tom Maloney shifted position wearily, it seemed to Dr. Ganga Roy, perhaps in an effort to keep his suit jacket from getting stuck beneath his ample backside. She was almost as bemused by her odd little class as she was by her remarkable classroom.

The main section of Nathan Stein's office, where they were meeting today, was twenty-five feet wide and eighteen feet deep. Its windows looked from the fifty-third floor over Manhattan north of the Battery. Stein's battleship of a desk occupied the southeast corner of the room, and the light behind him lasted all morning long. He set it up that way purposely. The light was so bright behind him it hid his facial expression from anyone sitting in any of the four leather chairs that lined up to face him across the desk. Ten feet behind them, in the middle of the room, was a brass-fitted glass conference table surrounded by a dozen very different, very expensive chairs. Beneath that grouping a large red Bactrian rug, perhaps a hundred feet square, bespoke the anguished labor of a thousand tiny fingers. At the far end of the office were a black leather sofa, two huge chairs, and a massive sleek black-wood coffee table. Two doors, set off to the right of that furniture, led to Stein's private bathroom and bedroom, so Dr. Roy supposed, completing his home away from all his other homes.

She'd stood and been ignored for the past twenty minutes, sunlight behind her, an easel at her side. Because she was standing, and because of the easel, where she stood became the head of the table.

Tom Maloney faced her from his least favorite chair, the unforgiving mahogany number that forced his body into an awkward forward lean. He was stuck with it because Nathan had chosen the velvet to his right.

Nathan Stein was a genius at making things as difficult as possible. Today he was at the top of his game, and no wonder. The Knowland business had just hit the fan.

Not twenty-four hours ago, when Tom first called Dr. Ganga Roy, he'd modestly introduced himself as Senior Vice President and Director of Mergers and Acquisitions. "Which is," he said, "when you come right down to it, just a lot of words." He'd heard from a research director he knew that Dr. Roy was quite good and "quite tiny," and hoped that the latter might have a soothing effect—that Napoleonfucking Stein, as he was known to so many at Stein, Gelb, Hector & Wills Securities, might find her smallness pleasing. This morning Tom had personally helped her set up the flip-chart easel she'd brought. He buzzed around her cheerfully until the others tromped in, none of them extending even the courtesy of a glance her way, and then Tom too acted as if she wasn't there. She might have been the cleaning woman patiently waiting to make some slight move without causing notice. And so she stood for twenty minutes as the others argued, Tom took his seat, and the spectacle progressed.

She gathered that the big black man, the one Tom told her was Wesley Pitts, had incurred Mr. Stein's disfavor. The matter had something to do with Houston. "Did you talk to Pat Grath *yourself*?" Mr. Stein was asking as they entered. Pitts said he'd talked to Grath and Billy MacNeal too. Now they were sitting, and she chose not to. Tom Maloney's chubby, English-looking cheeks seemed to sag as he followed the conversation. Pitts said, "They're all scared shitless. They've got hundreds of millions at stake." Now Stein snarled most unbecomingly. "Tell me again," he demanded.

Pitts's eyes were large and round, fraught with more than information—bulging with urgency, fighting an anxious tension. "Pat got a call from the plant manager in Tennessee. His name is Ochs." Pitts's extraordinarily large hands fumbled through a tiny notepad. "Floyd Ochs. One of his foremen, a guy named Wayne Korman, told him to shut down his line. He, Korman, said something about the readings being incomplete. Stuff was getting by untested. He said they'd been shipping out beef with E. coli bacteria since yesterday. He wanted to clean the whole operation, scrap the meat supply, and get new cattle before they started again. It seems they've been running around the clock. Ochs mentioned 'operator fatigue' to Grath. Anyway, Ochs told Korman not to do a fucking thing. He told him to take no action. He told him to wait for instructions. Then he called Grath. Grath told Billy Mac and Billy's shit turned to water. The IPO—that's all he thinks about. That's when Pat called me. And that's it, Nathan. That's all I've got."

"And what about Hopman?"

"I called Hopman myself," said Tom Maloney. "He wants to hear what we have to say and that's why we are sitting here now. That's why we need to do this now. We need to get a handle on the scope of this problem."

Silence at last settled into the room. They all looked at Nathan Stein and waited.

"Shit, Maloney!" he suddenly squawked in the strained, unpleasant voice of a student who understands nothing and blames that on the book. "Fucking sonofabitch!"

It surprised Dr. Roy only a little that they'd paid no attention to her, despite her doll-like beauty, despite her unconventional costume and easel. She was, she knew, a kind of servant—however well compensated. What amazed her was how freely these people talked in front of the help. She would certainly have excused her half-deaf Polish cleaning woman to ensure privacy for a sensitive phone conversation or a visit with friends. Where she came from, one accorded servants the very real respect due to those positioned to do one harm. Mid-level managers, research directors, whom she'd met by the many hundreds, did not behave this way. Now she knew those at the top were no different. Even faculty meetings were more discreet.

Now, Stein was looking at her, seeing her in his mind, she sensed, as the only one in the room not yet immersed in the troubles of Stein, Gelb, Hector & Wills Securities. "Sorry about all that," he said, attempting a gracious smile, "and you are Dr. Roy. Am I right?"

Maloney shot to his feet much more limberly than she supposed he could. He ran through her credentials and introduced her to Stein (Vice Chairman of Stein, Gelb, Hector & Wills; this man, she was sure, could only have gotten his crown by inheritance), and Pitts (described as the firm's invaluable Vice President for Client Relations, whatever that might mean; he was very likely an ex-athlete, almost certainly some kind of salesman). And then there was the only female at the table, Louise Hollingsworth, a tall, stiff-necked, sharp-featured woman, small shouldered and lean, wiry hair unfortunately blonde, not at all flattered by her rich floral scent, black skirt, pink silk blouse, and heels. Maloney described Louise as "our most Senior Analyst, but in reality, much, much more." Louise rose uncomfortably, unhappily, to shake hands. Even in her midthirties, even under the corporate get-up and ill-advised touches, Dr. Roy pictured a girl spending her best years free of lipstick and casual friends, haunting the stacks of a cozy New England college—Hampshire, Marlboro, maybe Bard—writing very long papers.

Stein got down to business by picking up the report he'd brought with him. He waved the document in the air and made his scrambled, inflamed speech about agar. The fleeting impulse to gallantry was now dead. He'd remembered what he did not understand. He continued:

"Agar's on first and agar's on second. No, agar's on first, smack's on second, crack's on third. It reads like I don't know what." No one appeared to disagree. "Let me ask you this, Dr. Roy. What's this stuff about 'Consequential Developments'? I don't know what the hell it means but I don't like the sound of it. Where do you get that from anyway? How do you know what will happen?"

His bratty-student voice rose even higher. "Isn't that a medical conclusion? You're a Ph.D., right? Rockefeller Institute?" He held up the cover of the report and pointed to her name.

"That is correct. I am Ganga Roy, Ph.D."

"Well, damnit, that's what I mean!" Stein exploded. "What we've got here is just some technical bullshit. Thank you Dr. Roy for your technical report. But all this crap about consequences—am I confused or what? Isn't that a medical thing? A medical kind of judgment? Don't we need a medical expert to make a call like that?" He stared at the Indian woman, eyes expectant, all but asking, "Aren't we one man short here?"

She could not have imagined a more delicious turn to the conversation.

"Oh, I certainly agree. I certainly do." She flicked an eye toward her new friend Tom, to see whether he was in touch with the joy of the moment. He gave no sign of it. "And most certainly you have the medical opinion upon which you rightly insist. I am also Ganga Roy, MD. I am also a medical doctor, you see. Much like agar-agar, Mr. Stein, you may wish to regard me as doctor-doctor. And, if I may add, with some modesty, I consult for many firms as well as your own, precisely because I am qualified to provide the very thing that you have aptly identified, which is to say, an expert opinion."

Which was, after all, why Tom Maloney had called her yesterday requesting a "detailed and complete" briefing on the subject of potential problems associated with E. coli contamination in ground beef.

Dr. Roy, a fellow at the Rockefeller Institute and professor of medicine at Albert Einstein College of Medicine, consulted with many firms. She billed on a "per day" basis: fifteen hundred dollars for research and reports (plus a thousand more should she appear at a meeting, like this one, to explain her work); five thousand a day for depositions or court appearances. Last year this arrangement brought her eighty thousand in extra income, which included nine thousand in research fees from Stein, Gelb, Hector & Wills; several of whose functionaries had, in recent months, asked her to investigate the practices of companies in which Stein, Gelb had taken an interest. She reported that the objects of their interest did or did not pollute, were or were not at risk for regulatory sanction. Something like that, she presumed, drove Tom Maloney's agenda now.

Until yesterday she hadn't heard of Tom Maloney. During their initial chat, he insisted with unexpected force, though never impolitely, that she present the following day. She told him her schedule would not permit. He doubled her rate to offset the inconvenience. She resisted. He persisted. She gave in before he got to the point of indicating the dollar value of those who sought her counsel. She would have guessed that the woman got a million or two; the black man something more than that; the others even more. Her guesses would have been far short of reality. Further, he did not mention the name of the specific firm in which they had taken an interest. He did emphasize that her audience would be unacquainted with the subject matter. This input was unnecessary. Dr. Roy understood that Stein, Gelb, Hector & Wills Securities did not, themselves, process meat.

She followed her rebuke to Nathan with a slight, charming smile. That crossed his wires sufficiently to quiet him for a moment. Tom saw his opportunity and slid a hand onto Stein's shoulder.

"Just part of the job," he thought, "but not *just* part of the job." Keeping Nathan Stein on an even keel in times of crisis had become

Tom Maloney's most important task. It hadn't always been so. Twenty years ago, Tom recalled, Nathan had been just as hard-ass about things, equally as aggressive, maybe more so, and probably meaner than he was now. But it played better in his late twenties than in middle age. Ambition is a garment best worn by the young. Tom knew that just as well as he knew who Nathan Stein was the first time he met him.

Tom was standing at the crowded bar waiting for the bartender to make his drinks. His friends were seated across the busy, noisy barroom. Lancers was the name of the place. It had changed names a half dozen times since then, but in those early, heady days it was the Wall Street equivalent of a cop bar. But Lancers, instead of serving as a home away from home for the city's armed and dangerous blue-collar workers, was filled with stock traders and brokers unwinding as they came off the floor, trying to do two things at the same time—overhear any nugget of news they might make money with, and looking to get laid. Naturally there were the secretaries seeking to better themselves, carefully deciding who to fuck and who not to. The raptors, of course, were there too. Raptors was the name given to people like Nathan Stein. They already had the power and they still had their youth. Some of them made it on their own. Many had more than a little help here and there. A few, like Nathan, were lucky enough to be born into it. Their name was on the door. "Grandson of Ben." Everybody knew him as that.

Nathan could have done as some did: played golf and fucked every woman he could. And there was no shortage of them to be found at Stein, Gelb and every other firm in the neighborhood. He might have paid little or no attention to the real business of business. Tom often wondered how some men could squander opportunity in such a manner. "Good Christ," he thought. Had he been fortunate enough to be a son-of or grandson-of, he would surely have done what Nathan Stein did. He would have grabbed that golden ring in his cradle and . . . just give me the chance! Tom wished. He didn't know him personally, but he admired Nathan Stein. What he didn't know was that Nathan Stein admired him.

Nathan didn't have big dreams. He had big plans. He knew, and so did Tom Maloney, the difference between the two. Anyone could dream. Only the powerful could make plans. And Nathan had every reason to believe he would bring his to fruition right on schedule. After all, his name *was* on the door. He viewed Stein, Gelb, Hector & Wills Securities as the major leagues, the NFL, and he saw the rest of the financial world as his farm system, his own private version of college football. He scouted, spotted talent, watched it develop and mature, then drafted accordingly. Although Maloney didn't know it, Nathan had his eyes on Tom for a while. Maloney was a definite first-round draft choice.

"Maloney," said Nathan Stein, maneuvering his way next to the big Irishman. He stuck out his hand. "Nathan Stein."

Tom said, "Good to meet you. I'm Tom Maloney."

"I know who you are and you've no idea how good it is . . . for you."

"Beg your pardon?" The bar was very noisy and the two had to shout at each other only inches apart to be heard. "What?"

"Come see me tomorrow, early as possible," said Stein, handing Tom his card. "You're coming to work for me."

"I am?"

"Give them your notice, Tom. We'll work it out in the morning." Then Nathan Stein looked into Tom Maloney's eyes in the way only the wealthy can when they see someone who is not, someone who has just hit the jackpot. "You're a rich man now, Tom."

That memory ran through Tom's mind as he kneaded Nathan's shoulder gently and looked at the lovely Indian woman. He said, "Dr. Roy, if you please, start from the beginning."

"Yes, thank you Mr. Maloney. I shall."

She'd stayed up all night fine-tuning her notes, preparing several dozen flip charts framing brightly printed words, illustrations, and simple diagrams. She referred to these as she went along.

"Bacteria," she began, "is the dominant life form on earth. I'm sure you all know that cockroaches and sharks have remained essentially unchanged for hundreds of millions of years. They are newcomers, I assure you. Bacteria have been here for billions of years and will be here for billions more. Oh, yes! When our planet is only dead rock it will teem with bacteria. They will have evolved, mutated, no matter the conditions. Imagine a life form so quick to protect its own interest that when you kill it you instantly make its kind stronger, the more difficult to kill again. The more ways you find to kill it, the stronger you help it to be. Bacteria as a life form is impervious to destruction."

She paused very briefly to gauge the room. They might be masters of money, but they were now her students. Even this disordered Stein could not resist the music in her voice, or the menace in her words.

"Did you know that NASA has tested the viability of bacteria during interplanetary travel? A species of bacteria called *Bacillus subtilis* withstood the rigors of space trapped in an absolute vacuum for more than six years. It emerged alive, and, as it were, ready for action."

She flipped the NASA experiment chart over.

"And here on earth," she continued, energized by the concentration flowing to her, "you know all about the Great Plague of the fourteenth century. Did you also know Napoleon lost an army of twenty thousand in Haiti without a single battle? Did you know twenty million died in the year 1918 from influenza? Imagine that. What we cannot imagine are all the plagues over millions of years, all the millions of humans, pre-humans, non-humans taken with none to remember and none to record."

She took a slow, deep breath through her nose, exhaling from her mouth. It satisfied her like iced lemonade on a hot, dry day. But the ecstasy she felt was in the teaching.

"Now," said Ganga Roy, "let us think about E. coli."

She explained that as bacterial cells are everywhere, many will, in the normal course of their travels, acquire genetic information from various sources. The flip chart listed these sources: bacterial viruses, plasmids, slices or chunks of DNA floating around and about.

"By chance or purpose, bacteria have the knack of continuous self-improvement. They pick up information. This information may come in handy. It may help them survive, which is all that they really care about. The term 'E. coli' describes a group of bacteria. And that, I fear, brings us to the very unfortunate connection between E. coli and human beings."

The next sheet contained a blue-bordered box, surrounded by an attractive swirl of multi-colored dots. Inside it she had artfully printed these bright red letters and numerals:

O157:H7

"This," said Dr. Roy, "is the primary cause of danger to humans emanating from the E. coli world. How has it become such a dangerous organism? Long ago a single cell acquired a bacterial virus, a virus adapted to life within bacterial organisms. This particular virus had the ability to insert its own DNA into the bacteria's chromosome without harming the bacterium, and it did, remaining there over the countless generations ever since. Each time this bacterial cell divides, the virus DNA, which is now part of the bacterial DNA, is part of every succeeding cell. These daughter cells of the originally infected bacterium constitute the E. coli strain of which we speak: O157:H7."

She decided to skip the E. coli testing process—the agar and sorbitol and smack—leave it for later, avoid another outburst. At this point she could not imagine it helping the flow. Briefly, she checked the group. She wanted no loose ends distracting them now. Nathan Stein obliged her with a swagger. "So all of these E. coli come from the first one."

"Precisely," she said, rewarding him with her first unguarded smile. "Much to our distress as human beings, this virus's genetic information—the virus that is now inseparable from the bacteria—contains instructions for the production of a toxin, or poison, which is called 'Shiga-like toxin' or 'SLT,' also called 'Vero toxin.'" By now they were all taking notes, except Tom Maloney.

As her next flip chart illustrated, "Our friend the E. coli O157:H7 has no choice at all but to produce this toxin. Why is that bad for us?" she asked Nathan Stein, paying him the improbable courtesy of suggesting that he might know. "The toxin is a protein," she said. "That protein can cause severe damage to intestinal epithelial cells—cells that line the wall of the gut."

"What kind of damage?" again she pretended to ask Nathan Stein, presenting her next sheet, simple but disturbing. "The protein degrades the epithelial cells, causing us to lose water and salts. But does it stop there? I am afraid not. It damages our blood vessels as well. The result? Bleeding. A very great deal of bleeding."

She cast her glance around the room, grappling every eye to her own, preparing them for the capper:

"Hemorrhaging!" she declared, showing the sheet with the terrible word leaping off the page.

The next sheet depicted children at play—elegant, inventive, stick-figures of children.

"Those in the most danger are children. Why? They are often too small to fight the effects of blood loss and loss of bodily fluids. And what else may happen to them?"

Dr. Roy knew they were now on terrain where Nathan Stein was likeliest to rebel. They'd arrived at the section of her report entitled "Consequential Developments." She introduced a more somber note to her voice.

"In some cases another syndrome may also be involved. It's called hemolytic uremic syndrome, or HUS." And there they were, all three letters: large, red, ornately inscribed.

HUS

"HUS is characterized by kidney failure and loss of red blood cells, and is most dangerous to children. Perhaps 5 to 10 percent of the littlest ones will progress to this stage of disease. In the most severe of these cases, they will suffer permanent kidney damage."

Now came two more stick figures, one in a bed, one stooping over a walking cane.

"The presence of the E. coli we are concerned with also presents potential for traumatic events among the elderly and people with chronic debilitating disease. For older people who suffer with respiratory or heart disease, or one of many conditions weakening their immune systems, to become infected with E. coli 0157:H7 is often deadly."

She paused. The sudden unease in the room was positively physical.

"Deadly?" asked Louise Hollingsworth in a hushed, and surprisingly but distinctly disgusted, voice. "*How* deadly? I don't mean *how* do they die; I mean *how many* of them die."

The next few flip charts presented the numbers.

"The latest available data from the Centers for Disease Control show seventy-three thousand cases of this kind of E. coli contamination for the latest year studied."

Dr. Roy became brisk, even cheerful again, referring her group to the flip chart pages, and to the tables at the end of her report.

"The hospitalization rate for cases with extreme complications, meaning a progression to HUS, is a jot less than three tenths of one percent. Very few developed HUS. Among those who did, however, 28 percent died. That means the annual total of deaths attributed to O157:H7 was sixty-one. For all patients progressing to HUS, considering all causes, the death rate is between 3 and 5 percent. Among the elderly," Dr. Roy said, "it will kill about half."

"Half?" Stein cried out with startling force. "You mean half the old people getting E. coli are going to die?"

"No," Dr. Roy told him, unruffled, quickly taking in the others. Pitts looked grave, but by no means threatened. The morbid cast to Louise's brown eyes had deepened, and perceptibly. Maloney kept his focus on Stein, reacting only marginally to the unhappy news in the air.

She thought she'd made the figures clear. Perhaps they were misunderstood. Most likely, Mr. Stein had jangled their nerves and their brains. She wanted to say, "Now, everyone, take a deep breath."

Instead, she raised her small right hand in calming benediction. "Those estimates are only for the demographic group generally referred to as elderly and infirm," she explained, as though it were truly excellent news. "And it only includes those within that group who contact the E. coli, and *then* become ill and progress to hemolytic uremic syndrome, or HUS."

She attempted a reassuring smile.

"And why is that again?" asked Wesley Pitts.

"Excellent question, Mr. Pitts." She was handing out bon-bons to everyone now. "Contact with E. coli 0157:H7 is most often only mildly harmful. However, ingestion of it through a ground beef product introduces the bacteria to the digestive system. It may subsequently leave the digestive system and enter the bloodstream, where it may break down red blood cells with its SLT or Vero toxin. After that, the damaged cells lodge in the kidney, causing kidney failure."

"Can you tell us," asked Pitts, "how you assess the risk mathematically?"

She was off the flip charts now.

"If your meat was contaminated, it would be about one death for every twelve hundred people hospitalized. I said there were about seventy-three thousand people hospitalized yearly with E. coli symptoms. But that figure reflects 150 million cases of food poisoning. Maybe more. Many get sick from agents less harmful than E. coli. Among those exposed to E. coli, we're talking *only* about confirmed cases with hospital admission. Many others fall ill but never go to the hospital. Even when they do, many are undoubtedly misdiagnosed. Clinical medicine is often hit or miss. The heart stops in everyone who dies, but not everyone who dies does so from heart failure."

"So, it's not too bad," said Nathan Stein hopefully.

"As I understand it," said Louise Hollingsworth, "there is some potential for a bad outcome, but the numbers are actually quite favorable."

Dr. Roy nodded. "In my opinion, the science indicates that it would take many thousands of people with food poisoning to result in a single death."

"I know it's in your report," Tom said. "Tell us again how you test for E. coli."

"In order to do that, one must be able to make a definitive identification. For that, one must conduct a stool test using the sorbitol-MacConkey agar. This is a substance resembling gelatin, in which the test may be performed. Without such testing no positive finding for the presence of E. coli bacteria can be asserted."

"Does that mean," asked Maloney, "that in the absence of such a test, any claim that E. coli was present would have no legal validity?"

She smiled the smile that she always smiled when declining to render legal advice. "I am not a lawyer, Mr. Maloney. What I can say is that no scientific credibility would attach to such a claim without the SMAC test. I don't believe a trained medical professional, Ph.D. or MD, would testify to the presence of E. coli without testing—proper testing—as I have described it."

"Tell me," said Maloney, "how readily available is the sorbitol-MacConkey agar in small-town hospitals in the southeastern part of the country?" Maloney had certainly read the report, quite likely more than once.

"It is readily available," Dr. Roy replied. "I would anticipate no difficulty in testing for E. coli in even the smallest of cities. Samples could be sent to any large hospital in the region. Any doctor who suspected E. coli poisoning could get immediate help from Atlanta or Birmingham or Charlotte, for example, or any full-service general hospital."

"We need a month," said Stein.

"I'd like a lot longer," added Wesley Pitts.

"Let me ask you this," said Tom, "in your expert opinion, what would be likely to happen if a substantial supply of E. coli–infected meat was widely distributed in the southeastern states in the next week?"

She should, of course, have seen this coming.

It suddenly dawned on her that she had not been involved in a remotely normal corporate consultation. She was not, and had not been, merely an academic fan-dancer doing her stuff, as she had done so often, for corporate mediocrities whose breadth of mind encompassed little more than expensive lunches and modes of theft.

Whatever this was, the brilliant Dr. Ganga Roy felt entirely out of her depth. She was now almost certainly being asked about real people dying.

She rallied, but not without effort, not without some of the mischief deserting her spirited manner. "The symptoms of this type of food poisoning caused by E. coli O157:H7 usually begin appearing in two to four days. Serious complications within a week; deaths thereafter."

She felt a little lightheaded now, but plucked up the courage to ask, "What do you mean by 'widely distributed?'"

"Hard to say, exactly," said Maloney. "These people make ground beef for a variety of brand names. Most of them house names, named for whatever chain it's being sold in. It's hard to keep track of everything."

"Not entirely," said Louise Hollingsworth, her voice more robust than before. "Competing supermarkets in the same city sell the same product under their own names. Shoppers don't know where it comes from. But the company knows. And the distributors know. They know where every bit of it goes. Of course, at the store level, it often gets mixed together with meat from other suppliers, and that could make positive identification difficult."

"They said that it was only one line," said Nathan Stein. "How much meat could that be?"

Dr. Roy had command of herself again. "If we are talking about a processing plant, there is no such thing as a small problem involving a single machine or production line."

Magically, she seemed to have forgotten the tangible corpses at issue and focused again on relatively cold facts. "Let us say that a single line has reported a problem. Those on other lines may or may not have recognized it as well. They may or may not have seen fit to report what they saw or suspected. Inspectors may find some and miss others. Moreover, if one machine or one product line has E. coli, it is likely to have spread. The entire plant is suspect."

"And that means what, Dr. Roy?" said Maloney, not bothering, or able, to suppress the slight quaver that persisted as he spoke. "Let's say that tens of thousands—perhaps hundreds of thousands—of pounds, maybe millions, get distributed to hundreds of outlets, maybe more. That means *what*?"

She did not respond.

"Dr. Roy?" The others were bearing down, straining from their seats, Louise on her feet, Stein poised to spring like a feral cat, restrained only by Tom Maloney's heavy hand. But it was Maloney who spoke again.

"Let us say, Dr. Roy, that a universe of three hundred thousand people eat this meat. If everyone among the three hundred thousand gets sick, and I realize that's farfetched, and let's say that half are children and elderly, about nine hundred would end up in the hospital. Am I right? Of the nine hundred, perhaps forty-five would advance to HUS. Of that group, with a death rate of 3 to 5 percent we might expect between one and a third and two and a half deaths. Since we can be fairly certain that all three hundred thousand will not become ill—if only half do—that brings the projected deaths to less than one person, doesn't it?"

"You must understand," she said. "If the numbers give us one death for every twelve hundred infected people, that doesn't predict which of the twelve hundred will die. It could be the first or the last. It could be the first ten who die, then ten thousand who don't."

She continued, looking to Maloney as the only one with whom she had any personal link. "Based on your scenario, it is not realistic to suppose that there will be no deaths. There will be deaths. People will die. Some people will die."

"And what's the *worst* that could happen?" Maloney asked, shockingly calm again.

"Well, the worst," she said, looking over their heads, thinking what she had just said was already in the *worst* class, "would be that you are not dealing with E. coli as we know it. The very worst, if that is what you are asking, would be a newer, stronger, heat-resistant E. coli. Bacteria are killed by heat. That is why steam at high temperature is employed in the slaughter of beef. If you cook beef to a hundred and sixty degrees you will kill the E. coli. Not all bacteria are killed at the same temperature. Salmonella, for instance, requires a higher temperature than E. coli. If our E. coli bacteria mutated to the point at which it could withstand higher temperatures, we could have quite a crisis. Other mutations are also possible, perhaps probable. You should be aware that this deadly strain of E. coli was first identified in 1982, and, while we have learned much about it, that is not long ago. A newer, mutated form of the bacteria may also have a highly increased level of quorum sensing."

"What is that, 'quorum sensing'?" asked Pitts.

"Bacteria, E. coli included, communicate with their own kind. They talk to each other. Dr. Bassler at Princeton has shown that in concentrations above a certain point, E. coli O157:H7 gang up, coordinate behavior, and act together, in community, to regulate virulence. They do this using a technique called quorum sensing. This E. coli is a formidable enemy and it can only improve. Perhaps today it will kill ten times as many as it did yesterday. Tomorrow, perhaps a hundred times. I'm sure that one day, somewhere, we will encounter such a strain—a bacteria that may perhaps kill everyone it touches. The worst possible scenario would be that today is *that* day and your meat company is *that* somewhere."

Dr. Roy was now depleted, but she looked to Tom Maloney and said, "If I may say so, Mr. Maloney, surely there's a scientific as well as a moral obligation to deal with such an event by notifying the public and recalling the meat as soon as possible and insuring that no more of it is distributed. Lives may be saved."

Maloney brought the meeting to a close. On behalf of everyone at Stein, Gelb he thanked Dr. Roy for her "super" contribution. Clearly, he explained, this situation required immediate and ongoing attention.

Then he put his hand, protectively, featherlike, on her very narrow, yellow silk shoulder, and spoke almost in a whisper, not secretively, but in confidence. He would remember speaking to her this way years later, when Walter Sherman spoke in very much the same confiding way to him near the kitchen door in Billy's Bar.

"Dr. Roy," he said, "we will need your exceptional expertise, perhaps at a moment's notice, for the next thirty days at least. I know you have a busy schedule. Still, I would like you to make yourself available as needed."

"I regret to say that I do have a full schedule. Perhaps I could—"

"We would expect you to bill us as though you were in court seven days a week, until further notice. Before you leave, I will have Mr. Stein's secretary give you a check for a month's fee at five thousand dollars a day. Can I count on you?"

As a very young child, Ganga Roy had had the same dream several times. In it, she was reading a book her mother had told her not to read. As she turned the pages, she grew fearful, certain that something bad would leap from one of those pages and do her great harm. But so overwhelming was her curiosity that she could not stop. As she turned the pages, they began to turn themselves. She awoke from each of these dreams drenched in perspiration, trembling uncontrollably, never having known what it was that leapt at her from the pages.

Tom was smiling down at her, piteously, it seemed. If ever a man stood in need of a helping hand it was certainly he. "Very well," she said, in what she hoped was a cool, offhand tone, "I shall make arrangements." She started to take down her flip charts, but Tom touched her arm.

"Thank you again, everyone," Tom said. "And before you go I'll need your notes. Leave them here with your copies of Dr. Roy's report. I'll need a communications review on your computers, and this is," he added sternly, "a 'voice only' matter."

Wesley Pitts and Louise Hollingsworth left empty-handed, without further conversation, each nodding politely to Ganga Roy.

"Dr. Roy," said Tom Maloney, Nathan Stein at his side, "I'm so happy you'll be helping us. If I could have whatever copies of your report are in your possession . . . and if you could get me your notes, I'll need them as well. And I'd like to keep those, too. " He nodded at the easel. She handed him the reports.

He asked if she'd used a computer to prepare for this presentation. She nodded.

"At the institute or the school?"

"At home. Last night."

"It might be best if you removed everything relating to this matter from your hard disk. Copy it to one of ours. If you need computer time we'll give you whatever you need right here. My office will call you to make arrangements. Let's try to keep our work in the building."

"But of course, Mr. Maloney," she smiled again, theatrically. They shook hands and she left.

"Tom," said Nathan Stein when Dr. Roy was gone, "what the hell was that? What do we need from her?"

"Loyalty. Silence."

"Are we looking at a shithouse?"

"Could be, Nathan. Yes."

"Then why not give her some real money? If we need to buy her, let's do it."

Maloney shook his head. "Nathan, you make too much fucking money. You got what, forty-three, forty-four million last year?" Maloney smiled. "You've lost all perspective. We just gave her a check for a hundred fifty-five thousand dollars. To normal people that is real money. And it's money she is honor-bound to earn." Nathan looked unconvinced until Tom said, "Take my word, she *belongs* to us."

TWELVE

New York

ELIZABETH REID HAD LUNCH delivered to Nathan Stein's suite at twelve thirty. She ordered from Cippriani's because Nathan was especially fond of their fettuccini with clams. For Tom Maloney she ordered the salmon. Both men had taken a walk after their meeting with Dr. Roy ended. She was ready for their return. Ms. Reid had been Mr. Stein's secretary for seventeen years. She eschewed the inflated title "Administrative Assistant" while gladly keeping the inflated compensation it carried. While she was only two years older than he, she looked upon Nathan Stein as a nephew or cousin who needed assistance. She was loyal beyond any question, privy to most of his secrets, and quietly instructed her sister in buying and selling stocks about which she had acquired some overheard knowledge. Perhaps, she thought, it might be questionable, although she never for an instant thought it might be illegal. Everyone in the higher reaches of Stein, Gelb benefited in some way, and she was content to consider such things part of her pay package. Of course, she never overdid it.

Her sister's account, maintained at a distance at Smith Barney, was worth hundreds of thousands, not millions.

She saw Wesley Pitts and Louise Hollingsworth leave the meeting, followed shortly thereafter by the lovely Indian woman, Dr. Ganga Roy. Tom Maloney had given Elizabeth an envelope with instructions to hand it to Dr. Roy as she left. She knew there was a check inside. "It has to be a large one," Elizabeth thought. The envelope was sealed.

She arranged the lunch carefully on the table in front of Mr. Stein's couch. When Nathan and Tom returned she told them the food had arrived. Then she left them, closing the door behind her.

"What is it we're sure of, Tom? Actually *know,* not surmise."

"We're certain the Knowland & Sons plant in Lucas, Tennessee, has turned out beef, ground beef, that's testing positive for E. coli and that it's happening too frequently for them to disregard. They're thinking of shutting down and recalling the meat."

"How frequent is too frequent?"

"The problem seems to be that they've been cited for violations an awful lot. In and of itself, that's not big news. Every meat plant's got E. coli violations. It's all part of the game. But now there's so much bad meat going out, and they've got so many violations, they think they may push the inspectors too far, which is hard to do. Ordinarily, they might recall the meat, shut themselves down, get cleaned up. That costs money, but sometimes it has to be done. Except now, MacNeal is worried about the deal. He wants to know how bad it will hurt to shut down. He wants to know if we can put off the IPO or pull some other rabbit out of the hat. He's scared and he's looking to us for direction." He stopped and listened for signs of progress.

"How can they turn out beef with E. coli? How does that happen?"

"Well, I'll tell you, Nathan, but you probably won't eat beef anymore." Tom laughed and took a forkful of salmon and spinach dripping in sesame sauce. He hoped the walk, the food, and the casual laughter would put Nathan's mind at ease. For all of his faults, Nathan Stein had a keen sense of what to do in the trenches. "That's where we are for sure," thought Tom, "*in the trenches.*" He wanted Nathan clear-headed and sharp as ever. He reiterated the process Billy Mac and Pat Grath had already outlined, complete with its potential downside effect. Tom had been sitting with Wesley Pitts when Billy Mac and Grath were on the conference call. Grath explained the concept of "captive supplies" and the money to be made speculating in live cattle. Knowland had done that, and the herd in question was, they thought, limited to the Tennessee plant. They were almost certain of that much. However, they had also been "mixing" more than usual—this on Billy Mac's orders, which he freely admitted. By "mixing" foreign beef with their existing domestic supply they could increase profits dramatically in the short run. Billy Mac's emphasis was now completely on the short run. He was selling the whole shebang and he wanted cash flow at the highest possible level in anticipation of the stock offering. The plant was also operating around the clock—three full shifts. Everybody in and around Lucas who could walk, crawl, or be dragged into that plant was working there, most six days, and some seven days a week. Almost all of them worked overtime because they always had trouble staffing the third shift. "Like it or not," Billy Mac said to Tom and Wes, "we got drunks, junkies—amphetamines are real big around there—poorly trained incompetents, and men who haven't had a night's sleep in a week. Hey, look. you want the production, you get it any way you can. We got lines running three hundred cattle an hour!" Pat Grath had already talked about "operator fatigue"—a problem that haunted the industry—and he pointed out that the injury rate was now the highest in the company's history.

"It's a fucking time bomb," said Billy Mac, "but who gives a shit. Soon as this thing goes down, we're outta there."

Very nice, thought Tom. However, Billy MacNeal conveniently overlooked the fact that another Stein, Gelb client, Alliance, would inherit his problems and pay a handsome sum to do so.

Grath had explained how the cattle are killed. Tom, obligingly, passed the information along to Nathan. One by one, he told him, the cows were herded into a chute, big enough for only a single animal. "Cows are dumber than shit," Tom recalled Grath saying, with his usual, West Texas, semi-arrogant laugh. "But you'd be surprised how many of them get real antsy right about then, moving around, sort of trying to get out, you know, eyes all funny, squealing like pigs. Almost like they know what's coming." And what was coming was The End. The Knocker—that's what Grath said they called him—used a handheld device that quite literally thrust a steel bolt in the cow's head. "The cow goes down," Grath had said, "usually dead. But when you're running a line at three hundred head an hour, well, goddamnit, you're pushing one through every ten seconds or so. Some of them don't die. They're still alive." After the cow went down, it was hoisted, hung upside down with chains. Its throat was cut. Most of the animals that were still alive died then. However, a few didn't. Federal law was quite specific on this point. The animal had to be "insensible" to pain before butchering was allowed. Grath had snorted at this point in his recitation. "What are they gonna do? Call Johnny Cochran?" The next stop on the line was the giant scissors. They looked like scissors, so that's what Grath called them. Here the cow, dead or alive, had its legs cut off. As Tom told all this to Nathan Stein, he felt an irrepressible urge to laugh—the kind of laugh people have when something awful happens to someone else, the kind of laugh that says, "I'm so glad it's you, not me." He also saw that Nathan was queasy, visibly shaken by the image of anything hung upside down and having its legs cut off.

"You alright?" he asked. Nathan just nodded. Having successfully stifled his nervous laughter, Tom continued. The carcass gets skinned and split in half, he explained. Then it's subjected to Steam Pasteurization, during which the meat is blasted with steam at 180 degrees while passing through a stainless steel chamber thirty-two feet long. When the beef emerges from "SP," as Grath called it, another operator does a Steam Vacuum. The "SV" process is just like a carpet cleaner, he told them. It uses hot water and steam in a vacuum to pick off any remaining hair or fecal matter. "That's cow shit for you fellas in New York City," Grath said with a chuckle. He knew they knew he had never been close to cow shit.

After this, according to Grath's running commentary, the meat was cut up and finally tested for contaminants. Tom stopped at this point to eat the last of his salmon and check Nathan's intestinal stability.

"You okay?" he asked, patting his own stomach.

"Yeah," said Nathan.

"Here's the thing," Tom said, "there's always some meat that tests positive for E. coli. What they do with that meat is sell it to people who make chili—"

"What!"

"No, no. Don't laugh. It's true. They sell the bad meat for chili and dog food because it's cooked before it's sold to the public. Remember, if you cook beef to 160 degrees the E. coli is killed off. It's only a serious problem when you eat those burgers rare. Grath said he himself adds prune puree to ground beef before making a burger; it's supposed to suppress the E. coli, and, he says, makes the burger taste better if its cooked well done. So anyway, it's the chili folks and others who make precooked beef products who get all the contaminated meat."

"Holy shit," Nathan said. "Do you eat chili?"

"No, I don't."

"Me neither. Not anymore. Is that legal? Selling it for chili?"

"It's either legal or nobody much cares. Pat says that's SOP. But what happened here is they needed so much meat to make their own quota that, first, they didn't test as much of the meat as they're supposed to. A lot of it went straight to the grinders. Second, some of the inspectors were tired, hungover, whatever—not up to their usual standards. Those guys work for the government, but they're local people too. They were driving the line. Production was beyond plant capacity and they cut some corners. When they grind this stuff, according to Grath, it all gets mixed together, sort of like putting dressing on a salad and tossing it. The E. coli present in one batch spreads to others, and the whole thing with ground beef is that it's so thoroughly combined the bacteria shows up everywhere."

"Just the ground beef?" Nathan asked.

"No, not just the ground beef, but it's a much bigger problem than with steaks or other cuts of beef. Once you clean those they're apparently okay. Keep in mind, Nathan, I'm telling you what Pat told me. He said there are more than a hundred million cattle in this country, and we eat thirty-five million of them every year. I've got no reason to doubt him on these technical issues, but we can't be a hundred percent sure."

"Dr. Roy didn't tell us any of this," said Nathan.

"Meat packing and animal slaughter is not exactly her area of expertise."

"Yeah, I know . . . all that doctor-doctor shit." Nathan got up from the chair next to his couch, went to his private bathroom, and emerged a few minutes later. Tom was still sitting there.

"So, there's no way there's nothing to this?" the wiry little man asked Tom. Tom could see Nathan was physically trying to squeeze out of this—weasel out if he could. He'd seen Nathan Stein like this before. Just tell him there's a way out and he'll take it, and when it blows up in your face, he'll blame you. On the other hand, Tom knew, tell Nathan Stein *he's* in a bind, that the monsters have surrounded *his* house, and he becomes a single-minded fighting maniac. Tom decided that's what was needed now.

"No," Tom said. "Billy Mac is fucked. That means we're fucked."

"I want to know what our options are."

They decided to meet again later that afternoon and have Wes and Louise join them. Tom's responsibility was to coordinate with the others and present a battle plan for Nathan's approval. The meeting would be in Maloney's office, where he knew Nathan felt comfortable.

They gathered at three o'clock. Wesley Pitts spoke first. He nodded several times. "Let me give my conclusion first, and then explain my logic." He'd been working on this all day, calling around, putting out feelers, checking with players who mattered. He'd spent the last hour and a half thinking about his alternatives, trying to come up with new ones. At the end he hadn't budged from the first idea that came to him on the phone during Pat's initial call, but he'd steadily built up a weight of anxious concern. Now he was more than ready to pass it around.

"If we tell Billy MacNeal to recall his meat and take his plant off line, we are fucked. There is no way around it. First we are fucked with the mutual funds. I went all out with them. I put my credibility on the line, the credibility of this firm. You know it hasn't been easy. Some of these people have doubts. They don't like that much cash going into Billy's pockets. They think we're generously structured. It's taken a lot to keep them in line. If we pull back for a minute, postpone, show any weakness, they will walk. And then there will be a stampede. After that we won't have a second chance. Not only will they not commit a cent, they will laugh at me for trying. And that's just the beginning. Some of these guys do guest shots on cable and *Wall Street Week*, and the rest. We drop the ball on this and they will be talking about it. They will make it, and us, a joke."

Wesley wiped his forehead with a monogrammed handkerchief. To Louise, the shining cotton looked like a bandage raised to a flowing wound. She'd never seen him quite this way, caught between fear and fury. Usually that part was under wraps. Nor had she seen him this eloquent. His normal act was a powerful mix of intellectual force and locker-room vigor. She considered him unique, morally righteous. How many ex-professional football players actually married a woman—a girl, really—he got pregnant? Pitts did. And while Pitts lived in Manhattan while his wife and daughter lived in Detroit, Louise thought she understood. She admired him.

He led with his meticulous grasp of facts based on research; delivered his pitch with celebrity panache, a winner's edge of certainty. And he closed with the knack of knowing the answer before his opposite number thought of the question. He typically spoke slowly, weighting his words with belief. He wasn't speaking slowly now. Louise was fascinated. She was also thrilled.

"People will want to know what went wrong. And it won't take them long to find out Billy shut his Lucas plant because it was putting out poisoned meat. And it won't only be Lucas. All of his plants will have to go down. Pat and Billy swear the other plants are clean, but who knows, and the government doesn't care. If Billy shuts down Lucas, the public will demand he shut them all. And he might even have to shoot his whole captive herd. The minute he recalls one pound of meat, they won't have any choice. It'll make a helluva story. Stein, Gelb, the Texas tycoon, and the horse's ass." Nathan seemed about to say something, but Pitts refused to surrender momentum. "I'm just getting started."

Louise flicked her eyes to Nathan. He looked like a dreadful statue, mouth frozen half-open, stone eyes locked on Wesley, Adam's apple painfully sharp. With this kind of news, Nathan would be looking to her. She'd be his real hope now. Tom would try to soften the edges, but she could turn it around. And Wesley was setting the stage. She felt the excitement build inside her as Wesley thundered on.

"Now, let's move to the mutual funds that currently hold Alliance stock. They've been expanding positions based on what Hopman's putting out on the Second Houston deal. We postpone and they start asking questions. The deal looks weak and Alliance drops three or four points. Now those guys are in Hopman's face. Is he fucking with them, or what? Here's what they start to believe: We are peddling Billy Mac's bullshit and Hopman's peddling ours. Here's what I think we're looking at. First, no Second Houston IPO, now or ever. Second, busted credibility with the funds I've been working, and the funds holding Alliance stock. Third, a foreseeable parting of the ways vis-à-vis Hopman and everyone he knows."

Wesley looked from one to the other. Louise narrowed her eyes when he got to her.

He grinned ferociously. "But wait; there's more. Our own special accounts, all the big ones we've been working, our favored clientele. A deal like this goes down the drain, they never look at us the same. Next time they want this kind of action they go to Morgan Stanley, Prudential, East Bumblefuck Financial. Anywhere but here. We will have our best private accounts holding their noses when we come around. And what about all the assholes on the street? There are plenty of people who hate us as much as we hate them. They will take a thing like this and beat us with it until we are broken. Pretty soon, someone like Ben Stein will be picking through our ashes."

He paused. When he continued, Wesley spoke slowly, choosing his words in the old familiar way. "And then there are the dollars we lose. If this falls through, Stein, Gelb watches seven to eight hundred million dollars slip through its fingers, plus sunk costs, which is the fifteen million we have already tied up in this. All down the drain." Wesley coughed, took a sip of water, and went on.

"Knowland is the principal income stream for Second Houston. A government shutdown, a recall of bacteria-infested ground beef, perhaps just the implication, and you've got trouble pricing and selling the IPO and it no longer looks like a great move for Alliance to purchase control of Billy MacNeal's company. And let me tell you something else," he said, looking particularly at Tom, "Billy MacNeal may be a goddamn billionaire, a colorful character, all that cowboy crap, but to the people I talk to, he's a fucking shitkicker, a wealthy fucking shitkicker, but a shitkicker nonetheless. Folks like us won't run out in the street to stop the bus when it runs over him. We deserve better than to go down in flames with a guy like him."

Nathan looked at Louise. She was busily going through her notes. Tom waited several seconds, then said, "Louise?" She felt ready. Nathan was waiting for her to dish up magic. Confident she had the stuff, Louise was equally aware of the importance of taking it out of the box just right. She opened her attaché case and spread her notes in front of her for easy reference, point by point.

"This is very difficult, especially after hearing Dr. Roy, so let me just lay it out." She paused while Tom cleared his throat and Nathan shifted uneasily in his chair. Then, she dove in. "Six plants distribute ground beef to the same market as Knowland's Lucas plant, which is to say the southeast. Each of the six is owned by a different company. When something like this occurs, it's not all that easy to track down the exact source of the meat."

"You know this to be so?" Tom said.

She saw the nascent glimmer in Nathan's eye. "I do. There have been a surprising number of E. coli incidents over the past ten years. They usually locate the source, but it takes time. And sometimes they never quite get it at all. The stores mix meat, one plant with the other, and it's not as easy as you might think to separate out one from the other. The story is the people getting sick. By the time the source is identified the story has played itself out. Bad hamburger makes page one. Five or six months later, the story about who did it ends up on page fourteen, in a box. Few read it, and most of them forget it before their second cup of coffee. But," and again she paused for effect, "assume things do go badly. Assume that someone does get sick, or worse. Assume the legal vultures all come down from the trees. They will. But they don't know who to sue. So, they sue all six companies. The packers either settle or deny. That's a lawyer's decision. If you settle, you have it sealed. Probably Knowland settles. Why? If someone does get serious, there will be records. How much went to the chili and dog food people? That's all written down. There is documentation. It may not all be accurate, and may not exactly follow the rules, but it's there. Sooner or later some plaintiff's attorney will put it together. The other five may feel they have nothing to hide, in which case they will deny. One or two may have problems of their own we don't know about, stuff they don't want looked into. So maybe they settle. That's what Knowland does. Purely a lawyer's decision. No admission of anything. Confidentiality rules. No investigation that means anything. And all of this is months down the road."

Wesley said, "At what cost? How much?"

"Less than what you were talking about. Twenty to fifty thousand for someone who's hospitalized. And if, God forbid, there's something else, a half million, a million, tops two or three. Historically, that's what it's been."

Tom said, "Something's not clear. Aren't there inspectors crawling all over the plant? Why don't they do the recall and shut it down?"

Louise felt high as a kite. Meeting a twenty-five-year-old bartender as horny as she or a delivery boy with unlimited stamina also made her feel this way. She heard her voice, symphonic, in the distance.

"They don't have the power. The system is built the American way. It's there to protect the industry as well as the people who eat the meat and do the work. We are not Communists here. If you want to take a plant off line, or do practically anything else, you have to report it up the chain. And that's when things slow down. Reports get lost. Reviews take time. There are always appeals. You want to know about recalls? The entire Department of Agriculture cannot order a recall. All they can do is recommend."

Nathan, suddenly back from the dead, joyously barked: "You know what? This is the greatest country on earth."

Louise reached into the spread of notes. "Let me read you something. It's from the *New York Times.* This is purely mainstream." She held up a printout. "It's about a plant called Shapiro, similar to Knowland. Dozens and dozens of violations. Nobody lifted a finger. Inspectors everywhere. All of them know what's going on, but they also know the law. They know they can't do a thing. This is a quote from several inspection reports. They wrote this over and over: 'Preventative measures not implemented and/or not effective.' Do you follow that? What does that mean? Nothing. It's not supposed to."

Louise beamed at her colleagues. "Until 1992 nobody thought E. coli could kill. Then a couple of people died from eating Jack in the Box hamburgers. That's a fast food chain on the west coast. After that they tweaked the system. Passed some regulations. All of which led to what? The rates of E. coli did not change and life goes on."

Tom said, "This is great to hear. But where does it get us?"

"The inspection system is set up to fail," Louise said. "Imagine the worst does happen. People go to the hospital. Maybe one or two succumb. It was bound to happen. And everyone's exposed. The industry, the government agencies, politicians, whatever. The general trend is to cover it up and make it go away. Some people, a couple of liberal papers perhaps, show a little interest. Otherwise, what happens? Cable and the networks march along. They take the message they're given and work it. What I'm saying is that as a practical matter, we may find that moving ahead need not impose prohibitive risks."

Nathan said, "We keep the plant running?"

"I'm not saying that, Nathan. That's something I cannot say, especially after hearing Dr. Roy. That's not a decision I want to make. I'm saying that if you decide to go that route, there may be ways to manage it. I'm not saying it will be easy. We'll have a lot of mountains to move. But as a practical matter . . ."

Tom said, "Thank you, Louise. Frankly that's more good news than I expected." Then he sat back, fingertips touching.

"As I see it," said Tom, "we have three options. First, we can advise Second Houston to recall its ground beef and then postpone or cancel the IPO, with all the consequences Wesley has outlined. Second, we can advise Second Houston to say nothing about any bad meat already out there, hope it takes weeks for the stink to reach Knowland, if it does at all, go forward on our end with the IPO, and deal with adverse effects later on. These will include exposure to Alliance, Second Houston, and potentially to us, in terms of the clients we put into this, and perhaps the value of our own warrants and options down the line. Third and finally, we can advise Second Houston to go forward, to publicly deny any responsibility for anything, and to settle claims on a confidential basis following advice of counsel. We move our clients in and out of both Second Houston and Alliance a bit more quickly than we planned. Simultaneously, Louise starts working now to position the following message: meat packing is not a pretty business, and it's absolutely un-American to scapegoat one company out of many."

Nathan said, "What happens to the price of meat?"

Louise said, "I'd expect a hit to the industry. But it shouldn't last very long. I think we'd see some short-term losses, but no lasting damage. Obviously there are no guarantees."

Wesley said, "I can't think of anything else. One puts us dead in the water. Two puts us waiting to die. Option three gives us a working shot. All we need is a little nerve."

Tom said, "There's one more point that should be made. By allowing this IPO to move forward without disclosing what we know, we are in violation of statute. I'm not suggesting we let that taint our judgment. I just want to have it clearly said, because it's a part of the picture."

Tom Maloney's job as Senior Vice President of Mergers & Acquisitions meant he would be the point man for such a deception. He hadn't reached these lofty heights by being stymied by bad news. He calculated the odds of success in his mind, looked at Nathan, and nodded in agreement. Wesley Pitts watched Tom's eyes and immediately signaled his support. Only Louise, whose analysis led to the third option in the first place, seemed to hesitate. "Dr. Roy said 'people will die.' People will die," said Louise.

"People die every day, Louise," Tom said.

"Like this?" she asked.

Wesley Pitts said, "Remember the natural gas deal we had two years ago? They had a labor problem that held the whole thing up for weeks. When they sent me their plan, do you remember what it said?" He was talking directly to Louise and he waited for an answer. He knew she remembered, but he wanted to hear it out loud. Finally, she said, "Yes, I remember."

"Two million dollars and two lives," Pitts said. "Two million and two lives."

"There's a budget for everything, Louise," said Nathan.

"I know," she said, "I know. But what if Dr. Roy's worst case scenario emerges from this? A lot of people could die. What do we do then?"

"Not going to happen," Nathan said. "And what about our people? What happens to all the people who depend on this firm? We get hurt. We get hurt bad. What do you say to the guy in our Seattle office who's got two kids in college? Or the young hotshot in Chicago who just turned down a job at Merrill or Morgan Stanley because he's confident his future is here, with us, with Stein, Gelb, Hector & Wills? We have people all over the country like that. For more than seventy years our people have trusted their management. That's not going to change on my watch." Nathan stood and waved his arms around as if the act of doing so enabled him to take the entire company and hold it to his breast. "What about all these people right here in New York, right here in this building, on this floor, outside that door? What do we say to them if, today, we make a decision in this room that brings the kind of results Wes talked about?"

Tom Maloney, much to his surprise, choked up. He hadn't heard Nathan talk like that in years. He was reminded of how he once admired the man. Wesley Pitts paid no attention at all to what Nathan just said. It seemed he'd heard that kind of crap from dozens of coaches all his life. He did, however, sense the thrill of victory. "The kind of results Wes talked about." Those were Nathan's words.

Louise Hollingsworth looked at Nathan Stein. She knew he trusted her, relied on the opinions she offered, and demanded unanimous consent for a move like this. Option three was hers. She felt the pressure to support it like rocks stacked on her chest.

"Okay," she said. And with that simple, single word, all doubt vanished from her mind. Her energies were already concentrated on success.

"Sell this," Nathan demanded.

"I'll call Billy Mac," Tom said.

"Call Hopman too," said Nathan.

THIRTEEN

Houston

Billy MacNeal was an OTO: a golden boy among those energetic, innovative Houstonites who owed their wealth to ventures Other Than Oil. As a kid he'd been called by two names: Billy Mac. When he grew up (in his mind becoming a millionaire in his twenties qualified him as a grown up) he decided to add the final note. Thereafter, most folks called him Billy MacNeal—emphasis on the "Mac."

He was a handsome boy: tall, slim, blonde, Texas to the core. He had an engaging way about him. People just naturally loved Billy Mac. At twenty-three he started a company called First Houston Holding. Using practically no cash, he bought undeveloped land no one else seemed to want. His very first purchase included a commercial parcel that he sold to Wal-Mart forty-eight hours after buying it. That, as he enjoyed telling newly-met admirers, really got him started. In the following months he bought a small fishing fleet in the Gulf, two restaurants in Dallas, and a charter bus company connecting Houston, Oklahoma City, and Phoenix, Arizona. In the following year he bought a record company in New Orleans and five radio stations in Louisiana and Mississippi. He didn't care what the company did as long as he could buy it cheap, find a way to inflate its numbers, and sell it for twice (more or less) what he paid.

While attending community college he took up with one of his teachers. They fell in love and got married. Billy Mac was twenty-two. She was thirty-one. She left him three and a half years later, taking their baby son and too much of First Houston Holding for Billy's tastes. That's when he started Second Houston Holding, which in less than eight years accumulated nineteen businesses, including golf courses in Florida, ski resorts in Colorado, a shipping company in the Philippines, textile producers in Central America, half a dozen television stations in the central plains, and several U.S. food processing concerns. The largest of Billy's companies, Knowland & Sons, operated five meat packing plants in the Midwest and southeast.

It was Tom Maloney's idea to make Billy MacNeal a billionaire. He and Wesley Pitts worked out the details with Billy Mac and his top man, Pat Grath. It took only ninety days to reach a substantive agreement, and Tom told Billy to expect a successful IPO within six months. They planned to take Second Houston public and structure the deal so that another, larger holding conglomerate, Alliance Inc., would act as the major buyer. Stein, Gelb, Hector & Wills Securities would sell Billy MacNeal's company to Alliance and others for a total of $1.85 billion. Maloney's meticulous plan allowed for Billy himself to bank four hundred million dollars while retaining a substantial stock position in Alliance Inc. Billy MacNeal's net worth would then exceed a billion dollars.

Getting married again was Billy Mac's idea. Carol Ann Cheetham stood five feet ten, with big tits, a small waist, a pretty face, and the longest, reddest hair you'd ever want to see. Her physical gifts pleased Billy almost as much as her gentle, accepting nature. She had not, in the two years they'd been seeing each other, refused him anything. Nor had she been the one to suggest that every billionaire should have a wife. That was entirely his idea. And so, at nineteen, she became his.

The wedding took place at his home just north of Houston, and for months conversations throughout the state focused on how much it cost. Did Willie Nelson really get a half million, or was it more?

There was no honeymoon. Billy Mac was a workaholic, as Carol Ann imagined most thirty-three-year-old billionaires must be. She sensibly considered her entire life a honeymoon, and waited only for Billy, in one of his many special ways, to grace the towering sundae of her good fortune with a fat, sweet cherry.

Aside from her, Billy's only recreation was diving. Every morning without fail he'd brush his teeth, put on his Speedo, and head for the pool. He'd had it and its three-level diving board apparatus designed and built by the best he could find. The ladder was padded. Most days he'd stand at the midpoint of the second board, twelve feet above the water. He'd breathe as his high-school coach had taught him to not that many years ago: slow and calm to smooth the muscular fibers and settle the jelly in the brain. He'd take three measured steps, bend his right leg at the knee, extend his arms upward, step down, and spring. Once airborne, he'd flip, twist, lay out, and float until he hit the water—long legs straight, feet joined at the ankles, toes curled in. Then he'd swim in one easy stroke to the edge, haul himself out, and do it again and again. His mantra, Pat Grath called it.

Carol Ann liked sitting at poolside reading the paper, lifting her eyes to catch the moment when Billy Mac rose like a god, or an angel. On this particular morning she was looking at the new issue of *Fortune* and her eye caught a story she figured might interest him. Depending on the look in his eyes, the look that told her how much of a good time he was having, she might mention the story when he got out, or wait until he was done for the day.

When she lifted her eyes from the magazine to see him jump, she saw that Billy Mac lay on his side, along the length of the diving board, left leg dangling, something dripping into the water. She screamed, and as though the vibration launched a hideous wind that pushed him off, he rolled over and hit the water, making a sickening splash. Carol Ann fought to bring his leaden form to the side. Once she had him out of the water, white and floppy, on his back, she saw the walnut-sized hole in his chest and the rivulet of blood creeping across the smooth terra cotta surrounding the pool. The blood was coming from what proved to be a ragged crater beneath his left shoulder blade.

The last thing on Carol Ann's mind as she yelled for the servants and fumbled at her cell phone was the name she'd heard Billy mention more than once before, or the unhappy fate of Christopher Hopman, whose story had caught her eye a scant ninety seconds before.

FOURTEEN

New York

A MONTH AFTER CHRISTOPHER Hopman's murder, Isobel Gitlin found herself preparing an obit for Billy MacNeal, the baby billionaire. Also shot to death. Also by high-powered rifle, from a distance. Also taken in silence, the crime absent any trace of perpetrator identity, possible motive, or useful physical clues. Absent, in any case, evidence the police admitted to having. Hopman on a golf course, MacNeal on a diving board. The two of them tied together by a billion dollars.

Isobel snatched the glasses from her nose as though they threatened her view of the truth. What magnitude of coincidence could possibly account for a thing like this? She shook her head and replaced the specs. At seven thirty that morning, Isobel began reviewing the histories of companies comprising First and Second Houston Holding from their inceptions. Now, midway through her third container of coffee, she noticed that Second Houston, which, she remembered, had been sold to Hopman's Alliance Inc., was also parent to the villainous Knowland & Sons. Isobel felt the kind of thrill she imagined her hairy ancestors experiencing with the mind-shaking revelation that the sharp stone embedded in their heels might do the same to a rabbit's belly. The caffeine did not calm her down.

She told her editor that she had discovered a link between the killings of MacNeal and Hopman, and therefore a possible story. He told her she was suffering from the heat. She outlined the facts she had, but he only heard her out; he did not listen. "Jesus!" he thought, as Isobel talked, "doesn't she know this is the fucking obituary page." Then he shook his head and said, "Very hard case to make off what you've got. Really. Not worth pushing further." He wanted nothing more to do with it, or her, for that matter. When he considered Isobel Gitlin, which was hardly ever, Ed Macmillan had only contempt for what he figured was her free ride. He had worked to get where he was. Macmillan was New Irish, very much in favor at the *Times*. He was not the red-nosed, hard-drinking Fordham product native to New York newsrooms in nostalgic yesteryears. He was in his early forties, Cornell, health-club fit, a white wine drinker. No spots on his one-hundred-dollar tie. He did, however, affect a manner that he believed echoed an earlier, ballsier day. He imagined himself a menacing Lou Grant. Isobel knew him to be a complete asshole.

"Look," he said to her, "if it's news, we have news people working it. If it's an obit, it's you. That's what you do. You write obituaries. So go do one." She pushed back, starting her pitch all over again until Macmillan interrupted her.

"Dog days of summer," he told Isobel, with a cold, dry chuckle. Then he sought to end the matter by saying, "The heat's getting to you. We don't sell the *New York Times* at the supermarket checkout. Why don't you try a weekend at the beach?"

Isobel watched Ed's little smirk spread and become a chaste, hence pointless, leer. His undistinguished, knob-nosed face turned into a caricature of adolescent self-regard.

"Do you know where the term comes from?" Isobel said. "'Dog days of summer'? Do you know what that means?" She stuttered severely on "do" and "dog."

He shrugged, condescension rising with sweet cologne. "Sweetie, even the dogs can't take the summer heat. They walk around with their tongues hanging out, huffing and puffing and beat to hell. It makes their little doggy minds go whacko. Watch out it doesn't happen to you."

"No," replied Isobel. "It's from the da-da-Dog Star. It's how the Indians knew it was the height of summer. The da-Dog Star is the brightest object in the night sky in August."

She paused, attempting to follow that up with her most ferocious, cobra-snaky stare.

He rolled his eyes and waved her away.

Isobel Gitlin's byline topped Billy MacNeal's obituary, but nowhere in it was she permitted to mention Hopman's name.

FIFTEEN

New York

Tom Maloney thought it was a very strange thing for Nathan Stein to say. "That could have been me," he said the day after Hopman was murdered. "Hopman was always asking me to play golf with him. 'Come up to Boston and bring your clubs.' Shit, I hate golf." And then Nathan said it once again: "That could have been me." The little man had entered Maloney's office seconds before, shoulders hunched, shuffling. He leaned over the front of Tom's desk, gray eyes moist behind silver-rimmed spectacles, voice subdued, mouth showing no tension, almost at rest. Tom said nothing, but it struck him that Nathan Stein obviously believed Christopher Hopman's killing had been a random act of violence, that Hopman was murdered purely by chance. No such possibility ever occurred to Tom. Why, he asked himself, did he think it might not be? A man like Hopman, he reasoned, a man who played under the boards with elbows flying, had enemies. It was only a thought, and Maloney quickly relegated it to a far corner of his perpetually crowded mind. "You know, Nathan, many people think there's a reason for everything." In rare moments Tom's better nature got the better of him and he could not deny or conceal his continued affection for Nathan Stein. Somewhere in the daily strain of minding, handling, nursing, he could actually experience sympathy for the small man around whom his life revolved. This was such a moment. He wanted to give it oxygen.

"You really think so?" Nathan looked at him with a curious, sentimental expression.

"At times I do believe that," Tom said, nodding benignly.

"Well, I guess you may be right. Thanks for being here, Tom."

Maloney didn't think about Hopman's killing again until a month later when reviewing a proposal by the Whitestone Broadcast Group, which desired to compete with the industry giants and required $465 million to do it. Tom liked the package. Broadcast ownership fascinated him. You get your license, your exclusive franchise, straight from the federal government and pay nothing for its asset value. Not much different from getting a driver's license. You make money—often a fortune—using the public's airwaves, and when you've grown tired of it, or for any other reason that strikes your fancy, you sell the now inflated asset value of the very same license you got for nothing. "What a racket," Tom thought. The Whitestone people didn't have a chance in hell of achieving their goal, and with a flicker of regret Tom tossed it on his pile of deals he'd have nothing to do with. CNBC was droning from one of the lineup of monitors on his wall. Tom heard the cute anchor, the one with the tiny waist and the collagen puffed lips, announce that Houston whiz-kid Billy MacNeal had been murdered. It happened at his home, she reported, right in front of his wife. On his diving board. Maloney was astonished. Mother of God! "In his own fucking house!" he thought. Jesus Christ!

Nathan Stein did not see it on TV. His secretary got a call. This time he did not shuffle into Tom's office. He barreled in, chin out, shoulders held rigidly back, thrusting his toes outward, strutting as he did when adrenaline drove him. He went straight for the liquor in the corner and poured himself a bourbon and water.

Maloney's office was traditionally decorated: restful dark woods and carpet, and modest lighting from a few table lamps and two floor lamps, each smoothed by heavy brown shades. The glass wall overlooking Manhattan was framed by a soft, shadowy, maroon window treatment. He kept the white, translucent drapes closed. Tom cultivated an understated, old-school look. It made him feel more than successful; it suggested to him that he was comfortable with success. Nathan often sought escape from the overwhelming sunlight and dramatic cityscape pouring into his own brash fantasy of an office. When stress rose within him, threatening to bust him wide open, Nathan came here looking for nurture, and Tom's décor seemed to help. Nathan threw a couple of ice cubes in his drink and plopped himself down on the oxblood leather couch in front of Tom's impressive array of televisions.

"A little early for that, isn't it?" Tom suggested, pointing at the whiskey.

"Maybe it's a little late, a little too late." Nathan took a long swallow. "This MacNeal business," he said. "I don't like it. Hopman a couple of weeks ago—"

"Last month," Tom said.

"Yeah, a couple of weeks ago. Now MacNeal. Christ, Tom, they said Hopman was cut in half. Can you imagine that? Have you thought at all about—are we both thinking what I am?"

"Anything's possible, Nathan. You want to check into it?"

"Fuck yes, I do. If this has anything to do with that mess, we've got a double shithouse on our hands."

"I doubt it," Tom said. He'd spent the morning thinking the complete opposite of what he just said to Nathan Stein. Maloney knew

Stein had his gifts, and he was often at his best in threatening situations, but not when he envisioned personal jeopardy. That sort of danger, perceived or real, more often than not threw Nathan into confusion and paranoia. Tom was determined to do his utmost to keep Nathan on an even keel. "I'll take care of it," he said.

"How?"

"Put it out of your mind, Nathan. I've got it covered. I'm sure there's nothing here, but it never hurts to look."

"If we have a problem, it's got to be fixed. You understand?"

"Nathan, put it out of your mind, please." Tom walked slowly to the couch and put his arm on Nathan Stein's shoulder, offering him a familiar reassurance. "We know people who know people. I'll get someone on it immediately."

"People for *this*? We never did *this*."

"Well, we're doing it now," said Maloney.

Tom Maloney made two telephone calls and then told his secretary to cancel his appointments and transfer certain calls to Wesley Pitts. He left the office and didn't return until late in the afternoon. On his way back he called his secretary, who confirmed that Mr. Stein was still in Tom's office, having left only once, presumably to use his own bathroom. Tom found him, drink in hand, on the couch.

"Been sitting there all day?" Tom asked.

"I like it here," Nathan said. "Watch a little TV. Have a little something to drink. Take a nap if I want."

"Mi casa, su casa," said Tom while thinking, "You've got a bedroom, for Christ's sake."

"So, what have you got?" Stein asked, suddenly alert and impatient.

Maloney told him he had spoken with "a friend" right after their earlier discussion. The "friend" gave Maloney a name and a number. "I called him. We set up a meeting and had a good talk."

"Where?" Nathan asked.

"A deli on Queens Boulevard. Great corned beef. He's on the job already. We got the right man for the job."

"Really?" said Nathan Stein. "You don't look so sure."

"Well, look, Nathan, we don't have much to get him started. I certainly didn't share any sensitive information—not that he wanted to know—but I couldn't tell him who to look for, could I?"

"Right," said Stein. "I know that. You think he'll find out who this guy is?"

"We don't even know if it's anyone at all. These things may be totally unrelated. Either way, it's under control."

"Sure," Nathan said, playing with Tom's universal remote, switching channels on the various monitors. Then he sat straight up and looked directly at Tom Maloney. "Who does this kind of work anyway?" he asked.

Maloney was afraid he'd ask that. He had devoutly hoped not to have to answer that question. It was better left unsaid. "Actually," Tom thought, "everything about this is better left unsaid." But Nathan Stein was the boss, and the boss wanted to know. "We retained a team, Nathan. There are always people who do things like this. Our 'friend' referred me to such a person." Tom hoped he could leave it there, but Nathan's narrowed eyes told him otherwise. He explained that he had met with an FBI agent who had described ex-cops, former FBI agents, and even some retired military who hire out. They work in teams. The teams are led by individuals still active in law enforcement. The best teams—and that's exactly what Maloney had been led to—often have an FBI agent as team leader. The FBI agent runs the whole operation. He provides direction as well as damage control. If they fuck up, Tom was told, the leader pulls down a mask to make the whole thing look official, or have it evaporate in thin air. But things don't fuck up. They invariably go well. And then the leader's official connections shield the client absolutely.

"We got to somebody like this so quickly? Just like that?" Stein eyed him with admiration and suspicion.

"We have many friends, Nathan. We help a lot of people. There's nothing mysterious here. We always get the help we need, do we not?"

Stein stood and began pacing. He started to huff—almost a full-blown wheeze—and switched on a determined look. He was pumped up like his Andover wrestling coach.

"They know to kill him, right?" he said. "Right?"

"Right," Tom answered, angered that Nathan had actually said the words out loud, in his office. "They know, but, Nathan, you're getting all excited about nothing. There's nothing to indicate these incidents are related. There's even less reason to assume that any of this has anything to do with us."

"You're sure these guys are the best we could find?"

Maloney believed they were. A couple of hours earlier he called Special Agent Robert Wilkes. He introduced himself only as Tom and mentioned the intermediary. Wilkes suggested meeting at David's Deli on Queens Boulevard, near the Woodhaven Boulevard exit, anonymous territory for both. Tom began describing what he would be wearing and Wilkes interrupted, saying, "I'll know who you are. Don't worry about it." They both laughed and the phone went dead in Maloney's hands.

Wilkes was right. He had no difficulty recognizing Tom Maloney. The late lunch crowd was sparse. Tom Maloney had to be the only customer who ordered a corned beef sandwich on white bread or wore a suit that was well pressed. Wilkes watched him from a booth near the back, thinking, "These rich ones, they couldn't hide in an empty cave."

"Hello, Tom," he said, walking up to the counter where Maloney's sandwich was being handed to him. "Bob Wilkes." He held out his hand and Maloney shook it warmly. Wilkes was six feet, lean, and trim, even with his overcoat still on. His narrow, square shoulders supported a thick neck dressed in a white shirt at least a half-inch too large.

"I'm glad you could make it, Bob," Maloney said. Tom turned on the combination of charm and unspoken power that was his trademark. It was like a faucet, and he opened it wide. Tom said that one man may have killed both Christopher Hopman and Billy MacNeal. He did not say why. Each of these men was a friend as well as a customer—an extremely important customer. Tom wanted the assassin found and "taken care of." Maloney had given a lot of thought as to how to say that. He'd never done this before. Not quite this way anyway. He'd considered "Eliminate." "Terminate." "Neutralize." The phrase "rub out" crossed his mind in the midtown tunnel. As he entered David's, inhaling the scent of mustard and garlic, he settled on "taken care of." Wilkes seemed to understand and accept the term, and with that, Tom felt mild relief.

Wilkes had a surprisingly deep and gentle voice. "Done," he said. He then explained in specific detail the composition of his team and how it would work. No names of course, referring only to "our guys," "subjects," and "clients." From the looks of him, Wilkes figured, Maloney needed no assurance. Nevertheless, he added, "We know what we're doing. This sort of thing is not unusual. But there are lines we can't cross, people we won't touch. We can handle things everywhere, across the country, anywhere. We've got 'friends' too—people in every major city—and they have their own circles of influence, which I have described. Philly, LA, Chicago, New Orleans, Seattle. You name it. And the ones I interact with personally have been my friends for twenty years."

"How will we know you've got the right man?" Maloney asked.

"If you're not happy, we're not happy. More than that I can't say."

And then Wilkes asked, "Who is he?"

That was the tough part, Tom told him. If the two shootings are unrelated, no further action is required. If they are, you resolve it. "Either way, you get paid in full. That won't be a problem for you, will it?"

Wilkes had just been told the job was more complicated than he thought. Maloney could see he was not pleased with that prospect. Wilkes frowned, but did not reply. He stared absently past Tom, at the heavy waitress tapping her fingernails at the far end of the counter, near the steamed-up deli window.

"Double." Wilkes's voice was mellow as ever, but Tom glimpsed tension in the fingers gripping his coffee cup. "The price is double."

"How much?"

"Two hundred and fifty."

"Half now. Half when it's done," Maloney said. "I'll have two hundred and fifty thousand ready for you in an hour."

"Two hundred and fifty *is* double," Wilkes said. Maloney couldn't be sure if it was the shock or a pang of moral conscience.

"I know," Tom smiled, "but there are some things it's always best to overpay for. I think this is one of them, don't you?"

SIXTEEN

Gatlinburg

Floyd Ochs was one of those small, wiry, middle-aged Southern white men who look twenty years older than they are. A woman who worked in his processing plant described him, within his wife's hearing, as ". . . the kind you *really* don't want to see naked." Floyd was a man of few words and fewer smiles. Given the choice he'd rather be fishing. Ochs was born and raised in Lucas, Tennessee. After high school he fixed cars, pumped gas, worked some construction, and spent a couple of months carrying parts around a Memphis motorcycle engine warehouse. Then he joined the Marines. Germany and Korea failed to broaden Floyd's ambitions. After the service he bee-lined for home and the processing floor of Knowland & Sons.

That same year he married Hazel Cummins, a heavy-set, plain-looking girl he'd met in church three weeks before. They enriched the community with three boys in less than five years. Floyd's good points stood out in his end of Lucas, Tennessee. Unlike most of his friends, he didn't drink much. He never hit his wife or made trouble with anyone else's. He enjoyed life at home. He loved his boys and did whatever he supposed a good father should. And Floyd Ochs showed up for work every day.

In the late 1970s the industry was transformed by a series of management consulting reports. One of these changed the way meat packing plants were run. Historically, plant managers had been company executives, ambitious, college-educated men eager to gain combat experience in the field. The company saw them as men on the move. Whether punching their tickets in Iowa, Michigan, Tennessee, or Nebraska, they were not local people. Locals correctly perceived them as outsiders arriving from someplace en route to someplace else, making their way up the pole. That began to change after 1980. The consultants suggested a less expensive way to run plants. And as suggested, meat packers began promoting local employees to responsible positions, to more than foreman and supervisor. To qualify, such men had to show up every day, sober and respectful. Floyd headed the line. Gradually, some of the chosen moved off the floor and into the front office.

By 1985 Floyd was an Assistant Plant Manager, one of six—many more than needed; corporate headquarters hadn't a clue as to how many would last. In 1992 he was Plant Manager, with only the two assistants he required. In less than twelve years Knowland & Sons had replaced its entire on-site management echelon at less than a third of its previous payroll cost. The new men managed efficiently and cheaply, did exactly what they were told, and were by-and-large accepted by the work force as exalted elder brothers. Headquarters called them "townies." Best of all, neither Floyd nor his counterparts ever thought of leaving home, of becoming real corporate executives. They craved upward mobility even less than their bosses hoped they would.

Floyd and Hazel took the same vacation every year. In August they visited Gatlinburg for a week. When the boys were young, Floyd and his sons fished together. Nowadays, he fished alone. For one full day Floyd left Hazel to her shopping and drove to the Hiawassee River. This year was no different from last year.

As he always did, he parked almost a mile away, tramped through humid fields, and made his way carefully down a steep, heavily wooded, rock-studded incline to the river. From its edge, jutting twelve feet into the tumbling water, a whale-gray rock measured thirty-seven feet across, just about flat as a board. Floyd and his sons had taped it out, and knew every inch of its surface. This stretch of the Hiawassee was wild, which made for fine fishing because it was not navigable; no boats nosed about to disturb the underwater life. Standing at the edge, Floyd could see a quarter mile in all directions but behind. He reflected once again on his deeply held, immensely satisfying belief that he and his boys were the only ones ever to fish from this beloved rock—most certainly the only ones since far-off Cherokee times.

He listened to the steady sounds of river and forest, rushing water slapping rocks, summer air in moving branches; smiled at the arguing jays and austere hawks wheeling high then disappearing into and behind the sweet-smelling pines. Floyd Ochs set down his fishing rod and opened the basket of sausage and beer beside him. He took out a Bud and pushed down on the tab. He loved the snap of the can and the fizzy noise he'd been hearing since his Daddy showed him how. As he lifted the can to his lips and felt the cold, wet metal on the tip of his nose, he thought he heard footsteps behind him. He started to turn as the force of a spinning bullet took his head from his shoulders. The sound echoed through the river valley, scattering the birds. His car was discovered that evening, a few hours after Hazel reported him missing. His head floated downstream to a state camping area, and was found the next day. But it took three more days to find the rock and the rest of Floyd.

SEVENTEEN

St. John

THE OLD WOMAN, CLARA, brought Walter a cup of beef bouillon. Walter liked the clear, hot broth after dinner. It complemented the sweet cool in the evening air. He'd tossed a creased and crumpled bit of paper onto the marble table. The names on the paper were smudged beyond recognition because he'd handled the thing like worry beads: Nathan Stein, Tom Maloney, Wesley Pitts, Louise Hollingsworth, Christopher Hopman, Billy MacNeal, Pat Grath, Wayne Korman, Floyd Ochs.

As Tom told it the day he and his gang were here, he and Stein developed a plan for Christopher Hopman's Boston-based company, Alliance Inc., to buy a sizable block of stock in another Stein, Gelb client company, Second Houston, which was owned by Billy MacNeal.

Second Houston would go public as an IPO. "So," as Maloney put it, "when the dust settled, Second Houston would be publicly traded and Alliance would be the controlling shareholder."

This was a billion dollar deal. "That's 'billion' with a *b*." Maloney had arched an eyebrow then. Almost a fourth of that was to go into Billy MacNeal's pocket.

Hopman's stock options in both companies would net him more than a hundred million dollars. Shareholders would come out ahead because Second Houston and Alliance would certainly soar on the news generated by favorable analysts' reports, and moves by some of the larger mutual funds.

"Wesley Pitts did a helluva job on the project," Maloney said, nodding toward Pitts, whose round face suddenly hardened into a genuine smile. "And Louise Hollingsworth is the Senior Analyst. Her reports and the publicity they received were essential to the success of this effort."

Maloney added that Stein, Gelb, Hector & Wills received sizable fees for facilitating this complicated transaction. "In all candor," he said, looking Walter pointedly in the eye, "this deal meant a lot to us."

"How much is 'sizable'?" Walter had asked.

"Our fees and other compensation—warrants, options, and so forth—were absolutely in keeping with industry standards for a deal of this magnitude."

Walter pressed: "How much?"

"All told, fees plus projected gains, in the midrange nine figures." Maloney hung his head just a little. His voice went sorrowful. "It was a honey of a deal until the shit hit the fan." That's how he'd put it hours ago, sitting right over there, across from Walter.

Walter picked up the list of names again, spun them around in his head, put them in order. Wayne Korman, first. He went to Floyd Ochs when he learned the processing line was dirty. He thought the meat might be dangerous and did the right thing. If he wanted to make a living he had to go back to work. Wife and kids. Car note. Mortgage. Visa bill each month. Ochs sent him back to work. He went.

Floyd Ochs next. He reported the problem to Pat Grath in Houston. Could he have done more? Halted production on his own? He didn't. Cost him his life?

Pat Grath told Billy MacNeal. The two weren't partners, Maloney said, but Grath was close to Billy. Everything he had, reportedly a lot, he got through MacNeal. He was not in charge so he went to Billy. What more could he do? Maybe that's why he's still alive.

That's when Maloney and Stein got into the act. Pat Grath and Billy MacNeal took it to Wesley Pitts. Fair enough. Hundreds of millions of dollars of Second Houston IPO money came through Wesley Pitts. That's why the guys in Houston went to him and not his bosses. Follow the money. It's always the money. Deep Throat *was* a deep thinker.

So, Pitts goes to Maloney, Senior VP, Director of Mergers & Acquisitions. He brings Christopher Hopman into the picture. That's what Hopman does: merges and acquires.

As far as Christopher Hopman's concerned, Stein laid out the plan for Alliance and Second Houston to follow—before the bottom fell out and people started dying. Stein and Maloney tell Hollingsworth to crank up the hype machine, manage the lie, put everyone off the smell of the thing.

Hopman goes first, then MacNeal, and now Ochs. And Grath no doubt pissing his pants, hiding behind a tumbleweed in Amarillo or somewhere. Three down. Six to go? Among them Stein, Pitts, Hollingsworth, Maloney? And then there's Ganga Roy. Dead two years by suicide. Really? She was the one he couldn't get out of his mind. According to Maloney she'd told them E. coli would make people sick, but nobody would die.

According to Maloney.

And if she really killed herself, why?

And why all this shooting now, two years after it was over?

Where's this guy been? Six out of ten still walking the earth. Why them? Who's next? And who the hell was he looking for? Walter knew where he had to start. He went inside and booked the morning flight, first class, from St. Thomas to New York.

EIGHTEEN

New York

AFTER READING THE *Times* for an hour each morning, Isobel Gitlin accessed the online editions of nearly fifty newspapers nationwide. She looked for flares of human interest, compelling hometown eulogies (the late mayor once jailed for smuggling parrots, the plumber who croaked fitting brass at ninety-six); little, sparkling, readable bits headed nowhere but for Isobel's keen, unquenchable eye. Amid the endless obits crossing her screen, Isobel noticed other things. Now, on the page beside the obits in the Memphis Commercial Appeal, she glimpsed five lines on the death of Floyd Ochs. When "Knowland & Sons" bounced up from the screen, she called Laticia Glover, the reporter at the Memphis paper.

Twenty minutes later she was storming the office of Ed Macmillan's boss, a man known mostly by his nickname, the Moose. She said, "I've got a triple connection on three murders, two of them very high profile. My information indicates a single killer for all three deaths. And I've got them all connected *to the big E. coli meat disaster*." He nodded his head to confirm the seemingly impossible. Then she injected a bold, ironic note: "It practically wiped out the South?"

"Yeah, I heard about it," he said.

"Nobody has this story yet." The last part seemed to get his attention.

Waiting for a reply, Isobel noted with pleasure that she'd not strangled a single sound.

Mel Gold was twice her age, and, as everybody agreed, closely resembled a moose. His thick gray hair fell forward exactly as a moose's might. His pendulous chins obscured a brown necktie resting at half-mast on his mountainous paunch. A disconcerting forward thrust lent vigor to his tan, wrinkled, endlessly bumpy face. Gold was rumored to be ill-tempered and grim. She'd avoided him until now. "Close the door and sit down," he said, in the street-tough rumbling voice that, in fact, sounded like that of a moose. "Exactly what the fuck do you think you have?"

Having done its heroic best when she needed it most, her stutter returned with moderate force. Gold, unlike others, did not seem to notice. She supposed he'd interviewed too many toothless people, and some, no doubt, without very much of their faces left in place.

Pacing herself, Isobel outlined the history: MacNeal's sale of Knowland to Hopman's gang, and the link created between those two and the great E. coli disaster. Then, hard on those killings, the Ochs affair and all that she'd learned from the Memphis reporter of Ochs's connection to Knowland & Sons, and the subsequent talk about who was asleep at the packing plant switch at the time, and all of them—Ochs, Billy Mac, and Hopman—blasted to bits out of nowhere, all gunned down and hooked up by corporate ties, all circling around a single, deadly drain. "If this is a supermarket story I'll be the first to s-s-say so," Isobel ended, eloquently she thought. "There are no news people on this, are there?" His silence told her all she needed to know.

She asked for time and resources. Gold made another rumbling sound; one, she thought, if very much louder, might have attracted females of his persuasion. Moving that ponderous head to the side for a one-eyed view of the Fijian wonder (he'd heard all of that without interest), Isobel thought he might very well have smiled. She'd heard him called the Moose, and even once someone referred to Mel Gold as an ancient elk. She could not have known then, but now there was no mistaking it: he was no elk, ancient or otherwise. The elk, Isobel knew, was a herd animal. The bull moose walked alone.

He gave her a week and a barely adequate budget, assured her that she would get no other help, and declared himself a fool for fools and children.

"I need to report directly to you," she said. "Otherwise this will get killed."

It did not wash. "You give whatever you get to Macmillan. If he doesn't think you've got anything, that's what you've got."

"Bu, bu, but—"

"No buts at all. You've got a week. Take it, and do not make me look like the asshole I probably am."

By mid-afternoon she was on her way to Houston. Two days later she landed in Memphis, rented a car, and drove to Lucas. By week's end she was in Boston. She shuttled to LaGuardia late Friday and took a cab to her office at the *Times*. Saturday morning she met with Ed Macmillan. The next day she saw her article situated two inches below the fold of the most influential front page printed in America, the Sunday edition of the *New York Times.*

> *Killings May Be Connected to E. coli Disaster*
> By Isobel Gitlin
> NEW YORK, Aug. 23—Law enforcement officials in three states have acknowledged the possibility that three unsolved murders

> may be connected to the E. coli outbreak of three years ago that left 864 people dead and thousands more sickened. Three men shot to death since June—Boston businessman Christopher Hopman, shot while on the golf course; Texas tycoon Billy MacNeal, gunned down in Houston; and Floyd Ochs, murdered in Tennessee—all have ties to a Tennessee meat-packing plant implicated as a source for the E. coli–tainted meat. Alliance Inc., where Mr. Hopman was CEO, was involved in a complicated buyout of Mr. MacNeal's company that counted among its assets the packing plant of Knowland & Sons. Mr. Ochs was the Knowland plant manager in Lucas, Tennessee. Police officials in charge of all three cases tell the *New York Times* they are now actively investigating the theory that these murders could be connected.

Isobel's story made the networks and cable news channels. Much of the old E. coli disaster tapes found new life on TV screens across the nation. She took calls from CNN, FOX, the network morning shows, PBS, and NPR. They all wanted her to tell her story on the air. Isobel refused, but did not say that her stutter was why.

There were plenty of other talking heads eager to analyze and dissect the story. The increasingly obvious fact that they knew nothing except what they'd read of Isobel's reporting (and frequently misunderstood even that) qualified them fully for the work. In a slow news cycle their ongoing blather gave the story durable legs. In her absence from the screen, Isobel's name was mentioned often, and was almost always praised. At Isobel's request, the *Times* did not issue a photo of her, and holding that line required a good deal of bellowing from the Moose. Without having made a single appearance, Isobel Gitlin became—for no more than the allocated fifteen minutes she hoped—a media personality.

Isobel's story and her insistence on personal privacy caused a stir at the *Times*. So many of the paper's reporters fantasized about breaking a story like this one. In daydreams they saw themselves on *Hardball* and *Crossfire* or sitting next to Woodward or Bernstein at Larry King's desk. Isobel had won the lottery, they thought, and refused to collect the prize. People who previously had nothing to say to her went out of their way to greet her. Others looked upon her, and the story of the triple murders, with more than a little skepticism. It was highly unusual for anyone's byline to go from the obituary page to the front page overnight, and even more unusual for it to stay there. One thing particularly puzzled her: Why hadn't other, more senior, reporters tried to muscle in, push her out? She asked Gold and the Moose told her bluntly, "They wouldn't touch it with tongs."

"Wh-what the hell does that mean?"

He looked at her and for a long moment tried, with his tongue, to loosen a piece of food stuck between two of his upper teeth. In that brief time Mel Gold realized he needed to protect Isobel against the reality of her chosen profession. "A lot of people think it's bullshit," he said with as fatherly a tone as he could muster. "The whole thing is crap, and not the kind of crap that belongs in the *New York Times.*"

"Oh," said Isobel, shrugging her shoulders, a hint of a smile across her lips. "Wh-wh-what about you?" The Moose rolled his eyes and plunged the last half of a glazed doughnut into his mouth.

"If you're worried somebody's going to horn in and steal your story—don't. Believe me, it's all yours."

"Thanks," she said, and her smile told him she knew it was she riding the tiger and him holding the whip and chair.

She went back to Lucas to write a *Sunday Times Magazine* cover piece. The story played out across two pages with grainy photos of three dead men layered above an eye-catching shot of ground beef, and behind it was a black and white mural photograph of the one story, brick-sided, Knowland & Sons meat-packing plant. The article began:

Who Is Seeking Revenge?
By Isobel Gitlin
The Knowland & Sons processing plant sits on fertile flatlands next to the Smoke River, dominating the landscape as well as the economy of this small Tennessee city. According to town fathers, pioneer hunters once roamed the Smoky Mountains' foothills looking for deer, bear, and other commercial game, and settled in Lucas in the early 1820s. "Meat made this town," says Ezra Combs, a city councilman with twenty-three years seniority. "Still does," he adds with a good-natured wink. Like everyone in Lucas, Ezra knows that meat packed in this plant may have caused the deaths of 864 people and made more than seventeen thousand ill three years ago. "There's good people living here and working hard every day at the plant," Mr. Combs insists. "I know the folks at Knowland, known them for years. And each and every one of them is doing what's humanly possible to find out just exactly what happened over there and make sure it don't never happen again."

Despite Mr. Combs's assertion, someone, it appears, is seeking revenge. Whoever it may be is still unknown, and authorities have little to show for their efforts to identify him.

NINETEEN

New York

BEFORE THEY FINISHED BREAKFAST, Tom Maloney, Nathan Stein, Wes Pitts, and Louise Hollingsworth had all read Isobel Gitlin's August 23 story in the *New York Times.* Pitts, who always liked being known as "football's workaholic" and brought the same zeal to his career at Stein, Gelb, was the first one. His daily routine got him out of bed at four fifteen in the morning, shaved and showered by four thirty, and drinking tea and reading the *Times,* which he had messenger-delivered to his fifth floor condo on East 64th Street. At ten minutes to five, Monday through Friday, he greeted his doorman and slipped into the same limo. His driver, Laurence, a hefty black man in his early forties, was a night driver. He ferried club hoppers, pill poppers, the wealthy "wild childs," and the idle rich too bored to go home at a reasonable hour. Pitts was always his last fare before quitting time. Laurence thought of Wesley Pitts as a man to be proud of. Laurence had driven enough rich, black athletes and entertainers to take them, one by one, as he found them. Mr. Pitts was in a class by himself. A black man, a star athlete, and now a man of real importance. He wasn't sure what Mr. Pitts did, but he knew it had to be something really important. Why else would anyone so well off be going to work so early? Family and friends loved hearing Laurence's stories about the big tips he often received from celebrities whose names they knew well. But no one treated him as well as Mr. Pitts did. Twice a year, at Christmas and again at the end of June, Mr. Pitts gave him five thousand dollars. Those two envelopes with their ten thousand tax-free dollars paid most of a daughter's private school tuition.

"Morning, Mr. Pitts," he said. "Everything alright, sir?" The gentleman's strange expression made Laurence apprehensive.

Half an hour before, Wesley Pitts read Isobel Gitlin's August 23rd story in the *New York Times.* As the headlines and the first two paragraphs penetrated his newly-awakened mind, his stomach twisted, and for a moment Wesley thought he might lose his tea and toast. He tried desperately to regain focus. The control of the adrenaline rush that he had cultivated since high school enabled him to calm down. *Fourth and goal with one second left.* It always worked. Why, he wanted to know, hadn't Pat Grath told him about Ochs yesterday, or the day before, or the day before that? They had not spoken for more than a week—perfectly unremarkable—but Grath would certainly have to call with news like this. Was he dead too? Wesley did not have Grath's home number, nor was it listed. His cell phone did not respond.

Wesley figured that anyone able to connect Hopman, MacNeal, and Ochs would soon finger Stein and Maloney. And that would shove him, and Louise too, into the picture. What to do next? He put the odds of getting shot, right now, right here in this limo, at zero. The chances of becoming cowardly he put much higher. Wesley Pitts had built his life and two careers on a bone-deep refusal to give in, but however often he'd beaten the impulse to let the frights take over, he'd not yet outrun his dread of losing the battle. Wesley feared fear itself. He decided to go to work. Once there he'd hear what the others had to say. He told Laurence not to worry, his upset stomach would right itself soon enough.

Pitts was always the first high-echelon executive to arrive—usually by five fifteen. Occasionally one or two of the junior people on his floor would be there before him, just to be able to say "Good morning, Mr. Pitts," hoping they were noticed and remembered. This morning the floor was empty. He unlocked his suite, passed through the small outer office where his secretary sat, and walked into what some people called the "third kingdom": an office less splendid than Stein's and Maloney's, but far grander than those of even his nominal superiors. He'd have his senior partnership soon, and that would complete the picture. Sometimes he even saw himself, older by twenty years, sporting white hair, astride the mountaintop. He could never totally escape the fantasy of his childhood friend D'Andre walking into the Chairman's office and saying, "Ma nigga, waz up." But not this morning. What's up, he thought, was some crazy motherfucker trying to kill him. Hopman, then Billy Mac, and now this guy Floyd Ochs. Floyd Ochs. Pitts remembered the name well.

Maloney failed to arrive as usual at seven thirty, and Louise Hollingsworth was also a no-show. Pitts began to worry. The thought that they might be dead crossed his mind. Nathan Stein called him at seven forty-five.

"Listen, Wes," he said, "you get up so fucking early I couldn't get you until now."

"What's happening, Nathan?"

"I'm in the car. I want you to meet me. Tom and Louise are on the way too."

"Meet you where?"

"My house in Wevertown. You know it?"

"No, I don't. Where's Wevertown?"

"An hour or so north of Albany. No planes, you understand? No planes, no records. Get here by car and don't let anyone you can't trust know you're coming." Nathan gave him directions that were pretty simple until the I-87 exit at Warrensburg. After that he needed to navigate the small roads, some of them unpaved, until he reached the house secluded on a small lake in the Adirondacks. "Leave now," Stein said. "We're only a half hour or so ahead of you."

Pitts's call woke Laurence from a pleasant dream. From his home in the Cobble Hill section of Brooklyn, Laurence opted for the Brooklyn Bridge instead of the Battery Tunnel. A stalled truck on the expressway made that a mistake. It took him almost an hour to get to Stein, Gelb's offices. He called Mr. Pitts's office when he was a few minutes away, and when he pulled up in front, Wesley Pitts was waiting for him, looking almost truculent, hands-on-hips, at the curb. Pitts handed the directions to Laurence, and they were away.

Nathan Stein's mountain retreat was about what Wesley expected from any man who measured his net worth in nine figures. Tom had been there a few times before, and told Wes he never understood the attraction the place held for Nathan. Nathan hated nature and all its abundant pleasures: mountains, lakes, forests, chilly evenings, and all the rest. "What in the hell did he do here?" Wesley wondered. The property was certainly picturesque: heavily wooded with only enough cleared land for the house and a few cars. There were no paved roads nearby, and no neighbors as far as Wes could see. Maloney told Wes he remembered Nathan saying something about twenty-six acres. But for all he knew, it might be a thousand and twenty-six acres.

The house itself was built on a ridge overlooking the lake. Behind it, a path led down to the shore. A boat dock, where a rowboat and a canoe were moored, extended a few feet into the water. A large barbecue pit stood near the dock close to the water's edge. Decks sprouted everywhere on the lakeside of the house, on all three levels. No matter where you sat you had a panoramic view of the water and the pristine, undisturbed forest encircling it on all sides. The house had seven bedrooms, each with a private bath. Four were on the first level, two were on the second level, where the main living space and the kitchen were also located, and where the three of them now congregated, and the master suite was on the third level. Trees surrounded the house so close to the building that the bedrooms on the first and second levels were always shaded. The house faced east and west, allowing a torrent of morning light to flow into the third floor master bedroom, and bathing the whole structure in the richness of the afternoon sun.

It was an exquisitely beautiful setting about which Tom and Wesley shared an unspoken agreement. Each was sure Nathan didn't give two shits about any of it. As far as Tom knew, Nathan had bought the place, sight unseen, from a cardiothoracic surgeon flattened by divorce, anxious for immediate cash. Supposedly, Nathan's wife, Susan, hated the place too, and they rarely went there. No surprise to Tom. Nathan and Susan had been married twenty-five years, at least, and paid little attention to one another. She raised the children and ran the household. He ran the business. That was the deal, the deal they had been born to, the deal they chose themselves. What the hell, Tom figured. He hadn't done much better.

At one o'clock Nathan's driver showed up with pizza. The drivers ate at the dock, where they set up a little table and played gin rummy. Laurence slept nearby on a yellow blanket. On the expansive second level deck, Louise and Wesley told Nathan what they thought in as low a key as they could manage. As he always did, Nathan demanded repetition and they complied willingly. Wesley leaned forward to avoid towering over Nathan. Louise Hollingsworth, in a director's chair, clutched her cup of coffee, the sun catching her wiry, blonde hair. She turned toward Wes when he spoke, her hawkish profile and dry smile unable to hide her fear.

Tom Maloney was the last to arrive. He pulled into the small area cleared for parking at a quarter to two that afternoon. With three Lincoln town cars already taking up all the space, Tom squeezed his Lexus coupe in between a couple of trees. It was silly, he knew, but the drive made him crave a cheeseburger, so he stopped at the Black Bear Diner in Pottersville. Cheeseburger and a beer and Tom felt great. He was the only one of the four who drove himself, and he used traffic as his excuse for his late arrival. Nobody seemed to care one way or the other.

On the deck off the living room, the four compatriots (the term "unindicted co-conspirators" raced through Wesley's thoughts) sat adrift in the same sinking boat. The more the others spoke, the easier it became for Louise to hold her demons at bay.

Tom examined each of them, concerned that the palpable fear might soon overcome them all, himself included.

"I thought this was taken care of," Nathan said. Wes and Louise assumed he was talking to Maloney, since neither of them had any idea what Nathan referred to.

"Obviously not," Tom said.

"Yeah, obviously not," Nathan echoed. "Louise, what's your assessment?"

"Hopman," she began, well prepared after thinking of nothing else since early morning, "even Billy Mac. I can see that. The logic seems straightforward. They're high profile, easy to identify. Their names are all over this. But Floyd Ochs?" Louise shook her head—scared, bewildered, amazed. Maloney and Pitts were unsure. Nathan had no interest in her emotional state. He hung on every word, however. He often said, though never to her face, that Louise Hollingsworth was the best analyst he'd ever known. Her insight into companies and the people who ran them was not only more often right than wrong, it was plain spooky. She could spot a loser when he was at the very top of his game, when people proclaimed him a genius, and she could see the future success of a company when no one else could. Nathan had seen the firm make tens of millions, sometimes hundreds, by following her recommendations. He respected her opinion and now he badly needed it. Louise did not mistake hard work and promotional instincts for sorcery. She was happy to have Nathan's favor, and fearful that her first really bad move would quickly erode it. Now, as always, she did her best and hoped to stay a step ahead of the game.

"If he knows Floyd Ochs," she went on, "he knows everyone."

Nathan's eyes glistened. "Who? Who?" he demanded.

"Who's everyone?" Pitts asked.

"Well," Louise said. "Besides Hopman, MacNeal, and Ochs, there's Pat Grath and us."

"What about whatshername . . . Dr. Roy?" said Wes.

Tom and Nathan looked at Pitts the way his line coach had when the game films showed him missing a block on a crucial play. "You asshole," seemed written in their stare. Some things were not necessary for Louise to know.

"I doubt that," Louise said. "How would anyone know about her, and besides, she's dead. But if you want to start at the beginning, there's also Wayne Korman."

"The foreman," Maloney said. "Why Ochs and not him?"

"There's no way to know," Louise said. "Why Billy Mac and not Pat Grath?"

"Billy Mac was this morning," Pitts said. "By dinner Pat Grath may be dead too."

"Why Hopman first?" Louise continued. "He wasn't the first to know anything. As I recall he didn't know anything except what you told him, Tom. Right?"

"I believe so," Tom said.

"So why start with him?" Pitts asked.

"Nathan," said Louise, "let's look at this. In addition to the three already victims, there are at least the four of us, Pat Grath, and the foreman Wayne Korman. Possibly others too at the plant level; maybe some within Knowland, Second Houston, even Alliance. We don't know. We can speculate about Grath—Wes has been unable to reach him—but there's little or no point. We know he's involved. We just don't know if he's still alive. Why one and not another? At this time we—"

"Who the fuck cares?" Nathan shouted. And once again he said, "I thought this was taken care of!"

"What are you talking about?" Pitts asked.

"Dr. Roy's notes may have outlived her," Louise continued, "quite frankly, Dr. Roy may be a source of information for this person. She was present when you, Nathan, discussed Mr. Hopman's role with Wesley. As I recall it was a heated exchange. She may have written that down somewhere and failed to surrender her computer records and destroy her notes as requested. When she was robbed it's at least conceivable that such information fell into the hands . . . what?"

The three of them were staring.

"That was us," Nathan said. "The burglary was us. We had people break in and take her stuff. They got a CD with everything on it, the works."

Louise let her mouth fall open and shot a furious glance at Wes. "You did a burglary?" She felt her composure snap and Wesley saw it go. "A burglary in her apartment?" Her eyes were darting now. Her thin hands moved in the air. Her expression reddened and she said,

"Are you fucking crazy? What have you involved me in? I told you not to go through with it. I told you from the start. It's one thing to make a goddamn mistake. Now you're talking about burglary! Did you *kill* her too?"

Wesley was surprised to see both Tom and Nathan immobilized. He leaned forward, as Tom often did with Nathan, and put his hand on her shoulder. He pitched his voice deep and soothing.

"Nothing like that. I give you my word of honor. We would not even contemplate anything like that. You know in your heart we wouldn't." By "we" it was understood between them that he meant only himself. She looked away from him, at the lake, waiting for her fury to ebb. Wes patted her shoulder. Tom kept silent. Nathan tried but could not contain himself.

"Absolutely not," he shouted, aiming for an indignant effect, "whatever she did to herself, she did to herself."

Louise looked sharply at Tom, certain in the moment that he could not successfully lie.

"It's the truth," he said. Was that regret or guilt she heard in Tom's voice, or something else foreign to her experience? She had no time to figure it out. She looked away from them all, upward at wisps of wind-driven clouds. The others gave her respectful silence. When she spoke again her voice was calm and hard. Wesley expected practical questions going to self-preservation.

"What else don't I know?" said Louise.

Nathan glared at Tom and spit as he spoke. "*Tell* her, for Christ's sake! Tell her what she doesn't know."

"Don't overreact, Nathan," Tom Maloney said. The world was falling apart in front of him and yet it was all Tom could do not to wonder how long it would take to canoe the length of the lake and back. For a moment he questioned his sanity. "Steps have been taken," he said.

Wesley Pitts seemed to breathe easier. He knew from experience that if Maloney was on top of something, he had nothing to worry about. He hoped that was still true. Louise's expression did not change perceptibly, but she crossed her legs, something Tom noticed she did only when she was at ease. When discussing anything with Louise Hollingsworth, Maloney knew to look at her body language. Legs straight, knees together indicated stress and uncertainty. Crossed legs meant she made her point, was comfortable with it, and fully expected agreement. She painstakingly taught herself to control her hands, which were constantly in view whenever she spoke, but her legs gave her away.

"We have people on this," Tom said.

"They're doing a great job, Tom," Stein said. Tom glared at him.

"What people?" asked Wes Pitts.

"We made certain arrangements after Billy MacNeal was killed," Tom continued without directly answering Pitts. "Suffice it to say, we've arranged to have the assassin found and taken care of. The people we've hired are used to pursuing their objective with somewhat more complete information than we've been able to supply. They—"

"What the fuck are you talking about!" Stein exploded. "When you pay somebody to 'take care of someone,' you expect they'll 'take care of it.' Am I wrong? These mystery men can't find the bathroom without a flashlight, *can they*?"

"Take it easy everyone," Tom said. "We have topnotch people on this. But, frankly, they have to know who to go after. We can't tell them that. This is not something these people usually do. Finding out who they're looking for may be a little beyond their scope."

"Five hundred grand, and it's 'a little beyond their scope'?" Nathan's voice was screeching with frustration, and Tom was certain anger had ignited the fires of Nathan's uncontrollable fear.

"Take care of them . . . ?" Louise said. "Does that mean—"

"Damn well better mean that," Pitts said. He mumbled something foul.

Tom delivered his next line to Louise. "Nathan is justifiably disappointed. I'm disappointed myself. The people I've hired have not been able to identify our man. Once we have him identified and know where he is, I'm sure they'll do as expected. And that's really why I'm a little late. Before I left the city I made a few phone calls."

All three were leaning forward now: Wesley hoping Tom had it locked at last; Louise feeling snug at the center of things; Nathan turning again to his only friend. Tom met each set of eyes and said, "I want to tell you about a guy. His name is Walter Sherman."

TWENTY

New York

Isobel Gitlin had celebrity thrust upon her, and she did not like it a bit. At least, not at first. The Moose tried to counsel her. "Let them see you and get it over with," he said. "These things have a shelf life of a day and a half. Go with it. Let it happen. Before you know it, it's over." She rejected his advice. She thought it was stupid that anyone would make her a part of the story of the E. coli disaster and the deaths that now seemed to follow. "It's nonsense," she told Gold. He followed her wishes. He held out for a while, demanding that the *Times* withhold her photographic image. That lasted a week, during which time the cable networks filled their empty afternoons with experts, some of whom actually claimed to know Isobel Gitlin, and they offered up details to which they considered the world entitled. Things changed when a former boyfriend sold an old but flattering photo to the *New York Post.* Murdoch's New York newspaper front-paged her face with the headline, "What Does Isobel Have to Hide?"

Isobel glumly watched a local TV report from a Manhattan perfume store she'd never heard of, where the girl at the counter described the fragrance advice she'd given Isobel just last week. A determined flock of paparazzi formed, not in the same league with the Jackie O/Princess Di eras, but large enough to frighten a normal person. The absurdity of it all amazed Isobel. Nevertheless, a friend procured a bag of discounted wigs from a Borough Park store for Hassidic women. Isobel wore a different one every day, and a blue jean jacket, and that was all it seemed to take.

She thought it all ridiculous. But lest Isobel miss any subtleties, Mel explained the dynamics: her week of faceless celebrity had tantalized the marketplace, precipitating, once the picture was out, a near-hysterical gathering of "the birds of the air." That's how the Moose always referred to television "journalists." The hook for the story was, of course, her investigative reporting: the link between the murders and the plague. That positioned endless replays of the desolation of the South by the mighty marauding E. coli bug. Television ran with it as if it were Sherman's Second campaign. They disinterred the grief of those days like fresh meat and served it up all over again with Isobel Gitlin as gravy. Cable wouldn't let it rest—not as long as the story pumped revenues. And the regular networks could not but follow. Thus was Isobel informed that she ought to go on TV. Management said she really ought to do it for the *Times*, for herself. She ought to do it. Period.

Upon hearing that, the Moose advised: "Too late, kiddo. You might have smiled at the assholes and gotten rid of them in the beginning, but not anymore. You need a war or some particularly gruesome celebrity murder to get the dogs off your behind now. You're the flavor of the month, and they all want a lick. You do it now and it won't be pretty."

"How about tolerable?" she said. "Can I d-do that?"

The Moose said, "Well, nothing lasts forever. They want their pound of flesh, and when they get it they'll be done with you. Make a list of words you can manage. You know what I mean. Say them out loud a few times. Put together some sentences. Then, when you go on the air, repeat them a lot. Doesn't matter what they ask. Just say the things you've practiced. That's what everybody does. If it gets to be too much, just look at the camera," he chuckled, "and say: 'F-fuck you!'"

"Thank you. Th-thank you very much," she said in her best imitation of the King. The Moose had not offended her. She worked on her delivery in a studio owned by the paper. To her astonishment, the camera helped control her stutter. She planned to write a piece on that, perhaps with a neurologist.

Her story, with her picture, made the cover of *Newsweek* and an inside, double-page feature in *Time*. Totally fabricated stories appeared in respected publications describing Isobel's role in briefing the FBI, advising the mayor of Boston, consulting with Houston's Commissioner of Police. There was gossip about a book deal, a movie, an HBO special. The info-tainment shows and one especially sleazy tabloid linked her with rock stars, actors, athletes, even an in-your-face lesbian poet.

The paper had gone through tough times. Management saw in Isobel a chance to recoup intangible losses, the slippage in prestige that sloppy and fraudulent reporting will bring on. If Isobel Gitlin had made the *Times* the new leader in investigative reporting, they were happy to run with it. Her face and legend inspired an instantly devised subscription promotion theme: her image appeared on posters advertising the *Times* in subways and bus stops. Her salary increased commensurate with her new private office upstairs and an Administrative Assistant. She was told to consider herself "at-large," and report to Gold for the moment. He had her continue to hunt up additional angles on the E. coli story—fly here and there, peer under rocks, and, above all, scour the Internet. In an industry that looked to generate heat, she was boiling. Her father warned her, "Boiling water evaporates, my dear." And something told her to hold off on getting an agent.

She invited the Moose upstairs for tea. She did not expect him to be impressed, or contemptuous, and he wasn't. She did not expect him to hand her a lecture on what was bullshit and what was not, and he did not do that either. What surprised her was his certainty that she'd soon be back in the basement or on the street. He could not lay out a scenario, but reported this news from deep in his world-weary gut. Isobel did not doubt him for a moment. "Evaporate," her father had said.

Her descent began with the arraignment of Harlan Jennings for the murder of Floyd Ochs. Isobel felt the chilly winds blow the morning the first reports hit the AP. Macmillan and Gold were upstairs moments later. Her door slammed behind them. If Ochs was killed by a redneck named Harlan Jennings, a shit-kicking peckerwood unconnected to Hopman or MacNeal, or anyone sickened by meat-borne E. coli—all of which seemed to be the case—then Ochs's murder could not be tied to Hopman's or MacNeal's. The three-by-one murder story was dead. As for Hopman and MacNeal, they had business dealings, yes. But those involved many diverse ventures, which implied a sprawling universe of potential satisfaction seekers. They could be anywhere. Maybe a vengeful or a chemically imbalanced ex-employee did in Hopman and/or MacNeal. Possibly it was someone—anyone—who had been let go, downsized by one of his or her takeovers. Somebody who, perhaps after losing his or her job, had to pull the kids out of private school or move to a lesser neighborhood; someone whose life went bankrupt in a very bad way. "Why not?" inquired the Moose. Hopman and MacNeal had those and other abuses in common. Without the E. coli angle the thing fell flat. The question facing them all right now—and facing their Olympian betters—was sadly and simply this: had Isobel Gitlin made the *New York Times* a laughing stock *again*?

Macmillan, whom she expected to gloat, did not. He seemed to believe that he would get caught in the gears, and his frat-boy confidence never made an appearance. He was all about looking around the room and twisting his Cornell ring. Mel Gold, who did most of the talking, struggled to retain his sense of humor. Having said his piece, he encouraged her to "... continue looking under rocks, but do it a little faster."

She called Laticia Glover at the Memphis Commercial Appeal. She began to introduce herself, but Glover got the stutter, "Girl, you're in a shit-storm now."

"Perceptive of you to point that out." Her infrequent spasms of irritation, like the camera, helped limit her stammer.

Laticia laid it out. Harlan Jennings had been an assistant plant manager for Knowland & Sons in Lucas. When Floyd was promoted, Jennings was one of several assistant managers suddenly deposed. Two guys went back to working on the line. One got a job in a lumber yard and had no hard feelings. According to Laticia, Jennings punched the executive who told him Ochs had the manager's job. That got him fired on the spot. Some weeks later, drunk as a coot, Jennings went after Ochs in a bowling ally. Threats were made and a lot of people heard them. Maybe, some thought, Jennings would eventually calm down. He never did.

The Tennessee authorities worked slowly and methodically. When the cops talked with Harlan Jennings he was drunk and uncooperative. He tried to hit an officer and went to jail for that. Four shotguns were found in his basement, two recently fired, all seized. Awaiting his assault trial, Jennings was charged with the first-degree murder of Floyd Ochs.

"They got this guy cold," Laticia said. "They have witnesses saying one time he was shooting shotguns and laughing and saying he wished he was shooting Floyd."

"What was he doing shooting shotguns?"

"Yeah, hold on." Isobel heard pages turning. "I got it here somewhere. He was out at The Canyon."

"The what?"

"A shooting place. A firing range. We've got a lot of them here."

No response.

The Memphis reporter stifled a chuckle, catching the question in Isobel's silence. "That's what they do down here. They go out and shoot their guns."

"You mean a canyon outdoors, where people shoot at targets?"

"A special building. Like in New York. You all go out and play racquetball. We got shooting ranges." She laughed again. "Too bad about this Jennings thing. You were 'in the house' for a while. But where does it leave you now?"

"F-fuck you, Laticia," Isobel said, as cheerfully as she could.

"Always happy to help the *Times*."

"Did Jennings confess?"

"Hell, no. He says he's innocent. Claims he's being railroaded." Now she let out a full, deep chuckle.

"Why's that funny?"

"Poster boy for Tennessee crackers kicking and screaming he's going down for a crime he didn't commit. Tulia, Texas upside down. Gets my funny bone is all."

"Is there *anything* tending to exculpate?"

"Nothing I've heard about. They got motive and opportunity. They got the murder weapon. Hard case to beat, Isobel."

"Hard case to beat." The phrase echoed after the call. Macmillan said something like that when she tried to sell her story. He told her it was a hard case to *make.*

As soon as Macmillan figured out that he was in the clear, that Mel Gold would catch whatever came down, and probably take more than his share, Macmillan's other side would surface. He'd be dancing soon enough.

As she expected, Jennings's arrest played big. This was no routine murder. This was a *counter* story; a harpoon in the side of a helium whale. Her own paper ran an article casting doubt on Isobel's earlier work, without mentioning her name. But that would not take long. She expected a mea culpa on the editorial page. That would be the fat lady's song. Once-eager new pals were already steering clear. Her private office became a no-go zone from the minute Macmillan and Gold walked out. Next day, the *Washington Post* and *Los Angeles Times* suggested that the *New York Times* had once again been suckered by a youngster with an imagination.

The *New York Post* ran a full-page headline: "Times Tainted." This time the photo of Isobel showed her ducking paparazzi. "Fuck you," she said, throwing a copy of that paper in her wastebasket. Other papers across the country ran stories stating as fact that Harlan Jennings's capture disproved the three-by-one theory. Many suggested that Isobel Gitlin invented the connection, developed it like a piece of fiction, sold it to her editors (and what kind of editors were *they*?), and thereby hoodwinked the national press, the cable stations, the networks, and, yes, *the American people.*

The talking heads asked each other when would they learn? They berated themselves as too damned trusting. They wondered what would become of us all if things like this continued to sap America's faith in its media. And who, after all, was this Isobel Gitlin? No friend of theirs, to be sure. None of them knew her.

Isobel still had her salary and her office, and Mel Gold was there to do what he could. Nevertheless, she saw herself near the end of a very short branch. That was when Walter Sherman called.

"Miss Gitlin," he said. "We have not met, but I know that you're right. I'd like to talk it over."

"What do you mean you know I'm right? Right about what?"

"Hopman, MacNeal, and Ochs. I know things that you don't. I know things that you should know. Where would you like to meet?"

"Who are you?"

"My name is Walter Sherman. Meet me in the restaurant of the Mayflower Hotel. Six o'clock. I'll be sitting at a table next to the window facing Central Park West. I'll be wearing a camel-hair blazer. You'll be relieved when you see me. I'm old enough to be your father, and harmless as a pup. I know what you look like. I'll see you come in. I'll be dining and I hope you'll join me . . . if you have any appetite nowadays."

"Mr. Sherman," she said. "I will have a gun in my purse. If you are f-fucking around I will shoot off your b-b-balls."

The tables by the window are actually in the bar. The first entrance from the lobby brings you there. A single line of tables sits against the plate glass, inches from the street. The bar's a step up. In between the tables and stools, a row of planters is filled with large, leafy triffids that keep the rooms apart. Walter watched Isobel walk past him outside, wearing a green summer dress and yellow sweater, chin on her chest, stepping quickly, hands clutching a green, beaded purse. He stood up, smiled, and waved as she moved inside.

"It's a pleasure. I'm Walter. May I call you Isobel? Please have a seat. And please leave the gun in your purse."

She shook his outstretched hand, sat, and felt an awkward silence roll in. He liked awkward silences. They sometimes offered a window into the subject's state of mind. The quality of the smile, or frown, the posture, the steadiness of the gaze—there were things you could often tell from signs like that.

Walter Sherman's own manner had nothing much to offer. He seemed relaxed but purposeful, self-assured but diffident. What he said next suggested telepathy:

"See? Old enough to be your dad."

"I'm older than I look," she said. "You could be younger."

Now his pale-blue eyes showed her something nice: he was at least a little impressed. "Drink?" he said, flicking a finger. A smiling waiter leapt forward. She ordered a vodka martini. He asked for a Diet Coke.

"Is that quite fair?" she asked him.

Walter said, "I'll have wine with dinner. We can talk about sports until then."

Isobel could hold five martinis long before she left London.

"You know about me. Everyone does. It's ugly." She was stammering only moderately, and felt unexpectedly at ease. Now she saw a curious light in Walter's bright blue eyes. She tried a telepathic turn of her own:

"I spoke English and very good French at home. As a child I spoke Hindustani every day, and Bauan as well. I still can. My parents tried to keep my speech white, European. I rebelled against that, which could have produced my stammer. They say I pronounce my English like a little black village girl. That may help to explain the inflection you hear. I cultivate it because I like it. Do you?"

The surprise in his smile seemed to confirm that she had, in fact, read his mind. Then came the martini. She felt its first effect before the alcohol hit her blood. Coffee worked the same way. She got her first rush from the smell. She became aware that this was becoming a "jolly bash," as her suave, determined father might have said. And a jolly bash was not what she had in mind.

"Now let's hear about you," she said matter-of-factly. "What do you do besides advertise your antiquity?"

"I find missing people," he said.

No question: he'd said the same thing hundreds of times before. He could certainly have lied; anything else would have sounded more likely. She got the sense that he liked going straight to the point. Did he really find that practical? When did circumstances permit that kind of candor? How would it work for a catcher of people? Or was it a nifty affectation?

"Why do you do it?" Isobel asked, all pretty eyes and ears.

"People pay me to do it."

"Why don't they call the police?"

"Most do, but some are embarrassed, and some are afraid of ridicule, the risk of humiliation. Sometimes they need a private way to find whoever's lost."

"First you said 'missing.' Then you said 'lost.' Which is it?"

"Sometimes there's no difference. Some people want to be missing. They are not lost. Once in a while they don't know where they are. Then they are lost."

"What do you call yourself, professionally? What's the name for it?"

"I usually don't, and I don't know," Walter smiled again. She noticed the skin crinkling around his eyes and mouth. She thought him mid- to late-forties, but she thought he looked sixty because of the tan—what it had done to his face. Her father and mother avoided the sun, out of European vanity. She was afraid of sunburn. This one, like many Americans, seemed to pursue melanoma.

She said, "I never imagined anyone actually did what you say you do. I imagined it was all in the movies."

"Well," said Walter, "just goes to show."

"Your . . . what do you call them, clients? I assume they're celebrities, public figures? People who don't want the world to know that their daughter—I'll bet it's always the daughter—ran away with a Hell's Angel gang, or a circus, or wherever they go. And, that's where you come in."

He seemed a little less charmed. Her flippancy was doing its job. She expected to get a look at him now. "That's where I come in," he said, just a little shortly.

"I feel like calling you Robert Mitchum. Except he'd be somewhat older, if he were alive."

He didn't like impertinence. Probably took it for disrespect. He was sipping his Diet Coke silently. Sullenly? No. Not quite that.

"What makes you good at doing it?"

He said, "I really don't know. I just am. I know where to look. I know what to ask. The right things come to mind. Experience helps. I know when a hunch is worth chasing. What makes you good at what *you* do? What makes anyone good?"

Isobel sipped the last of her drink. She put down the glass with emphasis.

"What do you have to do with Hopman, MacNeal, and Ochs?"

"There are other people on the list." Walter was looking into her pupils, expecting a reaction. She gave him none. He went on. "Some of the ones who are probably on the list hired me to find the killer."

"Who are the others?" Stupid, stupid, stupid. It was a stupid thing to say and she knew it, but too late.

"First I have to identify the guy, assuming it's a *him*."

"What will you do after you know who it is?"

"I will find him."

"After you find him, what will you do?"

"I won't 'do' anything." The tone of his answer rejected her plain implication—that he intended to rub someone out. He was past his impatience now. He seemed pleased to be talking simple business.

"Most of the time I'm bringing somebody home. All I'm doing now is finding a guy."

"And what do you think your friends will do when you find him?"

"They're not my friends. Just my clients. And what they do is their business. They're not killers themselves. From what I've seen they will buy him off."

"So you think he survived the E. coli disaster and lost someone he loved? Wife, child? Something like that?" She paused long enough for him to let her go on. "Then how do you buy off a person like that?"

Walter stopped, took in a long, deep breath through his nose, then turned his gaze to the park across the street for only a moment. "What's the largest amount of money you've ever thought of having?" he asked, turning to look at her.

"I already have it. My people are not poor. I struggle only because I prefer it. Actually, I don't struggle."

"How much? Give me a figure."

"I am not a materialist. I think in modest terms."

"How much?"

Isobel took a moment to ponder. Before she could speak he reached out and touched her hand, his fingers surprisingly warm.

"In dollars. Do you have a figure in mind?"

She did, and she nodded.

Walter sat back. "Now double it, triple it, quadruple it."

"Oh, m-m-my," said Isobel.

"Think about Hopman and MacNeal. Think about their money. How much was their life worth? Think of the people we're talking about."

Another flick of the finger, another waiter. They ordered, and Walter went on without losing a beat. She had the somewhat creepy feeling that Walter believed he knew all about her. In retrospect now, his impatience seemed measured, as though he were tolerating expected girlish antics. She suddenly felt—absurdly, really—taken for granted. She also felt a little like being understood. His apparently genuine inclination to talk straight had an effect. She found herself tending to accept his words at face value.

He said he wanted Isobel's help in identifying his man; he was sure that she'd done more research on it, and gathered more good information, than anyone else in the wide, wide world. He also said, quite matter-of-factly, that while Isobel's research would speed his work, she could not realistically expect to identify this guy without him.

And he left it precisely there.

She thought long and hard, and he did not attempt to hurry her.

They ate in silence for what must have been quite a while, as New York passed on the street outside, and waiters danced through the room, and diners, all nicely dressed, a surprising number of them older, hummed at each other over their food.

She suddenly saw that he'd ordered a bottle of white wine. As the waiter poured, Isobel understood that her mind was made up. She explained that she'd turned her West Side apartment into a photo gallery. She said she had pictures of hundreds of adult survivors—parents and spouses and brothers and sisters and grown-up children of those killed by Knowland meat. She also had spreadsheets designed to connect the dots, to correlate factors likely to narrow the field, to grind the data down to a workable list.

She had a rough timeline tracking who died when. She knew who lost a child, a wife, a husband, a brother, a sister. She included cousins when evidence showed they were close. Many of their pictures were taped on her walls. On her kitchen wall, her "wall of fame," hung photographs of all who had lost two or more close relatives. She and her assistant spent days on the net assembling facts and likenesses, then dumping them into a system of folders she had designed for that purpose.

Walter expressed neither admiration nor surprise, which disappointed Isobel and left her somewhat irritated, which irritated her all the more.

"You have the data," Walter said. "I have the skill and experience. We need to help each other."

"I am not without skill and experience." Now this old man was getting on her nerves. "Besides, I have the *New York Times* behind me." She wished she hadn't said it the moment she did. Behind her with a pitchfork, maybe. Walter certainly knew that.

But he played it like a gentleman, just as her father would. "My guess is that that anyone who knows you finds it impossible to believe that you were dishonest or sloppy. I'm sure that many colleagues believe you, but I do not *believe* you. I know for a *fact* that you are right. And you know that I'm the only one who does."

They both knew the deal was done.

And so was dinner. He suggested dessert and coffee and cognac. She signaled that she needed a rest by saying she'd never been inside the Mayflower before. He said that he based himself here when he stayed in New York. She thought to say that the senior contingent probably made him feel very young indeed, but she sipped her coffee instead.

Walter said, "When I was a kid in Rhinebeck, it took a couple of hours to drive down here. In high school we'd do it sometimes, get drunk, and drive home. It was a change of pace. At the time there was a notorious call girl ring in this building. It was all very high class and got some play in the papers when they busted the ring. I told my friends to drive by. We went around the block half a dozen times. After that I used to imagine walking down the street right out there, and one of these girls comes out looking like a movie star, and she wiggles her finger and there I go. And I'm sitting around in this penthouse with dozens of girls, drinking scotch and all the rest of it. The thing was, I'd seen an actual place that was in the news. I felt a connection. The first time I had to stay in the city for business, I came right here. I've done it ever since. I've sat at this table more times than I can count. As you can see, I'm a very popular figure here."

"And the girls . . . ?"

"Long gone by the time I landed."

She was greatly encouraged by her meeting and ongoing work with Walter. It helped her keep her chin up during the next couple of days, as the criticism continued. She spent the next day at home, working with him. She went to the office the following morning, more than a little bucked up. On top of the pile of her morning mail was an envelope bearing no postmark, no stamp, and no return address. The computer-generated label showed only her name. Whoever sent it had gotten it into the *Times*' internal system. It contained a single sheet, unsigned. The following words in 16 pt. bold were printed across the center:

I killed Floyd Ochs.
It was not Harlan Jennings.
Details to follow.

Very carefully, holding it by a single edge, she placed the envelope between two sheets of paper and stapled them top and bottom. Later, she learned there were no fingerprints on either the envelope or the note. Then she placed the evidence in her top drawer and sat back to focus on her breathing, trying to get her heart under control.

TWENTY-ONE

St. John

"Best towel I ever used was in Aruba," said Walter, wiping his face with the relatively clean specimen Billy had produced from behind the bar. "Big orange ones. They handed them out when you got to the beach. Real thick, but not too heavy. They smelled good too. You'd come out of the water and wrap one around you. It was just about perfect."

"When was that?" Billy said.

Walter shrugged. "A while ago."

"You wasn't alone. I can sure see that." Ike tilted his head sympathetically. Respect for Walter's privacy forbade him from speaking his thoughts: "Everything comes back when you see that orange towel. The good and the bad. It all comes back. I can see it in your face right now."

Instead, he looked at the ceiling and said, "Best one I can remember was New Orleans, summer of '49. She was a whore, you know, but she was a high-class woman. Told me she was twenty-four. Come to find out she wasn't but seventeen. No matter. Woman like that make an old man young and a young man feel a lot older."

"Lucky she didn't kill you," Billy said, heavy lids showing more of his sad brown eyes than usual.

"Man, she made me feel like I never did before and have not since," said Ike.

"I thought this was about towels," Billy said.

"I'm getting to the towels. When I was done, which was none too quick, I was soaking wet. I was covered with my sweat and hers. And we're in this hotel room with a big open window and doors leading out to a little terrace. Had a fan, but damn sure no air conditioning. It was hot and sticky too. She stood there by that open window and the moonlight shined off her in a way that made her look like, I don't know what—an angel, a statue like you see in a museum—except I knew she was never no statue. Never seen a woman beautiful as that. Next thing I know, she had a towel and sat down beside me on the bed and went to wiping me off. That's the best towel I ever had."

Walter said, "Hell of a way to get old."

Ike nodded. "I was half your age at the time, but I growed up a lot *that* night."

Billy suddenly stood up straight behind the bar, surprising Walter and Ike with his height. Unslouched, he was a different man. "My mother used to put a clean towel on the bathroom door every time I took a bath."

"Your mother?" said Walter.

"What's wrong with that? She took a towel out of the closet and hung it up on the bathroom door. It was clean and it smelled good. Every time I took a bath. Anything wrong with that?"

Walter's eyebrows jumped.

Billy bent toward him: "You want to hear about towels? Wrapped around people's heads after they got their brains beat out behind some warehouse? Towels all covered with blood so you didn't know what color they were? Believe me, Walter, I seen plenty of towels."

"I like your momma's towel fine," said Ike.

"Write it up, Billy," said Walter.

"What?"

"New Orleans, Aruba, mom." And to the general satisfaction, that's what he wrote on the rimless blackboard leaning against the mirror.

TWENTY-TWO

St. John

WALTER WAS HAPPIEST ON St. John, with the heat and the quiet, the privacy, and the pace. He was at his best on his deck, looking out at the rock. Whenever he came back, Clara said, "Walter? You have a good trip?" If he had, he'd tell her so. If not, he said, "Good to be back." That was enough for her. She lived in his house and she felt that she knew the man. She was old enough to be his mama.

He was glad to be home, but he couldn't get Isobel out of his mind. Three days in her apartment had yielded Walter a dozen names. He'd taken them from the pictures obscuring her kitchen walls. Each picture was tagged with a name, one or more street and e-mail addresses, and cell and landline numbers. He had their stories in his head. He worked without notes. He kept no records.

Isobel lived on West End Avenue, in an elegant building with a full-time, uniformed staff. Her sixth-floor apartment overlooked 84th Street. It opened into a short foyer with the kitchen on the left, the living room straight ahead, and a hallway ending at two bedrooms side by side, each with a full bathroom. The wall between the kitchen and living room had a chunk taken out and an archway constructed. Two large, potted trees guarded the archway. The kitchen floor was dark red tile. The rest of the floors were parquet. Her furniture was costly but thrown-together, comfortable everywhere. Live plants in all rooms. Piles of books, periodicals. Two very large living room paintings filled with big, colorful, abstract shapes faced each other across the room, the 84th street windows between them. Her bedroom was the place for family photos and personal displays: intricate seashell designs arranged in frames, a child's Tower of London.

The other bedroom was crammed with books. They were stuffed into bookshelves, piled on tables, stacked on the floor. The beds were made and the kitchen was spotless. Even the recessed light fixtures were dust free. "Isobel had help," he thought. He liked the place, except for the artwork.

"Lovely joint," he said. "You mentioned that your people are not poor."

"Obviously not," said Isobel, opening the refrigerator, not looking up. While the coffee brewed they sat at the kitchen table. She filled him in on her "perfectly ordinary" past.

Maurice Gitlin, her father, traded—in the great tradition of Englishmen who roamed the globe seeking to buy cheap and sell dear. He'd involved himself in deals pertaining to just about everything legal, and rumors persisted that from time to time he may have lost sight of the line. "Prosperity is the mother of invective," he counseled Isobel whenever she asked if the stories about him were true.

Isobel spent much of her youth in Fiji, but called London and Paris home as well. She was into her teens before she realized that only *some* people had homes in the South Pacific, England, and France. After Oxford University, where she learned to trade on her village-girl accent and treat her stammer as less than a problem, Isobel felt an itch to try America. She'd visited many times. At twenty she enrolled in the Western Classics program at St. John's in Annapolis. There she spent five years reading Plato, Virgil, Kant, Dante, and Nietzsche. She also wrote a regular column: "Sex and the Serious Student." It was extremely popular, exciting much mail. She was thought "witty yet substantive," "frank and irreverent," "self-contained," and "strangely, refreshingly modest." She responded to letters from graduate students with references to the classics, judiciously laced with reader suggestions on how to find G-spots and execute blowjobs, and she was not averse, on occasion, to finding out for herself.

Isobel asked to be titled Associate Editor of the publication, which had, over time, been called many things, most recently *Freethinker*. Then she went to New York and applied for a job at the *New York Times*. Her editorial background and roots got her in, she told Walter, then added, "And my father, of course, has always been a help."

They spent the rest of that day immersed in Isobel's files. Of all the survivors, the ones on the kitchen walls seemed most promising to Walter. Isobel gave him details of their lives and losses. She knew a lot. She'd even tracked down most of them in their present circumstances. A few were hard to find, but she had a list with addresses for nearly all. Walter had a professional's appreciation for Isobel's work. Murder was a state, sometimes even a local, crime. Every cop involved in one jealously guarded territory. Homicide was the top of the pyramid for cops. After chasing car thieves, burglars, bad-check bouncers, and wife beaters, every policeman in America yearned to catch a homicide. Small-town cops looked on such a happening as if they had won the lottery. They dreamed of solving a killing. They saw themselves in the papers and on the evening news, famous just like the football coaches and NASCAR drivers. Big city detectives saw big news murders as career builders. They sought them out like Infantry officers; eager for a star, they seek out combat. However, just because a killing is notorious, just because it makes the *New York Times* front page, doesn't mean it gets the attention of the best homicide detectives in the business. Jurisdiction was the whole ballgame. In Dallas, nearly half a century after the fact, they still smarted at losing the JFK murder to the feds.

Walter's work took him to so many jurisdictions, he had a real sense of the differences in police competence. He did not like to make judgments. It's just that he knew the importance of experience. He knew a murder like that of the little girl in Colorado, the beauty queen barely out of her toddler years, would have been solved in a New York minute—*in New York.* As it was, with an investigation lost in the boondocks of the west, he was just as sure no one would ever be arrested, tried, or convicted for that crime. If you're going to kill someone, Walter knew, the best place to do it was somewhere they don't have any murders, because that means they don't have anybody who knows how to solve them. Boston and Houston were not, of course, the same as rural Tennessee. But if Boston cops needed information available only in Houston, which they undoubtedly did, or vise versa, Walter knew they could forget about it. If your suspect list contained hundreds of names, living in hundreds of places, he knew you would need the cooperation of hundreds of police departments. Not a chance in hell, he wagered. Left to their own devices, the police might never identify this killer, and the FBI would only gum up the works. No one in the know was any longer unaware that the FBI hadn't caught anyone important in decades.

Isobel, or someone like her, was the only way. She had answered many of the most important questions, all by herself, long before any law enforcement agency could or would. It impressed Walter that she even knew the questions, no less was able to get so many of the answers. What Walter also knew was that she didn't know how to take the answers she had, the data, and spin them into a single, definitive, correct identification. He was confident he could.

Her descriptions were concise and detailed. And they were interesting. She spoke of these people as if she knew them; treated their stories like her own; tried, with great success Walter thought, to get behind their eyes. From time to time he asked questions. She nearly always answered "I don't know." They quit at eleven and ordered Chinese food.

"What was the point," asked Isobel, chewing Mu Shu pork, "of asking me questions you knew I could not answer?"

Walter looked at her carefully. She'd gone through the process for hours, never suggesting the slightest awareness of what he was up to. But she'd sniffed some purpose in him all the while.

"It's been my experience," Walter said, "that when people are telling you everything, you can ask them a question, any question, and if they don't have the answer, they will say so. They'll say 'I don't know.' But if they are holding back, they will not do that. They won't say 'I don't know.' They'll always give you something, true or not, just to be sure that you don't suspect them of covering up or trying to mislead you."

"F-fuck you. You were testing me all day and night."

Walter winced. "That's not the way to look at it. I have no reason to think you're holding back. I didn't. That's not why."

"Then, w-w-why?" That was the first time all day he'd heard her stutter. He felt a sharp pang of regret. It startled him because he hadn't felt anything quite like it for a long, long time. At that point Walter became aware of a growing attachment, the nature of which was anything but clear.

"Everyone forgets important details," he said. "You think you've said it all and then someone asks a question and another detail comes back. Talk to a doctor. Patients leave out all kinds of things when they talk about their symptoms. A cardiologist I know says patients with pacemakers often forget to tell him they have one. He doesn't know till he listens to the chest. If you want to know every relevant thing, you have to ask. You must be persistent. It's the question that brings it all back. That's all."

"You *are* an old shit," she said. And the hint of hurt in her voice, and the certainty in Walter's mind that she knew he was still not being completely honest, put a painful edge on that feeling of regret. He leaned forward and put his hand, very delicately, on hers.

"Listen, I test people as a matter of reflex. It's what I've been doing for thirty years. I knew I didn't have to do it with you, and I tried to stop several times."

She stared at him with a blank expression.

Walter smiled sadly. "I really did."

"I can live with that," she said, doing her best to conceal her delight in the sorrowful look on his face and the soft, tightened sound of his voice.

During the next day and a half, while Isobel was at work, Walter taxied from the Mayflower and worked in her flat. He sat in her kitchen reading the hundreds of pages of printouts she'd left him. Then he read them again. He focused on where the "A-group" survivors lived, how their lives had been changed, who'd moved, who'd quit jobs or been fired, gotten in trouble, divorced, found a new sweetheart or spouse. Who sued and what was known about how much they got? One by one he wanted to know: Where were they at this moment?

He knew how loss creates fresh separations: between survivors and friends, neighbors, relatives, each other. When a hamburger's killed one of your children, how do you ever send the others to McDonalds? How do you explain why they can't go? What do they tell their friends? Survivors are reminders. How many parents protect their kids by keeping them apart from the ones who lost parents or brothers or sisters? Men sometimes moved, like divorced men sometimes do, away from their old neighborhoods, away from the couples they knew when they were a couple too. Many people changed jobs, suddenly strangers with people at work. Amid the routines of devastation, Walter searched patiently for the abnormal. He made calls, discovered employers and co-workers, neighbors and friends, turned up new girlfriends, old flames, estranged family members. Most were easy to talk to. It was no surprise to Walter. This was what he'd been doing for years. He knew how to approach people, how to help them tell him what it was he needed to learn.

When Isobel returned in the evening she told him about the magical note: "I killed Floyd Ochs."

"*Who* killed Floyd Ochs?" she asked Walter. She told him some called it a fraud or a very bad joke. She suspected that some considered her to be the note's author. She told him it was a blessing because it confirmed what she thought she knew. Walter said he was glad it made her feel better, but it didn't change very much for him, except for what it told him about the killer. They had a drink and walked up to Broadway and found a place to talk about survivors.

When Walter was ready to leave New York, he kissed Isobel on the forehead and told her, "I have what I need for now. I do my thinking better at home. Come visit me. You'll like it." He promised to call in a day or two.

Clara gave him a message from Tom Maloney. He'd called while Walter was in New York. Walter called back on Tom's twenty-four-hour number. He said he was making progress but had nothing to report. Then he said, "I don't work this way, Tom. I tried to make it clear before. If I need to talk to you, I'll call. Otherwise, back off and let me do what I'm doing." Maloney said he would. Walter knew he wouldn't, not for a while anyway. Years ago, Walter had rejected the notion of being supervised. Making it stick wasn't always easy. The people he worked for supervised whom they pleased. He quit one job and sent back most of the money. But that was the only time it came to that. Otherwise, he delivered a real conclusion, happy or not.

Two days later, Walter identified Leonard Martin.

When he did, he found it odd that he had been hired to find this guy, or that this guy went where he did. Walter knew the Caribbean as only a resident could. Isobel had a Jamaican address for Leonard Martin, and something about it rang a bell with Walter. Leonard moved from Atlanta, retired from his law firm, and set up housekeeping in the Bahamas. He ran from his loss like so many others. He just had more money than they did. Checking out Leonard Martin's address was easy *and* confusing. Walter knew the Jamaica slum where Leonard bought his house. People with money didn't live there. No white tourists or exiles, certainly. They avoided places like that for very good reason. And there was no marina for miles around. A boat in that neighborhood had oars. Red flags started waving.

Unless he'd gone Rasta, nuts on weed, or both, Leonard Martin was nowhere near Jamaica. Walter called bars, restaurants, even local stores. No one knew a white man named Leonard Martin. The only fat, troubled American Walter heard mentioned was a priest named Ryan who drank heavily for a year or so until he met a local woman named Claudia. Now they fished together on their boat and apparently lived a happy life.

The deeper and wider his search for Leonard Martin, the more he discovered about him, the less he knew where to find him. Walter called people in Atlanta. He put together a detailed version of Leonard's life and downward spiral. He learned about his family, his law firm, his habits and tastes, even the Community Players and Barbara Coffino. He quickly got past the Bahamas dodge, but stymied in Jamaica. Did Leonard ever get there? If not, where did he go? Where was he now? What had he done? As a matter of very intense professional interest, what would he do next? Finding people was an art, a practiced and disciplined activity Walter Sherman had developed to its highest degree. It seemed simple, but no element of the process was more important than knowing when your goal was reached. A journey of a thousand miles always began with the first step—everyone knew that—but how many could spot the finish line with equal precision? The authorities couldn't. Walter was sure of that. Leonard Martin was a big target. No one's loss had been greater. But as soon as the cops began investigating him, they'd have learned he moved to the Bahamas and took twelve million dollars with him. His former law partners would have vouched for him, as would anyone else the cops might have talked to. If they even bothered to check, they would have found the house and property he bought in Jamaica, and the boat too. Soon enough, Leonard Martin's file would have been tossed into the pile marked "Checked Out." Walter knew that's the way it probably played out because he'd seen it happen many times before.

But Walter also knew Leonard Martin was his man—no doubt about it. He'd cleaned out and packed up every aspect of his life, what was left of it, and disappeared. Most telling, he disappeared on purpose. Walter thought Leonard had good instincts. A man who intended to do what Leonard was doing needed to cover his trail, cut himself off from anyone capable of endangering him, isolate himself for the task ahead. Leonard Martin's trail was not cold. It was frozen.

Walter called Tom Maloney in New York. He told him he had identified Leonard Martin and gave him a brief explanation. He then offered Tom a choice. Walter could continue his efforts to find the man, as agreed, or Tom could release the name in powerful circles and rely on law enforcement to do the job. If he opted for the second choice, Walter said that would entail a substantial cash refund. "A million dollars is a lot to pay for what I've done."

Tom said, "Walter, I can't adequately express my gratitude. It's really wonderful news. You've more than justified your fee. I've got to go with your first option and let me tell you why. Between you and me, law enforcement is useless. Its incompetence will be a central theme in the social history of this country in the twenty-first century. We're not kidding ourselves, are we? I know some of these guys and I guess you know some yourself. Would you trust them to finish the job? I wouldn't. What's more, I don't want a bunch of civil servants out there scaring the fish away. You know what I mean? I want you to do your job and find the man. Once we know where he is, when you have him, I know we'll be able to handle it. Is that satisfactory to you?"

Walter said, "Just wanted to give you the option."

It took Tom half an hour to track Nathan down. A servant brought him the phone in the little man's penthouse gym. He took it on his treadmill. Maloney reported his conversation with Walter. Nathan stopped the machine.

"Is he fucking crazy? He can't call the cops. Under the covers. This stays under the covers. We don't need any goddamn cops."

"That's what I told him," Tom said, repeating himself slowly word for word. "I told him to complete the assignment."

"And keep it confidential."

"He doesn't need to be told that. You already know that, Nathan."

Isobel wasn't in her office. She and Walter agreed not to message by voice. Walter knew where he had to go next, but before leaving he left her an e-mail with no subject and only the number *8* as text.

TWENTY-THREE

Atlanta

HE LIKED OLD HOTELS, elegant buildings with high ceilings, ornate chandeliers, quiet bars, and round-the-clock room service. The smaller the establishment the better. The closest he'd find to that in Atlanta was in Savannah. Walter's work had taken him around the country and around the world—a lot of hotel rooms in thirty years; the best and the worst, sometimes the only. He learned a long time ago that "When in Rome, do as the Romans do" was sensible advice. When in Atlanta he stayed at the Ritz-Carlton, Buckhead. If you can't find old elegance, new will have to do. Last night, after realizing he needed to go to Atlanta, Walter called the offices of Stevenson, Daniels, Martin and left a message on Nick Stevenson's voice mail. It was short and concise, not aggressive or hurried, not too friendly; he left his name and said he wanted to talk about "a matter of shared concern." He'd be arriving in Atlanta tomorrow, he said, and asked Stevenson to leave a message for him at the Ritz-Carlton with a time and place to meet. Then he hung up. In the morning he ferried to the rock and flew nonstop to Georgia.

From the air the city of Atlanta appears to have multiple downtowns. In that sense it bears some resemblance to Los Angeles. Walter's view from seat 4A showed the original downtown, a collection of modern office towers, two stadiums, a massive dome, and a group of skyscraper hotels taller and more attractive to his eye than LA. Farther north another downtown of sorts sprung up. He could make out the rash of construction cranes, toiling in their never-ending endeavor, building the offices and high-rise condos of Atlanta's ritzy Buckhead neighborhood. He remembered reading that Elton John and Coretta Scott King lived in one of them, in the same building. "How could she afford that," he wondered? Somewhere nearby, where new money commingled with old privilege, Carter Lawrence lived. Beyond that, two more substantial groupings of tall buildings stood separated by ten miles of the perimeter highway that encircled the city. Looking south, through the window across the aisle, Walter could plainly make out all of Atlanta's growth to the north.

When he checked in, the desk clerk at the Ritz-Carlton handed him an envelope from Stevenson, Daniels, Martin, P.C. Attorneys at Law. Inside, handwritten on the firm's letterhead, was a short note signed by Nicholas Stevenson. It ended with, "Call me tomorrow." Walter was pleased. He showered, had dinner delivered to his room, watched a little television, and went to bed early. In the morning he called the number indicated on the note as Stevenson's direct line. Nick Stevenson answered with a cordial, "Good morning, Mr. Sherman." Caller ID had long ago taken all the surprise out of the telephone. Walter knew if the tiny screen didn't say Ritz-Carlton, Stevenson had familiarized himself with the hotel's number and recognized it when it rang. Either way, the thoroughness impressed Walter, who ranked preparation high on his list of admirable characteristics.

"Thanks for leaving the number," he said. "I often find it difficult to reach somebody when we're both strangers."

"Not at all. I'm not the President. I'm easy to get ahold of." Walter liked the accent and the casual manner that accompanied it. It registered right away that Stevenson's tone showed he knew this call had nothing to do with real estate.

Walter said, "Is it convenient to meet sometime today?"

"Why, exactly?"

"You want to know now? Right here, on the phone?" That sort of directness was unexpected. It irritated him a little.

"It's my private line, Mr. Sherman. Why not?"

Walter did not like being taken by surprise, especially on such a simple matter as arranging an appointment. It unnerved him, and he struggled slightly to regain the measure of composure he felt the situation required. A sip of coffee, a short cough, and then, "I'd like to talk to you about Leonard Martin. The people I work for . . ."

"And who might they be?"

Walter was unruffled. He felt completely in control of himself now. Did Stevenson know what Leonard Martin was up to? Could he be helping him? Questions that needed answers, but this was not the time. Walter could make assumptions on the phone, but then he remembered Sherlock Holmes. He needed to see Nick Stevenson, to sit face-to-face with the man before coming to any conclusions—any worthwhile ones. He said, "I'll be happy to give you all the details I have—everything—when I see you." Stevenson's office was only a ten-minute cab ride from the hotel. They agreed to meet there in a half hour.

The ride, short as it was, was straight north on GA 400, a highway designed to quickly connect Atlanta's richest suburbs with both Buckhead and downtown; a road built directly through one of the wealthiest neighborhoods in the city itself. It was a remarkable political achievement occupying a unique spot in the annals of American urban renewal and suburban sprawl; it displaced rich people to benefit others even richer. Its course ran like a vein graft in a bypass operation, pumping new blood to meet the increasingly demanding needs of the heart of Atlanta, the growth of business. And like a bypass, it was not a cure, just a temporary fix. It was not long before a new downtown budded, like the Bradford Pears that dominated the area along what was already being called the 400 Corridor. Stevenson, Daniels, Martin was on the fifteenth floor of the Queen—one of two apparently identical buildings of black reflective glass, each topped with a huge, but different, ivory-white architectural sculpture. They had the look of enormous chess pieces, especially at night, when their white crowns, bathed in light and held aloft by their black base, shone brightly against the night sky. Their identity as the King and Queen had been immediate. They stood adjacent to GA 400, just north of the I-285 interchange, surrounded by luxuriously landscaped grounds. As his cab approached, Walter examined the building tops and wondered if the King and Queen were what the architect had in mind.

Nick greeted him politely. Had they been anywhere other than the South, where such cordiality was the rule, not the exception, Walter might have called it warm and friendly. He took in the room at a glance. Simple, and, surprisingly, not comfortable. A large couch against the wall; one easy chair with ottoman; a low coffee table and three serviceable chairs for visitors. There appeared to be nothing special about Stevenson's desk, and there were very few personal items in the room. Walter figured Nick Stevenson for a man who liked to work at work and saw no need to bring his private life into the office.

Nick said, "And who are the folks you work for, Mr. Sherman?"

"Walter. Please call me Walter."

"Do you go by 'Walt'?"

Walter smiled. "No. No, I don't. Not since grade school."

"Never liked it, huh?"

"Never did."

"Well, Walter—and please do call me Nick—who are the folks you work for, and what kind of work is it you do?"

"I work for some people in New York. You wouldn't know their names . . ."

"Try me. I've been to New York."

"My client is a prominent person. Let's leave it at that," Walter said. "I don't divulge names. I'm sure you understand."

"I do. And I respect that. But I don't talk to people when I don't know who they are. I'm sure you understand."

Walter had no response. He just sat there. In a moment, Nick rose, extended his hand, and said, "Nice meeting you, Walter." In the next moment Walter made a decision completely foreign to his experience, one he'd never even considered. Nick Stevenson had information that could very well be critical to finding Leonard Martin. Walter's best guess was Nick wouldn't talk to him, not about Leonard or anything else, without knowing who he was really speaking to. He judged Nick as a man who could be trusted, and said, "I work for a New York businessman named Nathan Stein."

"He wouldn't be the Stein of Stein, Gelb, Hector & Wills, would he?"

Walter smiled again. "More than once, I see."

"I beg your pardon?"

"You've been to New York more than once."

"I have. Yes, indeed. Bought some stock too. Made a few deals, you know. Met a few fellas down on Wall Street."

Walter saw the mischievous streak in Nick, and he liked it. It reinforced the judgment he'd just made on which he'd risked so much. He liked Nick Stevenson too. He was more than just a closing attorney. "You handled the case against Knowland, didn't you?" Walter said. "I'll bet you did it all by yourself."

Now it was Nick's turn to be surprised.

"I don't know what you're referring to," he said, but obviously he did. His demeanor gave him away, and he knew it too. After an awkward pause he finally said, "What else do you know?"

"You can assume that everything that can be openly discovered, I've got—and perhaps some things that can't."

"Like Knowland?"

"Like Knowland."

"What are we trying to talk about here?" Nick said.

Walter asked if he could have something cold to drink. "Diet anything," he said. Nick buzzed his secretary, and almost immediately she produced a cold can and a glass with ice. "Thanks," said Walter. "My clients—and Nathan Stein is one of a group—believe your partner, Leonard Martin, is going to kill them."

"You never said what it is you do, Walter."

"I find people. I find people who can't be found or don't want to be found."

"A private investigator? Bounty hunter? You're surely not law enforcement."

"None of those. I'm no PI, no license, not for hire for that. I'm no bounty hunter either. I never work on commission. And I don't go around hurting people. I'm not a hired goon. I just find people."

"I didn't know Leonard Martin was missing."

"Nick, we can go round in circles for as much time as you've got. I've got nothing else to do today. But I'd rather get serious. I'm not an adversary, not to you or Leonard Martin, not to anyone. That's not what I do. Nathan Stein wants to find Leonard. He can't do it himself so, he hired me."

"Why?"

"Why did he hire me or why does he want to find him?"

"The latter."

"Stein and his crew," Walter began, leaning forward in his chair to be closer to Nick, who reclined as far as he could behind his desk, "they believe that the same person who's already killed other people, including Christopher Hopman and Billy MacNeal, will try to kill them. They don't know yet who this person is. They came to me. Long story short, that person is Leonard Martin." Walter looked closely for any reaction at all from Nick Stevenson, anything that might tell him if he knew about this already, might even be part of it. He saw it: a quick halt in Nick's respiration, then a return to normal. Not enough by itself to draw a meaningful conclusion, but enough to raise certain questions. Perhaps he knew what Leonard was doing. Perhaps he was part of it. Perhaps he was worried he might be found out. Perhaps, also, he knew nothing and was shocked to hear the allegation, but careful enough not to give himself away. Perhaps only Walter's experienced eye caught the momentary change in Nick's breathing pattern. He probed further.

"He's not in the Bahamas—you know that?"

"I know about Hopman and MacNeal down in Texas. I read the papers too. Now you're telling me Leonard Martin is a killer, a cold-blooded murderer? That he shot these men? That's not possible."

"Nick, I've been doing this kind of work for more than thirty years. Take my word for it—anything's possible. When Leonard Martin left here, more than two years ago, you say he went to the Bahamas."

"No, I didn't say that, but you seem to know anyway. Leonard said that."

"Yes, he told you he'd bought a place there—a boat too, I believe—and left. Is that right?"

"Yes. That's what he said."

"And you probably got a letter from him some time later, perhaps even an address, and my guess is you haven't heard from him since."

"What is it you want, Mr. Sherman?" Nick Stevenson was getting a bit testy.

"Hey," Walter said, holding up both his hands in mock surrender. He most certainly did not want this meeting to spiral into distrust and anger. "Please, it's Walter. I'm only trying to let you know there are things I already know. We don't have to do this this way. I'll tell you straight out that I do not know what you know, if you know anything, about Leonard Martin's whereabouts and activities the last few months or the past two years. All I'm looking for is to communicate with him. I have to find him before I can do that. If you can help me contact him, or do it for me, that would more than satisfy my needs. That's all I want. Will you help me?"

Nick buzzed his secretary. When she picked up he asked her to bring him some tea. They waited in silence while his tea arrived, and Walter said nothing until Nick had taken a sip.

"I mean no harm to him, Nick. You have to believe that. That's not what I do. I need to talk to him or with him. It's in his best interest. Will you help me?"

Nick Stevenson shook his head, grimaced, and took another sip of his hot tea. "No," he said. "I can't."

"You haven't—"

"No, I haven't. I haven't seen him since the day he said goodbye, haven't talked to him since the day he left, and haven't communicated with him since then—except for the note I received, as you said, with Leonard's address in the Bahamas. Are you sure he's not there anymore?"

"Never was. It was a decoy. You're a real estate lawyer. You must have seen these kinds of purchases before. With his expertise my guess is that he flew in, closed on the property and the boat—if you can call it that—and flew out. Might not have spent even one night there."

"You're sure?" asked Nick.

"I live in the Caribbean, Nick. I know the area he bought in. I've checked thoroughly. He was never there."

"It's all Knowland, isn't it?" Nick said. "Knowland and your clients too."

"Yeah, it certainly is," Walter said. "At some point, probably shortly before he left Atlanta, Leonard came across information about the people who were involved in that sorry episode. He fashioned some sort of list of those he felt knew about the scope of that disaster, understood the danger in advance, and now he's killing them, one by one."

"Because they didn't stop it?"

"Because they didn't stop it."

"Leonard Martin is my friend. My partner. Thirty years and you think you know a man. Then his entire family gets wiped out and he doesn't recover. How could he? It's all quite amazing," Nick said. "'Revenge is the wet nurse to madness.' You know who said that?"

"No, I sure don't," said Walter.

"Me neither. Forgot. But I liked it since the first time I read it in college. It's true, you know. Tell me, how do you know this killer isn't one of any number of others who suffered a similar loss?"

"I can account for all the others. I won't bore you with the details, but—"

"Yes, of course you found the others. You find people, don't you?"

"But I can't find Leonard Martin. And it's because he doesn't want to be found. He's left behind all the earmarks of someone who's hiding."

Nick was as sad as he was puzzled. He told Walter he knew Leonard Martin to be a peaceful man, a man who despised hunting and never, to his knowledge, even touched a handgun or a rifle. Also, at the end, two years ago, Leonard was a pitiful figure of a man, fat and sloppy, out of shape. He just couldn't imagine him being able to do this sort of thing.

Walter said, "I'm sure you're right. Leonard is a man with a deep sense of character. That's why he's come forward to protect Harlan Jennings. I'm convinced he's a decent man with a strong commitment to justice. Isn't that what he's doing? His own form of justice? As for being out of shape, two years is plenty of time to get oneself fit," said Walter. Nick did not seem to be buying that line, and, frankly, Walter wasn't a hundred percent convinced himself. He knew Leonard Martin had gained weight steadily over a couple of decades and ballooned in the months following the death of his family. A man in his fifties, with that sort of history, doesn't often turn it around, no matter how much time he has. As for the guns, that too worried Walter. Leonard would have to start from scratch, and he would have to acquire the skills of a marksman without assistance. Not an easy thing to do, even in two years.

"I know people," Nick said, "who are fervent hunters. They damn near love it, but they're no marksmen. Some of them can't hit the side of a barn. I don't see how a man like Leonard Martin can begin at square one and be a proficient shot—hell, a goddamn sniper!—two years later. You can imagine the sort of weapons you're talking about. It doesn't seem possible they could belong to the Leonard Martin I know. It must be someone else. There must be someone you haven't found yet."

Nick Stevenson had been too young for Korea and too old to be drafted in the '60s. He had no military experience and was not himself a hunter. In fact, he had not fired a weapon of any kind, ever. Walter told Nick he'd been in Vietnam, where he'd known men like Leonard who turned out to be natural shooters. They had an ability to shoot at, and hit, targets that others who worked much harder could not. They came from all walks of life, all circumstances. They were few and far between, and there seemed to be no rhyme or reason to it. Perhaps Leonard Martin was one of them. Perhaps two years with nothing to do except hone those talents was plenty of time.

"Where could he do that?" Nick asked.

"I don't know," Walter said. "Not yet."

They talked a few minutes more. Walter again assured Nick he meant no harm to Leonard. He explained to him, as he had to Isobel, that he believed Nathan Stein would try to buy his way out of this mess. He said, "You've no idea what kind of money we're talking about." Nick said he didn't think money would count for much.

"Leonard has so much," he said, "and, if you're right, apparently nothing to spend it on except revenge."

Walter's conviction about Stein's ultimate solution remained steadfast. "These people are all about money. They believe in the power of money like some believe in the baby Jesus. 'Enough' and 'money' don't go together. If they don't have enough, nobody does."

"He must be paying you a handsome sum," said Nick. Walter nodded. It was clear to him now that Nick Stevenson knew nothing.

"If you hear from him, please give him my message." Walter handed Nick a small notepad page with the Ritz-Carlton logo at the top. On it he'd written a telephone number. "My cell phone," he said. "Call me at this number. Anytime. Day or night."

"You've not made my day any brighter," Nick said.

"I'm sorry," said Walter.

They shook hands and Walter left.

TWENTY-FOUR

Atlanta

Carter Lawrence lived in an apartment building on Lenox Road in the midst of what might reasonably be interpreted as luxury run amok. Walter was surprised at the modesty of his building, surrounded as it was by far grander and more gaudy residential achievements. It was an older, off-white stucco structure set back from the street, only five stories high. It appeared to lack most of the exorbitant amenities: pools, fitness centers, uniformed staff, and even valet parking, conspicuously available everywhere else nearby. Carter Lawrence had not been wealthy until the Knowland settlement. Walter knew that. He measured wealth as being able to maintain one's lifestyle simply on the earnings from one's assets. No aspect of work was required. "Rich" just meant you made a lot of money. In Walter's experience, he found many who were rich and few who were wealthy. Whatever amount Carter got from Knowland, he hadn't spent it on a new place to live. Walter thought that was a bad sign, particularly if he was part of Leonard Martin's operation. It would be difficult to tempt a man with money if he wasn't spending what he already had. Leonard, on the other hand, had obviously been spending his. The question was: Was he spending it all on this project? Were either of these men the type to be bought off? Then again, who could refuse the kind of money Nathan Stein had to offer? He pushed the thought from his mind. Contemplating that kind of money brought unnecessary complications. His job was only to find the man. That was always just his job, and he was content with it.

Walter had favors to call in from many places: former clients eager to be so obligated; past contacts who liked him and would gladly help him again; even law enforcement with whom he was cordial. And he cultivated that rich garden, harvesting its fruit as the need arose. A phone call was all he needed to get a picture of Carter Lawrence. Taken by a photographer from the Atlanta Journal Constitution, it dated back to the funeral of his sons. A staff member attending to one of Georgia's most well-known citizens had delivered it to him at the Ritz-Carlton. Fifteen years earlier Walter had been hired to find that man's wife. After an indiscretion on her part, and a bad reaction on her husband's, she bolted. Two weeks after she disappeared from her Tuxedo Drive mansion, he found her ensconced in a lesbian bar in Miami. The husband sent two other men to Florida to bring her home. The press was told she had been visiting friends in Boca Raton, and she was back in Georgia before anyone (except her frightened and angry spouse) missed her. Like all of Walter's cases, he did what he was hired to do—find somebody—and the details never became public. Clients like the one in Georgia felt they owed a life-long debt to Walter, and they frequently exhibited a need to show their gratitude. Anything they could do to help him, they would. No questions asked.

Around noon, Carter walked out of his residence. Walter saw him from across the street, where he had been sitting on a bench. He crossed Lenox Road and followed Carter into the parking lot.

"Excuse me," Walter yelled. Carter turned and stopped. Walter approached him, keeping a respectful distance. It was broad daylight, an open parking lot in plain sight. Nevertheless, he was careful not to appear as a threat of any kind. For all Carter Lawrence knew, this stranger wanted nothing more than directions to the mall. "I'd like to talk to you, Mr. Lawrence."

"What?"

"My name is Walter Sherman, and I'm looking for Leonard Martin."

Carter's obvious, growing agitation was a concern to Walter, and he knew, at times like this, that some people under stress could forget everything said to them. So, he repeated himself. "My name is Walter Sherman. I only want to talk with your father-in-law. Do you know where he is?"

"Who are you?" the skinny lad said, eyes darting, mouth and jaw noticeably tightening.

"Carter, I'm Walter Sherman. If you don't know where Leonard is today, when you hear from him can you give him a message? I really need to talk with him. Do you know where he is?"

"No," Carter said, still visibly uncomfortable, although he no longer looked like he was about to start running. "I don't know."

"When was the last time you heard from him? In the Bahamas?"

"No. Two years ago, that's when. After he left I never heard from him. Not in the Bahamas. Not anywhere. Who are you again?"

"If you hear from him, give him this," Walter said, handing the young man a page from the same Ritz-Carlton notepad he'd given Nick Stevenson. On it he'd jotted down his name and a telephone number. "Day or night. Anytime. Will you do that?" Carter reached out and took the note, folded it without looking at it, and held it tightly in the palm of his closed left hand. Walter thought the youngster was about to cry. He asked him, "When was the last time you saw Leonard?"

"I won't be able to help you, Mr. Sherman. It's more than two years since I heard from him." He said "him" in a way that made Walter believe Carter couldn't bring himself to say the name Leonard. He saw in Carter's face and the way he moved his hands a sadness verging on outright misery, a feeling of loss too heavy for his bony shoulders and pencil neck to carry. He knew, then and there, that Carter Lawrence had no contact with Leonard Martin. Walter looked curiously into Carter's eyes. He couldn't help wondering what it must be like to lose your wife—wife, ex-wife, there's no difference—and both your children at the same time, the same way. It was clear he'd lost his father-in-law too.

"Thank you," said Walter. He smiled and reached out to touch Carter Lawrence's arm. "I wish you the best. I really do." With that, he turned and walked away.

TWENTY-FIVE

New York

WHEN THE SECOND LETTER arrived, Isobel took it immediately to Gold, as prearranged. Ed Macmillan joined them, followed closely by two men and a woman—all stone-faced, pasty, suited; they might have been related. They greeted Gold, ignored Macmillan, and shook hands grimly with Isobel. These were *New York Times* lawyers. She turned to glare at Gold. "This is a real newspaper, not a supermarket checkout sheet. I am a real reporter, not an intern. I won't work in the presence of lawyers or people I don't know. Melvin? Is this your idea of a joke?"

"I beg your pardon, Ms. Gitlin," the oldest of the lawyers said. "You work for the *New York Times,* as do we. This case involves a potential for liability that is of great concern for the publisher and the parent entity. Mr. Gold was made aware of our need to be present. We're all part of a publicly held corporation, as you know. Accordingly, we have obligations to—"

"B-b-bullshit," Isobel said, slipping the unopened letter back into the folder she held very firmly. "This letter is mine. It is not the property of the *New York Times*. The story I write, after I write it, may be, but not the letter. I have no intention of sh-sharing its c-c-contents with you or anyone other than my editors."

Maybe it was her alliance with Walter Sherman. It could have been the adrenaline. More likely, it was her certainty that whatever the letter said would be her sword and her shield. Isobel Gitlin knew for a fact that she had nothing to fear from anyone East or West of Fiji.

The attorney's stream of patience flowed shallow, not deep. It was bone dry now. "You don't seem to understand, young lady—"

"You don't seem to understand, *old man*!" Turning toward the Moose, she demanded, "They go or I go. Mel?"

When all three had departed, she turned to Ed, whose bleary expression pleased her immensely. "L-l-lawyers?" She applied her village-girl sing-song with its version of a Mexican accent. "We don't need no stinking lawyers."

She cared not a bit that the joke fell flat. Macmillan had probably never seen the movie, and Mel wasn't in the mood.

"Read the fucking letter," said the Moose.

Dear Ms. Gitlin,

Harlan Jennings didn't kill Floyd Ochs. I can't allow an innocent man to be charged and perhaps even convicted. I killed Floyd Ochs. I killed Christopher Hopman and Billy MacNeal too. I did it and I'm not sorry. As proof, I offer you these details:

- *Floyd Ochs was shot with a Beretta S06, 12 gauge, Diamond Pigeon made in Italy, using an English cartridge by Gamebore aptly named Pigeon Extreme. Ochs was less than twenty feet from me when I fired.*

- *Billy MacNeal was shot with a 7.62mm shell fired from a Galil Sniper Rifle, sometimes called a Galatz, made by IMI in Israel. It's possible to mistake or misidentify this weapon as a German G3-SG1 or a Russian SVD. You can make sure the FBI doesn't make that mistake. The Galil comes with its own 6x telescopic sight, which was suitable since he was only 150 yards from me at the time. I also used a TPR-S suppressor to minimize the sound. At that distance I doubt he heard anything.*
- *I shot Christopher Hopman with a J. D. Jones–designed, Ed Brown–made, 50-caliber gun called the Peacemaker. I made my peace with him. This gun is a big one, but it doesn't have the full power of most 50-caliber weapons. For my purpose, it's strong enough, plus I used a 650-grain cartridge for extra speed because I was concerned that the can-type suppresser might not completely muffle the sound. I was exactly 453 yards from Hopman as calibrated by a Nightforce 3.5–15x50 Extreme Tactical Scope. Aiming downhill, that put him 1,318.2 feet from the position of the shell in my barrel. So, there you have it—the details.*
- *The authorities probably haven't identified all of these weapons, if they have identified any. If they had I think you would have known and printed it already. Now you can tell them. Without you, they may never find out.*
- *You can also tell them that for the next one I will use a Holland & Holland double rifle called Nitro Express. It has a beaded cheekpiece, double Purdey underbolts, and a Greener crossbolt with gold-line cocking indicators. You'll know it when you see it. Later I'll tell you where to find that one too.*

All the physical evidence mentioned in this confession, all the guns and associated equipment I've described, not including, of course, the Holland & Holland, will be found in a large suitcase

I've left in your name with your excellent doorman, Mr. Falikas. Your reporting on this has touched me, Ms. Gitlin. I ask only that you keep in mind that I seek justice, and nothing more.

The letter was not signed.

"Holy shit," said Macmillan.

Mel Gold's face had whitened by several shades. He'd become an albino moose or a man on the edge of shock. He spoke from behind the chewed pencil that quivered in his teeth. "Call your doorman. Tell him you'll be there within the hour. We will send two security people with you. Get a description of whoever left the suitcase. Security will bring it here. We will open it. Until then, technically, we do not know what's in it. We certainly cannot consider it evidence based on an unsigned letter. We are simply checking out what may very well be a hoax. That's our official position. I will get two very big security people."

"Could be another hoax," Macmillan croaked, nodding, out of nowhere.

Mel Gold gave him a quick, dismissive look, then hurriedly told Isobel: "Make the call from my desk. I'll have security pick us up here."

She could have floated out of her chair and bumped her head on the ceiling. She had *his* letter in her hand. And she had Walter's e-mail. Number *8*. Number *8* was Leonard Martin. But damned if she would tell anyone else.

TWENTY-SIX

Las Vegas

PAT GRATH WAS NOT in Amarillo hiding behind a tumbleweed.

But he wasn't much better off than that. He was laying low on the shore of Lake Mead just outside Las Vegas. He'd been there since the day he learned about Floyd Ochs. His estate house was back from the road a quarter mile and surrounded by thirteen acres, including four hundred feet of shoreline, which fronted a rolling lawn stretching from the back of the main house down to the lake. His family stayed in Texas. He brought nine bodyguards with him. He flew in a top security man to elaborate his house electronics, electrify the fences practically overnight, and add any other foolproof systems available ASAP. Still, Pat Grath was edgy.

He was a short, pear-shaped man just past forty with sandy hair and goatee, a snub nose, and a toothy smile. He'd always liked to have fun. He loved great food and beautiful women. But now he had no appetite. There were no girls in the party. He worried because the place was so secure. He thought his army of nine might grow complacent, and often instructed them not to. It was hard to make the point to his satisfaction. They all knew a twenty-four-hour camera covered the only road in, and one guy was always awake watching the screen. Two more, loaded down with weapons, manned the gate. Another two were always on patrol—the pool, the playhouse, the newly installed high-voltage fences, the lakefront lawn where Pat spent most of his time. The off-duty ones, if they weren't asleep, played cards with him or watched TV.

Pat thought constantly about what could go wrong. He couldn't come up with anything, and that made it worse. He was playing a round of croquet on the lawn, searching his mind for overlooked details. A bullet hit the end of his nose. The back of his skull and some of its contents were found as far as thirty feet back. The rest of him toppled like a log. The man on patrol who saw it happen called to the others and crouched his way to the body, handgun drawn, shaking every step of the way. He and the others threw frightened eyes rapidly from side to side. Had they known exactly where to look, they might have seen the tiny boat far out on the water turning quickly, heading toward the distant shoreline.

TWENTY-SEVEN

Birmingham

CARTER LAWRENCE WAS SITTING in the food court at the Riverchase Galleria Mall in Birmingham, Alabama. From where he lived in the Buckhead section of Atlanta, the drive had taken him two hours. Interstate 20 runs dead straight from Atlanta to Birmingham. Once outside the Atlanta metropolitan area, it's a dull drive, open spaces punctuated every so often by small towns. Gas stations, McDonalds, and Waffle House restaurants crowded themselves around the exits. This wasn't the first time Carter had made the drive. He remembered the strange billboard outside Oxford. It said "Jesus Is Lord Over Oxford, Alabama." As far as Carter was concerned, He could have it. Carter picked up an hour passing into the Central Time Zone and scheduled his arrival for ten o'clock local time. After what he'd been reading in the newspaper, watching on TV, and the trips to Raleigh, he looked forward to this day like no other in . . . years.

When he reached the mall he drove around a while looking for a parking spot. Traffic was brutal, more so inside the mall parking lot than on the roads. After finally parking he went inside. The place was jammed. He'd been sitting in the food court for nearly an hour, at a table between a cinnamon bun/coffee shop and a Japanese steakhouse/fast-food operation that was offering samples to passersby. The mad rush to find tables in the mall's food court was a sight to behold. Carter saw grown women pulling their own kids while pushing someone else's children aside to grab an empty place. Others hovered like anxious vultures—overeaters who appeared to be down to the last bites of their quick meals. It took Carter forty minutes to get his food and find a table. He rebuffed every effort to unseat him. "No," he said, "you can't take that chair." Still they came at him. "There's someone sitting there," he told not one, not two, but a half dozen or more eager shoppers wishing to lay claim to the empty seat at Carter's table. He waited patiently. The note he received in the mail a few days ago said only: "Meet me Friday in the food court at Riverchase Galleria, Birmingham—11 a.m." The letter bore a New Mexico postmark, but Carter Lawrence was sure it came from his father-in-law.

A few minutes after eleven Carter felt a light tap on his right shoulder. When he turned to see who was there, there was no one. From the corner of his eye he saw a figure moving to his left, and he turned quickly. There he saw a tall, lean, bearded man sitting down in the other chair. He did not immediately recognize Leonard Martin—not at first glance. But he was expecting him, and with that thought fresh in his mind he soon saw the man he remembered underneath the new veneer. For an instant Carter thought the new look might be a disguise. But, of course, it wasn't. No disguise can make you thin, can it? He was stunned, then greatly comforted, to see Lenny Martin, to know it was him. Carter smiled. Leonard saw the young man was near to losing it, quite close to tears it seemed . And then they came. Still smiling, Carter's deep-set eyes overflowed, tears dripping down his bony cheeks, falling from his chin to the table. Carter stifled a heaving sob when Leonard reached out and put his hands on the sides of his head.

"It's okay," Leonard said. "I'm here."

"I missed you," said Carter with a dry-cough mumble, trying as hard as he could not to cry anymore. He knew Leonard was alive, somewhere, because of the notes and the trips to Raleigh-Durham. But, now, seeing him, Carter's emotions got the better of him.

"I missed you too," said Leonard.

"Lenny, where—"

"No, no, stop," Leonard interrupted him, sternly waving both hands between himself and Carter. "No questions, Carter, please. Very important: It's essential that you never ask me anything. Not where I've been, what I've done, where I'm going. Nothing's more important. Do you understand?"

Carter looked at him, bewildered and confused.

Leonard said, "What you don't know can't hurt you, or me. If you get a card in the mail from somebody asking you to pick up a package and send it to another place, you don't *know* who asked you and you don't *know* what's inside. Right?" They looked at each other for many seconds in silence.

"Can I have some of those?" Leonard asked. He pointed to a plate of french fries. They were cold by now, but Leonard took a couple, dipped them in catsup, and put them in his mouth. Carter regained enough of his composure to drink some of his iced tea and take a handful of french fries himself. "You still hungry?" Leonard asked.

"No. I'm okay."

"Good. Let's walk." When they got up from their seats a flock of women, each with children in tow, descended upon the spot like ducks on pieces of white bread tossed into a lake. Carter couldn't take his eyes off Leonard, and Leonard said, "Don't look at me, Carter. Let's just walk. Not too fast. Not too slow. Do a little window shopping as we go." Walking just that way, the two approached the mall's main atrium and rode the escalator to the upper level. Halfway down one of the long arms of the Riverchase Galleria was a Discovery Channel store. Just outside the entrance to the store there was a young man, about nineteen or twenty, with long dreadlocks, a T-shirt with the logo of one of the popular bands of the day, and pants that were neither long nor short. He wore running shoes with colored laces and no socks, and he effortlessly flipped three multicolored balls about the size of grapefruits in the air. As he juggled, a small crowd of mostly teenage girls surrounded him. He laughed and joked with the onlookers, trying, in the time-tested tradition of carnival barkers, to get the people into the store. As the group dissipated, every few minutes or so new members took the place of those departed. The crowd changed size and complexion, but never went away. Leonard directed Carter to the women's clothing store directly across from this action. They stood outside. The store was crammed with young women shoppers all too busy to ever notice them.

"Let's stand here," he said. He could sense the nervousness in Carter's steps. "Nobody will pay any attention to us." He was right. The patrons walking past the Discover Channel store in both directions either stopped to join the group being entertained by the good-looking boy with the strange, long hair, or they turned to watch him as they went by. Carter noticed that Leonard carried a shopping bag from Nordstrom. "You want to be a shopper, you got to look like one, huh?" he said.

"Carter, I need your help—"

"I'll help you kill those bastards!" Carter blurted. "I knew it was you! I knew it!" Again, Carter Lawrence was crying; this time all hundred and forty pounds of him shuddered.

"Get hold of yourself," Leonard demanded. "You don't *know* anything." There was no sympathy in his voice, and that alone shocked Carter. It had the intended effect. He wiped his nose with a tissue Leonard handed him, and then asked, "What can I do?"

They stood there for ten minutes while Leonard explained what he needed: financial reports, SEC filings, income projections based on certain types of investments, personal asset data—a whole range of financial information, some of which would be easy to assemble, some of which would not. Exactly why Leonard wanted this data he didn't say. Carter had quickly learned to ask no questions if they involved Leonard's activities. He thought, "Just tell me what you want. It's yours."

"It's all here," Leonard said, handing Carter a list. "It's a couple of pages, I know. It won't be simple and it won't be cheap."

"Money?" Carter scoffed. "That's all I've got." Only Leonard could comprehend the sort of sadness and misery that could possibly be felt by a young man with six million dollars. "You know," said Carter, "I left it all in the bank. My parents don't need any, and my family . . . well, I just left it there where Nick put it. Now they're paying me almost twenty-five thousand a month just to keep it there. Twenty-five thousand. Fucking blood money," he said angrily. "And I'm still in the apartment. You know that already . . . the notes you sent me. There's a man—he came to see me—he's looking for you. Walter Sherman's his name." Carter fumbled through his pockets looking for something. Finally he handed Leonard a piece of paper. It was the note Walter had left with him.

"I know," Leonard said. He glanced briefly at the small note and put it in his own pocket. "I know about him. It's going to be okay, Carter. It is." Leonard held him close for just a moment, as a father might a son, and then they started walking once more. They talked as they strolled the mall, looking every bit the Thanksgiving Sale shoppers they wanted to appear to be. Leonard went over the data he needed again, this time pointing out certain details they might be interested in following up. "Don't forget this," he said, or "remember to get . . ." that. He wanted to be clear. He wanted to be sure Carter knew exactly what to do, what to put together. "And then what?" Carter's eyes asked. Leonard told him that when his task was accomplished—and he had only a few weeks to do it—he was to meet Leonard in the restaurant of the Holiday Inn in Clarksville, Tennessee. "I'll send you a note," he told him. "It'll only have a number. That's the date. Be there at seven o'clock. We'll have dinner and guests."

"Lenny," Carter said, his cheeks reddening and his eyes once more watery, "I'm sorry. I'm sorry. I want to kill them! Can I kill them? Can we do it?"

Leonard hugged his son-in-law, all that was left of his family, of his life, and said, "We're going to do something even better."

TWENTY-EIGHT

New York

THE BOX OF GUNS and ammo made a splash.

Authorities in Tennessee announced that while they had not the slightest doubt as to Harlan Jennings's guilt in the murder of Floyd Ochs, there was now the possibility that questions might be raised by some.

Harlan relaxed in his county cell, and Isobel was pretty much resurrected. The passing of Pat Grath began her beatification. She had written there would be others, and everyone remembered.

The *New York Post* ran her full-face picture again, somewhat misleadingly under the headline: "Meat Murderer Kills Fourth." The story began on page two, and there, she thought, the headline was even worse. "She Said There Were Others." Everyone knew who "she" was.

When the third letter came, she followed its instructions.

First, she told no one, not Mel Gold, not even Walter. She took the bus at 34th to Columbus Circle. She walked uptown on Broadway to 64th Street, where she turned east toward Central Park and continued walking. At the corner of Central Park West she turned again, south to 63rd Street. There, she stood across from the YMCA, her back to the park. After waiting exactly twenty minutes she started walking slowly westward. Halfway down the block, in front of what was once The McBurney School, a gray car pulled to the curb. The dark tinted window rolled down. The driver wore a black windbreaker, a large, turned-up collar, and a baseball cap, bill down, hiding his face. His voice was anxious, hoarse. "Get in."

"A-a-are you—?"

"Next to me!" As soon as she got in, the window went up, the doors locked, the car took off. "Put this on," said the driver, shoving what looked like a blindfold at her.

"Wh-wh-what?"

"Put it on or I'll shoot you." He sounded crazy and very young. She put it on as fast as she could.

After several moments, she said, "But you're not . . ."

Her blindness reassured him. His voice came back from the edge. "No, I'm not. Just sit there and don't talk. Take off your watch. Put it in your purse and don't touch it again until this is over. We'll be there when we get there."

She slipped off the watch and put it in her black purse. She'd been checking it every three minutes or so. Even for October it was cold. A freezing rain mixed with sleet and snow had fallen most of the day. The driver did not have the heat on. The two rear windows were open enough to admit a nasty breeze. The blindfold was uncomfortable. Her sense of smell was useless; the car had the odor of evergreen. She tried to keep track of turns and stops and the seconds between. At the end she had no idea where they were. She was fairly sure they had driven for almost thirty minutes.

"Get out," said the driver, nervous again. "Don't touch the blindfold. Just get out." She stumbled over the curb. A thin, strong hand suddenly squeezed her arm. The man led her up three steps, which felt smooth and slippery like marble. In a warm building, a lobby, she smelled leather furniture. A carpet took them into an elevator. The building smelled like the Upper West Side. (That could have been hope playing games with her nose.) She tried counting passing floors, but the elevator moved quietly and the music drowned out the clicks. "Theme from a Summer Place" would stay in her head for weeks.

The elevator stopped. The man urged her gently, a hand on her back. He said, "Step out, turn right, walk straight."

She hesitated.

"Do it. Go!"

Several steps later a hand grasped her shoulder, a silent command to halt. Someone—her driver?—frisked her, first the front, then behind. Treated like this by airport security, her very cells would have raged at the insult. It was just business now.

Leonard Martin, she assumed, must have known she was unarmed, without a recording device, following orders. What did the searching mean? Was he paranoid? Unbalanced? No conclusion to be drawn; searching cost nothing. The cost of a mistake could be high. She would have had herself searched, probably much more thoroughly than this. Isobel remembered what a friend had told her about going through airport security with a pacemaker. The woman couldn't pass through the metal detectors for fear they might set off her pacemaker in the wrong direction. Everyone knows that, and they have a procedure for a hand search at every airport in the world. They usually do a pretty thorough pat down, but at no American airport, she told Isobel, does anyone actually touch her chest to see if she really has a pacemaker. "They're afraid to touch my tits," she said with a laugh only another woman could appreciate. That was until she arrived at the airport in Frankfurt, Germany. There they felt. Isobel had been to Frankfurt. The women attendants there looked like prison guards in a soft-porn cable movie. "I'll bet they had a good time doing it too," she told her friend. Compared with that, her blindfolded search was really quite respectful. She was used to having her tape recorder. She wished she had it now.

"Okay," the driver said, the frisk completed. And that was different. They were *acquainted,* more or less . . . and here this *person* had just been . . . "Do not remove your blindfold. Walk straight in."

"Asshole," she muttered, blind eyes forward.

Isobel adjusted the blindfold on her head and across her eyes as if she were taking possession of it in an attempt to regain her self-respect. She moved it up on the bridge of her nose, allowing her to see beneath it. "Shit," she mumbled. "I have to see where I'm walking." It did the trick. It was now hers, not theirs. She ran her hands through her hair. That smoothed the transition, helped restore some sense of control. She slipped through an open door—into what was for her a dark apartment. The door closed behind her.

"I'm in the kitchen," a pleasant, distinctly masculine voice called out. "Can you maneuver yourself here or do you need help?"

"Are you . . . ?" Isobel followed his voice finding the kitchen with ease.

"I am," he said. "Want some tea? I'm heating the water. Please, sit down. Make yourself comfortable. How do you take it?"

"Got any m-milk? Sweet'N Low?"

"Got 'em both. Glad you're here. Kermit's a nervous wreck. I hope he didn't upset you."

"Kermit?"

"Let's call him that."

"He—*Kermit,*" she tried to say it sarcastically, "was okay. Hi. I'm Isobel Gitlin." She extended her hand. He did not take it. "Don't bother to tell me your name. I'm pretty sure I know it. But what would you like me to call you? I mean, for the sake of c-c-conversation?" She felt herself prattling, and stopped.

The kettle started whistling. He removed it from the heat and poured two cups. He put them on the table, then moved one toward her until it touched her fingers. He handed her a tea bag. "Milk, sugar, Sweet'N Low, even honey if you want it." She refused his offer of help preparing her tea and managed it quite well considering it was a first for her. She was half blind for less than an hour, and already her other senses were noticeably heightened.

"Why the bus, the walk around the corner, and the twenty minute wait?" Isobel stirred her tea. "And the trip to Grant's Tomb, or wherever? Don't you trust me, *Bob*?" She aimed again for that elusive sarcastic tone. "Is 'Bob' okay? I knew a Bob in London. He could have been your son."

"In my position, who would *you* trust?" he said.

"Knowing me as I do, I would trust me."

"I do, Ms. Gitlin. I do indeed. But you know you could have been followed. You must know you're being watched."

"W-w-watched? I don't think so. I really doubt it. I seriously do. But let's not d-dwell on that."

"It's important for you to understand—"

"And the driver with the frisky hands? What if he was caught? Would he have given up? Did he really have a gun? Would he have sacrificed himself for you?"

"Sacrifice? The word has a different meaning to us. We have already *been* sacrificed. We have nothing left to lose. What should I fear? Harm to my family?" There was a cruel irony in that and she knew it. "Freedom. Isn't that what makes us so dangerous? Survival makes us free, doesn't it?" Then he muttered to himself. It sounded like, "Freedom's just . . ." She couldn't make it out clearly. ". . . to lose." It made no sense to Isobel. She wondered whether she'd heard it right, but did not ask; if he'd wanted to say it out loud he would have.

He reached behind for a box of sugar cookies, and offered one, which Isobel took. He did not notice that she reached directly in the box to take one. Perhaps it meant nothing. "Of course," he went on, "as a tactical matter, what I have day-to-day is not getting caught. If I do get caught, it's over." He went silent for a moment, made all the longer by her darkness. "Does this seem like some kind of game to you? Believe me, it's not. It's everything because it's all I have left. You should understand how important that is."

"I know who you are."

"Yes, I'm sure you do. I thought you would have known some time ago. At first I was concerned, but I'm not anymore. See, I told you I trusted you."

"What about your followers?"

That seemed to amuse him. "There are no followers."

"Do you act alone? What if something happened to you? What if you got caught?"

"If I were gone tomorrow, who knows? Someone else might come along. You think I should groom a successor? Do you think I want to be Robin Hood? Or Joltin' Joe—where have I gone? You think I should have an understudy?" He shrugged. "That's the last thing I want to think about."

There was no anger in his voice. His tone was warm and friendly. But this was a self-proclaimed multiple killer. How could such a person be normal, regardless of how he sounded? They sipped tea. Behind blackened eyes she flashed on two old men she'd seen in a Reuters photo last week: in the mountains of Armenia drinking tea from glasses through sugar cubes held in their teeth.

Leonard Martin drinking his tea might just as well have been one of them. Walter had signaled number *8*, but this Leonard Martin, was he the one in the photographs tacked to her kitchen wall? Was she sitting inches from the fat man with long blue eyes? Leonard Martin? Yes, of course, Walter was right. For a moment she wondered how often he'd been right, the same way, in the past thirty years. To be sure, she sat facing number *8*. Unable to see Leonard Martin's unhappy eyes, in her own mind's eye she put them, quite definitely, with the picture.

She asked, "Are you in good health, Mr. Martin?"

"I am in good health, thank you. I can't and won't, of course, confirm my identity. There are many things in life we think we know, but the list of things we don't is far longer. I may be Leonard Martin—then again, I may not be. You know, I thought you'd find me before I found you. 'Who Is Seeking Revenge?' That is a bit pretentious, don't you think?"

He continued sipping his tea. Isobel wanted badly to see him at that instant, to look at his hands on the cup. The sound of his voice hinted that he might be suddenly nervous. Was he staring at her? She tilted backward in her chair for just an instant. If she could only get a fleeting glance . . . and then she stopped breathing. "Oh, my God!" she thought.

"Are you alright?" he asked.

Isobel said, "I'm fine, fine." She took her notebook and Sharpwriter pencil from her purse, then, realizing she was in no shape to take notes, she laughed. Then she asked, "When did you meet your wife?"

"It's not that kind of story."

"No?" Isobel asked, "I thought we could get some background."

"No."

"What kind of story is it then?"

"A story you've never written before. Maybe nobody has," Leonard said.

For the first time, Isobel felt frightened.

"I am going to tell you about the people I've killed and the people I will kill. And I'll tell you why I will kill them."

The fright passed, but not the shakes. "Yes? And why will you be telling m-me that?"

"I don't want any more Harlan Jennings."

"I see. Well that's . . . a good idea."

"Are you ready to start?"

Isobel nodded, still working on her breath. "You rejected speaking in the plural before. You just said 'I' will kill, not 'we.' Can you clear that up for me? Are there others working with, if not for, you?"

"Others give me support. They don't know what I've done until you do. They read about it in the papers. The boy in the car knows nothing before the fact. He does not know anything that would make him a contributer to any illegal act. We avoid such conversations."

"You want me to write it just that way. You're a lawyer."

"Write it just that way. And you'll want to identify me quite clearly. You'll want to leave no doubt about who I am. I will help you do that. Your cup is empty. More?"

Isobel declined. "Why am I wearing a blindfold?" she said. She had recovered her composure. She had seen enough of him to go on.

"Do you believe we live in a just society?" He asked it with a studied calm, a kind of forced serenity. Very much like a teacher too much in love with his subject—like one of her professors at Oxford who'd dry up and die without Dante or Francis Bacon. "Do you, Isobel?"

"What is that to the price of eggs? You haven't answered my question—the blindfold." She pressed the point to see if he thought she had seen something of him underneath her blindfold. He went on with his own question.

"Do you believe what your government tells you?" he asked. "Your church? Your media? Do you believe what your own newspaper prints?"

"I don't have a bloody church." It surprised her to hear her father's voice jumping from her mouth. "The newspaper sometimes gets it right. Politicians lie, most of them. But what's that got to do with the price of bloody eggs? And why, damnit, can't I see you, straight out?"

"You will hear the names of people who will soon be dead. I'm going to kill them. You will know why they died. When the public reads about them, they'll know too. These people are premeditative mass murderers. They did a cost-benefit analysis and made a decision to kill my family for money. I do not believe that they deserve to live."

"Let's take that as given. I'm still at a loss. Why is identifying you so important, and seeing you forbidden?"

Leonard said, "I am a lawyer, Ms. Gitlin. So long as you do not actually see me, and I believe you have not, you cannot actually *know* it is me. You *believe* I am Leonard Martin. That's fine with me. But you can't know it, and so long as you swim in that stream of uncertainty—the high waters of doubt, as a law professor once put it—you avoid the label of accessory. New York's press shield law notwithstanding, the FBI would draw and quarter you." He let that sink in, then continued. "Do you think I'm crazy? I think you know that I'm not. And here's my point. I don't want the story spun in that direction. I know how these things work. Think ahead."

Instead, Isobel focused on the very immediate present. A self-proclaimed killer was asking her to think about murders he planned to commit and to speculate on how they'd be handled in the press. It all seemed very singular. She'd let herself drift for half a second. He was still talking.

"You know how it works. Let's say a CEO gets killed by someone—someone who is not me. Someone I never heard of. And let's say this CEO had nothing to do with purposely selling hundreds of thousands, millions, of pounds of poisonous meat. Someone—not me—kills a banker in Cleveland, a software entrepreneur in San Jose, a guy who makes widgets somewhere. You pick one. What happens when they start speculating about it? ABC, CBS, NBC—all of them? All of them—CNN, FOX—you know, 'the most trusted names in journalism.' What happens when they start calling in the experts? You want to improve your ratings? Bring me into it. Stir Leonard Martin, or whoever I am, into the soup. You should know. The media devour people. Look what's happened to you, and you haven't killed anyone, have you?"

Isobel said nothing.

Now his voice roughened, found an accusatory note. "How do the media handle stories like that? However they want. If they call it terrorism, that's it. The country says 'terrorism, sure, must be.' Why? 'I heard it on the news.' If they say it was a terrorist, then it was. Who is to say otherwise?" He was no professor now. He mumbled again. This time she thought she heard "weapons of mass destruction." Anger and misery flooded his voice. She could see his trembling hands on the table and she imagined anguish in his eyes. "I'm no terrorist," he said. "Killing Hopman, MacNeal, Ochs, and Grath was not terror. It was a just and rational act. My family can't get justice. They were murdered as certain as if they too had been shot. These people chose to do it, they made a conscious decision to kill, and so have I. I won't be marginalized. For that I need your help, your cooperation, your honesty. I won't let them hang a Halloween mask on me, and most importantly, I won't have acts I do not commit attributed to me. Have you got the logic?"

Isobel felt helpless. Apparently, it showed.

"They have reason to make me mad or evil."

"*They*? Which people are you talking about?"

"The people who run the news. They'll turn me into Freddie Krueger. That's good for a couple of rating points, don't you think? They'll talk to the local cops. Ask about that screwball; that's what they'll call me. They'll line up two or three police chiefs—a fat white guy, a black career cop, a woman from somewhere. Great television. What does your now-famous local police chief say? At best he says he can't rule anything out. At worst he claims to have seen the evidence and brands me a certified madman. Livens things up all around, don't you think?"

"You want credibility. You want me to protect your image."

"I want you to write the truth. Only the truth."

"And what *is* the truth?" asked Isobel with a hard edge to her voice, the edge of her own anger? Her fear?

"The truth is," Leonard said, "that the public wants criminals to get caught and the cops want to catch them. And nobody seems to care very much exactly who gets caught. The truth is that if I did it, it's *just* me. If someone else did it, then it's *not* me. That's all the truth I need."

"You're asking me to take part in a conspiracy—"

"The hell I am! I'm acting alone. There's no conspiracy. There cannot possibly be one. That would require two or more people acting in concert. You and I are not partners. I have no partners. We already talked about that. Christ, you're blindfolded, brought here against your will. How could you be my co-conspirator? If I conspire with anyone it's with the spirit of my wife, my daughter, my grandsons. And it's not about the other people, or their survivors. I'm not avenging them. I speak for no one but me, and I act only for myself. Don't get me wrong. I'm no anarchist. I'm not waging an anticorporate crusade. I have nothing against the capitalist world. The system's been very good to me. I am, after all—if I am who you think I am—a rich man. This is only about justice for my family, for me."

"Justice or satisfaction?"

"What's the difference?"

"I can't be any part of this." Isobel shook her head. She felt like stamping her foot. "You can't just kill people."

"Really?" he sipped his tea, looking into Isobel's face, sadly, as if he'd tried and failed to make a fundamentally obvious point. She could not see him, but she thought of her father scolding her twenty years ago, despairing as she withheld any sign of understanding his point of view.

Leonard said, "Eight hundred and sixty-four people were killed. Was anyone arrested? Was anyone indicted? Did anyone go to trial? Is anyone in prison? You can't just kill people? Of course you can." His voice drifted off. *"You can't just kill people?"* he said.

"I'm sorry for your loss. What about Nina and Ellie and her boys? Let me tell your story. That will build public awareness. The people you're talking about, who want to shape the story their way? They'll have to deal with public opinion informed by the truth as you want it presented. Your personal story can be your greatest asset."

"My aim is my greatest asset," he said, "just me and Bobby McGee." I want it on the record. I don't need public support, or yours either. I only want you to be my voice." He waited a moment. Isobel said nothing. "You won't refuse."

"Why do you think so? Because I broke the story?"

"You broke it and you got it right. But also . . ." he paused. His demeanor changed and Isobel sensed it. Suddenly he was off the soapbox, down from the lectern. "You write about the dead. That's very important to me." He had pushed the button. Robert McG. undid her.

"Who are the others?" she asked.

"Pour yourself some more tea. We have a ways to go."

Leonard began in Tennessee and Georgia, took her from Texas to Boston and through the Byzantine canyons of Wall Street. He introduced her to all the people who knew—who drew their calculations, made their deals, went home to sleep . . . and let it happen. He acquainted her with each link in the chain, schooled her in its twists and turns. Isobel felt a chill on her back, cold and wet as ice. It grew colder and wetter and deeper as she listened, carefully, for two more hours.

TWENTY-NINE

New York

Leonard studied Isobel as he spoke. Before deciding to meet, he'd learned what he could about her. He'd read nearly every obit she wrote, and a few of her local stories. The more he read, the more he liked her style and the sensibility he thought he sensed behind it. She struck him as involved in the lives she summarized—however few words she was given to describe them. He thought he saw a weakness for the undiscovered truth. There were no great revelations in the obits and local stories. But there were small ones. And she seemed to want to highlight the unexpected. It took a while for that distinction to settle itself in his mind, and as it did, he also came to believe that Isobel might harbor another agenda—one she might not be aware of. In some of the obits and some of the local stories, Leonard heard notes of indignant sympathy on behalf of the victims of municipal neglect, the has-been inventor denied full recognition in his day, a bus driver beaten and left blind the same day his wife gave birth to twins. It became easy for Leonard to imagine that Isobel was chained to a sense of justice. He tried to dismiss the notion as too pat, too seductively sweet.

And he thought he glimpsed one more thing: a puritanical interest, possibly an obsession, with simple accuracy. He saw it in her face, her expression when they talked. He wished he could have watched her eyes. And Leonard was keenly aware that behind her impulse to accuracy, with nothing at all to lose by it, stood the *New York Times.*

He wanted to harness Isobel and her fast-emerging celebrity.

After a lengthy inner debate, he decided on the meeting. Nothing that she'd said, and nothing in her manner this evening, led him to alter or regret his assumptions. She seemed moved as she listened, and he felt her making unwritten notes, but he would not know the outcome for one, or two, or three days. When they were done, she seemed exhausted.

It might have been Kermit who drove her back, or someone else. There was no talk between them. She made no effort to track the time. Her mind was a tornado. The car pulled to a stop. The engine died. The driver's door opened and shut. She sat for a while, blindfold still in place. When she took it off she was alone in a parked car on 63rd Street, off Central Park West—the exact spot where she had been picked up.

It wasn't any warmer or drier, but Isobel walked home. Her windsore hand clutched the computer disc Leonard gave her. Isobel knew why Hopman, MacNeal, Ochs, and Grath were dead. She knew the names of the ones to follow, and why, in Leonard Martin's mind, they must. And she knew something else—something special—about Leonard Martin. She nodded to the doorman, who asked if she felt well.

She sat on her bed, reconstructing her mental notes with her coat on. In a notebook she wrote with a pencil, clarifying the squiggles whose meaning she'd lose by tomorrow. She cleaned the notes for almost an hour, then summarized and bulleted, and committed it all to her hard drive, her back-up, and another that was safely tucked away in Fiji. She did the same with Leonard's CD, knowing she would not open it until tomorrow.

Words and sentences brought back how Leonard sounded, and she struggled to put pictures with them. Her imagination created fragments that filled in what he did not describe: the unbelieving look that must have been on Korman's face when Ochs instructed him to leave it alone, when he said, "Wayne, you just leave it to me"; the faces and voices and gestures along the chain of panicky phone calls that followed; the Stein, Gelb office argument bemusing poor Dr. Roy. She imagined the flip charts in Dr. Roy's presentation; the devil's loose in Ganga Roy's head, her quick, black eyes struck wide as she made her bargain; the face of Tom Maloney in front of hers.

Isobel knew she was stuck with it all, for good.

She'd worked in her coat for hours. Now she needed a very hot shower. Not long after, flat on her back, wearing the fluffy white robe she stole from the Palace Hotel in Madrid, she called Walter Sherman, expecting to wake him up.

"You go to bed too early," she said when he grumbled. She told him, "I need to talk."

"Where are you?"

She heard the cobwebs shredding like whispers in his mind.

"I'm home."

"Come here," he said, as though speaking from down the hall, sounding so close she almost glanced that way.

"I met him, tonight, just a few hours ago."

"Number *8*?"

"He sent me another note. I met him here in the city. I don't know where. I had to wear a blindfold." She thought of saying more, but didn't. "The thing is, Walter, he confirmed to me that he is who we think. He told me who else is on the list."

"Do you want to inform the police?" Walter said. "Go to the cops?"

"I don't have to do that," Isobel said. "New York's press shield is absolute. I'm not an accessory or anything like that. I really should file the st-st-story before I go off island hopping, don't you think?"

"If he gave you a list I doubt he'll act until you publish it. Otherwise the list wouldn't have any meaning and he'd have no reason to give it to you—unless he's entirely crazy. Do you think he is?"

"I don't believe he's crazy at all. He gave me the list for a reason."

"Write your story on your way down. File from here. You can't get it into print any sooner. There's an early morning flight to St. Thomas from Newark. Book it right now. Take the St. John Ferry. You should be here by lunchtime. Come straight to Billy's."

"Where's that?"

"Directly across from the ferry. Look for an old guy. He's got a baseball cap and a beard. He sits out front during lunch."

Walter was fully awake and elated.

"See you tomorrow?" Isobel said.

"Set your alarm. It's an early plane. And for God's sake, wear something comfortable."

He hung up thinking her voice sounded different, unsettled and unsettling, revved up, but grave, and also eager, and maybe . . . what? There was certainly something different there. Or maybe not. Maybe a part of his mind remained in his vanished dream, or maybe he was listening too closely, hoping to hear something . . . else.

THIRTY

St. John

"Some things don't need no argument," said Ike. "One thing is an argument, the next don't have no argument attached."

Back in the shadows, at the other end of the bar, Billy repeated a point he'd made several times to no one in particular: "Too many fucking choices. How am I supposed to know?"

He was, in fact, studying a catalog that pictured and described ice-making machines. He already owned two, one in the back just off the kitchen, and a smaller one in front of him under the bar. The second was on the fritz. Once it was Frogman's, now it was past repair.

"It *is* a goddamn argument," he insisted. "The argument is between which fucking machine I should buy." He spoke with frank irritation now.

"How so?" asked Walter, drinking his Diet Coke. He'd not ordered lunch. He expected to have some with Isobel, though he'd not yet mentioned her to Billy or Ike.

"Steak," Ike said to Walter, preempting Billy. "That's one. You grill it. No argument about that."

"Unless you're a vegetarian," Walter said.

"That's no argument," said Ike. "Vegetarians don't like steak grilled, fried, or any way, so that's no argument."

Walter said, "People who eat vegetables and people who eat steak. They argue all the time."

"Could be," said Ike, smoke emerging from just about everywhere. "But that's an argument about one or the other, not about one. You see? You got nothing in common, you got no argument."

Walter said, "Ike, every question has at least two answers."

"Well," said Ike, "then just answer me this. What you like better, fuckin' pigs or goats?"

Billy looked up from his catalog. "Ike, you're crazier every day."

"Follow me here. Walter? I tell you I like to fuck a goat better. That's my personal preference. What about you?"

Walter turned to face Ike head on. He made his face as straight as a ruler. "I have never fucked a pig or a goat and don't plan to. Therefore, I have nothing to say on that."

"Then we ain't got no argument. That's my point exactly." Ike blew a grand cloud of smoke and waved it toward the outside air.

Billy returned to business, "Walter, one's fourteen hundred dollars. The other's two grand."

"Same size?" asked Walter.

"Yeah."

"Any other difference between them?"

"Not that I can see."

"You want to save six hundred bucks?"

"Yeah."

"Well?"

"Done," said Billy.

Ike stood and bowed in all directions, basking in his self-appointed victory, then reached inside his shirt pocket to fish out a bent and gnarly butt and hang it from his lower lip, "No argument at all. Why you even got to ask?" He winked at them both and lit the cigarette.

Billy scurried to the register, mumbling something, grabbed the blue chalk, and wrote:

$1400/$2000/No Argument

And he made the chalk squeak extra loud.

THIRTY-ONE

St. John

Isobel jumped off the ferry in blue shorts and a white cotton top with thin straps. Her open sandals showed ten bright red toenails. She pulled a small black travel case on wheels, and carried a brown coat with a fake fur hem and collar. She spotted Ike across the square. The sign above his head said *Billy's*.

She noticed a man lying in the grass in the middle of the square as she crossed. She wondered if he was homeless, or merely tired, or dead as a doornail.

"Hi," she said to Ike. "I'm Isobel Gitlin."

It had been a while since a lovely young woman grinned at him that way. He broadened his smile to present his lemon teeth like a row of golden amethysts.

"I'm Ike." He held out his long, skinny fingers, nicotine-stained, wrinkled by seventy-odd years in the tropical sun. "My very deep and eternal pleasure." He quickly stood, waving his pink cap above his head like a semaphore.

Ike felt, for an instant, a good deal younger than he was.

"I'm a friend of Walter's." Isobel took his hand. "He told me to look for you. He told me I could not miss you."

"I bet he did too," said Ike. "You can sit out here with me all day, and I'll do the best I can. Buy you a drink too. But if you want to see Walter, he is over there." He waved his hat toward the far end of the bar.

She slung her coat over her wheelie. "I'm sure we'll have a chance for a drink. I hope so." Then Isobel made her way through the people packing Billy's. From what she could see the lunch looked awfully good.

When Walter glimpsed her his face must have changed, because Billy, who was removing his empty Diet Coke bottle, dropped his long, heavy jaw, and said, "Walter?"

"You look great."

She twirled around for Walter to see. "I changed in St. Thomas."

"I'm glad to see you, whatever you're wearing."

"St. Thomas is not very pretty. Not like I expected." She hopped onto the barstool beside him, the one where Tom Maloney had been a couple of months before.

"I thought it was supposed to be some kind of paradise. I guess there may be resorts somewhere."

"On the other side of the island," said Walter.

"The cab driver told me I was on the wrong side of the island. To me it looks like Brooklyn. No charm at all. Anyway, I'm starving. They don't feed you on airplanes anymore, do they?"

"Except in first class," Walter said.

"It was full. I couldn't get in even at full fare."

Last night's sensation returned; she was definitely . . . different. Unsettled and unsettling. At first, when she turned around for him, she seemed flirtatious. Now, to his disappointment, she was not. She was just nervous.

Isobel ordered a club sandwich and fries. He did too. He watched her gobble it as he picked at his own.

"Anyway, the weather is nice here." She spoke as she ate.

"How is New York?"

"Miserable. Windy. Cold. Really. Just . . . fucking . . . miserable."

"You ever miss Fiji?"

"A lot. Sometimes. I miss London too. And Paris a little. I'm half French, but I was never *French*, exactly."

"How so?"

She went at the sandwich again.

"My mother had this thing about France. I think she really hated it. I bet something terrible happened there but she's never said what. I like to think it may have involved her mother. Not a very nice woman. I'll bet that's why mom went to Fiji. That's why she was so glad about my father. She was a nurse. She worked in Fiji although she didn't have to. She's retired now. We had a house in Paris. I spent some time there when I was little. Americans think the French don't like them. That is certainly true. But it's the English they really despise."

"You always liked London better than Paris?"

"Indeed, sir. I did and still do." No village sing-song there. She spoke her father's English.

"And Fiji most of all?"

"Fiji is heaven. The politics are rotten, of course. Where aren't they? But Walter, the Pacific—it's blue and clean and endless, not like this dirty shithole Atlantic, filthy and polluted to the bottom. Not here, I mean," she said, seeing the hurt in his face. "It's beautiful here. But the North Atlantic doesn't compare. There's no better place in the world than Fiji. No fucking better place."

Her expression changed in mid-sentence. She put her food down.

"I met him."

"I know. You told me last night."

She nodded.

"Tell me everything," he said.

"I will. It's very complicated. He sent me another letter telling me—"

"Not here. Finish up and let's go."

Billy leaned over the bar. He watched Walter and Isobel leave. Then he waved to get Ike's attention, but Ike only shrugged his shoulders and turned to see the two walk out of sight.

Billy shook his head and picked up a bar rag for which he had no particular use.

THIRTY-TWO

St. John

WHEN COLD WEATHER COMES to Connecticut, Grosse Pointe, or Georgetown, some pack up and head for St. John. Having tried it once, they may do so again. If they rent the same house two or three winters in a row, they are very likely to buy, and thus become one kind of local—the kind who maintain a northern home as well. The other locals live on St. John all year. Walter's Chicago apartment did not disqualify him admission to the second group.

Naturally, Ike belonged to the latter class: not rich like some of the full-time retirees, former snowbirds from here and there. But not by any means poor. He'd always been a worker, an entrepreneur and a saver like everyone in his extended clan. He didn't care at all what he looked like, but Ike watched his balances closely, with eyes like magnifying glasses.

Despite the moderate temperatures, Ike disliked this time of year because of the crowds. They turned Billy's into a madhouse. Billy's first-rate kitchen did not help. Nor did his well-stocked bar. The tourists wanted Billy's signature drink. It was called the "Bushwacker," a word locals also used in place of "tourist" to indicate the absence of respect and affection.

Except for lunchtime, when he preferred to sit outside and sneer at the Bushwhackers' colorful get-ups, the staff knew to keep Ike's table free even while he was out stretching his legs—a few yards this way, a few yards that—or in the back relieving himself, which could be a prolonged affair. His table was his until he announced that he was gone for the day. He didn't drive anymore, not at his age, and he couldn't walk very far. But one of his many grandsons was always somewhere around, ready to take him wherever he wanted. Grandson Roosevelt drove him most often, but today he was on another island attending to family business. Walter and Billy were never sure they knew all of Ike's family businesses. Ike himself was long since retired. Grandson Kennedy picked him up at Billy's soon after Walter and Isobel left. When Billy first arrived on St. John, he asked Walter if Ike's whole family had been named after dead Presidents. "Not the girls," Walter said.

Now Ike was back. He liked to walk in on his own, so Kennedy dropped him off to the side of the square. Ike shuffled into Billy's with the slow, elegant step that seemed to most a matter of choice. Jenna, a nineteen-year-old waitress from Indianapolis who'd been at Billy's almost a year now, said, "Hey," and looked toward his table, agreeably free of colonists.

"Seen Walter?"

"No." She had Ike's usual in hand, and set it onto one of Billy's fancy new bevel-edged coasters.

"Billy," he called out. "Where's Walter?"

"Beats me." Billy was boisterous with the huge success of the lunchtime shift. "Where's Jimmy Hoffa, Judge whatshisname, or the guys who really killed OJ's wife? They ain't here neither, in case you need to know."

Ike exchanged sympathetic glances with Jenna. He raised his glass to her and she smiled before moving on to other more profitable duties.

Ike saw Billy sending him a long, significant glance across the room. It said, "I make it a hundred to one they been fucking their brains out all day long." It also said, "What do you think?"

Ike fixed his mouth to turn his smile down at the sides. He did this to reinforce the silent message he sent back to Billy. The message was this: "More chance you fucked three different goats during lunchtime!"

In this kind of situation, Billy accepted Ike's "no argument" rule. These small subtleties mystified Billy, but Ike always seemed to get them straight.

At that moment Walter and Isobel were dissecting Isobel's meeting with Leonard Martin. In terms of method, they picked up where they'd left off in New York. That process exhilarated Isobel. It was what she'd tasted in Oxford, savored in Annapolis, quickly given up on at the *New York Times*: a truly pure collaboration; a protracted scientific conversation in words; an authentic treasure hunt of the mind—unencumbered by emotion; tightly disciplined. That was the word: "disciplined." This time, of course, there was an added element, a kind of secret. But it was metaphysical to the issue; strictly a preface to the play, nothing to do with the action; nothing to do with who, where, what. It was, in fact, about herself, nothing to do with, not precisely about, the business at hand. Certainly not the kind of thing to throw in the mix just now. Isobel kept her secret secret.

The magic was in the rhythm of the thing. Each led until it was time to switch; both knew exactly when that time arrived. As Isobel had the new information, Walter led with questions most of the time. When something came up that gave her a sense of direction, she led for as long as that lasted. Most of what they said was questions and answers, or back-and-forth construction of ideas. Parallel issues and brainstorm items got noted, or just remembered, and put to the side, then brought into play when a line of discussion had run its course. Things used to go that way with her father until he lost patience or interest. There were times she thought the Moose had potential.

Walter's focus was single-minded; he wanted clues to help him find Leonard. If he could not see how a fact or a thought would get him there, he put it aside for later discussion, if Isobel wished, but not for immediate scrutiny. Isobel could only report that Leonard had refused to talk about the past two years. He only wanted to lay out his case. They spent some time on that. They went over the four targets Leonard had named for Isobel, and his brief against each. They went over and over each one. But Walter said he was suspicious; for all they knew, Leonard had mixed in details designed to mislead. His purpose was to not get caught—or help Isobel prevent another crime. All Leonard had to do was give details after the fact, as he'd already done in letter two, which saved Harlan Jennings. Walter wasn't sure why Leonard wanted to meet her at all. Leonard knew she would publish the points he wanted made. He'd already given her journalistic presence. Why should Leonard doubt that she'd continue to serve? He had other ways to plead his case for preventing false convictions: via e-mail, snail-mail, telephone, throwaway cell phone—many safer ways. Why risk a meeting at all? It baffled him. And why the blindfold? Why refuse to acknowledge his identity absolutely? Leonard's lawyerly explanation did not sell with Walter. When he asked Isobel, she shook her head, returned his searching look, proclaimed with her eyes that she only wished she could offer an explanation.

Ganga Roy's complete report was on the disc Leonard gave Isobel, together with her notes and written comments about the rancorous, ominous meeting in Nathan Stein's office. They printed out two copies and each of them worked from their own. What Leonard told Isobel about Ganga Roy's revelations, what they could plainly read for themselves, and what Tom Maloney confided in Walter did not jibe. They spent an hour on those points of difference, talked about Ganga Roy's notes—her presentation and observations—and speculated briefly on the inner struggle that very likely ended in suicide. Walter never assumed that Tom Maloney had been fully truthful. He allowed as much for every client. The Roy materials helped him draw a more confident picture of where Tom lied. What else had been a lie? Walter kept thinking about Maloney saying, "How do I make the check out, Sister?"

They went over and over Isobel's "kidnap" and interview. She repeated the story twice from beginning to end, printout in hand, original notebook next to her. Isobel told Walter how she told Leonard Martin she knew who he was—even repeating her assertion that she couldn't see him—and of his refusal to admit his identity. Despite that, they spoke of details exclusive to Leonard's experience. There was no doubt in her mind that she met with and spoke to Leonard Martin. When Isobel described her pique at being felt up by the driver, something seemed to flash in Walter's eyes. Something boyish . . . jealousy? That did not seem right, anyway, not enough. "Do you *know* who that guy *was*?" she asked again.

Walter did not respond. Given the rhythm they'd established, his hesitation signaled a moment. She felt it. Probably he did too. "Do you know who Kermit is?" she said.

"Maybe." Walter said.

She gave him what she intended to be a curious, dissatisfied look. Then a series of unconnected thoughts brought Laticia's voice to mind and she knew *that* must be leading somewhere.

"The b-bloody canyon!" she squeaked.

"Canyon?" His face made it clear that he knew she had something. She had the thrilling sensation of something approaching a boil.

"I think we should look at the guns. It's something we know, something we actually have. Jennings was a shooter. So is Leonard. They have to use a firing range. Laticia said you can't shoot off guns wherever you please."

Walter picked it up. "Some of Leonard's rifles have a range of fifteen hundred yards or more. He killed Hopman from four hundred fifty yards. Who knows how far out on Lake Mead he was?"

"Locate the ranges. We narrow the whole thing down. Ranges or wherever else he could practice undetected."

"You can buy those weapons on the net. They're expensive. The Holland & Holland double rifle goes for about twenty-seven thousand dollars," said Walter.

"The other stuff, the equipment he left for me, it's all top of the line, six, eight, ten thousand dollars apiece. How do you get things like that? If people see things like that they remember. We work it from the guns, where they came from, where they went. Can we find that?"

Walter said, "They're not as hard to get as you might think, but he's not walking in and buying this sort of equipment over the counter. He must have a shipping point, a drop, maybe even a dummy name. Wherever that is, that's where you'll find the firing range. Unless—"

"Unless what?"

"Unless he's been using his own range. Unless he's got open space. He bought that hut in Jamaica. Maybe that isn't the only place he bought."

"You mean someplace where he's been living?"

Walter was nodding, trying as hard as he knew how to rid himself of a nagging doubt. "Everyone has to live somewhere," he said quickly, adding, "you have to avoid making judgments, Isobel, coming to conclusions based on speculation. Speculation is good, but only if it leads you in one direction or another. Eventually there has to be evidence. Physical evidence. Something you can see and touch. Something real.

Work with what you know, not what you think you know. You never get everything right all the time. Errors happen, but if you have a starting point that's beyond question—you go back and take another turn. And what do we have that's beyond question? The guns. We have the guns. Begin with the guns. Nice going." Walter leaned back in his chair, a visible sense of relaxation having come over him. Isobel saw it. She imagined this to be the work product of a man who's been through this very process many times. The effect on her was exactly the opposite. She was exhilarated.

"Now tell me about the other thing," she said, her excitement spilling out with her words. "Kermit."

"I already did. I only said maybe."

"Are you going to make me guess? I'm the one who got abused." She tried to work up some indignation but couldn't quite bring it off. She tried a smile, but Walter was serious now.

"It's just the way I work," Walter said. "Some things I keep to myself."

"I tell you everything I know." Her eyes grew wide, implying hurt. She hadn't forgotten about her secret, but she had convinced herself it didn't count.

"I tell you too," he said. He meant that he shared everything he *knew*, and that was true, but not everything he *thought*.

Like Sherlock Holmes, whom he read soon after getting into this business, often behind warehouse crates, Walter made a practice of drawing no conclusions, and certainly sharing no half-baked ones, until he had sufficient facts in hand. The revelation that Sherlock Holmes observed this rule lent grandeur to what had been a chafing, sometimes desperate need. Walter had left Vietnam, but had Vietnam left him? His mother saw the root of it as soon as he got back. Or maybe she heard the screaming in his head. She demonstrated her love by keeping her distance; allowing him to do the same. His work—finding people—eased his troubles.

His clients craved privacy, but Walter craved it even more. His work not only gave him a living, it allowed him to hold on to his secrets. And when he finally found whoever it was he was looking for, everything was all right again. No one held the secrets against him because he'd helped; he'd done the work.

His wounded nature reshaped itself around a peculiar structure of isolation. That peculiarity killed his marriage. It kept her out. And who wants to live with that? Gloria waited for him to let her in, but he never did. After four years she told him she had to go. She loved him, but that was all she could do. He knew she was right and he hated being without her.

He tried to try, but whenever she threatened to touch him at a certain depth of feeling, an iron door shut hard in his head. And when that happened he froze her with the look in his eye and the deathly sound of his voice. And all that lasted until his mind relaxed and his shame unclenched and he could think and act like a normal man. It happened, and happened, and happened because the threat was unrelenting. Both of them came to understand it. When she left, Gloria told him, "You'll be fine Walter. You really will." He never doubted it. And she had been more right than wrong. That iron door had grown rusty over the years. No one had wandered back there for decades.

And now, he thought, this girl. And this idiotic thing about who drove the car—Kermit. For reasons he could not imagine, he felt the rusty hinges move. Yes, he had a fine working method, and it should certainly be maintained. No point at all to pointless speculation. Never bend the rules that matter most. But he'd never had a partner before. He'd made that rule number three (after not promoting himself and never accepting supervision). And it's different with a partner, like it or not. You have to exchange ideas in a different way. Besides, they *had* conjectured together. They traded hypotheses, worked them to theories, set out conditions for proving facts.

"Are you okay?" She looked concerned.

Walter knew he'd broken a sweat. He knew that she saw his agitation, had to have glimpsed the fear. At the moment it thrashed and towered. It felt like a wave breaking over and inside his eyes. The door squeaked louder; he could hear it. Once it thundered shut he would shiver and freeze again after all those years.

But if he let this other thing out . . .

He confronted the prospect of thirty years of heavy protective machinery wrecked around him. He wondered what the arrangement would be after that.

He said, "I think he's Carter Lawrence."

And then, to his amazement, he slumped quite comfortably into his sturdy bamboo chair, remembering the time he and Gloria flew to Denver. He'd loaded her up with valium to cut her fear. He'd held her hand as the plane taxied into position. He'd smiled at her as she turned to look out the window. And when the engines fired up and swept them into the smooth silk sky she put her head on his shoulder and giggled. He'd done that. But it was long ago.

"Kermit," Isobel said, ". . . is Carter Lawrence?"

"I don't know. I'm not even sure why I think so." Walter felt more than comfortable now—he felt euphoric.

He enjoyed a deep breath of moist Caribbean air. His thoughts jumped like unruly pets.

"So where does this leave us?" said Isobel.

He went to autopilot. "If Carter's the guy, he may help a lot. There's always a way when people are . . ." He waited for the word. They waited together. "Vulnerable," he said. "He may be vulnerable."

Isobel offered ideas for going at Carter, reworking their background, designing a quick, simple plan of action aimed to open him up.

By then Walter's mind had shifted back to the point he needed to care about most: the widened gap between what Tom Maloney had told him and the version Dr. Ganga Roy gave to Leonard Martin. To the extent that Roy had it right, and Walter had no reason to doubt it, Maloney and Stein were far from the relative innocents Tom described, mistakenly targeted by a madman. They were the ones who set the death train in motion. How did Leonard put it? He labeled them "premeditative mass murderers." Accused them of making a cost-benefit analysis. And he said they "decided to kill my family for money." That altered the picture. It suggested questions. What else didn't Walter know about his clients? And what did they really expect for their million dollars?

THIRTY-THREE

New York

"I'M TURNING INTO AN addict. Prozac doesn't do it anymore. I get up at five and swim sixty laps. I have an agitated depression. Exercise doesn't help. My shrink is useless too. He doesn't listen. I don't listen. I dream about getting shot—over and over again—which might be alright, but it never kills me. I can't even die for a minute."

Louise Hollingsworth's eyes were inflamed. She'd been flying apart for weeks. Nothing she wore seemed to match. Her stiff yellow hair was at war with itself. Her high hawk nose and razor mouth had become unattractively mobile. She paced like a neurotic crane. Her thin soprano voice had developed a rasp.

"Every time I leave my apartment. Every time I leave the office. Every time I go anywhere. It's all I think about. I am decompensating. Nothing is worth this experience. Not all the money you can . . ."

The meeting had been a bad idea. Getting them all together like this had only reinforced the shared perception of danger. Tom Maloney tried again to offer a drink.

"I'm loaded up with Prozac," she wailed. "Prozac and whiskey? I don't think that's wise."

"I've done it a hundred times. Maybe you can take a nap. You can take a nap right here."

"Bourbon," she sniffled. "But not too much."

The others watched as he fixed her drink and got her to sit in one of the black leather chairs.

Tom was calmer than he'd been in months. In the past few days he'd worked out some ideas. He thought his new thinking might help the others get a grip. But today in Nathan's office was proving to be the wrong time and place.

From the other end of the room, Nathan watched Louise with momentarily calm contempt. He moved the odd-shaped crystals on his desk as though he were playing chess, a game he never understood.

"What's with Sherman? Where's the report?" he asked when Louise was settled. "Didn't he call you, Tom?"

"He doesn't call. I got an e-mail." Louise looked up from her drink. Wesley Pitts in the other black chair grunted curiously.

"He knows who it is," said Maloney.

"No shit!" said Wes, on his feet, athletic again for a second. He clapped his hands. "He's going to get him. He's going to nail his ass."

"Who is it?" asked Louise. "Anyone we've looked at?"

"I don't know," said Tom. "He's a fellow named Leonard Martin."

"Well that's great, just great. Why didn't you call him?" Nathan shouted, no longer calm and composed, out from behind his desk, heading for the other three. "We know the guy. Where is he? What's the story there?"

"I called him," Tom replied. "He doesn't like to talk."

"He doesn't like to talk!" Nathan climbed the register. "Fuck him, he doesn't like to talk. He works for me!"

"I work for you. We all work for you. Sherman's an independent. Very independent. When I called him he told me not to do it again. He meant it. That's how he is, whether we like it or not. He'll be in touch when he thinks it's time."

"What did the e-mail say?" Wesley Pitts's enthusiasm died. There was a flag on the play.

"Just that he knows who he is."

"So, where the fuck is this . . . Leonard Martin?" demanded Nathan.

"He'll tell us when he's ready. The entire country wants this guy. Walter Sherman found him."

"Did he say he 'found' him?" Nathan's anxious face turned shrewd. "Or does he just say he knows who he is?"

"He didn't say he found him. But it's only a matter of time. That's Sherman's history. That's why we went to him. He will get the job done."

Wesley had slumped back into the chair. "Somebody better kill this guy in a hurry. I can think of a couple of guys who will do it for a car."

Tom Maloney looked at Nathan Stein; they needed to talk. He said, "You two stay here a while. Relax. Unwind. Support each other."

He led Nathan into the private apartment. Nathan flopped onto the king-sized bed, head on pillow, short leg dangling over the side.

"Why aren't we dead?" Tom said, looking down.

"Why are you asking me?" Nathan whined.

"There's a reason for all this," Tom said. "I want to tell you first, before I talk to the others. I don't think it's all that bad."

"Oh? What's the good news? Maybe this nutcase won't boil us in oil before he blows our brains out?"

The grandson of the founder of Stein, Gelb, Hector & Wills turned his face into the pillow and sobbed. "He's gonna kill me because of some shitass meat."

The sound filled Tom with satisfaction. He heard his voice deepen triumphantly. "We'll hear from Walter soon enough. But that's not what I'm talking about." Tom had already come to the conclusion that Leonard Martin had stopped killing people because there was something *else* he wanted. He didn't know what, but felt certain it would be revealed. If Leonard Martin wanted a deal, that was fine with Tom Maloney. Dealing was his life's work.

"Nathan," he said. "I strongly suspect we're as safe as cows in Calcutta."

THIRTY-FOUR

St. John

THEY WOUND IT UP at six. Isobel badly wanted to go to the beach. "I am a beach girl, you know," she laughed. "And you are a beach man, aren't you?" They changed, jumped into Walter's open-top Jeep, and took off down the hilly road heading toward the sea.

"Where are we going?" she asked, her girlish enthusiasm bubbling over. "Wheee!" she shouted, smiling, spreading her arms high and wide in the open air as Walter sped down the hill.

"Cinnamon Bay," he said.

"What a wonderful name," said Isobel. "Cinnamon Bay."

There were four beaches, he told her, one after another. Caneel Bay was the first. That's where the island's biggest resort was. Then they would pass Hawk's Nest and Trunk Bay before finally arriving at Cinnamon Bay. Once there, Isobel quickly threw off her long shirt, dropping it at Walter's feet, and, not looking back, dashed to the water, kicking up sand behind her as she ran. She wore a two-piece black suit with the bottom cut low, very low, and the sides, no bigger than the straps on her blouse, rose high on her hip. Walter felt an unfamiliar stirring, watching her from behind as she raced into the surf. "Oh, shit," he said to himself, "I can't stand here like—this." He pulled off his T-shirt, slipped out of his sandals, and ran after her. He didn't stop until the cold water covered him above his waist. He had a hard time looking at her and she knew it. She splashed him and he dove headlong into the Caribbean.

Later, Walter offered to throw some steaks on the grill, but at Isobel's insistence, they went back to Billy's for dinner.

She'd arrived that morning unnerved and uncertain; the siege with Leonard burdened her, strung her out. When she spoke with Walter on the phone she'd fought against feeling unhinged. Today had dissipated that. She felt a much greater sense of control. She felt that she had a stronger, more subtle grasp of the facts. Her working alliance with Walter made her feel good. It gave her a deeply reassuring groove. And quite aside from that, she'd found a new sense of comfort with herself, some traction on how she felt about her story, some certainty about what to do next. All that and it was still early. She remembered the dishes she'd seen at Billy's and passed up for a sandwich. She'd promised Ike a drink. She'd been feeling a sexy edge for a while, and she wanted to let it sharpen. A long and promising night lay ahead. She wanted some dinner at Billy's.

"Back again?" Ike piped up. "I was just on my way out of here, but if you're ready for that drink, I'm staying."

Isobel smiled at him, wondering if he ever really went home. It was too early for the dinner mob. The place was far from empty but hardly full. Billy stood behind the bar, at the far end, as usual, reading what looked like a menu from one of his competitors.

"Drinks and dinner," Walter called to Billy, and then to Ike, "got room?"

"My treat, if you don't go overboard." Ike garnished the offer by raising his cap and showing off his teeth again.

Billy towered over them. "Diet Coke. Usual. And for the lady?"

"Vodka martini, plain as day." She unleashed her smile at him.

"Don't look at the menu," Billy said to Isobel. "I'll take care of dinner. Everything's good, but I know what's best. These two don't know nothing." He left with what looked like a wink of his own. That was just as well. She'd left her drug-store glasses at Walter's; the menu would be useless.

Ike squinted intently, as though he were trying to see through her skin. It was not an unpleasant sensation. "Is something wrong?" she said.

"Where you from?"

"Fiji."

"That's an island too?"

She nodded, charmed.

"Out by Australia, in that direction?"

She gave him the coordinates. He nodded and sipped his usual, visibly satisfied. "Always like to learn new things. You sound like some kind of island, but . . ."

"I don't look it?" she laughed a wondrously full, strong laugh, and looked at Ike as if they shared a secret—which they did: white girl and black man, both island people.

She asked if Ike knew the old man sleeping in the park. "The Poet," Ike said. He told her everyone did. "You heard of Clarence Frogman Henry? Very good singer, sadly departed. He could sing in three different voices: high, low, and medium. One song goes like this [Ike threw his head back and tried out his partly mended falsetto]: 'I'm a poor little frog and I ain't got no home.'" His ancient feet kept time loudly beneath the table.

He sipped his usual, cleared his throat, and then told Isobel, "That was in the song. Difference is, the Poet don't *want* no home. He's what you call the outdoor type. He's the only homeless person we got, to my knowledge. Also, he is a poet. He'll say one for you if you ask, if you got a little money. Sometimes they rhyme. Sometimes they don't. The Poet sell some stuff right here. Got a young boy lives on a boat down here. What's his name, Walter? Kenny something? I don't know. He's got a *really* great big boat. Boy is a famous performer. Sings rock and roll songs all over the world. Got records and all the rest. And he lives on a boat right here. My boy Truman rebuilt his engine couple years back. That man's got some boat. You can see it from Walter's house most of the time. He bought poems from him and paid him some money too. But the Poet prefers to be homeless and everyone shows him consideration, looks after him very good." Ike looked around to see where Billy was and then leaned forward toward Isobel and said in a low whisper, "Even Billy feeds him, and won't admit to it neither."

Isobel quickly came to admire Billy's kitchen. Curried goat, jerk pork kabobs, coconut jasmine rice, sweet potato wedges. Ike warned her off the scotch bonnet peppers. Isobel took care not to stuff herself and noted with deep satisfaction that Walter was eating light. He took it very easy from first to last. At one point Ike said, "You feel okay?" then covered himself with a friendly chuckle. "No reason to get no fatter than you are." He talked at some length about his family's predisposition to leanness of body and limb, tactfully excepting from this description two cousins on his long-passed father's side and several of their daughters. Very fine girls, but not thin.

"Dessert's on the house," Billy announced, Jenna trailing. Billy pulled up a chair. Jenna had brought four portions of Billy's Island Pudding with the coffee. "The recipe dies with me," he said. "I brought it down here from . . . all I can say is one word: 'Bacardi.' And that's the only word I'll ever say about Billy's Island Pudding."

He noticed Jenna standing behind him and shooed her away.

They talked a while about smuggling, and how American cops and Island cops, French and English cops, and mostly South American cops are basically the same, except for some being stupider and cheaper to bribe than others. Isobel rang the final bell by faking a generous yawn. As chairs began squeaking, she apologized, saying, "I've got to get an early plane." She and Walter thanked Ike for the dinner, said their goodnights, and left.

"Then why don't she take the ferry tonight?" Billy demanded of Ike.

"'Cause she ain't going nowhere tonight. She's going with Walter now."

"That's my point," Billy persisted. " Didn't you say it wasn't gonna be? Better chance I fucked a whatever, and all that?"

"That was then. Now is now. Everything is different now."

"No it ain't."

"Boy, you thick?" Ike's patience was not infinite, especially after paying for dinner. "They was not ready before. Now they had some drinks and dinner, they talked things over, and everything's different now. You saw how he didn't eat nothing. He need to be fit for what follows."

"There ain't no difference then or now."

Ike studied Billy's long face. "What are you talking about?"

Billy waved Jenna forward to clear the table. As she did, he leaned across so the girl had to scurry around him. His face was now barely six inches from Ike's: "I don't know who's fucking who. But he don't have a clue what's going on. It's been that way since she walked in. It ain't no different now or then. He's gonna wind up with towels he never heard of."

Billy did not have many theories, least of all about people. He did have one about Walter. Billy believed he knew why Walter had never had a girlfriend on St. John—or, as far as anybody knew, a date. He believed that Walter's wife would show up one day, and that Walter had a religious nature where that was concerned. He was waiting for his wife. Billy respected him for that, the way he used to respect the Church before his mother lost her faith.

Billy also had a general sense that the worst was most likely to happen. Once in a while he got a more specific feeling—that something was coiling to strike like a snake. He had that accurate intuition to thank for his presence here, in relative safety and comfort, in a business of his own.

He had that feeling the minute he saw the straps on Isobel Gitlin's little white blouse.

Clara brought Walter and Isobel ice in a bucket, and placed a pitcher of white sangria toward the edge of the black marble table. She made an interesting point of saying that she was feeling tired now and would go to bed if that was all right. In the cool repose of her room downstairs she opened the thriller she'd started the day before. Clara hoped Walter knew what he was doing. She understood quite well that the girl knew what *she* was doing.

Isobel had spent five years discussing great books, and she'd written "Sex and the Serious Scholar." She had few illusions, and none about this kind of thing. The horny goddess had taken her now for good and sufficient reason. She was overstimulated. The dread, and relief, and intimacy; the sudden rush of ambition, and the unexpected knowledge of her seductive power . . . do things to a girl. And here was Walter, bursting for her, walking around inside her head; a perfect gentleman, with really good eyes, an eminently decent sort, with what looked like a perfectly . . .

Oh, who the fuck cared why?

She'd had enough of gratification delayed. She sipped her sangria delicately and said, "I'll be back in a little while. I have to use the bathroom."

He told her he had plenty to think about. He did not confide that it wasn't easy because his thoughts were past controlling. He hoped she'd not seen that he was burning up inside.

Where sex was concerned, he had one rule: "Not with anyone close." That left women he met in the course of his travels—good natured, attractive women without expectations, who asked or implied no questions that required him to lie. Plus, of course, professionals. And over the course of twenty years, that had worked well enough, from time to time.

But now . . . now he was nervous as a kitten up a helluva redwood tree. He could not honestly tell himself when it started—not at the Mayflower, surely. Probably during those days in her apartment, but not as he could clearly recall. On the phone last night? Yes, it was in his head then, as soon as he awoke. Maybe she was in the vanished dream. And when she walked into Billy's, wearing that little white thing with the straps. . . . He wondered how he'd managed to think straight all day, and force his eyes off her, even for seconds, at dinner.

Minutes after Isobel's afternoon arrival, Clara had shown her to a cozy room under the deck beneath where Walter waited now. It had dark walls, a bronze tile floor with throw rugs, a wall of closets, a comfortable-looking king-size bed. She never even looked at the bathroom. Instead, she'd left the wheelie unopened, tossed her coat, and gotten her tour of the house.

She remembered Walter's room at the other end of the hall and stopped there en route to her own. Compared to Walter's, hers seemed awfully small. She peeled off her clothes and opened the bathroom door. The sight astonished her. It was half the size of the bedroom. The toilet and vanity set in a corner hardly seemed to matter. A vast, black-tiled shower filled most of the bathroom. It had no curtain and no wall. It was more like a locker room shower. You walked right onto the sloping tile floor, and you looked out through a huge glass door to the sea, the very same view from the deck just above. She looked for a curtain. There was none. She saw that the door could slide, and she moved it back. The warm, humid air flowed in. She turned on the faucet and water rushed down with extraordinary force from a very large showerhead. She soaped and let the water work on her body and her mind. She watched the ocean outside, the lights on the water; the boats still at sea, testing the darkness, strings of lights across their decks. She remembered Leonard telling her she was being watched. And if they were looking back at her? Fine. And if they could make her out clearly? "I hope they like what they see," she thought.

She turned off the water and stepped outside. It wasn't a night for a moon. The sky was black. She did not attempt to dry herself, but slid on the T-shirt she'd pilfered from Walter's room. She looked in the mirror. It stuck to her. She tied her hair behind, touched scent to herself, and went upstairs.

Walter heard her coming, smelled her coming, knew she was coming before she came. That drove his heart faster than fear ever had. The sight of her and the meaning in her eyes had him shaking. She knelt in front, undid his belt, and took him into her mouth. The act sent vibrations through her and she looked up into his eyes to let him see that. The sounds he made stroked her insides; she wanted them louder, and making them louder was all that mattered. When the throbbing started she forced herself back, sat on her heels, let him see her breasts rise with her rapid breathing, then stood. She pulled the T-shirt over her head and said, "Let's go to bed."

He took her first smoothly, expertly, with more than enough crazed urgency to set her off within seconds. He was strong and he quickly understood what she needed most. He showed remarkable stamina and excellent self-control. He shuddered when she wanted him to and he could get sounds out of her at will. It was like they'd been at it forever; like they knew each other before they'd begun. And then they began experimenting, and to Isobel's overflowing amazement, everything worked as well as it ever had. And when she could think, she thought she was getting what someone had been missing out on for years. She fell asleep after coming again—wondering whether it was the fourth or the fifth . . . and awoke still joined with him, awkwardly, at right angles. He was sleeping too. It was just after three in the morning. She watched the rise and fall of his gut. She shivered seeing the white of her leg against his dark brown belly. Walter was her first old man, the first one close to her father's age. He was a revelation, all right. But was he a one-time wonder? Could he ever do it—quite that way—again? Was it Viagra?

Walter woke up alone. Seven-fifteen. Clara would sleep till nine. He sniffed. Nothing was brewing or toasting now. He creaked out of bed, stepped into his shorts, made his way upstairs. He realized that he was smiling; he imagined his smile painted on, like a clown's. It occurred to him that he had not thought of his wife—not from the moment Isobel told him to wait. Not when she came to him on the deck, or in the blazing mindlessness that followed, or in the dreams that followed that. That was a first in twenty-five years. Walter felt better than fine. He did not dwell on the fact that he was thinking of Gloria now.

Nobody on the deck. He took the stairway down to the guest room. He found her asleep, on her belly, facing the shower and the ocean. A sheet had drifted over the small of her back, but her shoulders were bare, and most of her backside, and both of her legs, one of them bent at the knee. He noticed a twitch at the top of one shoulder; waited to see it again. Her mouth was open, just slightly. She didn't look nearly as pretty as she had. Her eyes seemed smaller, her nose somewhat thinner at the bridge, her skin looked like normal skin. He liked her a good deal better this way. She must have heard his boxers hit the floor. She smiled before she opened her eyes. When she saw him, she said, "Oh, m-m-y," and maneuvered onto her back with her arms outstretched.

THIRTY-FIVE

Nashville

THEY ARRIVED AT THE Nashville airport in late afternoon. The flight from Atlanta was short and uneventful. They looked like any two businessmen in town to make a sale, attend a seminar, or talk about a merger—each with a bulging attaché case in hand and a lightweight garment bag over his shoulder. Nicholas Stevenson, the older, bigger man, silver mane expertly layered and routinely trimmed, took long, easy strides. Harvey Daniels, the shorter man, dark-haired, rumpled, nervous, momentarily fell behind, quickened his step, fell behind again.

Through airport windows they saw Nashville blazing with Christmas lights refracted by pouring rain. They didn't join the line for cabs to the Renaissance or The Hermitage Hotel. Instead, they made their way to the rental cars and took the white Camero reserved for them. "They don't make Cameros the way they used to," Harvey griped.

The tallest of Tennessee's skyscrapers showed off bright decorations. "Sure as hell rather spend the night here," said Nick. He was thinking of dozens of times he'd been on Music Row, in the bars and clubs that line Nashville's streets, open night after night, proving, to his way of thinking, that Nashville will always be the musical heart of the South. And he said as much as they drove.

"You go to New Orleans to eat and fool around," agreed Harvey unconvincingly, not out of any great experience. "You're right Nick. Nashville is the only place for music."

The older man spoke slowly, more to himself or to the rain than to the one beside him. He said that young singers and songwriters flood this city. Some have honest-to-goodness talent. Others have little or none. "Kids come along and wash dishes in kitchens in all those bars all the time, dreaming of the stars, and once in a while, one of them makes it. That's the genuine optimism. That's the spirit that brings them here. That's the spirit that gives the city its deep-down sound and its moving force."

Harvey looked through the drizzle, "Everyone's getting ready for Christmas." Then he grasped another, more interesting thought: "You ever been to Branson?"

Nick Stevenson made a slow right turn and said, enjoying himself as he did, "If Nashville's the cradle of country music, Harvey, Branson's the nursing home. We went there once. Didn't like it a bit. It's like the elephant's graveyard—except they won't stop singing."

He drove the Camero on the darkened, rain-slick interstate to Clarksville, a Tennessee border town close to Illinois and Kentucky—home to the U.S. Army's 101st Airborne division: Air Assault! The signs shouted the mission at the headlights. The Camero pulled off I-24 and they registered at the Holiday Inn, just before you get to the mall and cinema complex. They took separate one-night rooms and paid cash. They signed in as Smith and Jones. An hour later they sat at a corner table in the motel's modest restaurant.

Debra Melissa Wallis showed them their seats. She figured them to order dinners off the menu; these were not buffet guys. They had things to talk about. They didn't want to be rushed. The manager, K. J. Singh, often asked her, "How in the world do you know such things?" She told him, "You just know." She figured these two for a good 20 percent; they were not local yokels. They were from someplace, here for a reason, money in their pockets.

The two were joined within minutes by a younger man, also wearing a business suit, but so bony-fingered and pencil-necked and seemingly fragile inside his clothes that his jacket flapped around him with every move—a scarecrow is pretty much what he looked like.

He smiled at the two at the table, and sat across from them. No names were exchanged that Debra Melissa could hear, no handshakes, although they clearly knew each other. She took their drink order. Scotch for the older gentleman. Margarita for his nervous companion. Amstel Light for the skinny one. Beyond that, not a peep, no small talk at all, just a long, unbroken silence; eyes in the distance, drinks, for the most part, ignored.

The fourth man showed up at seven thirty. He wore jeans, a blue down jacket, and a well-worn, brown, felt cowboy hat. The three stood; the cowboy held out both hands as if to say "no touching," and they sat.

He threw his coat and hat to a nearby chair, and sat next to the third one, the younger, skinny guy who arrived before he did. The older gentleman and his nervous friend made statements, like quick little speeches. Debra could not hear much, but they seemed to be using a lot of words she'd never heard before. By the time she'd worked her way close enough, all she got was the older one saying "turn yourself in" and the cowboy replying, "Thank you. I'll think about it."

They ordered steak and chicken, except for the cowboy, who wanted a caesar salad with hard-boiled eggs. When the entrees were placed before them, they started talking. They spoke until almost ten, the hour when the kitchen closed and the last remaining diners were chased away, when the minimum-wage employees made their way home, a chance to rest, to prepare to do it all over again tomorrow. Debra Melissa stayed to the bitter end, watching discreetly, betting her time on her intuition. These guys *are* big tippers—she was certain of that.

At the start, the young man sitting next to the cowboy opened an attaché case. He removed a stack of papers and publications: charts, spreadsheets, official-looking documents printed in tiny letters on flimsy tissue-thin paper; copies of memos, letters, and e-mails. From time to time the nervous one picked up a sheet of paper from the table, looked at it closely, and seemed to ask a question. Each time, the skinny one or the cowboy supplied an answer, and everyone seemed pleased with that. She heard some numbers tossed around, and for just a moment she was sure she heard "billions." "I must be hearing things," she told herself.

Eventually that work was done. There seemed to be no more questions. Now the cowboy ordered a sweetened ice tea. After that he talked for nearly an hour. From a distance he looked strong and sexy to Debra Melissa, determination all over his salt-and-pepper bearded face. After the tea he drank water, which she refilled several times. The two businessmen sometimes interrupted. The cowboy answered each question very slowly, taking his time, selecting his words carefully. When the cowboy was done they all looked at each other—not like businessmen do, but into each other's eyes for an awful long time. Debra Melissa didn't quite know what to make of that. Then they stood and started hugging, patting each other's backs. Each man went from one to the other until everyone hugged everyone else. The nervous guy held on to the cowboy the longest. He didn't want to let go. This was really something special, something she had only seen in the movies; movies about the mafia.

The cowboy put on his jacket and hat. The skinny one who came alone, the one who had all the papers on the table, left first. The gray-haired, distinguished-looking one, the oldest of the group, put his hand on the cowboy's cheek, touching it gently like they were kin, caressing the face like the waitress had seen wives do when the 101st deployed and they worried they'd never see their men again. The skinny-necked younger man paid the bill with his credit card and, sure enough, put down a 25 percent tip. Then the older guy, who knew the bill was already paid, put cash on the table, two twenties. He never looked back, but if he had, Debra Melissa Wallis would have offered her very special smile. She'd had it in mind all along that he was a gentleman you could be proud to know.

In the morning the two Atlanta lawyers checked out, drove back to Nashville, and flew home. The skinny one who stayed at a different motel one exit farther east on I-24 hit the road before six and planned to drive straight through the whole way home. The cowboy awoke from his hard, wooden sleep at seven. He showered and then enjoyed the complementary continental breakfast offered at his motel. He thought about why they called it that: a continental breakfast. He was sure Europe was *the continent,* and he'd never heard it called that there. He read *USA Today* with his coffee. The *New York Times* isn't sold at the Motel-6 near Clarksville. With coffee, cantaloupe, a small, round waffle, and three hard-boiled eggs inside him, he tossed his tall hat onto the seat of his SUV, turned west onto I-24, and headed for New Mexico.

THIRTY-SIX

West Texas

LEONARD MARTIN WAS SMILING.

Meeting with Isobel Gitlin had been a risk. He'd gone into it aware of the danger, unable to fully discount it. There were other ways he could have made his point, protected Harlan Jennings, prevented future cops under pressure from putting up other patsies. He could have done all that without compromising himself. If she had seen him . . . but she hadn't, had she? Had he, even by accident, revealed his strikingly different physical package, he might well have risked his anonymity. Leonard had taken a gamble, all right. And now, drinking coffee in a west Texas roadside diner, a day west of Clarksville and less than another's drive from Santa Fe, he knew he'd won.

Isobel Gitlin was no enemy. She might even be a friend. He'd just learned as much from the front page of today's *New York Times.* Isobel's two-column story ran in the upper right, the spot reserved for the day's number one event.

E. Coli Disaster Survivor Admits 4 Corporate Shootings

And below, in a smaller face:

Leonard Martin of Georgia Vows Others Will Die

What pleased him most was the picture above the fold, middle of the page. It was taken at a closing, one of the last he'd attended. It was cropped to show only him and the shoulder and arm of the buyer or seller—whoever was standing beside him. Leonard didn't remember the man or the closing. The picture showed him in a tan suit. The buttons were open, the double-breasted jacket parted over his bulky stomach and torso. His dark tie had flown away from his shirt. It stuck out crookedly over the front of his suit. The knot of his tie was askew and the top shirt button open. The suit was clearly wrinkled. He looked awful, and thought the paper's reproduction process made him appear even worse: pathetic. So much the better.

In the picture, Leonard looked distant and dazed. He was not smiling the way he always did in closing shots *before*. His face held only a vacant gaze. Nothing meant anything to him *after*, and it showed. His long hair was straggly, messy, uncombed. He was very fat. Even now he took a small shock on seeing how fat he had been. The caption read: "Leonard Martin in a Photograph Taken Three Years Ago."

The story told how Isobel had been blindfolded throughout the interview. She was unable to describe his appearance or confirm his identity as Leonard Martin—visually. Despite that limitation, she wrote that there existed no question the man she met was Leonard Martin. She was betting her reputation and future on it; so too, if to a lesser extent, was the *New York Times*. No need now to shave his beard, grow his hair, or keep the bottle of Grecian Formula bought on a fearful impulse somewhere in New Jersey. Meeting Isobel Gitlin had not given him away.

He assumed that faced with a situation in which Isobel could not or would not say she saw Leonard Martin, her editors had grilled her hard on her identification and bought into her position. He was absolutely correct. The photo editors at the *Times* had plenty of pictures to choose from, and Leonard was sure Isobel Gitlin was not consulted about which one to run.

He found no surprises in what she wrote. She described in detail how a gray sedan picked her up and drove her to the meeting. She did her best to draw a picture of the driver. She identified the meeting place as "an undisclosed location in New York City." She called Leonard simply "a well-to-do real estate lawyer from Alpharetta, Georgia." Isobel wrote about Nina Martin, Ellen Lawrence, and Ellen's two sons, Mark and Scott. She wrote that Leonard Martin had lost them all to an especially virulent and new strain of E. coli poisoning carried by Knowland & Sons' tainted meat. She described, very accurately he thought, Leonard's implacable anger, his determination to kill those he held responsible. Leonard was more than content with what she wrote and how she wrote it. She'd told the world what he told her.

The article described the deaths of Christopher Hopman, Billy MacNeal, Floyd Ochs, and Pat Grath with details that could only be attributed to the killer. He'd mentioned his practice on a small trampoline—a preparation vital to shooting Pat Grath from a small boat bobbing in the waters of Lake Mead—and she printed it. Her article stated that the *New York Times* had handed over "vital physical evidence" to federal authorities. It described the rifles and ammunition Leonard used and then left with Isobel's doorman. She wrote that the *Times* had also retrieved the Pat Grath murder weapon—an expensive, one-of-a-kind, Holland & Holland double rifle. It was found in the Nevada desert several miles east of Las Vegas (where he'd told her to look), and had also been put, by the *New York Times*, in the hands of the proper authorities. Leonard's second letter was printed in full within a half-tone margin. Reading it, Leonard did not think she could have done better.

Of course, she didn't tell everything she knew. Leonard correctly assumed that she was looking to other days and editions. En route to New York from St. Thomas, Isobel had in fact remembered a senior editor whom she met once, in her first week at the paper. He did his best to impress her in thirty seconds or less by saying, "Never forget, we have to print another one tomorrow." It sounded like tinny wisdom then. She'd made it an iron precept by the time the plane touched down.

Inside section one, the *Times* ran a half-page box showing guns and ammo with small-type insets on technical specs and retail prices. On the opposite page it ran a mafia-style table of organization. There were small headshots of all the players, with lines connecting one to the other: Leonard, his wife, daughter, and grandsons; Wayne Korman and Floyd Ochs from Knowland & Sons in Lucas; Harlan Jennings off to the side; Billy MacNeal and Pat Grath of Second Houston Holding; Christopher Hopman from Alliance; the Wall Street gang of four—still alive and breathing—perspiring, Leonard hoped, to the point of dehydration.

Dr. Ganga Roy's name was nowhere to be found. Leonard thought that the *Times*' bright lawyers might have fixed on the paper's relationship with the Rockefeller Institute and related liabilities. Leonard knew that Isobel could not *prove* the material he provided was, to a certainty, Dr. Roy's work product. Therefore, he suspected, the lawyers vetoed using her name. Isobel and her editors probably yelled themselves blue in the face. But as a lawyer he also knew that in the absence of proof absolute, legal had the better of the case.

Instead, the story credited "scientific data in the possession of the *Times*" together with "reliable sources" in support of their description of what took place in Nathan Stein's office. Leonard recognized everything Isobel wrote as the truth.

Isobel's news report, distinguished by her exclusive ID of America's most notorious home-grown desperado, offered no judgments on his crimes. Macmillan lobbied for a list of words and phrases: "corporate-terrorist," "serial killer," "unstable," even "deranged," a word that was dismissed by a quick, harsh look from the Moose. In light of his exasperation, that one wasn't even considered. The others were talked through and all rejected. Macmillan offered his ideas in a high-level meeting attended by Gold and other senior types. A senior editor suggested three names—all seasoned, experienced *Times* reporters, who might "step in and help you out." Isobel assured him, and everyone else, that she needed no help.

The same editor then offered the idea that Isobel ought not to write the story at all. "After all," he said, "to some degree she's now part of it. How can she be expected to write it?" He again brought up the same three names she previously rejected, and proposed they write the story "about you, and, of course, with your input." Isobel recognized each of the three named reporters. She'd had not so much as a "good morning" from any of them. She knew them only by reputation.

"I thought they thought the story was b-b-bullshit," she said. "You know, crap, and not the kind of crap that belongs in the *New York Times.*" The Moose couldn't help laughing. He quickly reached for a glass of water. Isobel said, "I don't need help, and," she smiled sweetly, "I always did poorly on the 'works well with others' marks." They all backed off except Macmillan. A few minutes later he submitted a paragraph questioning Leonard Martin's sanity, and citing the work of two forensic psychiatrists.

Had she asked him to, the Moose would have canned Macmillan right then, even in front of the others. Ed never knew how close he came to sniffing around the *Daily News*. Isobel felt her power building, not unlike the frightening force of a hurricane picking up steam over warm waters, hell-bent for landfall, God knows where.

The *Times*' unmasking of Leonard Martin dominated the media. Papers across the country drowned it in full-color ink. The Europeans noted it prominently, and even in Japan one paper's front page screamed "Crazy American" across the same picture of Leonard Martin the *New York Times* printed. The cable networks and talk radio raised the story yet again, like Lazarus from a shallow grave. Isobel was more than a property now. As she once saw Kevin Costner remark in *Bull Durham*, she was in "the Show." A second cover on *Newsweek*, and one on *Time* also confirmed it. Now the talking heads treated her differently—she was no longer the waif reporter. She had acquired gravitas. "I always believed in Isobel" pretty much summed up the general feeling. One deadpan prime-time showman used exactly those words. In New Mexico, Leonard watched it all unfold with more genuine pleasure than he had felt in years.

Isobel got calls from Time Warner and *Newsweek* offering her obscene amounts to join their stables. Rupert Murdoch himself called Isobel, his tacky accent bringing a whiff of Fiji bars that attracted Australians with schemes or lines of merchandise to sell. Rupert suggested that she decide precisely what it was that was she wanted, design herself a compensation package, and call him back. He emphasized that he felt she'd fit well on the air and in print. "Whatever you want, I already agree." He even crammed a delightful smile somewhere into his voice.

After thanking Rupert and promising to do as asked, Isobel reflected that, like Alice, she was now in a world where things had spun out of control. Later on, the Moose told her Murdoch was well known to make such calls himself. "I suppose he gets off on it," said Gold, adding that from what he heard Murdoch always reneged on the money part. The

New Yorker and *Rolling Stone* were asking her for cover stories. "Write about Leonard Martin," she was told by one. "Write any damn thing you want," said the other.

Page six in the *New York Post*, and even the hometown London tabloids, linked her to a new job daily. If, as in olden days, the *New York Post* published twice a day, she'd have been changing employment twice as often. The silliness reached ridiculous proportions when the supermarket tabloids reported on her fight against cancer, her joyful pregnancy, her fun-filled weekend in the Swiss Alps with a European prince who was twenty years her senior. "How do they get those pictures?" she asked as she and the Moose studied a photo of Isobel on the high Tibetan plateau, arm-in-arm with a movie star she'd never met and didn't recognize.

The heads of programming from every major cable news channel called with escalating numbers, some of which stood up handsomely against the print offers pouring in. They were encouraged no doubt by their edgy producers and highly stressed news directors. ABC and NBC let it be known that no cable outfit could make an offer that they would not match and exceed. CBS, hard-pressed to pay its ancient news performers whose packages reflected seniority and therefore weighed the network down, was forced to abstain from the frenzy.

Mysteriously, or so it seemed to many after the fact, no one in authority gave any thought to the notion that Isobel Gitlin might jump ship. She was not a contract employee. She worked at the pleasure of management; people *departed* at management's pleasure. Thus it had always been and would always be. A *New York Times* senior vice president's wife raised the subject at dinner one evening and was rebuked. In front of others, her husband told her, "People do not *leave* the *New York Times*. The *New York Times* is where they come to *be*!"

Isobel finally agreed to appear somewhere. She decided on *60 Minutes*. She chose it because CBS never offered her a penny, not even a job. In a world gone crazy, she judged CBS to be the last refuge of sanity. They told her Ed Bradley would tape the conversation at Isobel's apartment three days before the broadcast. She looked forward to the experience. The network promoted her all week. It seemed that every break had a promo promising "Isobel Gitlin, only on *60 Minutes,* this Sunday, after football." These messages promised the "whole story" plus "exclusive revelations."

"My God," she told Mel Gold, "is this my fifteen minutes? When will it end?" He only smiled. He'd already told her it was too late.

"You never know," he said. "Woodward and Bernstein got thirty years out of theirs."

By Thursday, she'd just about mastered the stutter, partly by learning to make the camera an ally. The awareness of its harmlessness to her worked like an umbrella in hand on a threatening day; more often than not it kept the clouds away. In her mind the camera became a machine intended to help her focus. She also had come to understand that the defect itself, the stutter, loomed large in her legend. "Oh my," she thought, "do I really have a *legend*?" Before the cameras rolled she asked Mr. Bradley if it was true that, as she'd heard, some producers at CNN, FOX, and MSNBC had lost their jobs for failing to book her. He told her it was possible. "This business eats people for lunch," he added.

That Sunday's *60 Minutes* show got its best ratings of the season. For CBS, it was one of the few times they didn't lose audience after football. Nonetheless, Ed Bradley's interview was not what he expected. At first, Isobel gave him no new information. She talked at length about things she'd already written about. Bradley's frustration surfaced when he came to understand that Isobel was skillfully holding back anything not already public knowledge. The blockbuster news he hoped for, expected, been told he was going to get, was nowhere on the horizon. What's more, she demonstrated devilish mastery of the process, especially in view of her reputed inexperience. Isobel had the infuriating knack of sounding as though she was offering new, exciting facts while revealing nothing. Eventually, her inquisitor threw up both hands and said, "Stop the tape." He glared with undisguised anger at Isobel.

"Something wrong?" she asked. A production assistant brought her bottled water. A makeup man worked on her forehead.

"Yes." He was trying, gentlemanlike, to take the edge off his voice. "I'm not getting anything here."

"What is it you want?" Isobel asked.

"A b-blockbuster's what we expected. Something new and exciting." She thought that it was absolutely odd that her own voice was strong as steel while he tripped on the always dangerous *b*. "Something we don't already know. I thought we were going to get into this. In all fairness, that's what we were led to expect."

"I see," she said, returning the water. "Something . . . b-big. I think I have it now. Get the tape ready and ask me how I feel about Leonard Martin and then about my future."

"Okay!" He yelled at the crew, and they bustled.

Bradley was all ease and purpose again, speckled beard glowing in the meticulous lighting. "Tell me, if you can, what do you think of this guy? How do you feel about Leonard Martin?"

Isobel said, "When I was a child, in France, my grandmother told me about a neighbor. During the war the Germans occupied the neighbor's house. They threw him out—him and his wife and his children—into the barn. They made them servants of the Nazis. The man's wife and both small children died that winter from disease and hunger and despair. When the war ended, my grandmother's neighbor reclaimed his home. Many years later, she told me—forty years or more—a man came and knocked on the door. He was an older man, a German, traveling with a young boy. He was one of the German officers who had occupied this man's house. I suppose he wanted to show his grandson where he had been during the war. Well, when the neighbor recognized the German, b-both of them old men by now, he reached behind the door, got the shotgun he'd kept there for decades, and killed the German right there on his doorstep, in front of the man's grandson." Isobel paused to take a deep breath. Ed Bradley gave her one of his practiced looks; the one that asks, "What does that mean?"

Isobel said, "Leonard Martin sees himself as that neighbor."

"Do you?" Bradley asked.

"Do you?"

Bradley was speechless. It was a great look, and Isobel wondered how long it took him to perfect it. Then he said, "This has been quite a ride for you. I mean personally. What does all this mean for Isobel Gitlin? You've got a wonderful future ahead of you. So, what are your plans?"

Isobel's answer, as disclosed to the world on that Sunday evening, sent a wickedly rapturous rush through the breast of the wife of a certain *New York Times* senior vice president. Few people outside the business would care, but a Richter scale for the global media culture would have surely shuddered and shattered when Isobel said, "I have no contract with the paper I'm with now. [She didn't even call it by its name!] Who knows, I might like to return to London."

"Back to England. Back home? Have you thought about that?"

"Yes, I have. There are so many things I'd like to do. I'm not married to the newspaper, you know. [Once more she failed to identify the *New York Times.* The *New York Times*!] I feel an obligation to the unfinished obituaries of Christopher Hopman, Billy MacNeal, Floyd Ochs, and Pat Grath. Leonard Martin is really part of that. I started these stories, and until I've finished them I cannot walk away. You see that, don't you? But I've no desire to be celebrated, famous, or turned into a journalist with a capital *J.*"

Ed Bradley's face registered no expression at all. But for his unchanged posture he might have been pole-axed. Isobel Gitlin, a woman on the very edge of media stardom, fame, and riches—the crowning achievement of American culture—had just said she wanted no part of it.

"You just want to go back to writing obituaries?" Bradley asked.

She addressed herself to the friendly camera. "People die every day, don't they. The stories I write are the stories of their lives, and I would hope I do it in a way that's both interesting to the reader and respectful of the subject. I believe obituaries are a noble part of this country's freedom of the press. I continue to strive to live up to the standard set by Robert McG. Thomas."

She was careful not to say "our country." She was, after all, a proud Fijian, carrying a British passport.

"You're *leaving* the *Times*?" asked Bradley, having quickly refitted the smile that helped make him rich and famous. "You can't be serious about going back to . . . to writing obituaries. You've got big stories ahead, no? Books maybe. And you're thinking of leaving the *New York Times*? Leaving the newspaper business altogether? Going back to England?"

"I might," she said, light as a feather, and smiled right into the camera.

Watching the show at home in the Whitestone section of Queens, bourbon and soda in one hand, giant salted pretzel in the other, Mel Gold let out a grunt of epic proportions. His wife hurried in from the kitchen, fearing it was something to do with his health.

"Sonofabitch!" said the Moose, unable to wipe the smile from his face.

THIRTY-SEVEN

St. John

Back on the island, Walter read Isobel's story about the infamous Leonard Martin while enjoying breakfast in his usual spot in Billy's Bar. On St. John, the *New York Times* comes ashore with the early morning ferry from the rock. The distribution began with Billy's because it was right on the square, only steps from where the ferry docked, plus it was well known that Walter Sherman liked to read it with breakfast. They do know everything. The story detailed the things Walter and Isobel talked about, and, while it was news on the most striking order for the world at large, it provided no new information for him. He read every word, examined every graphic: the rifles and ammo, the player chart that was spread out on the page as if they were each key members of the underworld. He couldn't help feeling there was something missing. He didn't know what, but he knew enough to keep that uneasy sense in a special file for future reference.

That Sunday he watched the interview with Ed Bradley on the television Tom Maloney had thought of as Radio City. Clara saw it too. She knew something about Walter's job, although she had never heard him refer to what he did as a job. He did something for people they couldn't do for themselves, something important, something she was sure was dangerous—that she knew. All those trips he took. Now, looking at Isobel Gitlin talking to one of her favorite TV personalities, that handsome Ed Bradley, telling him she had discovered this man, Leonard Martin, all by herself—Clara wondered just what it was that Mr. Sherman really did.

THIRTY-EIGHT

St. John

"STILL GOT NOTHING TO say?" Billy asked. Walter had been sitting in his regular seat at the bar in silence nursing the same Diet Coke all morning. He hardly ate his breakfast, and the *New York Times* lay folded on the bar, unopened. Walter muttered something at Billy, nothing he could make sense of.

"I knew a man once," Ike said. "Didn't say nothing to nobody for damn near two months."

"Who was that?" Billy asked, astonished.

"Isaac. You know him, Billy? Runs that Budweiser stand over near the beach."

"The hot dog place?" Billy said, clarifying things. "It's got that big Budweiser sign on it? Yeah, I know him."

"Well, like I said. Nothing to nobody for two months."

"You said 'damn near two months,' not 'two months.'"

"Thank God A'mighty!" hollered Ike, managing not to cough in spite of the prodigious puff of smoke coming out of his mouth simultaneous with his words. "Walter, you *can* talk."

"Better than the two of you."

"I talk pretty good," Billy said, a tiny bit of hurt in his voice. "You know, you can't run a bar, not one as popular as this, and not be a good talker." Walter nodded, but clearly not in agreement. Ike took another deep drag, the sound of the burning embers racing toward the butt, carrying all the way to where Walter sat.

"Christ, Ike," he said. "You're going to explode. So, are you going to tell us?"

"Tell us what?" Billy said.

"Alright Ike," said Walter, putting on his best third-grade teacher voice, "why didn't Isaac say anything for . . . however long you said?"

"Well," Ike said, "I can only tell you what he told me—later on, of course. He said he didn't have nothing to say." Walter stared at Ike, the question of the old man's credibility written all over his face. Ike, as always, smiled.

"Best talker I ever heard was Hitler," Billy said, and neither Walter nor Ike could think of what to say next. They looked at each other with flat amazement. Finally, Walter said, "Hitler?" And Ike followed with, "Shit," sounding more like bed linen than anything else. Billy rose to his own defense.

"Hey, I don't like him. I'm just saying, did you ever hear him speak, talking? I've seen him on The History Channel. I don't even know what he's saying, but I couldn't take my eyes off him. And then that crowd—all those Germans—yelling like that. All I'm saying is I never heard anyone else talk that way. That's all."

"I have," Walter said. "Ever hear of Martin Luther King, Jr.?"

Billy picked up a rag and began wiping down the already spotless bar. His embarrassment was painful. Walter knew Billy wouldn't be the next to say anything. Then Ike spoke up.

"Minister Henry Broomfield," he said. "Come here a long time ago, must be forty years. Preached three weekends in a row, mind you. Out by the old slave battleground. In a tent. Went back and stayed on the rock during the week. Everybody went that first weekend. Ain't that many of us here, right? And not much to do neither. But we went back again the next week, and then again another time just to hear that man talk. Spellbinder. For a few days after he'd gone I was this close to seeing Jesus myself." Ike held up one finger on each hand about a foot between them. He laughed, and Walter did too.

"Powerful, huh?" Billy said, feeling a bit rehabilitated. Jesus and Hitler were equally irrelevant to him.

"And that wasn't the best part," said Ike. "You see, Minister Broomfield come here only once and leave. But he come back a few years ago—thirty, thirty-five years later. He sets up his tent in the same exact spot as before. We all went. Why not? My wife—" Ike stopped and took a very deep breath, this time without the cigarette. Walter remembered when Sissy died about a year before Billy arrived on St. John. The old man needed a minute. "We all went," Ike continued, "and my wife wanted to speak to Minister Broomfield after his services, so she waits in line to see him and I'm waiting with her. Well, Sissy finally gets to shake his hand and she says something like, 'I bet you don't remember me, but I heard you when you were here before—twice, actually.' That minister looked right into her eyes with a big smile, held her hands with both of his—you know, sort of like he was Christ himself—and he says to her, 'Of course I remember you, darlin'. And your sister too.'"

"That's impressive," Walter said.

"Let me tell you," Ike went on. "I was shocked. How this man remember Sissy's sister? Sissy's so happy she just sort of drifts away and

I'm left standing there, just me and Minister Henry Broomfield. I look at him and say how could he remember my wife's sister after maybe forty years? Her *sister*! That man put his hand on my shoulder, and with that same smile he just gave my Sissy he whispers to me, 'They all got sisters.'"

The three friends were silent. What more was there to say. At last Billy said, "Sonofabitch. You want me to write it?"

"That's good," Ike said.

"How can people vote for this one?" asked Walter.

"How can they vote for any of them?" said Billy. "Nobody's got the slightest fucking idea what this stuff is all about."

"Okay," Walter said, looking over to Ike for approval.

"That's good," the old man said again.

"Well then," Billy said. He rambled over to the chalkboard next to the ancient cash register and, for the time being, a miniature Christmas tree, picked up the blue chalk, and wrote, "Hitler/Martin Luther King, Jr./Henry Broomfield."

Walter ordered a fresh Diet Coke and Billy's special swordfish steak with everything—the salad and potatoes too. He was hungry at last. And he was thinking, "They all got sisters."

THIRTY-NINE

St. John

The chase was easy. The path well traveled. It was a foregone conclusion that he would find what he was looking for. At the heart of it all lay what people call "intuition." Walter understood intuition as hidden calculation, invisible counting, and weighing. It made some card players rich, told goalies where to stick the glove without ever seeing the shot, drove scientific breakthroughs. As Walter had tried to explain to Billy and Ike, the conscious mind can't find or control the place where these calculations are made.

Intuitive people get results through a one-way door in the mind. This worked better for some than others. Walter believed that to fully exploit intuition, people needed intelligence. What's more, high intelligence plus intuition equals genius. True, people of average intelligence also have hunches and often know how to play them. Walter considered himself an average man with better-than-average hunches.

These skills and the resources he nurtured in thirty years spent finding people gave him a great advantage over cops and associated freelancers. He was confident of that. He faced no bureaucracy or any of the other multitudes of institutions that claim to be so vital to human sociology, yet more often than not are designed primarily to make things harder than need be. He worked without warrants, court orders, or permission, unshackled by rules. He encountered none of the legal, political, or jurisdictional red tape (priding himself on actually knowing the origin of the term) that plagued law enforcement. Most of all, when he thought about what made him a success he credited much of it to the simple fact that he knew what he was doing. His natural affinity for the process, going all the way back to Freddy Russo in Saigon, was only sharpened by years of experience. He wasn't quite able to recognize it, let alone have such feelings see the light of day, but deep inside he knew he loved it. The plane rides, the long drives to the middle of nowhere, the finest hotels in the capital cities of the world and the cheap ones in towns nobody wanted to spend time in. He loved the solitude, the privacy, the assurance of being alone, the certainty he could not possibly run into anyone who knew him. Especially himself.

Over time, Walter accumulated and cultivated a list of people who could get him access to information he needed either to begin or continue his searches. He made a conscious point of staying in touch with former clients and others he met along the way who could be useful to him in the future, and he was a truly good friend to those among them whom he really liked. He learned to distinguish gratitude from relief. Some clients lost their gratitude fast. Some never had it at all. Some never lost it—and many of these were positioned to help. The well was deep, and now he drank from it yet again.

"Hoe gaat het, Aat," said Walter, sitting on his deck, the tropical sea spread out beneath him, the telephone resting easily on his shoulder.

"Walter, my friend," was the surprised and happy reply. "How are you?"

Aat van de Steen was a Dutchman, a man of rare candor with a ripe sense of humor and a self-confidence Walter knew to be of awe-inspiring proportions. If you asked what he did, he most probably would describe himself as a soldier of fortune. And he would do so with a flourish, a smile, and a twinkle in his eye. What did Aat van de Steen do? Who could be sure?

"How are you, old man?" said the Dutchman. "So wonderful to hear your voice again."

"Old man?" said Walter. "You're older than me."

Van de Steen laughed. "Not in the ways that count, my friend. For there I am forever young."

"Yeah, you and Zimmy."

"Zimmy?"

"Dylan. Bob Dylan. 'Forever Young.'"

"You think I don't know your Bob Dylan?" The Dutchman laughed again. "You are—how do you say—kidding me."

Walter said, "Good to hear your voice too, Aat."

The Dutchman was suddenly serious. "You must need some help, no?"

"I do," said Walter. "I certainly do."

Walter and Aat van de Steen first met in Laos in the summer of 1971. Both men were new to their trade, both blessed with special abilities, which, if handled with care and developed properly, were certain to make both successful. Van de Steen had begun with a few small deals with some Eastern European irregulars. He soon branched out to Northern Africa and the former Dutch colonies in Asia. It was through an Indonesian that he got his first contract in Laos. Over the years, the decades, in fact, Aat van de Steen had become one of the world's busiest and wealthiest arms dealers. From his headquarters in Amsterdam, on the city's fanciest canal, the Herens Gracht, he bought, sold, and controlled a lion's share of the movement of weapons—from handguns to tanks, helicopters, even heavy artillery—on every inhabited continent on the planet. "War is the most fundamental attribute of humanity," he once told Walter. "I serve the species." Over the years, Walter ran into him on his occasional trips to Europe. He made a point of it. At each meeting they renewed their friendship with genuine warmth, affection, and respect. Then, eleven years ago, Aat's brother suddenly disappeared when he was unable to pay a substantial gambling debt. Although Aat's reputation and unquestioned power protected his brother from harm, Jan van de Steen panicked and went to hiding. He left behind his wife, three children, and a brother who was a friend of Walter Sherman. It took Walter a month to find the younger van de Steen holed up in an apartment in Vancouver, Canada. By then, Jan was ready to be caught. Walter returned him safely to his family in Zoetermeer, and, of course, he refused any money from Aat.

Walter detailed the guns, the equipment, and the ammunition Leonard Martin used and deposited with Isobel. As Walter spoke and Aat jotted some notes, the Dutchman said nothing more than an occasional "okay." Had the two been in the same room, a nod of his head would have sufficed.

"I will call you when I have something," van de Steen said. "And Walter, you would do yourself well to come see me in Amsterdam. Not now because it's too cold here for an island man like yourself, but in spring—then we can sit in the Leidens Plein, drink coffee, and watch all the Swedish girls." He laughed again, and so did Walter. "In fact, Walter, I will tell you what I will do. I will take you to the Yab Yum. Yes I will."

"What's the Yab Yum?"

"You will not be disappointed, my friend."

A picture was developing in Walter's mind. After Leonard's family died, his ties to everyone in Atlanta began slipping. When he discovered what really happened—when he received Dr. Roy's CD—he cut the remaining shreds. Sources in the financial world had already provided Walter with Leonard Martin's history. He knew Leonard had gone to cash and the money trail led straight to the Caymans. "We all keep our money there, don't we?" he thought, and wondered if they shared the same bank. If so, Leonard's account dwarfed his own. The move to Jamaica had been a hoax; a cheap one at that. There was a deed with Leonard's name on it, but the property had been bought for only a few thousand dollars. It made no difference. Leonard was probably never there. But he was somewhere, for two years. Wherever that was, he had managed to stockpile weapons, some quite exotic and expensive, and found a way to use them proficiently, expertly. "Practice, practice," thought Walter. Like a golf pro hitting hundreds of balls every day, rain or shine, he envisioned Leonard Martin firing round after round, day after day, week after week, month after month. As Walter put the puzzle together, he guessed there had been no way Leonard could have used a commercial shooting range. He would have been like a pool hall junkie, hanging around for hours on end, day after day after day. That would have attracted too much attention. There was no way that happened. Isobel had told him about Leonard's use of a small trampoline, one he used to stand on to learn how to shoot accurately even while unstable. So where then did Leonard Martin stay? Where did he shoot? Something didn't fit. Perhaps the answers would come from Aat van de Steen. Wherever the guns went, Leonard was there. Walter would wait until the Dutchman called.

FORTY

New York

MALONEY WAS WORRIED. THE stories in the *New York Times*—Christ! Every day they print something else with his name in it. Photographers, TV trucks, reporters of all sorts hounded them everywhere. The publicity was making it impossible for him and the others to conduct the normal business of the firm. Day after day the public relations machine so much a part of the Stein, Gelb, Hector & Wills operation labored to deny, deny, deny. Nathan wanted Louise to direct this effort, but he was dissuaded when she looked at him in disbelief, the left side of her mouth noticeably twitching, and said, "That's madness, Nathan. None of us—and I mean none of us—can be seen touching this. It will explode in our faces. Get someone else. You've got resources."

Wesley Pitts said, "It's already blown up in our face, Louise."

"No it hasn't!" she shouted. "It's just a fucking newspaper article, some talking heads on the cable. Shit, nobody watches those goddamn cable networks anyway. It can't hurt us. It will go away!"

"I think Louise is right," Tom Maloney interjected, seeing the need, as always, to get things under control. He tried not to show how desperate he was to get them all calmed down before it was too late. He knew Louise Hollingsworth didn't believe a word she'd said. He could see fear in her eyes. Her reaction was visceral. She felt she was doomed. They were all doomed. Her emotions erupted into an open sore. Maloney did not share those feelings. No matter what the *New York Times* wrote, the killings had stopped. Leonard Martin had stopped killing people. Tom had earlier confided as much to Nathan, and Nathan, he thought, had bought in. Or so it seemed.

"We'll get someone to handle this," Tom said. "The real problem is that we can't operate effectively with any sense of routine. We can't talk to clients because all they're thinking about is what they saw on TV or read in the paper. No matter how many times the firm denies any involvement, it's still out of the question to call someone—anyone—and say 'Hey, let's have lunch.' Who wants to be near us? After all, who among us is willing to walk in the street like a normal person?"

It was a question not requiring an answer. Nevertheless, Pitts said, "Not me."

"It's not 'out of the question,'" Nathan said, "it's fucking impossible! The way they treat us you'd think we were priests, goddamnit! As of right now," he said, rising from his big chair, looking as tall as he ever had, "we're all on leave. Go home, or wherever you want to go, and don't come back until this is over. We'll stay in touch with cell phones."

The room was deathly quiet. The light behind Nathan's desk was such that none of the other three could actually see his face. Were his eyes darting from side to side? Was his nose twitching? They had no idea. Despite the brief outburst, his voice was calm and smooth, his demeanor subdued, not agitated. Louise and Wes took the moment as a sign of Nathan's leadership. Had they thought it through they would have seen the folly in such judgment, but they badly needed reassurance, and how they got it was of no importance. Maloney stayed seated and Stein stood, towering above him as Tom Cruise might be made to appear tall when shot from the proper angle. "He might be a wee little man," thought Tom, "but his name's on the door." Wesley Pitts and Louise Hollingsworth left.

"Let them go hide," Nathan said. "This is real horseshit, Tom. You know that. What the fuck is going on with Sherman? He knows his guy is Leonard Martin—the whole fucking world knows it. Results!"

"I haven't heard from him, but that means he's working, Nathan. That's what it means. The time will come when Walter Sherman calls, and Leonard Martin will be right there."

"You still think we're safe?"

"No, not safe, not the way you mean it. People we know are already dead, for Christ's sake! We're in the crosshairs alright, but Leonard Martin has something up his sleeve."

"Great. When do *we* find out?"

"If Sherman doesn't find him first, and soon, we'll find out when he wants us to. In the meantime there's nothing we can do, Nathan. Nothing."

Louise and Wesley went home, kept their blinds closed, and stayed away from the windows. She drank and he paced, talking to himself, cursing. They didn't hurt for any creature comforts. The very rich can have anything delivered. They were used to having things brought to them. Each passed off the new, higher cost of such luxury to market conditions. Their stocks were tumbling, and in the end they knew the servants would just as soon pick their bones as wish them good morning. For both of them, bitterness and anger grew in direct proportion to personal jeopardy. After a couple of days of this, Tom called to say Nathan wanted them to "take off," to go somewhere they won't be found and try to relax.

Under different conditions Wesley Pitts might have flown off to Cabo San Lucas or Palm Springs. Not now. Instead, he bought a first-class ticket with a private cabin on the Amtrak train that ran from Washington, D.C. to New Orleans. Lawrence made the long drive from Manhattan to Union Station in the nation's capitol. From there, Wes was on his own. Although his ticket was to the end of the line, he got off the train when it stopped for a few minutes in Meridian, Mississippi. From there he rented a car and drove the hundred miles or so to the tiny town of Hintonville. His grandmother welcomed him with open arms and a warm smile.

"Are you hungry, honeychild?" she said. "Oh, Wesley, I'm so happy to see you." She squeezed her grandson, although she barely came up to the middle of his chest. "I love you so, boy." She was not surprised to see him. Even in the backwaters of the Deep South people read the newspaper, even the *New York Times.*

Like Wes, Louise would have preferred La Costa or Vail. Unlike him, she had no grandmother who would take her in, no family who had been proud of her since childhood, eager to protect their loved one. There were many men she slept with, but none of them were of any use to her now. What she did have was an enormous amount of money. She called a real estate agent she found on the Internet in Brattleboro, Vermont. The same day she bought a house nearby, just north of the Massachusetts state line. She was adamant. She wanted privacy, off the beaten path, no neighbors. The agent suggested three properties. Louise chose the second one, a six-year-old cabin with all the amenities, three bedrooms and three and a half baths on two and three-quarters acres at the foot of what passed for a small mountain. The agent offered to fax Louise pictures of the property and directed her to a website where she could take a 360-degree virtual tour of the house. "Not necessary," Louise said. She wired power of attorney and approved a wire transfer from her bank to the realtor's escrow account in Vermont. "Close on it immediately," she instructed the agent. "Today, if possible. Tomorrow at the latest." She packed and began driving. She thought of Nathan's house in Wevertown and prayed the one she just bought would be as nice. It had to be, she figured. She paid almost six hundred thousand dollars for it.

Tom Maloney believed the best place to hide was in plain sight. He moved into a suite at the Waldorf, arranged for private security, and settled in for the duration. He was quite happy to get away from his current wife for a while, and she was so pleased with his decision she immediately left for Switzerland, telling friends she'd be gone until the spring.

Nathan Stein stayed home in the city for two days, then took off for the country, upstate. A day after arriving in Wevertown he was already going stir crazy. He called Maloney.

"Get a bigger suite," Nathan said. "Hell, get the whole fucking penthouse." By dinner he had moved into the Waldorf with Tom.

FORTY-ONE

St. John

The phone woke him at six o'clock the next morning. It was noon in Holland and van de Steen had other business to attend to that day.

"Hoe gaat het, Walter."

"Hoe gaat het yourself. What time is it?"

"It's nice to see you haven't lost all your Dutch."

"No, I still know how to say 'hello' and how to find the toilet."

"And the polar bear." Van de Steen laughed, recalling an old joke between the two men.

"Waar is de ijsbeer?" said Walter with a smile. "I don't remember much, but I remember that."

"Listen Walter, some of your man's arsenal is too common, too available to trace to any one individual. You knew that, of course, but not all of it. The Holland & Holland, a fine and excellent piece of equipment—truly a work of art—that one I am sure came from California. How do you say S-a-n J-o-s-e?"

"San Jose," said Walter. "How did he get it and where?"

"I cannot say for sure it was the man you are looking for, but the rifle itself was sold through a dealer, on the Internet, paid for in money orders."

"Money orders? I thought that gun sold for more than twenty-five thousand dollars. That's a helluva way to pay that kind of money."

"Yes. Quite normal, actually. And it was twenty-seven thousand, plus a dealer's fee and shipping."

"That's great, Aat. I think I can find the trail of a money order that size. Is there a name?"

"Not so quickly, my friend. These dealers never sell to people who use their real name. In your country there are many named Smith or Jones. It will be a name like that. Dealers know the name is untrue. They don't care. The name—whatever it is—will do you no good. And, you will not be able to track down a money order."

"Why not?"

"Most individual clients pay in this manner, and they do so with a group of money orders, none for more than nine hundred dollars, all of them purchased separately. It's an inconvenience, but it serves its purpose. Again, the dealers have no interest in the procedure, only the result."

"Where did they ship to?"

"Ah ha, now you are talking—what is it—turkey? Do you know where is Fargo, North Dakota?"

Walter listened as van de Steen told him how the Holland & Holland double rifle was shipped from an anonymous owner in San Jose, California to a PO Box at a private mail and packaging store in Fargo, North Dakota. The transaction was completed under the auspices of a dealer Walter's Dutch friend saw no need to name. He wasn't asked. The owner of the PO Box was listed as Evangelical Missions Inc. Van de Steen said the commercial mail store, following instructions, forwarded the package, knowing nothing about its contents, to a private address in Raleigh, North Carolina.

"Jackpot!" said Walter.

"The Israeli gun," van de Steen said, "I believe it too went to this address. Of that one I cannot be totally certain, but I think it is so. There are many of them—it too is a wonderful piece—and I believe at least one went to this place in North Dakota."

"That's great," Walter said. "The Holand & Holland is enough. That two of them were sent to the same place makes it a hundred percent."

"A word of caution, my friend. It was not on your list, but I can trace a Walther WA2000 to the same destination."

"What is that?"

"*That*, as you call it, is the finest rifle ever built in the sniper class. It is a NATO 7.62mm semiautomatic regarded by most people who are familiar with things of this nature, such as myself, as the most accurate long-range weapon in the world. And there lies the trick, Walter. The Germans—a people so good at making things like this—built only seventy-two of them. If you asked me to get one for you today—and you would be a rich man, a very rich man to do so—I could not."

"You're serious? *You* couldn't find one? How could a rank amateur?"

"He did not. It was no amateur. A Walther WA2000 is a transaction to be proud of. I think it could be sold for a hundred thousand euros, maybe more. A dealer I know in Hong Kong made just such a sale at the same time as these others, all bought within a few months of each other. I remembered hearing about it. We brag, as you Americans say, even in my profession. I called him last evening. He was bursting with pride still, and told me he arranged for it to be delivered to the same place—North Dakota. Be aware, Walter. With that gun you can kill anyone, anywhere."

"No need for the concern. My man doesn't want to kill me. He doesn't even know me."

"He will kill someone with it. When you do what *you* do you can never know what can transpire. If he does not know you, make sure it stays that way."

"Don't worry, Aat. But thanks."

Aat van de Steen said, "No man spends that much money for such a thing and doesn't use it. Besides, having played with it, practiced with it, held it in his hands and against his cheek and shoulder, taken it apart, cleaned and reassembled it, I am certain he will be unable to resist shooting it at someone. It must be so."

"Thank you, Aat," said Walter, acutely aware of the intensity in his friend's voice. It struck him as almost religious—sexual. Every business has its Holy Grail. "As always," Walter said, "I am in your debt."

"Quite the contrary, Walter. It is I who owe you. It is my pleasure to assist. Do not forget. I am planning on it. In the spring, the Yab Yum."

FORTY-TWO

St. John

When the address in Raleigh turned out to be an empty lot, Walter was not surprised. No delivery service—not UPS, not Fed Ex, not anyone—would simply drop a package in an empty lot and drive away. Someone had to be there when it arrived, and Walter was sure it wasn't Leonard.

He was certain, as certain as he could be absent real proof, that Isobel's Kermit was Carter Lawrence. He was convinced, although less certain, that Carter had been present at the empty lot in Raleigh. It must have been he who took delivery as the packages of weapons and ammunition arrived there. What did he do with them? Probably, Walter conjectured, he shipped them on to wherever Leonard was. Most likely Carter loaded the packages into his car and drove south on interstate 85 back to Atlanta. If he had sent them out again it would have been from there, from somewhere in Atlanta. And if the two men had seen each other, Walter was sure it was Leonard who had come to Carter, not the other way around.

For the last twenty years, at least, no contacts had been more valuable than those that enabled Walter to see credit card records. With friends in the right places, vital information could be gathered instantly. Walter knew the authorities could accomplish the same thing, but it would take them weeks, even months. There would be search warrants, court orders, and, of course, the inevitable screw-ups caused by multiple and overlapping jurisdictions. The cops would have to deal with their own internal politics. Somebody might have the idea to check out credit card records, and somebody else, often times the next guy up the line, would kill the idea, simply because it wasn't his. Walter's years in the business also taught him that even when the cops, the FBI, or any of a slew of government agencies got it right—when they knew what to look for and where it was—they still missed it at least as often as they didn't. Just as he once told Isobel the best way to follow someone can sometimes be to walk in front of them, he knew the best way to look for a clue was to know what you were looking for before searching for it. Easier said than done, but Walter trusted his instincts. For three decades they led him in the right direction.

Carter Lawrence's credit card receipts gave Walter the confirmation he expected. Gasoline purchases tracked him from Atlanta to Raleigh and back again, more than once. Walter could even see where Carter stopped for lunch along the way. And, best of all, UPS records showed shipments from Carter Lawrence to a PO Box in Las Vegas, New Mexico—no doubt a private mail and package store just like the one in Fargo. The shipments were in Carter Lawrence's name, paid for with his Visa card. The recipient was EM Inc.

After his ex-wife and two sons died, Carter hunkered down in Atlanta. Except for the trips to Raleigh, he went nowhere for more than two years. Some of his gasoline charges in Atlanta were separated by many weeks. He wasn't even moving around in town. The only vendor that showed up on Carter's records in any regular fashion was a Kroger supermarket. From the amount of the charges—never more than forty dollars—Carter was obviously eating alone. Then, only a month ago, charges appeared for gas and food in Birmingham, Alabama. "What was he doing there?" Walter wondered. This month there was another out-of-town charge. This time for a Hampton Inn in Clarksville, Tennessee—plus a restaurant bill of $130.46 at the Clarksville Holiday Inn. He wasn't eating alone that night. Another gasoline charge showed up the following day in Springfield. Walter opened the travel atlas he kept handy on top of the refrigerator and turned to the map of Tennessee. Atlanta to Clarksville was about three hundred miles. He traced out a route, simple and direct, going north on I-75 and picking up I-24 just past Chattanooga, going west right into Clarksville. The round trip was too long to make on a single tank of gas, and the refueling stop fit the trip perfectly. Springfield was just down the road on the way to Nashville. It was clear to Walter that Carter Lawrence had driven from Atlanta to Clarksville, eaten dinner with someone, spent the night at a nearby Hampton Inn, and drove home the next day. Walter had seen his share of Holiday Inns, from Maine to Montana and too many places in between. There was no way anybody could spend $130.46 in any of their restaurants—not alone. Carter had more than one dinner guest—at least two, more probably three, Walter figured. There were no more surprises after Clarksville. Carter wasn't hiding from anyone. He never thought to cover his tracks by paying cash. By now Walter expected to see the airline charge for Carter's ticket to New York. Yes indeed, he was Kermit. No hotel for New York. Walter made a mental note to check the addresses for Carter's brother and sisters. He was sure he'd find one of them living in New York City on the Upper West Side.

FORTY-THREE

New Mexico

WALTER'S PLANE DIDN'T LAND in New Mexico until late afternoon, and he had also lost two more hours by the clock. The trip had been grueling, but he felt momentum and didn't want to break it, didn't want to stop. Up at six, he had taken the ferry to St. Thomas and boarded a flight to Miami. From there he flew to Dallas, changed planes, and he was airborne again on his way to Albuquerque—his first time ever in New Mexico. Santa Fe was another couple of hours by car from Albuquerque. Walter had booked a room at Santa Fe's most famous hotel, Inn of the Anastasia. At the suggestion of the reservations agent, he got one with a fireplace. "Isn't Santa Fe in the desert?" Walter had asked her, mistakenly believing he was headed for a warm climate. "Yes it is," she told him, "but it's the high desert. It gets real cold here, Mr. Sherman. You'll see. There's snow on the ground right now. If you're coming from the Virgin Islands you need to bring a coat." She laughed a friendly laugh. Walter had a lopsided idea of what Santa Fe was all about, and he figured she labored under a similar misconception of the Virgin Islands, and most likely had never heard of St. John. "She probably thinks we're all walking around in shorts and T-shirts, with floppy hats and sunglasses," he thought. Then he realized if she did think that she wouldn't be too far from right. "Take the fireplace. You won't be sorry," she said. After landing, he rented a car and drove first to Sure Shot Shooting Supplies and Accessories at 5400 Holly NE. It took him less than half an hour to purchase a Glock, with bullets and holster, for $576.42.

The interstate is straight as an arrow, uphill heading north. Walter found it barren and sad. Occasional Indian casinos, their satellite motels and restaurants, were clustered along the sides. He noticed with wry surprise that the sun was setting, suddenly, behind ragged mountains. The Caribbean sun takes forever to disappear out past Puerto Rico. Here it drops like a rolling stone; daylight one minute, dark the next. "Not my cup of tea," Walter thought.

He didn't like the landscape, either. It was mostly scruffy sand, much of it overrun by alarmingly hearty, ugly weeds. It wasn't graceful desert like Arizona, Nevada, or even Aruba. Whatever it was, he'd not seen it before and would not miss it when he left. An hour later he stopped at a roadside restaurant, felt the chill stepping out of the car, and understood how cold it would be when he'd driven another few thousand feet up. The restaurant was not even much of a diner. Walter ordered a grilled cheese sandwich. It came on the thickest bread he'd ever seen.

He reached Santa Fe at eight, followed directions to the Plaza, and found his hotel. The whole town looked like a theme park. From what he'd heard, it wasn't. The city restricted construction to adobe old-west designs, but people did live in the houses. The Inn sat smack on the well-lit Plaza, a wide space filled with people moving swiftly in the cold. It was, Walter reminded himself, the Christmas season, which probably explained the seven hundred dollars he paid for the room. A bellhop led the way and started the fire. Walter found a Diet Coke in the mini-bar, set it next to the telephone, and fell asleep with the light on.

In the morning, after an early breakfast, he drove north for about an hour and a half to Las Vegas, New Mexico. The journey to Las Vegas led to a shopping center mail and package store. Walter expected as much. He already knew the address and PO Box number. The packages had been sent to Evangelical Missions Inc. Carter left a trail a mile wide. When Walter first encountered that name, he wondered whether he would again, or whether Leonard would use it just once. Walter was relieved to discover that Leonard was not quite that wise. Why should he be? This was his maiden serial rampage.

Had he been the kind of guy to offer advice to others in his field—if indeed there were others in his field—Walter would have told them first and foremost: *respect the obvious*. The easiest thing to discover is always the most obvious. Start at the beginning. As he had done countless times in the last three decades, Walter once more began at the beginning.

Evangelical Missions Inc. in New Mexico was the same as EM Inc., which owned the empty lot in Raleigh. Corporate records in North Carolina showed that the company had been incorporated just before Leonard Martin left Atlanta for the Bahamas. Further checking turned up an SUV registered in North Carolina to the same EM Inc. It didn't take Walter long to find a transfer to a New Mexico registration for the same vehicle. The plate location indicated a Las Vegas address, but Walter knew he wouldn't find Leonard anywhere near there. Not anymore.

Leonard could not have shown his rifles at any conventional range. Weapons that unique would have been noticed. He had to have practiced someplace else, free from observation. That meant he almost certainly bought land for that purpose, probably when he purchased the lot in Raleigh. Working backward from Las Vegas, Walter saw Leonard planning it out in Georgia and selecting a suitable parcel from the raw, empty stretches of west Texas and out-of-the-way New Mexico. Walter did his own search for Evangelical Missions Inc. or EM Inc. Coming up empty, he reached out.

Before leaving St. John, he had called a nationally known, flamboyant attorney from Reno, Nevada who had once sought him out, and for whom Walter found and returned a wayward young son. As with so many others, the attorney was forever eager to show her gratitude. Many times she told Walter that she was at his service for any legal work, anything at all. Discretion was the ironclad bond between them, and no questions were ever asked. Walter's infrequent requests were sometimes difficult but never impossible. What he needed now was a land search. From the attorney he requested data on land sales of parcels within a day's drive of Las Vegas. This time it wasn't easy. After turning up nothing for Leonard Martin, Evangelical Missions Inc., or EM Inc., Walter was sure Leonard had bought the land using another name, one totally unfamiliar to him. A dead end. His Reno client told him she'd look for quit claims filed between two and three years ago. She explained that property is often purchased by one party, and then transferred, or quit claimed, to another. This tends to obscure the transaction, but it cannot be entirely cloaked, because every quit claim deed must be filed with an appropriate state or county agency. You had to know how and where to look. Forty-eight hours later, Walter had a map showing 270 acres adjacent to the Kiowa National Grasslands, north of a speck on the map; a place called Albert, New Mexico. The property had been purchased by a North Dakota company (he should have known), quit claimed to EM Inc. of Raleigh, North Carolina, and then quit claimed again to Evangelical Missions Inc. of New Mexico.

In Las Vegas he showed Leonard's picture around—the same one that had been pasted across the front page of the *New York Times* and just about every other newspaper in America. But nobody had seen him and nobody cared. Walter was disappointed, although not entirely surprised. He doubted that Leonard had been to Las Vegas since his meeting with Isobel plastered his face on the nation's screens and front pages. Walter did not expect to find Leonard waiting for him here. He had hoped a Pac-Mail employee might remember a very fat man with pudgy cheeks on a fleshy face, and a belly bulging deep and wide. None did. "What about a guy who looked *like* this," he asked everyone. Cut his hair? Grew it longer? Changed its color? Even lost some weight? Still nothing.

"Never seen this fellow," the clerk at the mail store said.

Walter asked, "How about a man who picked up packages, big ones. Do you get many of those?"

"How big? Do you mean like refrigerators?"

"Not quite that big. Long, perhaps, but not bulky." He held his hands as far apart as he could.

"I wish I could help you, mister. I do. But we get so many deliveries like that. This is ski country, you know."

"So you don't remember anyone in particular who might have picked up packages looking like skis—maybe that long, maybe a little shorter, the size of a shotgun or something? About two years ago?"

"Two years?" said the clerk. "Why didn't you say? Except for the regulars, I can hardly remember two months or even two weeks ago. Two years? I'm sorry."

Walter got the name of two others who worked there part time. Before leaving town he looked them up and got the same response. Nevertheless, he felt a twinge of satisfaction, a sense of professional pride standing outside this Pac-Mail store in, of all places, Las Vegas,

New Mexico, knowing that the rifles that killed Christopher Hopman, Billy MacNeal, Floyd Ochs, and Pat Grath had passed this way. Perhaps, he thought, Leonard Martin had parked his SUV in the same spot where Walter's rental car was now parked. He pictured Leonard opening the back of his SUV, sliding the boxes into the vehicle, and driving away. Walter had a very familiar itch, an adrenaline rush he often felt when he was *near*.

Snow covered the ground and blew across the road. He was looking for a land parcel northeast of Las Vegas and about a hundred miles from Santa Fe. It looked like wilderness on the map, and close up too. No villages, towns, or houses. No filling stations or bars. He drove on small roads, long stretches paved with barely visible sand, oiled to harden in winter. Within the last hour, a pickup truck passed him, but nothing else moved his way. Three cars came from the other direction. The desert here was hilly and spare, less overgrown than near Santa Fe. His Buick handled the snaky white roads nicely. He hadn't thought to rent a four-wheel drive. Just as well. The Buick got all the traction it needed. He slowed, consulted the map that the attorney sent him, and turned left onto an unmarked road shown leading to the parcel owned by Evangelical Missions Inc. The car-width trail took him twisting in and around hills. Frequent sharp turns forced him to break. After ten minutes the cabin popped up ahead, as suddenly as the sun had set the day before as he drove north from Albuquerque. It was built into the side of a large hill, looking down on the road. Fifty feet in front of the cabin, the bumpy road stopped and widened, providing space for one car to stop and turn around. Walter parked and got out. The cabin door swung in. He saw a flash of white. Whoever was there had to have heard the Buick crunching ice—might have known he was coming a quarter mile away, or more. The door opened wider and Walter felt disappointment set in. A man emerged with a torso as strikingly muscled and as hard as a kid's. The man who faced Walter did heavy work for a living. He wore a clean white T-shirt, old jeans, work boots. His close-cropped gray hair and creased, sun-dark skin put him in his forties. The man wore shades, but used his hand to shadow his eyes against the white, glaring sun and the snow. He scratched his chin beneath a tight black and gray speckled beard. There could have been a pistol tucked at his back. Walter did not think so. He wasn't threatened now, but being closer might be different. Then, if intuition failed, Walter could only hope he'd get to the Glock in his coat pocket first.

"Evangelical Missions?" Walter shouted across the fifty feet.

"Yes it is. What can I do for you, sir?" He strained to be heard. Had the wind not been at his back, he would have been inaudible.

"I'm looking for Leonard Martin."

"Leonard Mart*ee*nez? He left two weeks ago."

"Where to?"

"I don't know."

"When will he be back?"

"Don't know." His soft voice carried the nervous regret of one who knew his place and wanted to give some kind of satisfaction. The measured rhythm of his speech suggested to Walter that he might be what is politely called "slow." "I don't hardly never see him. Never seen him but once or twice. He mostly has me come when he's away. He has me work on the well pump. I like that." He pointed west. "It works just fine now. He wants me to build him a fence. He lets me use the place if he's not here. Honest, he does. I'm allowed."

"Who are you?"

"Michael DelGrazo. I come by to work on the well pump and all."

"My name is Walter Sherman. Some people in New York would like to talk with Mr. Mar-, Mr. Martinez. They want to talk about something very important. Will you tell Mr. Martinez I was here?" He covered the distance between them, reached inside his coat to the pocket of his shirt, produced a small, yellow sheet from an Inn of the Anastasia notepad. "Ask him to call this number to get in touch. Will you give him this?" Michael DelGrazo reached out and took the note in his hand. He looked at it for a long time.

"I'll put the note on the table, but no telling when he'll come back. Walter Sherman? From . . . New York?" He wrinkled his forehead, puzzling over the slip.

"No, I'm not the one from New York, but it's okay. It's all right there. Be sure not to lose it. Just see that he gets it, okay?" He watched Michael nod, all seriousness. Walter looked around, then said, "Use your bathroom?"

Michael said, "Sure," and stood back from the door. Walter entered and Michael followed. "Over there." The blinds were up. Sunlight streamed in. The air inside was clear and bright. Walter took in a spacious, plank-floor room, a tattered, brown fold-out couch, a bleached wooden table and two wooden chairs, a propane lamp on the table, and a fireplace in the corner, with scrub wood stacked beside it. Everything looked tidy and taken care of. He peered into a much smaller room, bedroll standing upright in one corner, thrift-shop bureau against the far wall, no pictures in either room. The place had electricity, but no sign of anything plugged in. Walter surveyed the narrow kitchen: propane stove, plate and cup in the sink, a few cans and boxes piled on the floor. "Where's all the food?" he wondered. A big man has to eat a lot. Probably in the boxes, he figured.

Then Walter spent his time in the john and threw its small window open before he left. No sign at all of a gun or of Leonard Martin. Michael sat on the fold-out couch, now in a heavy, red-plaid jacket, nodding to himself, the hint of smile indicating a happy thought, looking like a blind man to Walter because of the sunglasses and the way he moved his head. Walter said, "Where's your car? Don't you need a car out here?"

Pleased to produce an answer at last, the friendly voice said, "Leonard took my car. I got a Toyota last year. My sister has one, said it's a good car. Said he don't want the truck for a real long ride. That's how come I know he's coming back. He left his truck and said I can drive it. Honest, he did. I'm allowed." They walked around back and both of them looked at the SUV. Michael studied Walter's face. Anxiously? For signs of disapproval?

"It don't drive as good as the car. But you should get a four-wheel truck if you're gonna drive around here."

"Maybe I will. Thanks again." They walked to the front, and Walter said, "I know Leonard's got some problems with his health. How's he feeling lately?"

"I don't know. He's awful fat. Fattest man I ever seen. Huffing and puffing. Huffing and puffing." Michael's grin became a full-throated laugh; he had all his teeth.

They shook hands in front of the house. The wind whipped. Michael, wearing a floppy felt cowboy hat to keep his head warm, still shivered, and said, "So long." Walter turned after Michael did. Walking back to the car, he put the chances that Leonard might call at maybe a thousand to one. Still, there was nothing to lose. Walter thought about Michael DelGrazo, middle-aged yet hard as a rock. Walter too needed to get in shape, lose some weight. Perhaps he would get a workout tape. Walter pictured himself on a chinning bar looking out at the sea as his muscles hardened; saw the look on Ike's friendly face when he walked into Billy's sporting an eighteen-year-old's abs. Driving away, he smiled at his own daydreams.

Walter had seen her paintings in books, and the Georgia O'Keeffe museum was within easy walking distance. After a bite at the Inn he went for a look. Distractions often helped when hunches were on the bubble, and plans needed thought. Someone had told him her work was symbolic; the flowers weren't just flowers. He spent an hour among them, looking for the symbols. Someone also said a cigar is just a cigar. Walter could never remember who. He'd always wondered why that needed saying. A flower, he now suspected, might also be just a flower.

Now that he had a reliable fix on Leonard, Walter considered how to play it. He had options. He'd go back and wait until Leonard showed up. Tonight or tomorrow morning. Did it really make a difference? He felt sure it did not. He'd already reconnoitered, gotten a feel for the property, found places where he'd park, sufficiently off the road to avoid detection, but close enough to see Leonard coming. "Or maybe," he thought, "what is the downside of getting an all-day, all-night flat, blocking the road, striking up a friendly chat with whomever happened by?" How did he know that Leonard would use the road? He'd left his truck behind, so it was likely. Was likely good enough? If not, Walter could go back to the cabin and talk to Michael again. He might learn more. That might be the easiest way. Downside of that? Still not entirely clear. In any case, the situation looked good, almost as good as he'd hoped. A couple of words with Leonard, a phone call back to Tom. Job done. Walter gone. Everyone happy. Or not. The only thing off was the feeling he couldn't completely shake, that very small grain of sand. The same feeling he had on the dock on St. John after reading Isobel's story.

Despite bitter cold, the sheltered Plaza sidewalks were crowded with blankets covered by silver and turquoise bracelets, necklaces, rings. Heavy Indian women sat together fighting the cold with coffee or something stronger. Walter wanted a gift for Isobel. The old woman in front of him brewed tea on a hot plate, an outlet set in the wall behind her. She had brilliant black eyes and a smooth, cheerful manner. She did not move easily, though; he figured she might have arthritis. She gave him a bluish stone attached to a silver chain. Walter held the stone in his fingers and raised it to the sunlight. As he moved it, the pendant seemed to change color and even shift its shape.

"It's a stone for love," the woman said, leaning slightly over her tea.

"Very nice," Walter said.

She winked suggestively. "It changes in your hand. It changes because of the sun and the warmth of your hand. It's a good romantic gift for the lady. She will like it very much. Two hundred forty dollars."

"I'll take it," he said, thinking maybe tomorrow he'd drive back to Leonard's place one more time.

FORTY-FOUR

Clarksville

He rejected seeing the slow-witted handyman Michael DelGrazo a second time, and, in the clear light of a New Mexico morning, realized that waiting for Leonard's return was useless. Instead, he decided to go where he knew Carter Lawrence had been, and where, he was almost positive, Leonard Martin had been too. Somewhere they might have been seen by somebody. Walter flew to Atlanta again, this time changing planes and continuing on to Nashville. From Nashville, the drive to Clarksville, Tennessee would be about an hour. Before he left St. John, he checked some of the credit card records for Nicholas Stevenson and Harvey Daniels. He knew they were the ones Carter had met in Tennessee—it had to be them—but he wanted to be certain. Preparation was always the key element in solving a puzzle. There were times when Walter had to act quickly without it, but this was not one of them. "Two plus two is always four," he told himself. No matter the certainty of the math, he knew it was always best to check your work. He set about that task. He knew exactly what he was looking for, and it took little time to find it. Both men had flown to Nashville on the same day Carter Lawrence drove to Clarksville. In Nashville, Nick Stevenson rented a car that he returned the next day with 117 miles on it. On the map, Clarksville was about fifty-five miles from Nashville. He found no hotel charges and he knew why. He smiled at their amateurism. They had paid cash for their rooms, thinking they would go unidentified. It might have worked if they hadn't rented the car. The airline tickets were fine, absolutely normal. "After all," Walter thought, "two lawyers from Atlanta traveling to Nashville for the day—happens all the time." The car gave them away. It is possible to rent a car for cash, but it's not easy. It's also possible to use your credit card to actually get the car and then pay cash when you return it. Thus, no record. But, of course, Walter knew you'd have to be experienced in the ways of such secrecy to understand things like that. If people realized how simple and quick it is to read the story of anyone's life via their credit card activity, they'd pay cash for everything.

The Pakistani gentleman who registered Walter at the Holiday Inn in Clarksville told him the restaurant was open for dinner until ten o'clock. He'd been flying since early morning, and the drive from Nashville was so dull he almost fell asleep at the wheel. A nap was what he needed. He awoke around seven, washed his face, changed his shirt, and strolled toward the restaurant. The dining room was half filled. Syrupy recorded music, heavy on the strings, played too loudly. Walter found a table next to the window as far from the smokers as he could. A young Korean girl brought him a menu. For a moment Walter wondered how an Indian or Pakistani ends up a hotel clerk in a place like this, and how a Korean woman gets to be a waitress in a Holiday Inn in rural Tennessee. Then he remembered that Clarksville was an Army town. Fort Campbell, Kentucky was just up the road. In his sleepiness he must have missed the billboards. There are probably wives around here from every place on earth graced with the presence of U.S. troops in the last half century. He assumed this girl was married to a soldier in the 101st. When she brought him his Diet Coke, he asked, "Do you always work the dinner shift?" The Korean girl didn't know what to make of this question. Walter saw her reticence and added quickly, "Have you seen this man?" He showed her a photo of Carter Lawrence.

"No," the girl said.

"You've never seen him before?"

"No. I am just filling in tonight. I don't usually work this late."

"Oh, I see," Walter said. "Thank you. Is there anyone else here who does who might have seen him?"

"I don't know. You can ask someone else. Maybe Melissa. I can ask her to come over."

"Please do. Thanks." Walter ordered a chef salad and some french fries. Maybe a gut as hard as a rock wasn't completely out of the question. When his waitress had taken the order, she walked over to where another waitress stood, killing time, hoping for a larger crowd later in the evening. Walter saw the Korean woman point to him as she said something to the other woman, who then looked in his direction too. Then the other waitress, a chunky, middle-aged white woman, walked over to his table. The little plastic pin above her right breast read "Debra Melissa."

"Thanks, Melissa. Thanks for coming over."

"You looking for somebody?" she asked, keeping her distance.

"No. Not exactly. But I am looking for someone who might have seen this man." Walter showed her the photograph of Carter Lawrence.

"You a cop?" she asked, then answered her own question. "You're no cop."

Her eyes gave her away, and Walter saw it. Of course he saw it. He'd seen that same expression many times before in many places.

She recognized the picture. "Of course I'm not a cop," he said. "You've seen this man, haven't you? You served him, right?" She said nothing. It appeared she was mulling it over, trying to decide if she ought to reveal anything to this stranger. "Where the hell is he from?" he imagined her asking herself. He was exactly correct. She was thinking, "Nobody comes in here with a tan like that just before Christmas." She remained silent.

"Look," said Walter, taking a hundred dollar bill and laying it down on the table, putting its edge just under his Diet Coke. "I just want to know if you saw him last month sometime." Melissa looked at the hundred; a sight she saw not often enough to please her. She looked again at the photo. It was the skinny one, the one with the long wrists and geeky neck, the young one who sat next to the cowboy.

"What if I have?"

"I take that as a 'yes.' The hundred is yours, if I'm right."

As she reached to take the money off the table, Walter's hand fell on top of it. "And did he have dinner with this man?" He showed her a photo of Leonard Martin, the one printed on the front page of the *New York Times.* The woman was startled. She hesitated momentarily, then said, "I've never seen him before." She put her finger on the picture of Leonard Martin.

"You're sure?" Walter said.

"Yeah, I'm sure. The younger one, the skinny one, was here. He was here." Poor Melissa was worried she wouldn't get the money.

"He had dinner with someone, didn't he?"

"Yes, he did, but not this one." Again she pointed to Leonard. "He and three other men. They ate right over there. Stayed until after we closed. I remember them. They had a lot of papers and things. Talked a lot, ate a little. This one," she tapped Carter's photo with her index finger, "but not this one."

"What about these two? Walter laid pictures of Nicholas Stevenson and Harvey Daniels on the table. All four photos were lined up in a row, facing Melissa. Walter removed his hand from the hundred and motioned for her to take it. She did. She recognized the silver-haired gentleman who'd left her the extra tip and the nervous one who sat next to him.

"Both of them. They were here with the first one."

"The three of them? Did you get any names?"

"No," she said. "There was another man who came later."

"The younger one paid, right?"

"How'd you know that?"

"Just a guess."

"You know," she said, "I'll never forget when they left. Hugged each other like there was no tomorrow. It was weird, like a movie."

"I know," Walter said. "I'm sure they did. Thank you, Melissa. You've been very helpful."

"Why are you looking for these guys?"

"Just routine. Our company checks the expense accounts of people who travel for us on a regular basis. I'm just confirming they were here, that's all."

"Bullshit," she thought. No one checks expense accounts like this, not with hundred dollar bills and photographs. And for damn sure not with any guy as tan as this one.

"One more thing," he said. "Who was the fourth man? What can you tell me about him?"

Melissa said, "You mean the cowboy?"

"Cowboy? What did he look like?"

"Well, he wasn't a real cowboy, you know. It's just he didn't wear a suit like the others, and he had on a hat, a floppy kind of cowboy hat, you know? Tall, thin, good-looking man. Short hair, sort of salt-and-pepper beard. Good-looking man. Forties, I'd say. That's all, but he sure wasn't this guy." This time she tapped the photo from the *New York Times* again. "He wasn't here."

A chill gripped Walter's gut and moved like electric current outward. It made him lightheaded, nauseated. *Respect the obvious.* He hadn't looked, hadn't seen, and now it was too late. The missing piece crashed into place and a second wave of nausea rose. He should have known all along. Instead he'd been blind as a bat. The Indian woman's pendant had shown him the mysteries of altered shapes and he missed it. Was he was losing it? Had he lost it already? His eyesight wasn't what it had been, nor was the hair on his head. And whatever Isobel told him, neither were his hydraulics. Henry Broomfield's punchline roared, an angry, reproachful, soundless voice, an unforgiving scold. *They all got sisters.*

FORTY-FIVE

New Mexico

LEONARD WAS GONE WITHIN an hour. He'd practiced playing the slow-witted Michael, planned on using it in case anyone made a wrong turn and stumbled onto his property. No one had until now. The business about Mr. Marteenez had been a spur-of-the-moment thing. It worked pretty well, he thought. Walter Sherman had been an unnerving surprise. Sure, Leonard heard the car approaching long before it reached the cabin, but he never thought someone would actually find him there; someone whose intention it was to seek him out. That frightened him. How could he have come to this place? And who are these people from New York? What was he talking about? Had this man been sent by Nathan Stein? And if so, how in the world did he know where to find him? Leonard knew he didn't have the luxury of contemplating these questions. He had to hurry.

He knew this man calling himself Walter Sherman was trouble when he asked to use the bathroom. It was obvious he wanted to look inside the cabin. Leonard didn't like it, but considering the circumstances he had little choice in the matter. How could he refuse? He didn't fear exposure. Clearly he was convincingly unrecognizable. The weapons and ammunition were all locked away securely. That was an arrangement Leonard had come up with at the very beginning. He was going to be away for long stretches of time: Boston, Houston, Tennessee, Nevada, and who knows where else. He couldn't risk someone finding his equipment, so he devised a storage compartment in his bedroom. To the naked eye it appeared as a closet, but behind the plain closet door was another locked door, this one made of steel protecting a safelike box four feet square and eight feet high. Inside were racks of rifles, shelves of special accessories, sights, stocks, cleaning materials, and boxes of ammunition. Walter Sherman could look around all he liked and never find a sign they were there. And Leonard was sure that was exactly why Sherman asked to use the facilities.

As soon as the intruder left, as soon as the sound of his car faded to silence, Leonard began packing. There wasn't much to it. He threw a few clothes into a bag, tossed in his toothbrush and other toiletries, grabbed three jackets hanging from hooks in the back room, and loaded it all in the SUV. It took about forty-five minutes to move the rifles and other stuff from the secure closet to a lock box in the SUV. When it didn't all fit, he decided to leave some of the ammunition behind. It was a risk traveling with weapons, but what choice did he have now? "Just make sure," he told himself, "do not get stopped by a cop on the highway."

Finally, he tucked a metal toolbox behind the driver's seat on the floor. It was filled with hundred dollar bills neatly wrapped in packs of ten thousand dollars each. Then he was gone. He would never return. He did not look back. There was no nostalgia. Leaving was not sad. Nothing pulled at his heartstrings. In the last two and a half years Leonard Martin had learned not to become attached to anything.

He'd shut himself off from feelings like that. He wouldn't miss the sunsets or the crisp, chilly mornings, the smell of a fire crackling in the fireplace, the sounds of silence in the high desert. He wouldn't miss them because he wouldn't let himself. He came to New Mexico with a single goal—learn to kill. Having done that—and now being discovered—it was time to move on. He drove south on route 39, past Ute Lake and Logan, and picked up I-40 at San Jon. He was in Texas by the time Walter Sherman was considering his options.

FORTY-SIX

New York

JUST AFTER SEVEN, ISOBEL met Walter in the lobby of the Hilton on Sixth Avenue. Dressed for winter, she wore a wide-brimmed woolen hat pulled down to cover her ears and forehead, and a heavy scarf on top of the coat with the fake fur trimmings. She passed unrecognized. "Celebrity," she thought, although her encounter with it was somewhat marginal and thus far short-lived, "was a crock of shit."

"Why here?" she asked, after greeting him with a kiss on the cheek. It was a friendly kiss and he felt disappointed. He hoped for more and hoped it didn't show.

"Dentists," Walter answered. "There's a convention of dentists here. The biggest one they have anywhere all year. Dentists love Christmas, and they love New York." Isobel laughed and dropped her coat next to her on the couch. "Go ahead," Walter said, "look around you. Every one of these guys pulls teeth."

"What about the women? What do they do?"

"Hookers," said Walter after only a slight pause.

"All of them? It appears, perhaps, that some of your American dentists prefer hookers who are, shall we say, older and a twinge on the heavy side."

"Wives," Walter said. "There's a few of them too."

"So, we're here to see the dentist?"

"No, we're here because the dentists do not want to see us—you, in particular. I don't need to be ducking photographers, but you do. By the way, how did a photographer get that picture of you and whathis-name in Tibet?" Isobel laughed, and so did Walter.

"It's a hoot alright, Walter," she said, "but honestly, I think it's a tub of crap. Hard to imagine any person, no matter how well known, who can't leave the makeup home, dress as casually as everyone does these days, and just walk about. I do it quite well, thank you."

Walter said, "So, no cloak and dagger stuff for you? I'm overdoing it, you think?"

"Absolutely," she smiled.

"We don't need the dentists? Or anyone to cover our movements?"

"We don't need no stinkin' dentists," she said.

Now he too was smiling. Isobel leaned over and kissed him on the cheek. This was more than a friendly kiss, and it thrilled him.

"No one knows who I am," she said, using her father's accent again. "I go anywhere and everywhere, just like the common folk."

"Well, in that case," Walter said, "let's go get a good steak. I'm starving and don't mind spending forty-five bucks for a piece of meat." They left the Hilton and cabbed the short distance to Ben Benson's, Walter's favorite New York steakhouse.

When their salads arrived, Walter said, "I saw him, talked to him, used his bathroom." Isobel was speechless. She knew he meant Leonard. A forkful of salad never made it to her mouth. Walter waited for something, but Isobel said nothing. Her eyes registered amazement.

"I found him in New Mexico. Way out in the middle of nowhere."

"How?" she asked. And he told her everything: the guns, North Dakota, and Raleigh; the trip to New Mexico, the Pac-Mail store in Las Vegas, and the lonely cabin north of Albert. He told her how a tall, rock-hard, bearded man with some marked limitations named Michael DelGrazo said he worked for a Leonard Marteenez, not a Leonard Martin. He described the inside of the cabin. He told her how he decided to follow up the lead in Tennessee, how credit-card receipts told him Carter Lawrence had gone there to meet Nicholas Stevenson, Harvey Daniels, and a third man. He told her about Debra Melissa Wallis and the man she called the cowboy.

"My God," said Isobel. "Michael DelGrazo is the cowboy."

"No. Not quite. Michael DelGrazo was a man who lost his wife and children in an apartment fire in Detroit in 1962." Isobel looked at him bewildered and confused.

"The apartment house was owned by a man named Robert Bass. It seemed Bass had paid off the fire department inspector, a man named Willard Cox, who, in turn, gave the building a clean bill of health. The place was, of course, a fire hazard, and it soon burned to the ground, taking DelGrazo's family with it. When DelGrazo learned all this from a newspaper investigative exposé, he hunted down both Bass and Cox and shot them dead. Michael DelGrazo died in prison in 1984, prostate cancer."

"Wow," Isobel said. "Then this Michael DelGrazo is . . . ?" Her question hung in the air. She knew the answer already, but Walter obliged.

"Leonard Martin."

"Oh, my God. B-but you said he looked like—"

"A man can change a lot of things in two years. Leonard did. I missed it, completely missed it."

"The blindfold," she said, remembering Kermit and her interview, in the dark, with Leonard. "That's why the blindfold." She felt bad saying it, but she said it nonetheless.

Walter described his misadventure in New Mexico again, this time in fine detail. Isobel strained to hear every word in the noisy restaurant. She asked, and he said he didn't think there was much chance Leonard would call. Their steaks arrived, although they hadn't touched the salads yet. The waiter insisted he would bring them new steaks, freshly cooked, whenever they were ready for them. Walter insisted the waiter leave the entrees. They would eat everything at the same time. The man was reluctant, but, as any good waiter would, he protested but consented. They ate everything he put in front of them.

"Don't be disappointed," Isobel said. "Don't be hard on yourself."

"I'm not," Walter replied in his trademark easy manner. "I know where he's been, where he's gone, what he's done. And I believe there's no rush. He's not killing anybody, is he?"

"I wasn't aware he had a schedule."

"There was a pattern to the intervals. Hopman, MacNeal, Ochs, and Grath. Then he stopped and what did he do?" Walter took a sip of his wine. He looked for a response. Finally, Isobel said, "I don't know. Nothing."

"Exactly. Nothing. Not yet anyway."

"That means something?"

"Yes. I think it does."

"What?"

"Now I'm the one who doesn't know." He smiled at her and she smiled back for lack of something better and smarter to do.

"You'll find him again?" she asked.

"I think he'll find you again before I find him. I have a feeling he's got something in mind. Whatever it is, he'll need you to tell it." Isobel did not reply. After a moment of silence, Walter said, "I saw you with Ed Bradley." She nodded. "You like him, don't you? Sympathize with him, right?"

"Bradley?"

"Leonard. You're inclined to think he's righteous. Am I wrong?"

"How would you feel?" she asked. "What would you do?"

"No, no," Walter said shaking his head, holding up his hands. "Don't ask me how I feel. Tell me how you feel."

"I do," she said. "It's not academic to Leonard Martin, not just numbers. They took everything from him. Can you imagine losing everything? It frightens me just to think about it—not only his family—everything. There's a curse in being a survivor. Yes, I sympathize with him. I can't help it."

"And the people he's killed? And those he means to kill? All of them?"

"I can't say," she said. "I can't say. I said I sympathize with him. That's not the same as saying I approve of what he's doing."

"It isn't?" That question remained unanswered.

Over coffee and a glass of Spanish port, Isobel asked, "Walter, why are we still working together? You were correct. I could never have identified Leonard Martin on my own. You did, and you did it before he contacted me. However, now we've both met him, talked to him. I know who he is and my story is no longer questioned by anyone. You know who he is. You say finding him again is no trouble. Why are we still in this together, Walter? What's left for us to do?"

"I represent the people who remain on his list—"

"Exactly my point. What's in it for you or your clients? Why do you need me? And what's in it for me?"

"And," Walter continued, "that puts me in a position to arrange a negotiated settlement, an end to the killing. When he reaches out to you, I can put him in touch with Stein and Stein's money."

Isobel looked at Walter out of the corner of her eye, her mouth a frown, skepticism written all over her face. She had been impressed with Walter's self-assurance and intelligence from the first time they met. She found his demeanor enchanting and not a little bit erotic. Now she began to question his approach and her own judgment.

"Stein's money," she said. "What in the world makes you think Leonard Martin wants any of it? And why are you still working for them after learning what they're all about?"

"I got paid," Walter said. Isobel shrugged her shoulders, recalling a film where Humphrey Bogart had a speech about some silly obligation he felt to his partner.

"That's p-p-plain ridiculous."

"I took the job. I got paid and I have an obligation to finish the job. That's not ridiculous. That's honorable. As for Leonard, don't discount him so easily. Remember when I asked you to think of a dollar amount and then double it or triple it? You'd be surprised how much money might be involved here. It could be an offer Leonard Martin can't refuse."

"No," Isobel said. "Not for any amount. Not this man. Not a man who uses the name of Michael DelGrazo. It's love, Walter. Don't you see that? There's no price on love. It's too important." Walter stirred his second cup of coffee, wondering what Ike would say to that.

"You're right. I don't need you to find Leonard," he said. "Now that I know what I know, a second time is only a matter of where and when. That's what I do, you know. I find people no one else can." He was looking down into his coffee or at his napkin or checking out the brand name carved into the blade of his steak knife. He avoided Isobel's eyes. He felt the rush of blood to his cheeks. He hadn't experienced this kind of helplessness since high school. Isobel could see he was troubled. She leaned across the table and took his hands in hers. She knew there must be more than the lame excuse he offered. "What is it?" she said. "It's something, but what?"

"I want to be with you," he said, terribly afraid he sounded like a sixteen year old. "It has nothing to do with Leonard. You're right. Find him or not. I really don't care. It's you, Isobel. I think about you all the time. I don't sleep. Tonight's the first time I've eaten a real meal since you left St. John. I want you."

Walter's needy desire, his awkward hesitation, his tender honesty—it all did the trick for Isobel. Her faucets ran wide open and red hot.

"You want to go to my place?" she said. The invitation and the promise it held thrilled Walter. Whatever disappointment he felt at her casual greeting at the Hilton was gone now.

"Would you like to see what a snow-covered Central Park looks like from high up?"

"Sure," she said. " The Mayflower's close enough. Shall we walk?"

Bundled up to stay warm on the windy, cold night, they walked arm-in-arm toward Columbus Circle and the Mayflower Hotel. It was close to eleven o'clock, but this was New York, the city that never sleeps, where the streets were always crowded. Kids, couples in their twenties (kids to Walter, anyway), ran past them toward the park, tossing snowballs at each other. Many stores and all the bars and restaurants were still open. "In New York the magic never ends," Walter thought. Tonight he was alive too. He pictured Isobel unbuttoning her blouse, slipping it off her back, her skirt dropping to the floor of his bedroom a few blocks away. His whole body tingled in anticipation. That was when the man standing by the window of an electronics store caught Walter's attention. Something inside him stirred, and it had nothing to do with the thought of Isobel's naked body against his own. Walter was sure he'd seen the same man near the Hilton. They passed the store and Walter glanced quickly behind him. He knew the man could easily see their reflection in the store window. Walter and Isobel continued walking. The man followed them.

At the corner of 60th Street, Walter put his hand on Isobel's shoulder. She looked at him, and the look on his face frightened her. They stopped right in front of the Trump Hotel. The man who had been behind them kept walking, past them. He stopped at the next corner. And he waited. Walter watched the traffic light at 61st Street go from red to green, and then to red again and once more to green. *Walk . . . don't walk . . . walk.* The man did not cross the street.

"Don't say anything," Walter said. "We go to this corner and turn left. Trust me." They resumed walking, and at the corner of 61st Street, where the man who followed them was still standing, they turned west, heading toward Broadway. That block is a dark and empty one. The side of the Trump Hotel has no customer entrance. The other side of the street is the southern face of the Mayflower. It also has no public entrance. There is only a solitary apartment building with its awning entrance well down the street on the other side. Halfway down the block, on their side, there was a service entrance to the Trump Hotel. It was an unlit, windowless metal door set back slightly from the sidewalk. Walter could make out the icy walkway in front of the doorway. He and Isobel were a few feet past that door, firmly on a patch of dry cement, when Walter turned.

"Got a match?" he said to the man, who now stood squarely on the icy spot. He was clearly startled by Walter's unexpected action. For just an instant the man seemed paralyzed. Then his feet moved, but all he could manage was an uncertain slip.

Walter lunged and grabbed him. He spun him around and slammed him face-first against the metal service door. He ripped the man's coat off from behind and seemed to jam his hand into the man's ass.

"You know what you're feeling?" Walter demanded. The man shook his head nervously.

"No," he said, the word barely escaping his mouth.

"Who are you?" demanded Walter. The man did not respond. "What you're feeling is the barrel of a small twenty-two caliber pistol. If you don't answer my questions, quickly and truthfully, I'm going to shoot you. Do you know what that means?" This time Walter didn't wait for an answer. "It means a twenty-two magnum cartridge will literally cut you a new asshole. It probably won't kill you. But the damage it does to your colon and your intestines will take years to fix. Maybe decades. You'll shit in a bag until you're an old man, and every time you so much as pass gas you'll think of me and regret whatever impulse you're feeling now to withhold information. Have I made myself clear?" Walter reached into the man's coat pocket and removed a pistol. He ran his hand across the man's chest and took a second gun from his shoulder holster. "You hear me, asshole!"

"Yes," the man said. Isobel could taste the fear in his voice. She too was imagining the lifetime of pain and discomfort that awaited the wrong decision.

"Who are you?" Walter asked. He pushed harder into the man's rectum.

"Jack Allen," the man said.

"And?" said Walter, pushing even harder.

"I'm a New York City police detective."

Isobel was shocked, certain they had stumbled into something that meant trouble for both of them. Holding a gun to the asshole of an NYPD detective. . . .

"Name," Walter commanded. This time he took the man's wallet and flipped it open. The badge was there and the ID card. "You want me to start counting? Because when I get to one your ass is on fire."

"Allen. Jack Allen. I already told you." There was panic in the man's voice. Isobel could feel how desperate he was to save himself.

"You're not on the job, goddamn it! Your ID is old, shitface. You're retired. Name who you work for, fuckhead!" said Walter.

"I'm an NYPD detective," said the man claiming to be Jack Allen.

"Fuck you, detective!" Walter growled in his ear. "I don't hear another name I shoot."

"No!" the man cried out. "Don't shoot me! I work for a man named Robert Wilkes. I really do. Wilkes hired me."

"To do what? Follow me?"

"No, no. I don't have any idea who you are, man. I'm following her."

A chill ran through Isobel's body, not unlike what she felt talking to Leonard Martin. She remembered. Leonard said she was being watched.

"Her?" Walter screamed. "Why? Hurry up now, Jack."

"Wilkes thought she would lead me to Leonard Martin."

"You fucking sonofabitch!" Isobel kicked him just below his knee. Allen stumbled, but Walter held him up, pushing the pistol as deep into his asshole as he could. He felt the man's pants tear.

"Then what?" Walter asked in voice more at ease than anything he'd said before. "Then what, Jack?"

"Nothing. Just go back and tell Wilkes where he's at."

"You won't hear the sound of this gun, you know that? When I pull the trigger you'll feel it like a hot poker ramming up your ass into your gut." The man, Jack Allen or whatever his name was, groaned and slumped to the ground. Urine was flowing on the sidewalk, steaming in the cold winter air as it inched its way to the curb. Walter had not shot him.

"You're out of business, Jack. Tell that to Wilkes and whoever he works for. I ever see you again, you're a dead man, got it?" Jack Allen didn't say anything. He was pissing and sobbing at the same time. Walter threw the wallet down on the street but kept the badge, the ID, and the guns.

"Come on," he said to Isobel. "Let's go."

"Sure," she said, but Isobel Gitlin wasn't sure of anything anymore.

FORTY-SEVEN

New York

THE SMELL OF FRESH coffee woke Isobel. The bedroom drapes were open and a brilliant morning flooded in through the glass. The city that never sleeps at least naps, and now its nap was over. It was wide awake once more. Horns blared. Traffic inched forward on the streets below. Darting through the bare limbs of trees in snowy Central Park, an occasional jogger could be seen. The sun was bright in a cloudless sky, although the air looked cold to her. Steam heat whistled from the pipes in Walter's suite. He always asked for accommodations on the side of the hotel that had not been renovated. He told her that the first time, when she met him in the restaurant. He liked his hotels old. He preferred steam heat over hot air. She heard him on the phone in the living room where the coffee awaited, but she was unable to make out what he was saying. Isobel stretched and yawned. The sex had been fantastic, and the pendant he'd put around her neck when they were both naked was beautiful. Intrigue and danger, mixed with the sweat of their bodies, had driven them to furious heights. "Wartime sex must really be something," Isobel thought. Violence, she already knew, went with sex like brandy with coffee. It made the moment more intense and the aftermath sweeter. She bent down and picked up the pillow on Walter's side of the bed. Holding it close against her face, she inhaled, smiled, and tossed it back on the sheets. Then she headed for the shower.

"Yes," said Tom Maloney, answering his cell phone on the first ring. His voice was cold with a touch of anger poorly hidden. Walter had no sympathy for the difficulties of Tom Maloney's existence. The *New York Times* was on Maloney's ass. They continued to talk about him on cable TV, and the liberal press wrote piece after piece, coming this close to saying that he and his gang of co-conspirators deserved to be shot. Leonard Martin, already regarded as America's most effective and efficient multiple killer since *The Terminator*, wanted him dead. Maloney's charmed life had turned to pure shit, but Walter couldn't care less. He was pissed about a retired NYPD cop and Robert Wilkes, whoever he was. There was no "*hello*" in his manner or his voice.

"Wilkes," said Walter. "Robert Wilkes."

"Sherman? Is that you?"

"Tell me about Wilkes, Tom."

"I don't know what you're talking—"

"If I hang up, Tom, you'll never hear from me again." There was only silence on the other end of the line. "Tell me about Wilkes."

"I don't understand," Maloney said. "How do you know about Wilkes? Does Wilkes know about you?" He thought, "What have I gotten myself into." Could it be that people like Walter Sherman and the FBI Special Agent Wilkes knew each other, traveled in the same circles like business associates or something? Could there be a world out there he knew nothing of? One that posed a new danger to him? Maloney hadn't said a word to Wilkes about Walter Sherman, and he certainly didn't tell Walter about hiring Wilkes first. Tom Maloney was, however, quick on his feet. "Nathan made a mistake in judgment, Walter. I didn't think you needed to know, and that was a mistake I made. I see that now and I'm sorry. But I still don't understand—"

"Isobel Gitlin," said Walter. "Just what the hell is that all about?"

"Mother of God!" Maloney thought, "that bitch," and he almost said as much out loud. "She's a reporter with—"

"I know who she is. Why did you sic Wilkes on her?"

"I didn't know—"

"You didn't know? Is that it? You didn't know?"

"I still don't know. What are you talking about?"

Walter shook his head in disgust, in frustration. He heard the shower go on. "Tom?" he said.

"Yes?"

"Detective Jack Allen. Does that name mean anything to you?"

"No."

"Never heard of him?"

"Never." Maloney had regained his composure and sensed that Walter had too. "Who is he?"

Walter told him about the encounter with Jack Allen. He left out the part about shoving his 22 magnum up the detective's ass—and, of course, said nothing about Isobel—but he made it clear he had taken control of the situation with Wilkes's man. Maloney was still in the dark.

"What an asshole," thought Walter. "An amateur, a total fuck-up!"

"You hired Wilkes to kill Leonard, didn't you?" he asked.

"Nathan—"

"Come on, Tom. Don't fuck with me. I have no patience for it. We both know Nathan couldn't hire anybody and get it right. You hired Wilkes."

Maloney's first instinct was to soothe his own hurt feelings. After all, he'd been hired by Nathan Stein, but he was scared. Leonard Martin wanted to kill him, and now Walter Sherman was heading in the same direction. "Yes, I did. I'm sorry I didn't tell you. I am. I am."

"What did you think Wilkes was going to do? How did you expect him to go about his business? Did you give any thought to that at all?"

Maloney said, "No. I hire the best professionals. I pay top dollar. Why should I inquire about details? I don't ask how, just how soon. I hired you, didn't I? As I remember it I gave you a million dollars. Did I ask you how?"

"You stupid shit," Walter said. "Wilkes was going to *kill* the girl!"

"Bullshit! He was going to kill Leonard Martin! You stupid shit!" Tom Maloney yelled at the top of his voice. He was not used to being talked to that way. His reaction showed Walter everything. Walter realized Maloney, for all his money and power, really didn't know how people like Wilkes operate. "It must be so easy to kill people when you don't know how they're going to die," he thought.

"Calm down, Tom," he said. "Let me tell you the facts of life here, fill you in on Wilkes's plan." Walter took Tom Maloney through it step by step. The more he disclosed, the more convinced he was that Maloney had no idea what he had started. When he was finished, Walter said, "I want you to know that if anything bad happens to Isobel Gitlin—anything at all—if she gets mugged, hit by a bus, falls down a flight of stairs, has a heart attack, is struck by lightning—anything at all—I'll hold you responsible, Tom. And if I ever see one of Wilkes's people again I'll make them very mad at you. You'll regret that. You understand what I mean?"

"Look, Walter, I—"

"Just say 'I understand.' I need to hear it, Tom."

Maloney cleared his throat which was very dry now and said, "I understand."

"Good."

"I'll cancel the arrangement with Wilkes as soon as you and I get off the phone. By the way, Walter, how do you know Isobel Gitlin?"

"That doesn't matter," Walter replied. "Now listen to me. You'll like this part. I'm going to tell you about Leonard Martin. I saw him. I talked to him. He's gone now, but I can find him again, easily. I gave him my number. He might even call me."

"You found him! That's great news—just great. When? Where? I knew you could do it. Am I allowed to or supposed to ask you how?"

Walter told Maloney about his trip to the New Mexico wilderness north of Albert. He told him about the empty tract of land Leonard bought, and the small cabin. He didn't mention Michael DelGrazo or Leonard's altered physical appearance. He considered that his own proprietary information. He saw no need to tell Tom about Clarksville. Carter Lawrence, Nick Stevenson, and Harvey Daniels were not part of his contract, just as Isobel Gitlin was not part of Wilkes's deal. When he finished, he asked, "What do you want to do with Leonard Martin? What do you want me to do? I'm just as anxious as you are to get this over, to go home. What's it going to be?"

"Jesus, Walter, this is fantastic. I can't tell you how good this makes me feel. I want you to come over to the Waldorf—that's where I'm pretty much holed up these days. Nathan's here too. We can go over our plans together. How soon can you be here?"

Walter listened. The shower was off. Isobel was only a closed door away. "Noon," he said. Maloney told him to call the penthouse from the house phone in the lobby when he got to the Waldorf.

Then Maloney spoke as if addressing one of his sales managers. "Congratulations. Job well done. We're all proud of you." For a brief moment Walter considered the possibility that Tom had lost his mind.

He opened the door to the bedroom. Isobel was dressed and brushing her hair. She had sprayed the same perfume she wore last night.

The scent excited him. Walter wanted nothing more than to grab her, throw her down on the bed, and make love to her.

"What did you mean if *'something bad'* happened to me?" She continued, brushing her hair while looking at him in the mirror. "I heard you say that. What did you mean? Who were you talking to?"

He had carried a fresh cup of coffee with him, and he put it down on the dresser in front of Isobel. "Thanks," she said. He walked over to the window. A faint draft of cold air from the window frame, which had no doubt gone untouched for thirty or forty years, drifted across his face. It felt good.

"Our friend from the New York Police Department worked for a man hired by Tom Maloney, a man named Robert Wilkes. I can't be certain, but my guess is Wilkes is either FBI or CIA, and, unlike Detective Allen, he's an active duty agent."

"W-what about—"

"No, Isobel. Don't ask me anything. Not yet. When I'm done there will be plenty of time for questions." She nodded, and Walter sat on the edge of the bed. He continued, "Wilkes was brought in to kill Leonard. He couldn't find him, of course. He didn't even know who he was hired to kill until he read about it in the *New York Times.* That's where you come in. Guys like Wilkes assemble a team, and so he got a retired cop, that's Allen, to follow you, hoping Leonard would contact you again and you would lead Allen to Leonard. If such a meeting happened—once you and Leonard were in the same place together—Allen would show up. He'd kill Leonard with one gun and then kill you with the other. He'd place the gun he used to shoot you in Leonard's hand. Wilkes then takes over and there could be many possible scenarios, but any way they do it, the official story ends up with Leonard Martin killing you and someone in law enforcement killing Leonard. "Courageous Reporter Murdered by Madman Killer: Hero Cop Kills Murderer."

Isobel seemed unfazed. "That's why Allen had two guns?" Walter shook his head yes. "You were talking to Maloney, weren't you?" Again Walter shook his head yes. "You told him if *'anything bad'* happened to me you'd kick the shit out of him. Did you tell him you would cut him a new asshole with that little pistol of yours?" Walter shook his head no. A smile spread across his rugged face. "You're a wonderful man, Walter Sherman. My hero." Isobel began unbuttoning her blouse. "I can always take another shower," she said.

FORTY-EIGHT

Northfield

In his *other* life, Leonard hated long-distance driving. If Nina hadn't shared the five-hour trek to Hilton Head, they never would have spent so many weekends there. He recalled those days now, now when things were so different. He had been impatient then. Now he felt safe in his SUV: secure, comfortable, at peace with himself. He enjoyed the hours spent on the interstates, the noise of the tires at high speed, the music on the radio, the truck stops and gas stations along the way. The first trip from Atlanta to New Mexico had not been the drudgery he expected, and the drive two years later to Boston had been downright exhilarating—a feeling Leonard credited to his mission. *Justice, at last.* Even though the unexpected arrival of Walter Sherman made it necessary to leave New Mexico quickly, Leonard was not upset. His mission was not complete and he had work to do elsewhere. On the road again.

He watched the high desert mountains and stony foothills of New Mexico and west Texas fade in his rearview mirror. He drove across the flatlands of Oklahoma into Missouri and Kansas. Traffic got heavier in the urban midsection of the country: Illinois, Indiana, Ohio. Still, the long, straight stretches of interstate did not conjure up the unpleasant memories of those sleepy, endless miles on I-16 from Macon to Savannah. And yet the sadness in his belly never left him. Nina was not there sitting next to him, reading her book, napping, ready whenever he needed to share the load. And he fought all thoughts of Dahlonaga.

The skies turned gray and the snows returned in Pennsylvania and western New York. Finally, Leonard arrived to find the mountains in Vermont thrilling, spectacular, and not at all like the unattractive jagged peaks of the Southwest. The beauty of New England's winter—icicles dangling from the branches of snowy forests, streams flowing rapidly, somehow oblivious to the sub-freezing temperatures, and quaint two-lane roads winding their way through small towns—had him thinking about skiing, although he had never even once tried it. The closest he ever came was playing golf on a trip to Aspen that he and Nina made one summer. Three days after abandoning the cabin north of Albert, Leonard was nearly euphoric as he checked into the Centennial House hotel in Northfield, Massachusetts. He was less than five miles from the Vermont State Line, and no more than twenty minutes from Louise Hollingsworth's new house. Perhaps, he thought, she didn't know—but how could she not? He was a real estate lawyer. Did she think she could buy property and escape his notice?

Dr. Roy's CD laid it out for him. Louise Hollingsworth, at a time of crisis and impending chaos, had a clear appreciation of the gravity of her situation. She had asked Dr. Roy directly about people dying. The others were cold, calculating, unfeeling bastards, but Louise Hollingsworth knew exactly what she was doing. She weighed the toll it would take on others and she made a conscious decision to participate when her protest might have stopped it. And then she stage-managed the coverup, a scheme that continued to this day. The murderers at Stein, Gelb persisted in their claim they were nothing more than ignorant servants in the employ of their corporate masters. Little more than hired help. They had done their due diligence, they said. Under Louise Hollingsworth's direction, assertions were made that experts (including Dr. Ganga Roy—conveniently dead and unable to speak for herself) told them nothing about the possibility of dire consequences. There had been no mention of a newer, different, more vicious strain of E. coli, they said. No talk of anyone dying. Leonard was not fooled. And, insofar as reasonable people might believe that the Gang of Four at Stein, Gelb were without guilt, Louise Hollingsworth was responsible. Her crimes were compounded. She had killed his family, then led the lie. It was all Leonard could do not to start shaking again the way he had during those first months in New Mexico. He drifted off into a troubled sleep on the floor of his hotel room, praying the dreams would not haunt him again, all night. His prayers went unanswered.

In the morning, Leonard found a spot where he could drive his SUV off the two-lane road that wound its way up and around the mountain overlooking Louise Hollingsworth's house. Unless someone noticed the tire tracks in the snow, there was no way anyone would suspect his vehicle was parked behind the trees in the bushes. There were a few pine trees, their branches fluffy white, but none where they might cause him some concern. The area was heavily wooded, but except for the pines, in December there were no leaves on the trees. His sight lines were clean, undisturbed. He sensed a gentle swirling breeze coming from the northeast. No problem. In only minutes he found a place suitable for the folding chair and the Y-shaped, pointed metal stick he brought with him. The chair was something Leonard had come up with on his own. He took an ordinary metal folding chair, one with a cushioned seat, and carefully filed down each of the legs to a sharp, spiked point. By planting it and pushing down on the cross-bars holding the front and back legs to the body of the chair, he could set it firmly into the ground and steady it, stable enough for sitting and shooting. He much preferred that to lying prone. The Y-shaped spear looked like a naked umbrella handle or one of those things rainmakers pretend to use in their act, and he drove it into the ground in front of him and rested the barrel of his rifle on the Y. How many times had he done just that in New Mexico? He'd lost track many months ago. He'd sat in that chair hour upon hour, in the mud, the rain, the snow, the scorching heat of the desert afternoon, and fired what seemed like a million rounds. Now, on a snowy hill in Vermont, he set up his position and watched Louise's house through the powerful scope sitting atop the gleaming barrel of one of the world's most spectacular weapons. His calculations told him the elevation was 247 feet 8 inches above the top stone step leading to her front door, and the distance was 1,380.2 yards from the door itself. Although he could have been much closer, he had no need to be. Leonard was dressed perfectly to withstand the weather. He had a thermos of Earl Grey tea and some hard candy. He settled in for the day. The stock nestled in his shoulder. The scope covered his right eye. The smell of gun oil was in the air. Sooner or later she would walk out that door and he would pull the trigger on his Walther WA2000 and watch her die.

Louise Hollingsworth was new to the area. The house was invisible from the main road. She was not missed. After two days of not calling New York—she had been phoning the Waldorf three or four times a day—Tom Maloney reluctantly called the police. They found her body lying in front of the doorway, still ajar behind her. Her contorted face, a Halloween mask frozen in pain, caused the medical examiner to conclude she took a long time to die.

Maloney and Stein were convinced he was headed for New York. They increased security at the Waldorf. When Tom called him, Wesley

Pitts was actually relieved, although he made sure not to let on. Vermont was a long way from Mississippi. He'd made the right choice going to Mississippi. He felt safe. Had he known Leonard Martin was already in New Orleans, Pitts would have shit in his pants.

FORTY-NINE

New York

Walter's meeting with Maloney had gone badly. After the morning's hijinks with Isobel, he fell asleep. The phone woke him. Isobel was gone, but she left a wake-up call for eleven o'clock. He was cranky when he arrived at the Waldorf. He spotted two men in the lobby, near the elevators, trying very hard to be less obvious than they were. When you're working a hotel lobby you have to be in motion. Walter knew that. How could these guys be so dumb? Move around. Check out the restaurant menu, the gift shop, read a paper, change seats every ten minutes, but always keep your eyes on the elevators. It wasn't brain surgery. These guys looked like they had been planted in cement. Walter wondered how much they were being paid. Too much. The elevator at the penthouse level opened to reveal a grand foyer, elegantly appointed, subtly lit. Six security agents, weapons at the ready, waited for him. Two stood directly in front of the elevator door as it opened. They frisked him immediately. He expected something like this and came unarmed. Two more were stationed a few feet back on either side. The last two guarded the door to the suite. "Not bad," thought Walter. He couldn't see the service elevator, but assumed at least two more men watched it round the clock. No one was going to get through this small army. Certainly not Leonard Martin. Of course, Walter knew Leonard had no intention of coming within a hundred miles of the Waldorf Astoria. One or two men, three if it made you feel better, would have been plenty.

Maloney was fully dressed, the same way he had been on St. John. It was all Walter could do not to smile. Did these guys ever get comfortable? They greeted each other coldly. Walter could not get it out of his head that Tom Maloney had hired someone who meant to kill Isobel Gitlin, and Tom would never forget being called "you stupid shit!" Nathan was here too. Walter knew that much. But the obstreperous little prick never showed himself.

Maloney had some lunch already in the suite. Walter wasn't hungry. He accepted a Diet Coke, but that's as friendly as it got. Maloney lied . . . again. What did Walter expect? He had no heart to argue with the puffy and pink Irish sonofabitch. They just wanted Leonard Martin to know how sorry they were and to demonstrate their contrition with an enormous amount of money. That's what Maloney kept saying. He practically begged Walter to find him again. The meeting was short. Walter felt all Maloney wanted to know was if Walter too might want to kill him. Nathan Stein was probably cowering behind one of the four closed doors leading God knows where. Walter had no idea how big the penthouse suite was, and no inclination to guess. Suitably convinced of his immediate safety, Maloney rose from his seat, signaling Walter that it was time to conclude their little talk.

"Walter," he said. "We know you've encountered some rather unusual expenses. This has taken more of your time than you probably thought it would. We want you to have this." Holding a bulky brown envelope in his fingers, he reached out to Walter. "It's another hundred thousand," said Maloney, as if he were talking about twenty bucks.

Walter considered turning and walking away, leaving Tom Maloney with his hand outstretched. His eyes caught Maloney's, and neither man blinked. Who could walk away from a hundred thousand dollars? *An extra hundred thousand dollars!* "Not me," Walter realized. He took the envelope, stuck it under one arm, and said, "I'll be in touch." The last thing he saw before turning to go was relief in Tom Maloney's face.

The next morning, instead of heading home to St. John, Walter was unexpectedly back at the Waldorf. Maloney had called him at the Mayflower. He was clearly panicked. Walter was already awake, eating his breakfast, contemplating his next move, hoping to take an afternoon flight home.

"Get over here right away," Maloney said. There was no sweetness in his voice, no pretense of fellowship or comradery. Definitely master-to-servant.

"What's going on?"

"Just be here." Maloney paused and Walter thought he heard a sigh. "He got Louise."

Thirty minutes later Walter was in the penthouse again. This time Nathan Stein was there too. Maloney filled him in on the details. The ME's report was not yet available, but the fact that the bullet struck her below the breastbone told Walter she had died a miserable death. Leonard gutted her. He was a better shot than Walter had given him credit for. The Hopman shooting involved such a powerful gun it ripped him in half, but a hit anywhere on his torso would have done that. MacNeal and Ochs were sitting ducks, and he may have passed over Grath's death without enough consideration of the difficulty of that shot. A long-distance shot from a floating boat. Maybe it wasn't a lucky shot. And now, a gut shot from somewhere on a mountainside. Walter worried. Had he misjudged this one too? He remembered what Aat van de Steen told him about the German rifle.

"Where's Pitts?" Walter asked.

"Some place in Mississippi," Tom said. "He won't even tell us exactly where."

The image of Christopher Walken trying to get Dennis Hopper to give up his kid came to mind. Walter scoffed at the idea that Leonard would try, or need to try, to get information from any of his targets. He's researched all of them thoroughly. And of course he caught Louise. *Christ, the guy's a real estate lawyer.* Her stupidity cost her her life. Or maybe it was the stress. Maybe it was a mistake she wouldn't ordinarily have made. Now Walter understood what Tom meant, back on the island, when he asked for some understanding of the stress they were under.

"He'll show there," said Walter, referring to Mississippi, "before he comes here."

"Show where? How the fuck will he know where Pitts is? Christ, we don't even know." Nathan's questions, taking the form of only a minor outburst, came without so much as a *"good morning."*

"How'd you know about my wife—ex-wife—my daughter, my bank account?" Walter waited, but there was no response. "You found out, didn't you? So will Leonard." That hurt. Nathan and Tom prided themselves—a foolish pride to be sure, assumed Walter—on being able to find out things about people, things they felt sure others could not discover. "A problem you guys have, among many, I'm sure," continued Walter, "is you live in a world where you think you know everything. As a result, you mistakenly underestimate your adversary. You think your resources are somehow exclusive. I haven't looked into it at all, but my guess is that Wesley Pitts has family of some sort in Mississippi, and my assumption is Leonard Martin knows exactly who they are and where they live." Silence filled the room. Neither Maloney nor Stein reached for a cell phone to call Wes and warn him. In the same tone of voice he might use to ask a waiter what the specials were, Walter said, "Did you guys kill Dr. Roy?" Nathan Stein leaped from his perch on the couch.

"You arrogant fuck! Who the fuck do you think you are!"

"Nathan, calm down!" Maloney cried. "Easy now." Stein was more given to outburst than real confrontation. Frustrated, he backed away. Walter hadn't moved a muscle.

"No," said Tom. "We did not kill Dr. Roy. She did that to herself." Nathan turned and was about to say something. Tom glared at him, and the frightened little man backed farther away, walking over to the French doors opening onto the patio. It was too cold to go outside, but he stood there looking through the glass, his back to Walter and Tom. He mumbled something, and then he was quiet again.

Walter said, "Why did she do it?"

Maloney turned to Walter with his very best "honest to goodness" look, and said, "We arranged for Dr. Roy's apartment to be burglarized. That's true. Made it look like some kind of hate crime. We were concerned she had made a record of her work for us. We needed to find out. We found nothing. But we were right, weren't we? She had it all on a disc, a CD she kept someplace else. And before she died, she obviously sent it to Leonard Martin. We didn't find anything, so we thought our concerns were unfounded. You know the rest of the story. But we didn't kill her."

"You guys are a piece of work," said Walter. "Good cop; bad cop. Out of control nutcase; Mr. Calm, Cool, Analytical. Lying bastard; fucking saint. This kind of routine, it really works in your business, doesn't it? Crock of shit! You knew what your interests were and you acted accordingly. People died and you knew they would. Dr. Roy told you, but it didn't matter. Leonard Martin's family died and now he's taking out everyone who knew and let it happen. You're all there on Dr. Roy's CD. You're all lies and bullshit. I'm going to send your money back to you. I don't want anything to do with you."

"No you're not," Maloney said. "You are going to find Leonard Martin and you are going to kill him for us. That's your job and you will do it."

Walter rose to leave. The anger he felt turned his face beet red. He didn't care.

"Do it yourself," he said.

Nathan Stein said, "Sit down Sherman." Walter did not stop or look behind. He continued walking toward the door. "Sit down!" As Walter's hand grasped the doorknob, Stein yelled, "Na Trang!" Walter froze.

"What, do you think we're fucking idiots?" It was Stein who was walking now. He went right up to Walter's back and said, "We know. We know." Walter's head was spinning. He had the look of a man about to pass out. The rules of the game were shifting. "Now sit," said Stein.

There is no such place as Na Trang and no one knew that better than Walter. But he remembered it. He'd spent the last thirty years trying to forget, but he remembered it. They dropped him by rope because they were too scared to put the helicopter on the ground. Too many warrant officers had touched down, never to rise again. As he reached for the rope, the crew looked at him in a way that Walter knew meant they never expected to see him again. He was less than an hour from a little village, no more than a collection of shacks and huts on the outskirts of a vast rice field. The map they gave to Walter was the only one this place appeared on. Not even captured VC maps showed anything here. Perhaps two or three hundred people lived and worked in what Headquarters had named Na Trang. They chose the name because it closely resembled the sound of a popular Vietnamese slang for "shithole." Another helicopter had gone down in this area the day before. The crew was killed except the pilot, who suffered injuries to his legs, but had survived and radioed his condition and location back to base. Then communications were lost. Na Trang, that shithole of a village in the middle of fucking nowhere, was the only place a captured American who couldn't walk could be taken. Walter's job was to locate him and bring him back. Nobody told him how to do it, just do it.

Crawling through the wet rice paddies, ducking down under the water whenever he thought he heard someone, Walter approached the tiny village at dusk. He carried his rifle, his bayonet, a 45-caliber sidearm, and eight grenades. His face and hands were covered in charcoal. The nearest he could get to the shacks themselves was about fifty yards beyond a small hut standing between him and the center of the village. As he lay in the wet rice—it sure seemed like weeds to him—he saw four young men, one in uniform, all armed with rifles. They emerged from one shack, stood in the dirt path outside, talking, and then three of them seemed to be getting instructions from the one in uniform, who turned and walked away, leaving them standing there. The three went back into the shack. A few minutes later, Walter saw the uniformed soldier return, accompanied by another soldier also in uniform. They entered the shack together. None of the other three had left. There were at least five men in there now. The American was undoubtedly there too. The sun was almost completely gone, Walter's vision already compromised. He decided to stay put. No one was looking for him, and with nightfall nobody seemed likely to stumble upon him. He didn't smoke and had no fear of being discovered. He'd adjusted to the water. He had brought a Milky Way bar with him and pulled it out of the small pack he wore on his back. He was careful to put the empty wrapper in his pocket.

The scream was so loud Walter thought it was right next to him. It was followed by another, and then a third. The horror increased in each one. The anguish and pain subsided slowly to a moan. He heard choking sobs. Two or three voices, all speaking Vietnamese, were yelling at the same time. More screams, and finally a moan that was endless. He couldn't lie there any longer. Clearly the man he was looking for was inside being brutalized. God only knows what they were doing to him. Walter scrambled out of the rice paddy. The small hut fifty yards away stood between him and any attempt to rescue the downed pilot. Walter looked, but there was no way around it. He would have to sneak past it. There were people living there. He saw light inside and the smoke from a cooking fire rising from the top of the roof. He crawled quietly, passing only a few feet from the hut. Whoever lived there was still inside. The awful moaning ahead never stopped. And then more bloodcurdling screams. Now they too were unending. He had to hurry. He took a big chance. He ran the last twenty yards. The screams and the moaning so close to him were more than he could stand. Walter looked through the loosely attached walls of thatched reeds and large, heavy leaves. He could not believe what he saw. The American, blonde, in his mid-twenties at most, lay on a wooden table. He was naked. Both legs were mangled at the knees, crushed in the crash of his aircraft. A knife was embedded in the table and stuck through his balls. Half his penis had been cut off. It lay to the side, still bleeding. Two of the men were slicing the fingers off at the first joint. The fingernails had already been torn out. Another was doing the same to the American's toes. The uniformed soldier, the last one to have joined the group, was actually skinning the man alive. He made long, thin cuts across the abdomen, and peeled the skin away as if he were cleaning fish. The longer the American remained conscious the more horrific his ordeal and the more gruesome his death. Walter could not imagine what sort of sanity could possibly remain in the man's brain. There was no way he could save the pilot, not even if he killed the five men and carried him away. The captured American would just as certainly bleed to death being carried by Walter as he would at the hands of his captors.

Walter did what he thought to be the most humane thing possible. He tossed a grenade through the open window. The explosion killed the American and the five Vietnamese. It blew the hut to pieces and started a small fire. Walter hit the ground in anticipation of the blast. Now he jumped to his feet and entered the smoking rubble. He grabbed a severed foot, knowing it was the pilot's because the toenails had been pulled out. He found the stub of a hand, a piece of skull, half an ear, each one obviously from a white man. He shoved the body parts into his backpack. Walter heard the village come to life. A fire had begun just behind the now demolished shack. People were running toward it. He removed two more grenades from his belt, pulled the pins, and threw each of them as far as he could into the darkness in opposite directions. Two explosions rattled the night. More fire. More screams. More casualties. Now people were racing in all directions, some ducking behind huts, others fleeing toward the rice fields. Voices everywhere, all yelling in Vietnamese. Walter understood nothing. He needed to deflect their attention to make his escape. He spotted the American's dog tags and reached to pick them up. A piece of skull with blonde hair spared by the flames lay next to them. He put both in his backpack.

Backing away from the village, the same way he had entered it, Walter had to pass by the outlying hut again. This time he could not move unnoticed. The family living there was standing outside, huddled together in fear, watching the chaos from a distance. There was no way for Walter to crawl past them. He decided the safest passage was the most direct. He moved out of the shadows and began walking slowly, but at a steady gait. He was only a few feet away when he could see them and they could see him. A man, a woman, a much older woman, and two small children looked straight at him. At that moment they realized what and who had approached their home. Walter returned their stare. Then, the man—Walter could not be certain how old he was—dashed into the hut. Instantly, he reappeared, holding a rifle he pointed at Walter. And just as quickly Walter shot him. The old woman rushed at Walter, her high-pitched scream barely audible through her tears. She lunged at him, grabbing his shirt and tearing the top button off. Walter shot her and she fell to the ground. The younger woman, undoubtedly the children's mother, drew her children to her. They held tightly to her side and she laid a hand on the head of each. All three were weeping. Walter stood there, looking at them, unsure what to do next. The shots he fired gave him away, and he could hear the villagers behind him. He had to go quickly. They would catch up to him in less than a minute. Which direction should he go? This way? That way? Whichever way he chose, this mother and her children would tell the others. He pushed them into the hut. They disappeared in the darkness, but he heard them. He heard the children crying and the mother trying to calm her babies. It may have been a strange language, but Walter knew she was comforting them, telling them, "It'll be alright. It'll be alright." He tossed the grenade into the hut and began running. The explosion was the most violent thing he had ever heard, much louder than its actual sound. It was the sound of a mother and her children being attacked by millions of tiny pieces of sharp metal, a shower of death. He did not stop and he did not turn around. He navigated the rice paddies and made it into the jungle on the other side. The search for him was relentless. He evaded soldiers and villagers day after day, hiding in empty caves, climbing trees, taking cover in leafy swamps. He ate insects when his meager rations were used up. Three times he stole food, again picking on the most remote hut farthest from its village. The first of these huts was empty and he walked off with enough to eat for almost a week. The other two times he killed the occupants and took their food. Once he sneaked up behind a teenage boy who had lost his right leg at the knee. He cut his throat. The last time he beat an old man and his wife to death with the butt of his rifle. He needed to eat to live. On the twentieth day since being lowered into the high grass on a rope, he spotted a patrol of

American soldiers. He didn't have the slightest idea where he was, but he knew he had made it back safely. The odor from his backpack sickened the soldiers who rescued him, but he refused to take it off until he could deliver its contents to Headquarters. Walter's report described everything that happened to him, down to the smallest detail. It made difficult reading for some. There were others who found it thrilling. All those who read it looked at Walter Sherman with a mixture of awe and fear. And there were the rumors. In time, Walter heard them all. He never believed them, but could not totally dismiss them. He'd been gone three weeks. In Vietnam that's as good as forever. Had officers at Headquarters really placed bets on whether or not he would return? Had members of his own unit done the same? After the first week, had some demanded payment? When the Colonel smiled and promoted him to sergeant, was he counting his money?

FIFTY

New York

MALONEY TRIED TO EASE things. He was an expert at that. In moments of self-doubt he often feared he was an expert at only that. Once more he saw a need to apply his gifts. Walter was still standing in front of the door to the suite. "Na Trang!" had stopped him in his tracks, but he had not yet turned to face the little man who knew more about him than he dreamed possible in his worst nightmare. Tom Maloney walked over to the bar and poured a Diet Coke. He approached Walter with it. "Take it," he said, his voice and demeanor very much the opposite of Stein—Stein the jackal, Stein the screecher, Stein the sonofabitch. "Go ahead," he said, handing the glass to Walter. He put his other hand on Walter's shoulder and guided him to the couch across the room, nearest the doors leading to the patio. He motioned for Walter to sit.

"A man's history," he said, taking a seat himself, "it's never a complete mystery. It's always there waiting to be unearthed, discovered, brought into the light of day by those whose interest is served by disclosure. You should know that as well as anyone. You've been a historian of men for many years, haven't you? Of course you have. And a brilliant one at that. Who else could have identified Leonard Martin and then found him? Leonard Martin, the most hunted man in America—perhaps in the entire world—and who else could have done that? No one, that's who. You are a historian, but you're fallible, Walter. You're just a man. You have your limitations, like all men. We do too. But we have resources to overcome those limitations. Resources you cannot imagine. You think we live in a world where we *think* we know things others don't? No. You're wrong." Maloney's eyes motioned Stein out of the room, or at least out of Walter's sight. "We *know* we live in that world. That world belongs to us." Maloney left Walter sitting there and moved to a chair in the middle of the room. Nathan Stein sat off to the side and behind Walter. He said nothing. Maloney was on a roll, and Nathan recognized it as he had so many times before. Finally, Walter sipped his Diet Coke. That single, simple act worked to return the color to his cheeks and bring his respiration back to normal. He looked up into Tom Maloney's angelic, Catholic face.

Maloney said, "Your past is safe with us. And your future too. You're 'the Locator,' and you've created a life in which you cannot be located. We've been over that, haven't we? We've no wish to disturb that delicate balance, unmask you before official agencies that are unaware of your existence, open your secret sores before your wife—ex-wife—your daughter, your grandsons. No one wants that. When this is over you go back to St. John, back to your past, back to your privacy. And you do so a rich man. Do you follow me here?"

"I do," said Walter. *"Sister, how do I make out the check?"* It pounded in his head.

"Precisely."

"But I don't do that any—"

"Walter, Walter, Walter." Maloney was on his feet, his voice louder than before, his tone harsher. His puffy Irish face reddened. He threw his hands and arms wide apart and said, "Who among us would not change the past if we could? You? Me? Nathan? Wesley, wherever the fuck he is? For damn sure, Hopman, MacNeal, Grath, that fellow Ochs, and now Louise. Leonard Martin? What about him? You think he wouldn't give everything just to change one single day for his wife and family? But he can't. They can't. We can't. You can't. Change the past? The past is the future, for all of us. And that means you too."

The iron gates had swung open against his will. The stone walls were breached. The enemy was pouring in. Nathan Stein—Na Trang—had changed the rules, changed everything, and Walter felt the heavy metal and broken stone weigh him down. "The future," he thought, "what future?" Maloney was right. The past is the future.

"You'll find Leonard Martin before he finds us, and you'll kill him. You won't do it for us. I know that. But you'll do it for Gloria, for your daughter, for your grandchildren, for yourself. Will you think of the mother and her two children crying in the hut? The one-legged boy whose food you stole and whose throat you sliced open? The American whose life you saved by ending it? I hope so. I hope so because the past will lead you to your future. Change the past? No. Embrace the past and recognize that you cannot change the future."

"Wilkes?"

"He's gone. I didn't get a chance to fire him. He bailed out as soon as you made his man. Chickenshit sonsofbitches; they only want the easy work."

Walter breathed deeply. He smelled that hotel smell, a combination of food, smoke, and alcohol mixed with the expensive scent of cleanliness. There was no escaping it, even in the penthouse of the Waldorf Astoria. That might have been sign enough for Maloney, but Walter further obliged with a nod of the head.

"Walter, you have my word that when this is done you'll never hear from us again, ever. We're not blackmailers. Quite the opposite. We're just clients. And, as clients, we want you to go home now. We know you're most comfortable there. Make your plan, then make your move. But move fast." Maloney stepped back, an acknowledgment of Walter's freedom to leave. Walter rose up from the couch as if his whole body ached with despair and regret. Maloney thought he seemed a smaller man than before. "By the way," he added, "we've taken the liberty of depositing some more money into your bank account." Walter just nodded again and started for the door. "Don't you want to know how much?"

The extra hundred grand still fresh in his mind, Walter asked, "How much?"

"Thirty million dollars."

"Thirty million dollars?"

"You never know when you might need some extra cash," Maloney said, glancing at Stein, whose attention seemed elsewhere.

"Thirty million dollars?"

Maloney just laughed as Walter walked out.

FIFTY-ONE

St. John

Watching the old man strike a wooden match he'd taken from his shirt pocket, Billy said to Ike, "Remember, it was you who once said 'some things don't have no argument.' Well, this is one of them things." As Ike lit up, the flame nearly exploded when it made contact with the tobacco. They were talking about the size of a certain boat. It was a boat belonging to a bigtime bushwhacker, an Englishman named Spence. By all accounts it was a large vessel, although *how large* was the question at hand. The boat was named "Lady Kate" after the Englishman's wife Catharine, a magnificently beautiful woman, no youngster herself, yet many years his junior. No matter how big the boat really was, instead of "Lady Kate" Billy called it "The Stugots" because he was sure Louis Spence—if that was his name—was mobbed up.

"I've seen it bigger," Ike said. "Sometimes."

"What the hell does that mean—you've seen it bigger, sometimes?" Billy was leaning over the bar, getting as near to Ike as he could get considering the old man was sitting practically outside. "Sometimes?" he repeated.

"Well, you know, there's times I see it sort of coming straight at me and it has a certain size to it. You understand? Then there's other times I see it going away—from behind—and it looks different."

Billy pulled two bottles of wine from a box on the floor behind the bar and shoved them in the ice cooler, the new one he bought when he finally replaced the small icemaker last week. Then he did the same with two more. "Looks different to you depending on which side you're looking from?" he asked. "That's no big deal. An old man like you can't see good no more." Billy looked toward Walter for confirmation.

Walter said, "That sounds like an argument to me."

"I think Billy's right," said Ike. "It's no argument. Not that I can't see. I see just fine, thank you. That boat though, it's all relative."

"Einstein," said Walter. "Albert Einstein."

"That's him," said Ike, releasing a huge cloud of smoke that caught the breeze coming in from off the water, blowing across the square and into Billy's Bar. The smoke was soon a long, thin, hazy blue line headed directly for the spot where Billy stood. He must have seen it, because, quick as a cat, he moved all the way to where Walter and Isobel sat at the far end near the kitchen. He mumbled something about Ike's cigarette and then looked up into Walter's eyes, searching for understanding.

"Einstein," Walter said. "You know, it's all relative. He invented it, or discovered it, or whatever."

"You know what it means?" Billy asked.

Walter smiled at the bartender. "No," he said. "I sure don't."

Ike said, "Well, it's like this. What you see coming at you is not what you thought it was when it passed you by." He sucked in an almost inhuman amount of smoke—Walter thought for sure the blazing butt would burn his fingers to a crisp—and while the smoke slithered out of both sides of his mouth and his nose at the same time, he added, "Just like life, boys. Just like life." Then he flashed his trademark smile for all to see.

"Pretty close," said Isobel, "pretty close." Being around Ike had already made an impression on her. She found herself too often repeating something in the way he did. Once she realized what she was doing she made a successful effort to stop it, but the old man had his effect. She was here, back on St. John, in Billy's Bar, sitting in the seat next to Walter, drinking a beer and munching on some french fries because the Moose had kicked her out of the paper until after New Year's. It was her own fault. She'd been summoned to his office right after Louise Hollingsworth was killed.

"Isobel, we can't print this," said Mel Gold, waving a sheet of paper in his hand as though her writing was on it, when in fact it wasn't. He couldn't remember the last time he read anything anyone wrote on paper. All he had done for years was read things on the monitor screen of his computer. The days of typing on paper were long gone, and, for many middle-aged newspapermen, sorely missed. "You know we can't do that." The Moose was more than a little pissed. Isobel had flown to Vermont and back by helicopter. She had her details, her interviews with law enforcement, even an exclusive—a preliminary report from the Medical Examiner. Her story began:

> Leonard Martin, who has already killed four men, continues his relentless pursuit of those responsible for the deaths of his wife, daughter, and two grandsons. Yesterday it took him to rural Vermont, where he shot to death Louise Hollingsworth. Martin's family died in the great E. coli poisoning disaster three years ago. The disaster, which paralyzed America's food supply for months thereafter, was perpetrated by a combination of business interests. Their identities became known to Mr. Martin

> later. The personal pain and anguish that gave birth to his violent campaign for a justice he feels has been denied, appears undiminished. Ms. Hollingsworth, a Vice President and Senior Analyst at Stein, Gelb, Hector & Wills Securities Inc., worked with a small, high-level group within her company. Sources say it was Ms. Hollingsworth and others at Stein, Gelb, Hector & Wills, including Nathan Stein, Thomas Maloney, and Wesley Pitts, who were responsible for allowing more than a million pounds of deadly beef to be sold to the public. Mr. Martin has sworn to kill them all. "I can only imagine how he feels," said Warren Kimbrough, Chief of the Vermont State Police.

The Moose shrugged, his mouth drawn tightly into a crooked line, one side pointing up, the other down. His chins seemed to take on a life of their own. He squinted in frustration, and finally, no longer able to control himself, grunted. He looked at his empty chair, knowing that if he sat down it would surely collapse and splinter into pieces from nothing more than the weight of his dismay. Isobel said nothing. She too chose to stand.

"It's '*advocacy.*' We don't do '*advocacy.*' Is this where you're going?" Isobel remained silent. "Are you a reporter—a *New York Times* reporter—or are you looking to go back on *60 Minutes*? Because this," he waved the same empty sheet of paper in the air again, "this is exactly what they like. 'The personal pain and anguish that gave birth to his violent campaign . . .' That kind of language doesn't belong in the *New York Times.*"

"Oh yeah," she said. "Being dead." That's all she needed to say, just two words, for him to understand. Everyone at the *Times* knew those were the first two words from a legendary sentence in the story about the State of New York's posthumous pardon of Lenny Bruce: "Being dead, Mr. Bruce is not expected to reap any immediate benefit from the pardon."

"That got in the *Times*," she said.

"Don't give me bullshit! Lenny Bruce said 'fuck you' a couple of times. He didn't kill five people! Now what the fuck is going on here?"

Isobel said nothing. Mel Gold tried to calm down, but he couldn't. "Come on, damnit! Talk to me, Isobel!"

"They tried to kill me, Mel." She spoke quietly, almost in a whisper.

"What!"

"Stein, Maloney, the gang of criminals at Stein, Gelb—"

"They—"

"They tried to kill me." This time her voice was loud and clear. He heard every word and thought he glimpsed a look of relief in her eyes.

Now the Moose sat down, confident his bulky frame wouldn't break anything. "Hey kiddo, what's going on here? There's something I don't know and I think you need to tell me. Sit down. Talk to me. Tell me."

She did. She told him all of it. Some of it he already knew, some he'd never heard before—from Walter Sherman's first call, to the incident with the former NYPD detective Jack Allen and the warning Walter gave Tom Maloney. She told Gold everything. Almost everything. She left out the sex. And, for reasons she did not fully comprehend, she did not give Gold a description of the "new" Leonard Martin. Whatever she saw of him remained her secret. She said he was "unrecognizable"—although only Walter Sherman had actually seen him—but she didn't describe his appearance even as Walter had related it to her.

"What the hell does that mean, 'unrecognizable'?" Mel Gold knew his voice was the wrong one, his manner delivering the wrong message. He wanted so badly to be more compassionate. He yearned to be a real friend to Isobel in her time of need, but he was a newspaperman. Like a soldier in combat, he newspapered on. "What does he look like?"

"I've never seen him," Isobel answered. "I was blindfolded, remember?"

"Sure, so what did Sherman say?" Isobel was silent. The Moose knew she was having a hard time giving him up. "Here's the deal," he said. "Listen closely, and if you don't understand, ask me, okay?" She nodded. "If you've never seen Leonard Martin you can't describe him. If Walter Sherman says he's seen him and if he can describe him, if he says Martin has changed or altered his appearance in any way, we have no way of corroborating Sherman's story, do we? We have only your word that someone, a third party—in this case Walter Sherman—told you something, right?" Again, Isobel nodded. "But we do have Sherman's description. Can we use it? Can the *New York Times* publish a story about a physical description of Leonard Martin that differs from the public record? Can we do that based solely on what you say somebody else said?" He paused for a long moment. Isobel said nothing and she did not nod her head. She waited. "No," he said. "We can't. If we don't have a first-hand sighting or a cooperative source, which I gather Walter Sherman is not, plus a second witness, we will not print a description for which we have no backup. Am I clear? Do you understand?"

"Yes."

"Good. Now go back and write it. Give me every little detail Sherman gave you about Leonard Martin's appearance. Do it on paper or on your own computer—not here. I don't want it showing up anywhere on anyone's hard disk or mainframe or wherever in hell all this shit gets stored. Print it out and give it to me. I'll keep it at home. You and I will be the only ones who know, but I must know. There has to be a record. Believe me, the time will come when there has to be a record. And you and I have to know what we're looking at when we see it."

"You won't share it with anyone? And we won't print it?"

"Absolutely correct. I know you speak French and some other languages, even some I've never heard of, but you speak English too. You heard me. You do understand me, right?"

Isobel smiled at the big man. "Eai, I, Han jee, Io," she said—yes, in Kiribati, Rotuman, Hindi, and the standard Fijian she spoke as a child.

Mel Gold grinned from ear to ear, then told her to get out of town until after New Year's. He'd get someone else to finish writing the Louise Hollingsworth story. She would get her byline with whoever wrote the final draft.

"Now get out of here. You're on the beach for a week or so."

"D-d-dog days of summer, eh, Mel?"

"What the hell are you talking about?" he said. "It's December. It's fucking Christmas, for Christ's sake."

Isobel gave him a kiss on the cheek, called Walter, and headed for the airport.

"Ike is close," said Isobel. "Einstein published two theories of relativity. The first when he was only twenty-three years old. Can you believe that? He called it the 'special theory of relativity,' and ten years later he published a second one he called the 'general theory of relativity.' Relativity takes into account different points of view—literally, like Ike pointed out—and says that what you think is real could be seen in a different way. Einstein was all about questioning the interchangeability of absolute time. And this fits because his theory holds that the idea that every object has a form and a mass that are constant is false. He also deals with heavy mass objects, saying they actually curve with the universe, which explains gravity, although I don't think that has much to do with the size of this boat."

"Damn," Ike said. Billy and Walter had nothing to add. They were indeed speechless. Each assumed the others, like himself, were still in the dark. "Damn. Where'd you learn that, child?"

Isobel said, "St John's."

"Not here you didn't," said Billy.

"That's for damn sure," said Ike, poking through his pockets, looking for another cigarette.

"I didn't mean here, St. John. I said St. John's, with an *s*."

"What's that?" Billy asked.

"It's a college," said Walter. "Unlike the three of us, this charming and lovely young lady is an educated woman."

"That true?" Ike asked. "St. John's a college?"

"It is," Isobel said. "A fine institution of higher learning. In Annapolis, Maryland."

"And you learned about Einstein?"

"I did Billy. I surely did. But don't hold that against me."

"You studied it, but I almost got it right, didn't I?" Ike was bubbling with pride and soon smoking with it too. Isobel smiled and nodded at the old man.

Walter said, "I still say that sounds like an argument to me. Write it up, Billy."

"Write what up?"

"Einstein, Stugots, and Isobel."

"I don't know what that means," said Ike, "but it sounds good." He shook his head, giving the okay to Billy.

"What's the 'Isobel' for?" Billy asked.

"Beauty," said Walter. "Beauty and knowledge."

"A mighty powerful combination," Ike said.

Once more the bartender with an uncertain past and more than one name picked up the chunk of blue chalk lying near the register and wrote on the familiar blackboard: Einstein/Stugots/Isobel. He poured himself a glass of tomato juice, took a swig, and said to no one in particular, "It ain't 'Stugots.' It's 'The Stugots.'"

FIFTY-TWO

New Orleans

Leonard rented a one-bedroom second-floor apartment on St. Ann near Burgundy, a block away from N. Rampart Street, the northern end of the French Quarter. He paid a premium holiday rate, taking the place for both Christmas and New Year's. He'd seen an ad for the apartment on the Internet and made all his arrangements by e-mail. The owner told him there had been a cancellation and he was lucky to find a place, any place, still available inside the French Quarter. Leonard e-mailed back that he wanted to rent the apartment through the month of January. He told the owner he and his wife loved New Orleans and this was a special surprise for her. He mentioned he was already in transit, and, as such, it would be more convenient if he paid in cash when he arrived. Leonard called when he was less than an hour's drive from New Orleans, arriving purposely after dark. The owner, a middle-aged gay man named Erubio, was waiting at the entrance to the building with the key. The transaction took only a moment. Leonard did his best to look away from the man's face as he handed him the money, and he wore a floppy, brown cowboy hat pulled down across his eyes. He handed the money over in an envelope, took the key, and disappeared inside. He never said where his wife was and was not asked. Although he paid for six weeks, he intended to be gone by the middle of January.

Leonard had been there ten days, far away from Vermont. Newspaper and TV reports speculated he was headed for, or already holed up in, New York City gunning for the rest of the crew at Stein, Gelb. The *New York Post* twice reported Leonard Martin sightings complete with fuzzy, grainy, out-of-focus photos in which, of course, his face was never shown. They were all photos of fat guys with long, light-colored hair. One such picture, supposedly showing Leonard leaving a movie theater on Third Avenue, made most of the major papers in the country. He saw it on page one of the *New Orleans Times-Picayune* over coffee and funnel cake loaded with powered sugar, in a tiny restaurant near Jackson Square. He laid the paper, photo up, next to his coffee cup on the small, round table and looked at himself in the mirrored wall. He looked as much like the man in the picture as he did like Santa Claus. His waitress came over and refilled his empty cup. Gazing at the paper, she said, "I hope they catch that guy, but I hope he gets all the others first." Then she smiled at the real Leonard Martin and asked if he wanted anything else.

New Year's Eve was already a thing of the past, and the Super Bowl still weeks from kickoff. The French Quarter was crowded anyway. Even the unusually cold weather didn't keep the crowds away or the best players from coming out to blow their horns. In the mornings, Leonard took the twenty-minute stroll to Jackson Square or Decatur Street down by the Mississippi River. He'd have breakfast in one of the many small coffee shops in the area, read the morning paper, and take in some fresh air. After two winters in the mountains of New Mexico, a chilly morning in New Orleans was like a spring day. The rest of the time he spent in the apartment, on the Internet, making calculations, checking the spreadsheets Carter Lawrence had sent him. Most nights he walked up the block to the corner of St. Ann and N. Rampart to Donna's Bar & Grill. He liked Donna's because the place had the casual atmosphere of a neighborhood bar or a slightly rundown Cajun hangout. Of course there were always a few out-of-towners and tourists, but Donna's was off the beaten path for the conventioneers at the Hilton or the Marriott, and certainly not the kind of place visited by the folks from Iowa in the Big Easy on a two- night, three-day package holiday.

The old man, Charlie, was always there, with Donna, and they were happy to see you no matter who you were. Leonard also liked the anonymity numbers afforded since Donna's was always packed even in the wee hours of the morning. The best brass band music in the world is heard there nightly. New Orleans has no second team. For musicians, no minor leaguers need apply. There are no off-nights, no such thing as a slow season. Donna's Bar & Grill was the place in the Quarter where the hornmen showed up after playing their regular gigs on Bourbon Street or the small joints over on Iberville or on Canal near the businessmen's hotels, where the Quarter ends and New Orleans becomes just another city. One after another they'd wander in, instrument in hand. A few were instantly recognized by some in the crowd and applause greeted their entrance. Even if they were unknown, anyone carrying a horn case, especially a black man, caused an immediate stir among Donna's patrons. No doubt, he came to play. As the hours passed the band got bigger or smaller as players arrived or called it a night. Sometimes there were as many as a dozen playing at the same time. Trombone and coronet players traded solos on "Tiger Rag" or "Bogalusa Strut" like boxers whipping their left jab into an opponent's helpless face—snap, snap, snap. Then—it was always the same, a kind of ritual—they stopped and smiled, the crowd cheered, and another boxer, dancer, painter, or poet stepped forward to pick up the gauntlet, accept the challenge. A couple of hours, a few beers, and Leonard could walk back to the apartment, hoping for a dreamless sleep. He was in Donna's every night for more than a week, until one night when Charlie greeted him with a friendly smile and a small nod of his head, acknowledging familiarity. Leonard could have none of that. He left immediately and never returned.

Wesley Pitts longed for the gym. His size and speed set him apart, even as a child. By the time he was ten or eleven his days of running free on the street or in the woods were over. Would-be and future coaches ushered him into the inner sanctum of high-tech body care. His birth certificate was altered to make him a year younger. That change delayed his entrance to high school by a year, allowing his high school football coach the luxury of playing him until Wes was almost twenty years old. During those years and the time to come in a bigtime college program and finally at the highest echelon of professional football, he had at his disposal the finest workout equipment and facilities in the world. Once he tasted steak it was unthinkable he would go back to macaroni and cheese. Now he found himself in the backwoods of Mississippi. The only exercise option around was running, so he ran twice each day. In the morning, before breakfast, he'd jog a mile and a half from his grandmother's house to the intersection with one of the two red lights before you get to town. On one corner was a small grocery store, and diagonally across the street a feed-supply warehouse. At seven o'clock in the morning neither was open for business. He'd turn around at the light and this time run—sometimes sprinting—all the way back. He repeated this at about four-thirty each afternoon. The round trip took at most twenty to twenty-five minutes.

On the morning of January 15th, Wesley Pitts jogged to the red light. He bent over, his hands on his knees, catching his breath, and turned around, ready to begin his run back. He had excellent vision, a seldom mentioned yet key aspect to his success as a receiver. Some people could judge distance by car lengths, others by city blocks. Pitts had a keen sense of distance measured in yards, in football fields. As he looked up he saw something he figured to be about two hundred and fifty yards away. It looked like a man standing in the middle of the road. The man appeared to be wearing a cowboy hat. He held something up to his shoulder or chin with both hands. The instant it took for Wesley Pitts to realize the man was holding a rifle was his last. The bullet struck him in the center of his chest. Almost at the same time, two more hit him. None of the three mortal wounds were more than two inches apart.

FIFTY-THREE

St. John

The phone rang at a quarter to eight. Wesley Pitts's blood still flowed hot on a Mississippi asphalt two-lane beneath a lonely traffic light. Walter reached over to the end table where he put his cell phone the night before. He rubbed the cobwebs from his eyes and tried not to wake Isobel.

He said, "Yeah?"

"Good morning, Mister Sherman."

"Who's this?" The voice was vaguely familiar. Walter sought to clear his mind, get his bearings.

"You may remember me as Michael Del—"

"Leonard Martin."

"Yes, I thought you knew back when—"

"What do you want?"

"Well, good morning to you too. It's time for us to talk."

Walter was struggling now, fighting what he knew was his stupid, damaged, ego-driven reaction. He tried to tell himself—quickly—that

Leonard Martin had fooled him with his Michael DelGrazo act out of a sense of survival. What could he have expected in New Mexico? Did he ever really think Leonard Martin would welcome him with open arms, buy him a cup of coffee, tell him his life story? What would he have done in the same situation? "Oh, fuck it," he thought.

"I'm glad you called," he said. "I am."

Leonard said, "Good. Let's get together tomorrow, in the afternoon. How does that work for you?"

"Where do you want me to meet you?"

"No need. I'll meet you. I like St. John. If Ms. Gitlin is there, I hope to see her too. Save me a trip."

"Let me give you directions," Walter said without skipping a beat. "Finding my house is not always the easiest thing. It can be confusing." How did he know about Isobel? How did he know Isobel was here? What did he know about Isobel? Does he know . . . ?

"I'll find it okay. See you tomorrow," Leonard said. And the phone went dead.

Leonard Martin was on a plane from Jackson to Atlanta before noon. While waiting to change planes there, he made one more phone call to Carter Lawrence. "Go ahead," he told him, "tell Nick to get started. Have him make the call." He landed on St. Thomas in the midst of the Caribbean afternoon's slow and glorious multicolored fade to evening. He took the first ferry for St. John. He meant to rent a car and had made an Internet reservation with the island's biggest rent-a-car agency, an enterprise owned and operated by one of Ike's sons. Ike's grandson Roosevelt met Leonard Martin at the dock. He held a sign in front of his chest with his customer's name in bold, capital letters. He did not make Leonard for a tourist, but Leonard saw him.

"Mister DelGrazo?"

"Yes," said Leonard.

Roosevelt introduced himself with a smile, a warm and friendly handshake, and a small apology. "I'm very sorry, sir, but can you bare with me a minute? I need to give a message to my grandfather. He's just over there across the square." He pointed to Ike, who was sitting at his regular table on the other side of the small square. "It will only take a moment, then we can be off to the paperwork and your vehicle. Then you can begin what I'm sure will be a wonderful stay for you here on our lovely island of St. John."

"Quite alright," said Leonard. "No apology needed. I've been sitting all day. I'd like a little stroll." Roosevelt grinned broadly and the two were off on the short walk to the open-air bar called Billy's. Not wishing to intrude on the young man's words with his grandfather, Leonard stood at a respectful distance. Only a moment later he tensed up. His heart rate increased and in his fear he considered that he might have made a big mistake coming here—here to this tiny island, here to a place where there was only one way out and it was behind him. He was a man on the run. Only a few hours ago he'd killed someone. Was he now trapped? Although he was a complete stranger, newly arrived, Leonard had an uncomfortable feeling he was being watched.

Someone was indeed staring at him. At the far end of the bar he saw Isobel Gitlin looking right at him. A sense of shock rolled over him. He was riveted to the ground, undone by the dread he felt that his carefully constructed cocoon of privacy and safety had been pierced. Did she recognize him? How could she recognize him? She was blindfolded all the time. She hadn't seen him, or had she? Then, next to her, he saw Walter Sherman. He was drinking from a bottle that appeared to be a Coke. Of course, Leonard realized with a comforting sense of relief, she had his description from him. There could be no other way. Unlike Isobel, Walter had not yet noticed him. Leonard chuckled. He tapped Roosevelt gently on the shoulder and told him to bring the rental car here, to Billy's.

"I'm sorry. I can't do that, sir," said Roosevelt, confused and a little worried he'd somehow offended a customer, perhaps by stopping to talk with his grandfather. "There's the paperwork, and I have to—"

"It's okay, boy," said Ike, not missing the stare that now both Walter and Isobel were giving to this bearded cowboy. "He ain't no bush-whacker." Leonard acknowledged the old man with a pleasant tip of his hat and moved slowly but easily toward the far end of the bar where Walter and Isobel sat motionless. Billy saw the connection too. His old friend Walter and his new friend Isobel looked right at this guy with the floppy, western hat. The surprise on their faces was unmistak-able. They knew him, Billy figured, but were they happy to see him? He couldn't tell. The cowboy seemed eager enough to see them. His gait as well as his smile was definitely friendly. Billy had reached for the base-ball bat he kept behind the bar. It had been so long since he grabbed a bat, or anything like that, with bad intentions. He broke a sweat, but as Leonard passed him, he realized it was uncalled for. He dropped the wooden club and, shaken, wiped his face with a bar towel. Walter had not missed Billy's clenched teeth or his hands beneath the bar. Even the sight of Leonard Martin could not overcome the nagging question in Walter's mind: *Who was this William Mantkowski?*

"Ms. Gitlin, a pleasure to see you—again," Leonard said, holding his hand out. She shook it and it seemed she was trying to say some-thing, but nothing came out. "Mister Sherman." Again, he tipped his hat politely.

Walter said, "Please call me Walter. And what should I call you?"

"Leonard will do just fine. I hope my deception can be forgiven between us."

"You look just like Walter said you would."

"Ms. Gitlin—"

"Isobel."

"Isobel, you're nervous. You know what I look like, so why haven't you printed it?"

"We can't. The *New York Times* won't print something we can't confirm to be true."

"Of course not," Leonard said. Even Walter caught that one.

"That's not a joke." Isobel was unnerved. Despite her education and experience, she believed in the integrity of the press in general and the *New York Times* in particular. Plus, Walter told her that Leonard Martin was coming tomorrow afternoon. Not now. Seeing him, like this, without even the semblance of a blindfold—she needed to collect herself. "Just because Walter told me what he saw doesn't mean I can print it. I didn't see it."

"No, I suppose you didn't and you can't. And you couldn't say that Walter Sherman saw me without explaining who Walter Sherman is. That I suspect would be just as difficult. So difficult that it will never happen."

Isobel said, "Yes. That will never happen."

A moment of awkward silence followed. Isobel had yet to fully digest what was going on, yet at the same time, she understood Walter actually encouraged moments like these. That whole character revelation thing, she remembered. Walter tried to gauge Leonard's state of mind. He seemed unfazed by the absence of conversation. Walter noticed he hadn't changed his clothes for a while. His boots were soiled and Leonard Martin gave off a scent Walter immediately recognized as country, rural, backwoods. No airplane ride was sufficient to hide this. This guy hadn't gone back to New Mexico, had he?

Leonard asked Isobel, "You haven't spoken to anybody today, have you?"

Isobel said, "No. I mean, who do y-you mean?"

"Check your messages. You have a call to return."

"This is not a good place to talk," Walter said. "Why don't we go to my house."

"I'm expecting a car here."

"You won't need one. Really, you won't. If you need to go somewhere afterward, I can have you driven, wherever. Or, if you haven't made arrangements, I have room. You can stay at my place."

"Thank you," Leonard said. "That's very considerate, but I wouldn't want to put you to any trouble."

"No trouble at all," said Walter. "Are you ready to go?"

Walter looked to Isobel. She answered his question with obvious uncertainty. "Sure," she said. "I'm ready to go." Walter left some money on the bar and the three of them walked out. As they passed Ike, Leonard stopped and said, "Please tell your grandson I won't need that car after all. And give him this for any trouble I've caused."

"That's not called for," said Ike, refusing the money, "but I'll let him know."

When they were gone, Billy yelled to Ike, "What the hell was that all about?"

"Don't know," Ike said, puffing like a locomotive running full steam ahead uphill. "Don't know. But I seen that guy somewhere, I think—don't remember, exactly. But something about him. I seen him, I think."

Unlike Tom Maloney, Leonard Martin did not seem to notice the beauty of St. John or the darkening sea below and beyond the mountain road. The setting sun, the clouds floating over St. Thomas, the sailboats leaving their sunlit silver wakes—they held no interest for him. He was oblivious to the condition of the roads and didn't bother to look when they passed a herd of noisy goats struggling to climb one of the hills. He sat in the back seat, alone and quiet. Walter thought he might have dozed off. He looked in the rearview mirror. Leonard had the brim of his hat pulled down, covering most of his face. Perhaps his eyes were closed. "If I had a gun," thought Walter, "I could kill him right here."

Even a man who's lost his sense of natural beauty could not resist the view from the patio of Walter's house. Leonard Martin was no exception. He stood, pressed against the railing, overlooking the steep mountainside and the sea. Walter seriously wondered what such a man could be thinking. He could make no guesses. Finally, Leonard turned to the covered table where both Walter and Isobel sat, took a chair, and accepted a glass of lemonade from Clara.

"This morning," Leonard began.

"I know," said Walter. "We know. We saw it on CNN earlier this afternoon."

"I hope that doesn't make this too uncomfortable."

"This whole thing is a little creepy, is it not?" said Isobel.

"It is a bit. I don't know," said Walter. "A black man shot to death in Mississippi on Martin Luther King's birthday." A statement or a question—Walter's words hung in the humid air.

"Judged by the content of his character," Leonard said.

Walter went on. "That you could kill a man in Mississippi in the morning and by evening be a thousand miles away, on a tiny island, sitting in the very same chair he once sat in." Leonard Martin showed no reaction. "What would you call that?" Walter asked.

"Serendipity?" said Leonard. "I can change seats, if you want."

Isobel's curiosity was near the bursting point. She said nothing, but inside her head she was screaming, "*My God! What are we doing here?*" Leonard tried to look completely at ease, but Isobel saw the movement of his upper lip, the increased respiration, and the occasional darting of his eyes. Walter had taught her well. His hat was off and the close cut of his hair no longer obscured his features. Looking closely—real closely—you could see it was him. From the corner of one eye she saw Walter, as calm as if he had been relaxing on the beach. His gaze was fixed on the other man, the one who used to be fat and blonde, the one who used to be a successful real estate lawyer, the one who used to be a husband and a father and a grandfather, the one who was now a killer.

"Isobel, I would really like you to check your messages and return that call while I talk to Walter. Please?"

"Sure," she said, getting up and walking into the house, closing the glass sliding doors behind her.

"I have a message for your employers," Leonard said when he and Walter were alone.

"Best I can figure, there's only two of them left."

"Yes, that's quite correct. And it's possible they may stay alive, die of natural causes in their old age." He reached down and picked up an attaché case he'd carried with him to the patio. Walter could not help remembering Wesley Pitts doing the same thing, reaching for his money-laden, million dollar case, in exactly the same place. His better judgment told him to keep such a remembrance to himself. Meanwhile, Leonard removed a file folder, stuffed with papers, and placed it on the table. "Stein and Maloney," he said, "will each make a contribution to a named nonprofit foundation with which I am completely unconnected in any discernable way, and that will allow them to live. Additionally, the companies of Stein, Gelb, Hector & Wills, SHI Inc., which used to be known as Second Houston Holding, and Alliance Industries Inc. will make similar contributions. I realize that Christopher Hopman, Billy MacNeal, and Pat Grath are already dead, and I acknowledge that those now running these companies share none of their culpability. The current senior officers and directors of those companies, however, still maintain and benefit from the proceeds derived from the sale and effective combination of the two companies. Therefore, they are to make contributions equal to the amounts of money they made in, and as a result of, the IPO of Second Houston, just as Stein, Gelb will and just as Stein and Maloney individually will. Failure of these executives and directors to comply with this requirement will have the effect of making them accessories after the fact. I make no immediate threats against them, but they hold the fate of Nathan Stein and Tom Maloney in their hands. Their failure to respond according to my instructions, even if Stein and Maloney comply, will result in the deaths of both men. What happens afterward is yet to be determined." He picked up the folder from the table, took a long drink of his lemonade, and looked at Walter. Walter looked back at Leonard Martin in amazement. Leonard Martin may be the most dangerous person he'd ever known. But he just changed the rules. Killing him was out of the question, totally unnecessary. The pressure on Walter had been relieved. He had nothing to say, and so said only, "After the fact?"

"You'll find the amounts for each contributor spelled out on the cover sheet, and the basis for them in the documents in this folder, which I'll leave with you. This will give all concerned the specific details as to how these amounts have been arrived at. These numbers are nonnegotiable. No one at the foundation, or anywhere else, will be authorized to make changes. I appreciate that this amount of money has implications that go well beyond the contributors. I have no desire to see the ramifications damage innocent people. Believe it or not, I grieve for the families of those I've killed. I do. Specific terms of payment—when, where, and how—will be worked out later, but it will be necessary for one half of one percent to be *donated*, in cash, within thirty days, and another one half of one percent within ninety days. After that, arrangements can be made with the foundation for delivery of the remaining funds. There will be a time limit. We're talking about a large sum of money. Assets will have to be divested. I understand that. Nevertheless, half of the total must be delivered within three years. The rest of the money must be in the possession of the foundation within one additional year. If, at that time—four years from now—if the full amount has not been paid, the agreement will be deemed to have been broken. Nathan Stein and Tom Maloney, and possibly others whose bad faith in this matter may make them responsible, will die. These payment requirements are also stipulated in the cover letter. Finally, it's important that all contributors know that any attempt to shift assets to a wife, a relative, an offshore subsidiary, for example, or to any entity, will be viewed as an attempt to avoid payment. Assure them that I will know if they try to bury it in their backyard or stuff a safe-deposit box in Malta. I will know and I will consider the arrangement broken. I will act accordingly." He paused and looked very carefully at Walter. "Any questions about what I've said?"

"Isn't this extortion?" Walter said matter-of-factly. "You can't get away with this. How can you expect something like this—"

"Extortion is a legal term, Walter. To be extortion I would have to receive the money or the foundation would have to be seen as acting as my agent, with a benefit accruing to me. Neither condition exists. There might be an element of blackmail in it—I grant you that—as it relates to me. It's no doubt accurate to say I'm making 'terroristic threats,' and, of course, killing someone is always illegal—even threatening to kill someone. But the foundation will not be a party to any of this information. They will just receive the money. No, this is more like a drug dealer getting ripped off by someone who gives the money to charity."

"That makes no sense at all."

"Sure it does. Don't thieves, even murderers, give money to charity? If a thief sent the United Way a thousand dollars or a million dollars, wouldn't they be free to accept and use it? Or what if somebody earned money and didn't report it, in fact didn't even file a tax return, but donated ten thousand dollars to the American Heart Association—would they be free to accept and use it? Of course they would, provided they have no knowledge of any illegality that either prompted the contribution or involved the source of the contributor's money. Enron made charitable contributions. Did they all give the money back?"

"And just how do you deal with all this without everyone knowing everything?"

"I won't tell. You won't tell. Stein, Maloney, and the two corporations won't tell. Instead, they will hold very public press conferences, admit to their ill-gotten gains, express their deepest sorrow and remorse, speak movingly of their desire to atone for the sins of previous directors, and then . . . then they will donate this money in the manner I've prescribed. They have stockholders who must support these noble efforts. And I'm sure they will. They must be seen to act willingly, openly, and publicly. Except, however, there will be no mention whatsoever of my role in this." The puzzled look on Walter's face merely encouraged Leonard to go on. "You will deliver these instructions to Nathan Stein and Thomas Maloney. They face the task of telling the key people—all of whom are named in the documents—at SHI Inc. and Alliance Industries Inc. to do their part. Under the circumstances, I don't think there's any chance at all anyone will name me in this matter. I'm sure the history of my 'bad acts' thus far will help Stein and Maloney convince their friends." Walter said nothing.

"As for Nathan Stein and Thomas Maloney," Leonard went on, "an attorney in New York—a lawyer who knows nothing, not even who his client is—will open a checking account for each of them. Every week he will deposit five hundred dollars in each account. That is all the money Stein and Maloney can use. If they spend a dollar more than that, I will consider that they have used hidden funds, worked for money, borrowed money, or received gifts—none of which are allowed—and I will kill them."

"Christ," said Walter, scratching his head, running both hands through his hair and down the back of his neck. "What if they refuse?"

"That's entirely up to them."

"This is—"

"Revolutionary?"

"Revolutionary? Jesus Christ!"

"I don't think he can help me with this."

"Help? You seem to be doing quite enough on your own. What about Stevenson and Daniels and Carter Lawrence?"

"Nick and Harvey know nothing. I can't be responsible for what they may think, but they know nothing. I'm sure they'll be cooperative with the authorities. They'll answer all their questions. They have nothing to hide and nothing to offer. Their truthful answers won't change a thing. As for Carter, what can I say? We share a certain immunity, one which I have surely violated and forfeited. But he has not. Carter is a victim. As this unfolds, I'm sure the press will present him in a very favorable light. For law enforcement to pursue and harass Carter Lawrence while the real culprits live and go free—that can't happen. And besides, he knows nothing or almost nothing. He never knew where I was, or when, and he doesn't know where I am now. None of them—Nick, Harvey, or Carter—have any of these details, nor have any of them been privy to my activities up to now. I've never admitted to them what I've admitted to you. I've never discussed it with them. If you think about it, you and Isobel are the only people with specific knowledge, directly from me, about what I've already done and what I plan to do in the future. You heard what Isobel said. What she knows can't be published without your own exposure, and even then, it lacks corroboration. Just your word. This conversation, for example." Leonard looked around the patio, out toward the open sea, then behind him at the closed sliding doors, shrugged his shoulders, and said, "We're alone. Just you and me, Walter. No corroboration."

"Michael DelGrazo," Walter said. "You might just as well have said Kaiser Zoesay."

"Do you have any more questions about this?" Leonard asked.

"Did you shoot Pitts with the Walther? Why did you meet Carter Lawrence, Nick Stevenson, and Harvey Daniels in Clarksville, Tennessee? How come—"

"No, Walter. Only questions about this." Leonard held up the folder with both hands. "You already know the answers to the other questions, most of them, anyway. And in time you'll figure out what you don't know now. But we'll never speak of it. Never."

"Dr. Roy?"

"Never."

"You think this is justice, don't you?" said Walter. "You're acting righteously? You believe that, don't you?" Now it was Leonard who chose silence. Walter continued. "Your wife, your daughter, your grandsons—they ate lunch and died. The meat killed them, and there were people who let that happen. What did you do? You killed those people, the ones who could have prevented it. One by one, you shot them down. For their complicity, they died." A touch of sarcasm, mixed with murky anger, rose in Walter's voice. "Oh, of course, you saved the best for last. The guilty must pay, and pay, and pay some more. What you're doing to Stein and Maloney is worse than death, at least for them it will be. Shit, they go from living on five hundred dollars a minute to five hundred a week. How are they going to do that? They can't live in their homes if their wives own and keep the property, or you'll kill them. They can't use a car that belongs to someone in the family, or you'll kill them. They can't wear the same clothes, make phone calls on the same cell phones, eat the same food, use the same health insurance—God knows what else they can't touch, or you'll kill them. But they can stay alive. That you'll allow. For men like that, they'd be better off dead." Walter leaned forward across the table separating the two men. Leonard was perfectly still, stoic.

"For Stein and Maloney," said Walter, "money is like drugs. They're addicts, and you know that. A lifetime of fabulous wealth, and now they're reduced to poverty. They can't make it. They'll cheat. Somewhere, somehow, they will. Maybe Nathan Stein gets some money—a hundred grand, two hundred grand—from one of his kids. You know, kids can have a hard time seeing their fathers suffer. Perhaps Maloney begs his wife to put some money in a Swiss bank account for him. It could happen, right? They take the money and you kill them. You call this justice? For whom? For Nina? For Ellen? For her sons? I don't think so. Vengeance, that's what it is. 'Vengeance is mine, sayeth the Lord.' And who the hell are you, God? Whose guilt are you killing for?" Leonard didn't say a word, the expression on his face remained unchanged. "Where were *you*?" Walter asked. "Where were *you* when it mattered?"

Now Leonard seemed about to say something, but instead, he breathed deeply through clenched teeth, sat back, and a small, almost imperceptible, nervous and hostile smile crossed his lips. He would not be baited.

"I know about Barbara Coffino," said Walter. The smile on Leonard's face disappeared. Walter could see him catch his breath before it choked him.

Leonard broke the awkward silence by asking, "Have you ever killed anyone, Walter? You look like the kind of man who's killed. Perhaps you've considered killing me. I suppose I'll never know. You also look like the kind of man who knows—*who knows*—killing is sometimes the only way. If I'm wrong, tell me. But I know I'm right and you know it too." They looked at one another, each man keenly aware, whether they liked it or not, they shared a common value, a common judgment, a common past.

Isobel returned to the patio, this time leaving open the sliding doors behind her. Walter could not interpret her look. The expression on her face, the tightness in her cheeks, the lines across her forehead, this was all new to him.

Leonard said, "I hope you'll take it, Isobel. For Nina, Ellie, and for the boys." He turned to Walter and said softly, "If you'll call a car I'd be grateful. It's time for me to go."

"Go where?" Isobel asked.

"Home."

"When is the next ferry, Walter?" Isobel said.

He shrugged his shoulders. "Not sure," he said, trying to recover himself.

"Doesn't matter," said Leonard. He knew there was a boat waiting for him in the harbor at Cruz Bay, and a chartered Gulfstream, fueled and ready to fly, on the tarmac at St. Thomas. Walter used his cell phone to make the call and told Leonard the car would be ready in ten minutes.

"If you'll excuse me, I'll wait at the gate. And I'll see myself out. Please don't get up." He shook hands with Walter, who was still seated at the table, his back to the water, looking in at his own house through the glass. Then Leonard turned to Isobel, where she stood. He smiled and extended his hand to her. When she took it, he covered hers with his other hand and held on to her tightly. "I hope you'll take it," he said before walking out. He did not look back.

Walter reached over for the file folder Leonard left behind. He opened it and began to read the first page of the first document, the one Leonard referred to as the cover letter. "Holy shit!" he said.

"Holy shit is right," Isobel said, her attention far away on one of the small, empty islands offshore, unaware of anything Walter was reading. "You don't know the half of it. That was Nicholas Stevenson who called me. When I called him back he offered me a job. He wants me to be the Executive Director for a new organization of which he and his partner Harvey Daniels are trustees. You won't believe this. It's a nonprofit foundation called The Center for Consumer Concerns. He wants me to come to Atlanta to discuss the details. Isn't that a bit strange, don't you think? Leonard Martin's law p-partners offering me a job, especially this sort of job?"

"Well," Walter said. "It's a foundation that'll have a lot of money."

"What are you talking about? Is this something you and Leonard discussed while I was away?" He told her everything Leonard Martin had said to him, repeating his exact words as best he could remember them. "And it says how much in there? How much money?" she said, pointing to the folder. Walter nodded. "How much?" she asked.

Walter leaned back in his chair, stretched his arms out as wide as they would go, breathed deeply, smiled broadly, and said, "A little short of six *billion* dollars."

"Oh, m-my," said Isobel.

FIFTY-FOUR

New York

Tom Maloney and Nathan Stein were still squirreled away atop the Waldorf Astoria, each keenly aware they were the only ones left. It preyed on their minds. It was the evil, ugly monster hiding in the closet, and they were ten-year-olds all over again, afraid to turn the lights out. Nathan couldn't sleep or eat or sit in one place or calm down long enough to simply move his bowels. Maloney could do little more than lay on the couch. They bickered.

"Safe as . . . what the fuck did you say it was? 'Cows in Calcutta' or some other Godfuckingforsaken place. You're full of shit, Tom. You're fucking full of shit! And it's going to get me killed." Maloney still just sat there, saying nothing. Stein paced. "Goddamn, MacNeal and Hopman and you—yes, you Tom—you're all getting me fucking killed!" Maloney was past the point of trying to soothe Nathan's spirits. He no longer possessed the energy to play that stupid, fucking game. Pretense had flown out the window and off the penthouse patio, carried by the winds to the four quarters of New York City.

"Fuck you," Tom mumbled.

All he could think about was Leonard Martin. Where was he? What was his next step? When would the executioner appear? Could Walter Sherman catch him in time? He considered sending more money to Walter, but what good would that accomplish? It would be of no use to him unless he found a way to get out of this mess. Besides, some things cannot be bought, not because they lack a price, but because they just can't be. No amount of money can change the past. How outrageous, he protested silently. Maloney had been a good Catholic boy and now he found himself thinking he was a rich man afraid Leonard Martin was pushing a camel through the eye of a needle. He would go to heaven, wouldn't he? In spite of everything? Jesus Christ had always been his Lord and Savior. Honest, he was. Did Jesus know he was here, in the Waldorf Astoria, in need of help? "Christ, I'm in trouble!" He trembled. He would have given the nun another million if he'd had to. A million? What's another million? His wife was in Switzerland. His colleagues dead. His friend, mentor, boss was half mad. Tom Maloney felt helpless, absolutely fucking helpless. Christ, he'd give anything to be rid of Leonard Martin. He poured himself another bourbon and made for the toilet. Diarrhea plagued him.

Isobel arrived in Atlanta the day after she and Walter met Leonard Martin. Nick Stevenson and Harvey Daniels expected her. She took a suite at the Hotel Nikko and asked that they meet her there. The three talked for more than two hours. The Center for Consumer Concerns was hers for the taking.

"Chase anyone," Nick said. "Anyone at all. Investigate at your pleasure. You'll be in charge. No limits, no interference."

"We're the trustees," said Harvey. "That's for legal purposes. We'll never tell you what to do or how to do it."

Nick added, "Just be true to Leonard Martin, Carter Lawrence, and all the others like them. Do your best to see there are no more of them."

Isobel took the job, and it was agreed she would give the *Times* notice through the end of the month. The Center for Consumer Concerns would lease a condo for her, giving her six months to find a place of her own. No problem, they assured her, especially with their real estate contacts. She could hit the ground running. The two trustees, both former partners of Leonard Martin, assured her they had no personal knowledge of the source of the funds with which the foundation would be endowed. All they could say was that they were confident large contributors would appear, and soon. Since she had not been present when Leonard explained the details to Walter, Isobel too had no actual personal knowledge. From a legal point of view the only three people associated with the formation of the foundation came to it with clean hands. Isobel remembered a sociology professor at St. John's who challenged her class to list the things they knew to be true, yet didn't believe were absolute. Love, honor, justice, truth itself. Where are the absolute moral precepts? She could be comfortable knowing how the foundation—her foundation—got its money without actually *knowing*. She called Mel Gold when she returned to New York. They met for a sandwich at Artie's Deli on Broadway. She told him the foundation, The Center for Consumer Concerns, had offered her the job as Executive Director and she had taken it. Her resignation from the *New York Times* would be effective January 31st.

"The Center for Consumer Concerns?" said the Moose. "Never heard of it." It was new, she told him. Headquartered in Atlanta. Just getting started. He asked no more questions and she offered no more details.

"Put it in writing, kiddo," he said, meaning, of course, her resignation. "They got great pickles here, you know that?" Somehow, she figured, some way, she had to tell him. She wanted to tell him. Perhaps he saw it in her eyes—perhaps not—but he reached across the table, laying both of his huge hands on hers, and said, "If he walked in here right now you'd know him and I wouldn't, right? And that's been so all along, hasn't it? *Unrecognizable*." He shook his head and smiled. "That was bullshit wasn't it?"

"Mel—"

"Don't tell me, Isobel. I'll have to print it." She leaned forward and kissed him gently on the cheek. Mel Gold tried to remember the last time a reporter kissed him. He couldn't.

Walter sat alone on his empty deck. The lights of St. Thomas flickered in the distant darkness. There was a slight chill in the air, for St. John, that is. Clara brought him a cup of bouillon and a light sweater.

"Put this on before you freeze to death," she said. Hardly a chance of that. "The woman has a great sense of humor," he thought. In the morning he'd call Tom Maloney and make another trip to New York. The specifics of Leonard Martin's plan were dense and complicated, and a good deal of the data and supporting materials were pretty much incomprehensible to Walter. However, it was his job to bring all this—this most amazing and unexpected turn of events—to his clients. After that, he hadn't the slightest idea what he would do.

Leonard Martin was gone.

FIFTY-FIVE

New York

"I HAVE NO DOUBT that can be arranged," Walter was saying. He was reviewing the materials Leonard had given him with Nathan Stein and Tom Maloney. Stein was subdued, perhaps resigned, to the futility of his patented outbursts. He'd just mumbled something like, "I'd rather be dead."

It was getting late in the afternoon. The sixty-seven degree temperature had been a record for New York on this day in January. Now it was cooling fast. It had been such a lovely day the doors to the rooftop patio had been open most of the time. The illusion of spring was disappearing now, together with the warmth of the setting sun on the Waldorf's Jersey side. Walter arrived with three copies of everything Leonard gave him. One was for him and one each for Stein and Maloney. He made no introductory remarks. He told them only that he'd met with Leonard Martin, who had given him instructions for them. With that he handed each a file. They took their pile of papers and read quietly to themselves for more than an hour. Tom didn't make a sound, and Stein only mumbled something from time to time. Walter could hardly make it out. He waited.

Dinner arrived unordered and unannounced. Walter was not at all surprised, figuring they had to know what he liked by now. Two room service waiters laid out a simple yet elegant tray before him. On it was a bowl of tomato-based soup of some kind and a Caesar salad topped with both blackened shrimp and grilled chicken. Rolls and butter, coffee for later, and a chilled bottle of Chardonnay completed the spread. Nathan Stein had a steak, which sat alone on the plate with no side dishes. He would eat less than half of it. For Maloney, just a club sandwich. "Whoever ordered this stuff," thought Walter, "has a pretty good take on whose life is in jeopardy and whose isn't." He had no idea it was Elizabeth Reid, patiently working out of sight elsewhere in the suite every day since Nathan Stein joined Maloney in this seven-thousand-dollar-a-day-tower prison.

"You've read this?" Tom asked Walter.

"I have."

"Why didn't you kill him?" Stein inquired, with only a small edge to his voice.

"He came to my house."

"On St. John?" asked Stein.

"On St. John."

"Gutsy sonofabitch," said Maloney.

"That. And dangerous," Walter said.

"Here's what I want you to tell him . . ." Tom started.

Walter laid his soupspoon down, shook his head, and said, "I'm positive, certain as I can be, that I'll never see or hear from Leonard Martin again."

"Then what the fuck do we need you for?" Stein said, more frustrated than angry. "Why are you here?"

"I'll be happy to leave—soon as I finish my salad, if you don't mind."

Tom said, "No, no. Don't go. Nathan's . . . upset. We're all upset." Walter continued eating as if nothing had happened. There were no secrets among them. Not anymore. Not Dr. Roy. Not Knowland. Not even Na Trang. Walter considered his surroundings. Three killers having an early supper, two of them trying desperately to stay alive.

According to Leonard, Alliance Industries Inc. had to come up with $3.8 billion. A lot of money, but not too much, said Stein, for a corporation that did not cook its books and was legitimately valued at somewhere between forty-five and sixty billion, and they had three to four years of lead-time. SHI Inc., Billy MacNeal's old Second Houston Holding, was a different story. Leonard's demands called for them to pony up $1.3 billion to The Center for Consumer Concerns. That was about three-quarters of the company's net asset value, according to Tom Maloney. That amount pretty much put them out of business. But, Maloney said, since Alliance owned a controlling interest in SHI, they could effectively buy that company with a stock exchange—Alliance shares for SHI Inc.—roll it into the parent organization, and even after eating the $1.3 billion, still add about five hundred million to Alliance. SHI Inc. couldn't survive on its own, but it didn't have to. Walter mostly listened as Stein and Maloney discussed this part of the arrangement with each other. "This is what they do with their pathetic lives," he thought. He realized they were actually enjoying themselves. After weeks jailed up here, they were finally working again.

When they were finished, when they had determined to their mutual satisfaction that the incredible amount of $5.1 billion could be successfully secured from the two corporations, they turned their attention to their own firm. To Walter, it seemed both men would do anything to avoid talking about their own individual situations.

Walter, as was his habit, had done his homework. He knew quite a bit about the company his clients directed and worked for. Stein, Gelb, Hector & Wills Securities Inc. traced its roots to a small investment banking company started in 1923. The partnership of two young men, Andrew Hiken and Michael Sears, known derisively on Wall Street as "the children," had only sporadic success, and always seemed as if it were on the verge of dissolution. In 1929, the youngsters were bought out by a more substantial investment banking house, Brown, Roote & Higgins. While Hiken and Sears ran with the cash, Brown, Roote & Higgins ran headlong into disaster with the Great Crash. After the flames of their destruction subsided, the smoldering embers of that esteemed partnership were rescued by Benjamin Stein and Henry Witherspoon. In time, Witherspoon gave way to Larry Gelb, who many thought was Jewish but was not, and after World War II Randolph Hector joined the crew. They maintained a subtle yet influential presence in the financial world with a list of topnotch clients that read like a roll call of the capitalist nobility of the twentieth century. Then, in the full bloom of the Reagan deregulation frenzy in the eighties, Stein, Gelb & Hector merged with Lumpkin, Hewitt & Wills, a full service brokerage firm. While Messrs. Lumpkin and Hewitt found themselves unemployed—rich, but out of work—Mark Wills prospered in league with his new partners.

Nathan Stein, grandson of Ben, joined the firm right out of school. His rise to Vice Chairman was not without merit, though a little too meteoric for some. When his grandfather retired, Nathan became the ringmaster and Stein, Gelb, Hector & Wills his circus. He knew where every dollar was hidden and was, frankly, astonished at how accurate Leonard Martin's analysis was. Nathan calculated his firm's income from the Second Houston–Alliance Industries deal at $716 million. Leonard showed him where he'd missed seven million more. Rather than argue with it, Nathan was impressed, and not a little disturbed, that the people who worked for him had failed to see it. He wanted credit for every penny. As for Leonard, he wondered who helped him with all this. One way or another, almost all the data was public, but very little of it was easily accessible. What's more, some of it required a sophisticated understanding of modern finance and an advanced computer capability to connect the dots. Leonard Martin had help, for sure. Good help.

Maloney and Stein agreed. Stein, Gelb, Hector & Wills could meet the payment schedule. True, this kind of money was certainly not chicken feed or chump change, but the discomfort of paying it could be managed in-house. Obstacles could be overcome. Besides, it was a matter of life or death. Theirs.

It was then they finally came to themselves. Both men had been astonished at the amount Leonard demanded: $123 million from Stein and $36 million from Maloney. Stein, in addition to the shock of his own amount, had been just as surprised and displeased with what he considered a low number for Tom Maloney. A careful review of the supporting data made Nathan more angry. He became both bitter and nasty. Walter sat there while the two went at each other, wondering why they would talk this way in front of him. True, he was familiar with the details of their contention, but still he was puzzled at their willingness to forego privacy. He had no way of knowing, of course, that Dr. Ganga Roy had encountered the same feeling in circumstances that were only slightly different.

"That's bullshit," Nathan said. "Thirty-six is a bullshit number."

"Are you serious?" Tom Maloney was shaken at the obvious inability of Nathan Stein to grasp what was happening. "We're being wiped out, Nathan. There's nothing left. You know—your money or your life—and you're more concerned with my number than your own? Are you out of your fucking mind?"

"I see what he did," ranted Stein. "He's left out everything in your wife's name. But not with mine!"

"Nathan, you don't have anything in your wife's name. You have assets jointly owned—you and her—but there's nothing of any value in her name only, is there?"

Nathan knew the score. He was just pissed. "Nothing worth anything," he said.

Leonard Martin had been very picky. He'd examined the voluminous data Carter Lawrence gave him and pegged each man's net worth, leaving out noncash assets held jointly. For stocks, bonds, mutual funds, and other financial instruments easily converted to cash, he'd figured the share for each man separate and apart from their wives, children, grandchildren, or any other partners. For real estate and other hard assets Stein and Maloney owned with others, Leonard assessed the value of their share. He required that the partner or partners in each deal buy out Stein or Maloney, and that the proceeds from such a buyout were included in the final figure for each man. Three to four years allowed more than enough time to make all these arrangements without damage to the equity position that would remain for Stein and Maloney's surviving cohorts. Leonard did not hold wives, relatives, or even business partners liable for the sins of Nathan Stein and Tom Maloney.

Nathan had always treated his wife with total disregard for her financial independence. She had come to their marriage with some money, her family was not poor. Over the years, he figured, she'd probably made some small investments he was unaware of, but he'd never given her anything except some jewelry. How much could that be? A half a million? A million at most. He really had no idea. He was the same with his children. Christ, he thought, they all had unlimited expense accounts. He never inhibited their spending, but they were always spending his money. He had never been one to share anything. Now, Leonard Martin meant to break him, leave him without any safety net of family assets. Nathan was furious, yet even while considering the very real possibility that he would be wiped out, he could not bring himself to regret not having given his wife or children anything of value. It was his money, goddamnit! And now this motherfucking sonofabitch was going to take it away. He wanted to scream. He wanted to yell it: "No! No! No! I won't do it, you fucking prick!"

Tom Maloney didn't have Nathan Stein's kind of money to begin with, nor did he share his temperament and general outlook on life. He'd also spent his a little differently. The departure of the first Mrs. Maloney had cost him a small fortune, his attitude at the time worsened by the knowledge that she meant to marry a man worth zillions immediately after the divorce. The second Mrs. Maloney paid a heavy price for that mistake. She signed an ironclad prenup. However, over the years, she cajoled, convinced, and insisted that he put some things in her name. He did, time and time again, thus she skirted not only the letter, but the spirit of her limitation. As he mulled over the demands Leonard Martin was making on him, Tom was relieved to think his wife had, on her own, something in the neighborhood of five to ten million. No matter what his tormenter took, that was a substantial fallback position. He gave only passing notice to the fact that his wife was in Switzerland. He dismissed all thoughts she might not return. Besides, unlike Nathan, who had unwavering faith in the invulnerability of the ruling class, Tom Maloney always felt, somewhere in the back of his mind, that a day like this might come. Tom realized the thirty-six million was everything he had—everything except a certain thirty million sitting in a bank on Grand Cayman Island. Nothing in the Caymans showed up anywhere on Leonard Martin's list of assets. Why should it? "Rainy day money," he thought, "and it was already coming down in buckets." Sure he would be wiped out. Maybe—oh, what the hell, there was a good chance—his wife might never come back. But he had his own safety net. For a moment he saw himself lying on the beach in Costa Rica, a piña colada next to him. In this fantasy, the beach boy was

Nathan Stein. Tom visualized the thirty-six million gone. Everything he had, everything except . . .

He smiled to himself. Outsmart them. That's what he'd done again. His parents, the nuns at school, the wives and all the jackoffs and miserable sonsofbitches he'd done business with. Now he'd outsmarted Leonard Martin too. Fuck him!

Walter smelled wood burning and felt obligated to warn his clients. The look in Stein's and Maloney's faces said they were thinking how they could get out of this one. Leonard Martin was not a man to fuck with. Couldn't they see that? "My god," thought Walter, "have they forgotten?" Christopher Hopman's body cut in two? Billy MacNeal being fished out of his bloody pool? Pat Grath flat on his back, his eyes still wide open? Floyd Ochs's head floating down the Hiawassee River? Louise Hollingsworth gutted like a wild animal? Wesley Pitts's perfect body slumped to the ground with three holes neatly grouped in his chest? He said, "Whatever you're thinking, it won't work. You're limited to the five hundred dollars a week. Spend any more than that, you might as well blow your own brains out." Nathan looked at him as if he'd forgotten Walter was there, seeing him for the first time. Fear was written all over his face. It seemed to envelop him, seizing control of his entire body. He trembled, which was all that kept him from collapsing on the floor. Could Nathan Stein—not a man like Nathan Stein, but Stein himself—could he survive the fall? Pu Yi came to mind. Walter had seen the movie *The Last Emperor*. The story of a man whose past haunted his future, whose personal history forced his life in a direction beyond his control, fascinated him. He studied the boy-king, the last emperor of China. Born in 1906, an Emperor at age three, deposed and restored, used and manipulated, Pu Yi lived in unparalleled grandeur, in splendid isolation—literally in the Forbidden City—an absolute monarch, served at his whimsy. After World War II, he spent six years in the Soviet Union living under a rather luxurious house arrest. However, in 1950 he was returned to China and imprisoned for nine years at hard labor. Released in 1959, Pu Yi spent the rest of his days working as a gardener at the Institute of Botany. He married a member of the Chinese Communist Party and died in obscurity in 1967. What sort of man could endure that? Nathan Stein? For a moment Walter felt sorry for the little sack of shit—for a moment. "I'd rather be dead," Stein was mumbling.

Maloney turned toward Walter. He looked almost happy. It was a look Walter hadn't seen since Vietnam, a battlefield euphoria that affected some men just before they died. But they were in the penthouse of the Waldorf Astoria, not the jungles of Southeast Asia. Maloney was alive and kicking, not about to die, and Walter knew it. He had something up his sleeve. Walter couldn't see it, but he knew it was there.

FIFTY-SIX

Atlanta

IN 1968 RALPH NADER assembled a team of dedicated, intelligent, and vigorous young people with an aim to investigate the Federal Trade Commission. These were true believers, children come of age in the sixties. They believed their government could be made answerable to the informed will of the people. They believed disclosure of wrongdoing and malfeasance would mean an end to both. It was a time when such things could be believed. Three years earlier he came to prominence with a book called *Unsafe At Any Speed*, detailing the deadly deficiencies of the Chevrolet Corvair. Corporate colossus General Motors fought back, thinking they could manhandle Nader, push him around, discredit him, consign him to the margins reserved for civic-minded nutcases. He sued, and funded his consumer-based operations with the GM money he won. So it was that America's largest corporation unwillingly financed the start of the most effective consumer movement in the history of the United States. A year later, in the summer of 1969, Nader's group was so well known that more than thirty thousand people applied for two hundred unpaid internships. William Greider, a columnist at the *Washington Post,* tagged them "Nader's Raiders."

Isobel saw the parallels between Nader and The Center for Consumer Concerns. Certainly they shared a rather unique funding source—the very corporations they sought to expose and change. She hoped her newly constituted organization would be the equal of Nader's in its formative years. That was a lofty goal she set. And she was equally determined that The Center not lose focus like Nader had. In 1971 he officially founded Public Citizen as a permanent organization, and in time it drifted into mediocrity and loss of influence mainly because it attracted a staff of poorly-paid nonprofit careerists whose internal politics closely resembled academia. Isobel had something to get her started that Ralph Nader never had—an enormous amount of money. She was determined to use it to build a staff of lawyers, analysts, researchers, investigators, and administrators who would be paid as much as the very best in their field might earn in the private sector.

As part of her plan, The Center would have the equivalent of a major industry marketing department, complete with writers, media people, and specialists in promotion and public relations. The work of The Center would be delivered to the public as effectively as if they were in the beer or automobile business. She knew influence would come with public acceptance. She also knew acceptance was as much the result of advertising and promotion as was brand preference and market share for laundry detergent or soft drinks.

For Isobel, just as the *New York Times* was regarded as the country's newspaper of record, she wanted The Center for Consumer Concerns to build a social position of equal weight. Nick Stevenson told her she had carte blanche. The trustees were there mainly to handle the legalities of forming and operating The Center. She started February 1st and they told her The Center would pull in about thirty million in its first thirty days. Another thirty million would follow in the weeks after that. Of course, she already knew that. She would be responsible for setting policy guidelines for delivery of the remaining pledges, within the framework of the three and four year time limits. She would work directly with the contributors themselves. With those as her only instructions, The Center leased office space near Colony Square in midtown Atlanta, and she got started.

It took only two weeks for Nathan Stein to call Nick Stevenson. He was prepared to transfer $29,910,000 to The Center for Consumer Concerns. Nick provided the routing numbers and other information needed to complete such an electronic deposit.

"We're so pleased with your generous support," Nick said. "All of us at The Center are grateful. Exactly how would you like this contribution attributed, Mr. Stein?" Nathan broke it down for him, listing amounts for himself, Thomas Maloney, the Stein, Gelb firm, Alliance Industries Inc., and SHI Inc. When he was done, Nick was once more effusive with his thanks.

Nathan said, "Are we supposed to play this game all the time, or what?"

"I'm afraid I don't understand you, Mr. Stein," said Nick.

"You don't, huh? You're Leonard Martin's partner, aren't you?"

"Former partner."

"Oh, go fuck yourself. The money's on its way." He hung up.

Walter called from the airport. "Good afternoon, The Center for Consumer Concerns," said a friendly voice with a delightful southern accent.

"Good afternoon to you too, but I think it's still morning, isn't it?"

"Why, no sir. It is truly afternoon. Twenty minutes after twelve noon." By the sound of her voice Walter could tell she was smiling.

"You know, you're right," he said, realizing where he was. "I just got off a plane from Chicago and I'm still on Central time."

"Well, welcome to Atlanta and the Eastern time zone."

"Thanks. Can I speak with Isobel Gitlin, please?"

"I'll put you right through."

"Very nice," thought Walter, "no 'whose calling' or 'what company are you with' or, the most hated of all demands, 'may I tell her what this is in reference to?'"

"Hello," said Isobel.

"Hello."

"Walter! Where are you?" He told her he was at the airport, changing planes in Atlanta on his way home. His flight to St. Thomas didn't leave until five fifteen. Could they meet for lunch somewhere?

"You want real food, or bar food?"

"Bar food is fine with me," he said.

"Good," she said. "Me too." Isobel gave him directions to Manuel's Bar on Highland Avenue. "Tell the cab driver to get off at the Presidential Parkway, otherwise you'll end up in Chattanooga. It's a great bar. You'll love it." The cab ride, she told him, won't be more than twenty minutes. "I'll be there, waiting."

Isobel was right. Less than a half hour later Walter saw her standing in front of Manuel's. He reached out to hug her and she kissed him just the way she had at the Hilton on Sixth Avenue. Once inside, Walter could see that the founder, Manuel Maloof, was something of a local personality. A large painting of Manuel hung over the bar. The walls were covered with old photographs, nearly all of them showing Manuel with some entertainer, politician, or sports celebrity. Walter recognized many of them, and those he didn't know looked just like the ones he did. Jimmy Carter was there. Bill Clinton with dark hair and Bill Clinton with gray hair. Andrew Young. Hank Aaron, Frank

Sinatra, and Carol Channing. There was one with LBJ and another that looked like young Manuel and a young Elvis Presley.

"This guy, Manuel, still alive?"

"I don't think so," she said. "I'm still new here."

They sat at a table in the front room just off the bar, the nonsmoking section of what Walter agreed looked like a terrific neighborhood establishment.

"You live nearby?" he asked.

"Not too far. I'm in a condo until I get myself settled. I think I'm going to buy a house in a neighborhood called Inman Park." Walter never did well at these kinds of conversations. He had no idea where or what Inman Park was, and, except for the fact that Isobel might buy a house there, no interest in finding out or being told. They started going through all the uncomfortable questions with all the meaningless answers. She asked where he was coming from? Did he have a good flight? Was he happy to be getting back to St. John? How was his health? Was he hungry? He asked if she liked Atlanta. Where the Center's offices were? Was the weather more enjoyable than the winter in New York? All the crap, and it continued even after their food arrived. Finally, he said, "Isobel, no more bullshit. This is going to drive me fucking nuts. How are you? Really?"

"Fine. I'm f-fine." It wasn't what he was looking for. Her eyes had no sparkle, her smile, such as it was, lacked the warmth he'd come to treasure, and her manner made no offer of intimacy. He reached out across the table to hold her hand.

"Is there someplace we can go. I don't have to be back at the airport—"

"No. No, I can't. I've got to get back to the office."

"What for?"

"This is a real job, Walter. I'm not running around chasing Leonard Martin anymore. And I'm not ducking photographers from the *Post* or the *Daily News*. No one in Atlanta knows who I am. Isn't that wonderful?" The food ran out before the small talk.

"I should be home by ten," he said. "I'll call you tonight."

"You don't have to do that. I'm not even sure—"

"When are you coming to St. John?" Walter asked. Now it was Isobel who leaned across the table to take Walter's hand. They sat beneath a photo of a middle-aged Manuel and two other men of the same age. All three stood next to Arnold Palmer. They were smiling. Arnold was young, in his prime, lean and fit, had dark hair, and a cigarette in one hand.

Isobel said, "Walter, don't go getting serious on me, alright? It was great, wonderful—I love you dearly—but we each have things we need to do. Don't we? Places to go. People to meet. We'll see each other again. We will." Her smile was breaking his heart.

"It's just, I thought—"

"Don't. Please don't."

"I love you, Isobel."

"Oh, Walter, you don't. No, you don't. You think you do, but you don't. It's been a long time for you. I know. But you have a life, Walter. We both do. We'll always be friends and we will see each other again. We will. I promise."

"Isobel—"

"Walter, Walter. Please don't. Don't be hurt. I never wanted to hurt you."

She was young and he was not. He was experienced, so experienced, and she was not. What was it about her? Time had not dulled all his senses. He'd missed some things, sure, but you always missed some things. You never got it all right. Why had it taken him this long? Why didn't he want to know? The pain. The pain. It came to him now. It came to him the way it always had, the way it had in Vietnam and Laos and ever since. The unease he sensed when she called him the night she met with Leonard—the feeling that something was missing when he read her article—the shock that went through him when Debra Melissa described the cowboy. It all came to him now like the floodgates had been thrown wide open. He looked at Isobel. Her eyes begged him to be silent, but he said it anyway. "You saw him, didn't you? You knew all along."

"Walter—"

"No," he said, looking away, waving her off.

He finished his drink. Isobel didn't touch her ice tea. The moment passed, although both knew the memory would last forever. She offered to drive him to the airport, but he said he'd catch a cab. He kissed her on the forehead when they said goodbye. His lips lingered a moment—too long? The scent of her hair caused him to close his eyes. He could tell it was an uncomfortable parting for Isobel. On the plane, he tried to convince himself she meant it when she said, "We will see each other again. We will." Didn't he know her? Couldn't he tell how she felt? Nor could he keep Leonard Martin at bay. He saw the fat, suburban attorney, disheveled and depressed. He saw the lean, trim Michael DelGrazo. He saw the cowboy in Clarksville—saw him in his own cabin. And Isobel knew from the beginning. He had opened the iron gate to his soul and let her in. Knowingly. He had shared with her things he had never shared with anyone. Purposely. He had kept no secrets from her. Gladly. He had loved her not at first sight. She was different, special. He earned this one. He had given himself to her. Completely. And she betrayed him. How had he missed it? There were so many things lately he failed to see, none more painful or more humiliating than this.

He fell asleep in first class, frightened he might never again run his hand across her bare hips, down her legs, across her knees; never again wake her in the morning, kissing her nipples, watching as she opened her eyes, smiling. In his dream he chased her across an open field. She climbed a flight of marble steps outside a large building, a building with no doors. He struggled to reach her as she stood atop the stairway. He climbed as fast as he could, yet made no progress, got no closer. He had trouble breathing. Then, finally, he was within reach of the top. Just as he was about to touch her, she stepped back out of sight. He crawled the last few steps, then, gasping, he looked up to see the Indian woman, smiling, offering him a pendant. And there was Leonard Martin. Behind him stood a young Vietnamese mother desperately clutching her two children. All three wept. Leonard had a rifle in his hands. He lifted the gun, shifting its weight against his shoulder, and pointed it at him. Isobel was nowhere to be seen. Leonard squeezed the trigger. Walter woke up trembling.

FIFTY-SEVEN

New York

Tom Maloney walked in the back door. It was an entrance he'd been shown months ago, when the idea of retaining Walter Sherman first came to mind. At the time he considered it no more than another skill available on the open market. True, the market he spoke of wasn't quite that open, and this particular skill was available only for a handsome price. Nevertheless, Maloney believed that if it existed, it was for sale. "If I want it—it's mine." Anything that was for sale could be his. Price was never a factor. How many kings had he ransomed in his day? What he'd acquired was indeed exceptional. "Crack and hack," it was called. Get in. Get the code. That's it. Simple? Sure, but close to impossible. Once you beat it, however, it's over. No one and no place was immune, not even the Caymans. Besides, he'd used it before. He thought it was strange that he'd been inside twice already, once just to read it, and a second time he actually put something in. He'd not taken anything out. Now he was about to use this technology, this mechanism, this mumbo-jumbo magic for the purpose it had been invented. When the message appeared on his computer screen, he didn't believe it. The chill that ran the full length of his body could have frozen hell. He'd gone to cash his lottery ticket and it was nowhere to be found. He lost it. He looked at the keystroke instructions. Letter by letter he read them half out loud. He canceled out his connection and started all over again from the very beginning. He was not far from turning the computer off and restarting it. He was like a man searching his sock drawer, frantically tearing apart the pockets of a coat he hadn't worn in years, desperately looking for his missing car keys. He knew they weren't there, but he couldn't help himself. The correct home page appeared. He typed his code in the special box, watching the letters and numbers as he pushed them down. They showed up as asterisks on his screen, and so, for no reason at all, he deleted them and did it again. One by one he pushed down on the computer keys until each one could go no farther. Of course the code had been correct the first time. He knew that, but he was no longer in control. Things were speeding up. His heart rate and respiration soared. He struggled to keep his thoughts straight. He began to sweat. He felt sick, lightheaded, about to throw up. The message popped up again: Account Closed.

FIFTY-EIGHT

St. John

February is high season. The Caribbean sun blazes from early morning until early evening. For those on the beaches, a sunblock with a number at least as high as thirty is recommended. Lean and pretty young girls in skimpy bikinis, and not a few middle-aged, fat guys in Speedos, seem to be everywhere. Even the rain, which comes down in short, sudden outbursts in the late afternoon, makes the tourists glad they're not in New England or the Midwest. "We're not in Kansas anymore," has been heard more than once on the streets of Cruz Bay. The island is as packed as it ever gets. In addition to the bushwhackers, day-trippers from St. Thomas crowd the shops and bars near the dock in Cruz Bay. St. John's taxis, pickup trucks with rigged canopies and benches for their riders, drive load after load from the dock to the beaches. The ragged, narrow streets are jammed, and every so often someone from Ohio or Iowa or someplace like that drives the wrong way on a one-way street. Traffic gets snarled, tempers frayed. New Yorkers in new shorts and pastel shirts show their true colors. All the island's restaurants are full, and for many, getting a table at lunchtime is almost impossible. Later in the evening, when the last ferry has taken the final load back to the rock, things get a little quieter. The best places still manage to turn their tables twice for dinner. A reservation is a necessity. February is a tough time for the locals. Even at Billy's, some days go by without Ike or Walter making an appearance.

"There's two kind of locals," Ike once said. "February and March." He wasn't talking about himself, about the *real* locals—those who've been on St. John for generations, the blacks born and raised there. He meant the newcomers. He was talking about people like Walter and Billy, and whatshisname, the pop singer living on his boat out in the harbor, and all the others who left their roots on the mainland to take up the island life. There were those who came for the lifestyle, flat broke or loaded with all the money they needed, and there were those on the run looking for a place to stop. These were the February people, according to Ike. They could be found eating lunch or dinner at Billy's alongside the tourists and visitors. Or they might be the ones waiting tables, crewing the charter boats, hanging out on the beach, living on the cheap. Walter was not a February person. "Never was," said Ike. He was a March person. He tolerated high season, taking comfort in the certainty that it would end, the crowds would lessen, if not leave altogether, and life would return to normal.

Walter came back from Atlanta and stayed home. It took Clara no time at all to see what happened. She wouldn't be seeing that girl Isobel around here anymore. She did what she could to care for him, but Clara had no medicine for Walter's blues. He moped. He sulked. He sat alone on the patio until all hours of the night. He didn't talk much. Clara told her sister. Her sister told her friends. They told theirs. Before long everyone knew. It's a small island, and they do know everything.

To make matters worse, Walter had that CD Clara had heard a million times, *The Best of the Cadillacs.* It was a rare day she enjoyed listening to that one. He played that one song, "Gloria," too many times to Clara's way of thinking. It was hopeless, she concluded. How could he miss both of them? At the same time? Poor man. His sadness was not a pretty sight. She figured he had to hit the bottom of lonely before he could pick himself up. She prayed it wouldn't take him long. Ten days into his depression, Clara said she needed to see a sick friend. "I'll be gone all day," she said. She gave Walter a list of groceries and household items and asked him to pick them up in Cruz Bay. "I can't be making you lunch either," she said. "I won't be here. You should stop at Billy's, get something to eat, and see your friends." She said she'd be back by eight o'clock to make him a late dinner.

Billy's was so crowded Walter almost decided to turn around and go someplace else. When Billy saw him he hurried to the end of the bar, moved the last two patrons out, and signaled to Walter his regular place was available. Both seats.

"Thanks Billy," he said.

"Anytime. Anytime, Walter. You doing alright?"

"Great. Fine."

"Hungry? You want something?"

Walter shrugged. Billy didn't budge. "A sandwich," Walter said. "Anything at all will do."

Billy said, "Coming up." He opened a bottle of Diet Coke, placed it on a coaster in front of Walter, and walked back into the kitchen.

Walter heard the familiar footsteps even in the noisy bar. It was a skill he developed early on. Perhaps it was a talent, something you had or you didn't. He was never sure. When you're following someone you can't always count on being able to see them or look directly at them. Learning to recognize someone by the sound of their footsteps had helped him many times and saved him on more than one occasion. He knew a blind man who said he could hear a friend coming a block away. He wished he were that good. Without looking up, he said, "Sit down, Tom." Maloney sat on the same barstool he used when they first met, the one next to the fan at the very end of the bar, near the kitchen. Walter looked at him. This time Maloney was comfortably dressed. He wore white pants, a cream-colored, loose-fitting golf shirt, and sandals on his bare feet. His cheeks and forehead were red. "He's been here at least a few days," thought Walter. Probably looked for him in Billy's everyday. Walter's elbows rested on the bar. He opened both hands and moved his arms out as wide as his elbows would allow. Without saying it, the look on his face asked, "Why? Why are you here? What do you want?"

Maloney's rigid shoulders made him appear as if he had no neck at all. His tight-jawed anger allowed him to speak only through clenched teeth. He said, "Where is it?" Walter said nothing. "It's gone, isn't it?" Maloney asked. "Where'd you put it? Where is it! It's mine, goddamnit!"

"Easy, big guy. Remember where you are. Show respect if you want to get some."

Tom Maloney may have dressed more comfortably than the last time he was on St. John, but he was definitely agitated. He tapped his feet and licked his lips. Walter sized up his loose-fitting outfit, looking to see if it was possible he might be carrying a weapon. A man with a big gut has a hard time concealing a gun in his waistband. Maloney was unarmed. He was just angry.

"What's the problem, Tom? What are you doing here?"

"The money. The account's closed."

"My account?" He looked at Tom Maloney with contempt. "You're surprised? What kind of a fool do you take me for? You gave me my exact balance the day we met, remember? When Pitts gave me the briefcase, I realized you didn't want my money, so I wasn't worried. Then you deposited quite a lot of money in my account, again getting access without me knowing about it. That's twice." Walter looked at him like a stern uncle might a recalcitrant nephew. Billy brought Walter's sandwich. He recognized Maloney too and spoke right up.

"Anything else you want, Walter? You need anything, I'm right here." Billy glared directly at Tom Maloney, then walked away.

"Lots of people do something once," Walter said. "Something they shouldn't. Once is not nice, but understandable. However, anybody who does something twice is telling you something. I can be fooled, but I'm not a fool. There'll be no third time."

He took a big bite of his sandwich. Obviously he couldn't keep talking with his mouth full. Maloney had already said everything he had to say: "Where's the money!" Walter swallowed and tried to remove a piece of ham stuck between his teeth with his tongue. "You shouldn't have hired Wilkes," he said.

Maloney had either forgotten Wilkes or had no interest in him. He was single-minded. "Where is my money!" he demanded.

"I thought by now most of it would already be earning interest for The Center for Consumer Concerns. Yours and Nathan's. You sent it, didn't you?"

"Look, you sonofabitch! Where's my fucking money? Not the money I had to turn over to that thieving murderer. Do you know what's happened to me?" A nervous, perhaps even dangerous, laugh overcame Tom Maloney. He was shaking. "I owe money. Me! I owe money!" He struggled to gain control. He stopped laughing. "Where's my money! Thirty million dollars. Thirty million no one could touch. Not yours! Mine!"

Walter was not a man to be called a sonofabitch, especially on his home turf. A warning was written all over his face. Maloney could not have missed it.

"Remember what I told you about Leonard Martin, Tom? Remember I said I was certain I would never see or hear from him again?"

Maloney gave him an angry nod. "You won't see him either, Tom. Everything has a price, right? Even life—your life. Pay up and live. Stiff him and you're dead. You talk about *your* thirty million. A little extra stashed away. You don't *have* thirty million. You *had* thirty million."

"You took that money. I want my money's worth. You find him again and you kill him. Get my money back from those sonsofbitches in Atlanta. Then it's your thirty million. Until he's dead you have my money. Do you understand me?"

Walter laughed. "Doesn't sound like my kind of work," he said. Maloney was beside himself. He raised his right hand, trembling, fist tightly clenched. Walter didn't budge.

"You threatening me, Tom? You just found a way to stay alive—complements of Leonard Martin. Don't push your luck. You don't need me to kill anyone. Not anymore. No one wants to kill you. The rules have changed. I want you to listen to me, Tom, carefully." Now Walter spoke to him softly, just as he had done once before. This time the message was different. "Fuck with me, *I'll* kill you. What I told you about Isobel Gitlin, that goes double for me. I even *smell* one of your goons, you'll wish you were dead already. Remember Na Trang? I'm no Leonard Martin. You'll never get off my hook. I'll cut your throat and watch you die slowly. The last thing you'll see is me cleaning my knife." Walter calmly picked up his sandwich and took another bite, followed by a long drink of his Diet Coke.

If Maloney was searching for any sign of nerves, he had the wrong guy. Walter Sherman was the last person Tom Maloney could intimidate. Maloney was crazed, but not crazy. He feared Walter Sherman more than any other man—Leonard Martin included. He knew he was right to do so. Walter could see him cooling down. He looked like a boiling kettle turned to a lower heat, its whistle reduced to a whimper. He was still hot, but no longer running out of control. And he had the look of a man definitely thirty million dollars poorer.

Walter said, "Now get the fuck off my island." Tom Maloney got up and walked out. In the mirror behind the bar, Walter watched him walk all the way out. Billy, a look of fierce determination and readiness on his face, pointed to Walter, his index finger definitely meant to be a gun—a sign of absolute support. Walter smiled at the bartender, thinking, "I wouldn't want to have William Mantkowski as my enemy."

The thirty million dollars Tom Maloney had sent to Walter's account in the Caymans was now sitting in another bank in Cyprus, in transit, on its way to its final destination.

FIFTY-NINE

St. John

THE NEWS ABOUT ISOBEL Gitlin and The Center for Consumer Concerns began to spread after the joint press conference for Alliance Industries and Stein, Gelb, Hector & Wills. Alliance announced their plan to absorb SHI Inc. using a stock switch plan effectuated by Stein, Gelb. Then they shocked the attending press, almost all of whom covered the business or financial beat, when they admitted to culpability in the E. coli disaster more than three years earlier and announced their intention to contribute close to six billion dollars to a new foundation, The Center for Consumer Concerns. They were confident the money would be approved by their directors and shareholders. No specific schedule had been worked out with The Center, but Alliance and Stein, Gelb promised to fully fund their pledge within four years. No one in the room, except for a hulking mass of a man standing in the back, known to a few people there as the Moose, had ever heard of The Center for Consumer Concerns. Questions came furiously. A silence, a pause punctuated by an audible gasp, greeted the news that

The Center's executive director was Isobel Gitlin. A murmur that could not be stifled followed the announcement that Nicholas Stevenson and Harvey Daniels served as the foundation's trustees. Before the press conference restored order, Mel Gold left to return to the *Times*. In a heated editorial meeting later that afternoon, he succeeded in having the morning edition of the *Times* refer to Isobel only as "a former obituary writer for the *New York Times*." He knew she'd be happy with that.

The normal news cycle—especially for the television networks and cable channels—is twenty-four hours. In a day, Isobel Gitlin was old news. Two days after the press conference no one was talking about her or The Center. Alliance Industries, and to a lesser extent Stein, Gelb, had become the darlings of the left. "Corporate Conscience—At Last!" cried *The Nation*. Even the libertarian Cato Institute praised the move proclaiming self-awareness and self-examination the best path toward curbing corporate abuse. Then, of course, they questioned whether such abuse existed or not. The stir in Atlanta lasted a little longer. It was a good local story. Still, by the weekend few were talking about it anymore. Isobel went about her daily life in pleasurable obscurity. In stores, supermarkets, and in the malls, the only stares she got were those always waiting for attractive young women.

Back home, Walter's mood improved slowly, if at all. The walls had fallen, the doors were cracked open. His vulnerability had been an open sore. He called upon more than a half century of resources to repair the damage. He went back to eating breakfast in Billy's. The company of his friends was a gift not to be taken lightly, but he'd been hurt and they knew it.

"Walter, you know that song—you know, that one—it goes," and Ike loosed his tortured falsetto on Billy's sparse morning crowd. "I found lo-ove on a two-way-y street and lost it on a lon-le-y high-i-way."

"Very nice," Billy said from behind the bar. "You want them all to leave?"

"Yeah, I know it," Walter said. "I can even recognize it when you sing it."

"Well, that's what I mean," Ike said, the smoke from whatever it was hanging from his lower lip blanketing his face.

"So what?" Walter said.

"The thing is, you found love on a lonely highway and lost it on a two-way street. That's ass-backward, ain't it?"

Walter said nothing. He drank his usual drink and frowned at Ike.

"Forget about it," said Billy, turning away from Ike, mumbling something else.

"No, no," Ike said. "Don't you never forgetaboutit." His attempt to imitate Billy was laughable. Billy and Walter smiled at each other. Ike continued, "Keep going, Walter. You'll find it. Damn if you don't find everything else."

Walter offered no reply. He had nothing to say. The song in his mind was "Looking For Love In All The Wrong Places." God, I hate country music, he thought.

Isobel flipped off the cell phone. She dropped the instrument on her kitchen table, right into the pile of real estate brochures. She covered her smiling face with both hands, almost laughing out loud. She should have known. Of course, she should have known. The bank had just called. They said a bank representing an anonymous donor called requesting wire instructions for a contribution to the Center. A few minutes later a bank in Cyprus made The Center for Consumer Concerns richer by thirty million dollars. "Oh, m-my," she said. "Walter, Walter, Walter."

EPILOGUE

St. John

"You got three," said Ike, blowing the usual amount of smoke away from Billy out toward where the Poet slept in the square. "Brando, Newman, and Dean. What's more to say? Ain't three better. Ain't three as good." He looked to Billy, standing where he always did, behind the bar, halfway between himself and Walter. Billy mumbled something as he wiped the already spotless counter. "What?" said Ike.

"Tinkers, Evers, and Chance," Billy said, this time loud enough to be heard. "There's three for you."

"Who the hell they?"

"Come on, old man. You're losing it. Tinkers to Evers to Chance."

"Un huh," said Ike, the same way his doctor often did after putting down his stethoscope.

"Chicago Cubs infield," Billy went on. "Best double play combination there ever was."

Ike said, "Oh, yeah. Now I hear you. Couldn't make out what you said. I heard of them. That was when only white boys played, so we'll never know how good they were, will we? Easy to turn a double play on a white boy. Can't run fast enough."

"Ahh," said Billy, waving his bar rag at the old man.

"Brando, Newman, and Dean," said Ike again. "And they all white. I am no prejudiced man. I recognize talent."

Billy said, "Walter, you got three for us?"

"Three what?"

"Three anything. Three better than Bran—"

"I heard him," Walter said. "You too. I'll go with the three ghosts."

Billy dropped his bar rag on the floor. "The Father, Son, and the Holy—"

"No, Billy. That's only one ghost, if I remember correctly."

"I think you're right, Walter," Ike said. "Only one."

Walter said, "The three ghosts. The ghost of Christmas past. The ghost of Christmas present. And the ghost of Christmas future."

"The past, the present, and the future," said Ike. "That's good. That's very good. I'll take the past, if you don't mind. I surely will."

"I'll take the present," said Billy, who feared the future and dreaded the past. "That leaves you with the future, Walter."

"It most surely does," said Ike. "You up to it?"

"The future," said Walter, raising his drink in the air. "Gentlemen, here's to the future."

Billy went to write it up.

THE END

ACKNOWLEDGMENTS

Leonard Martin's loss reminds us all that without family we have nothing. Everything I am I owe to my wife, Maria, my daughters, Jenny, Barbi, and April, and my son, Ben. How they put up with me is an ongoing mystery.

I want to thank the novelist Jeffrey Marlin, my friend through six decades, for his help in the earliest days, when I began writing *The Knowland Retribution*. I see his creative contribution again and again on pages from the first stages of this project.

I also want to thank those who were kind enough to read some or all of *The Knowland Retribution* and offer me support, criticism, and suggestions. Most noteworthy among them is Barbara Ross, who gave me wonderful ideas even though I'm sure she is still mad that I didn't make some things turn out the way she wanted. Thanks also go to Bob Marrow, Annie Korzen, Bill Swanger, Mike Lureman, Abigail McGrath, Marcelle Harrison, and my dear friends Andy and Laurel.

Finally, I am forever grateful to my agent, Julia Lord, without whom there would be no acknowledgments.

Read on for an excerpt from the
next Locator Mystery by Richard Greener

The Lacey Confession

Coming soon from Midnight Ink

November 22, 1963

The Czech—the one who had made himself known in America as Stephen Hecht—was a tall, thin man with a sallow complexion that, because of his high cheek bones, made him look rather sickly. On top of that, he rarely smiled. He brought the rifle with him. He carried it in a small bag, in pieces. He was recommended not only for his expertise, but for his attention to detail. It was a certainty that many times he had put the weapon together in just a few seconds, each piece clicking neatly and swiftly into place. With only minutes remaining before the motorcade would enter the street below, he sent his new friend away. He said, "I know you are hungry. Go down and get something to eat. It's okay, I'll stay here."

"Do you want me to bring back anything for you?" the other man responded.

"No, Lee. Thank you. Just go now."

Alone, the man whose name was not Hecht at all, but whose real name was Josef Gambrinus, calmly assembled the rifle, loaded it, and placed it on the floor under the open window, the one he had chosen carefully the day before. He stacked three shipping boxes—boxes once filled with textbooks but now empty—one on top of the other, and maneuvered them into position between the open window and the door leading onto the sixth floor. He meant to hide sight of the rifle from anyone who might happen to pass by. The noise of the crowd gathering below filtered up to him. He hoped the murmur of anticipation, followed by the expectant cheers, would erupt at the proper moment. The Czech would have liked it as loud as possible, but he realized, as he knew he must, that there are some things beyond our control. It was not realistic to expect every detail to fall exactly into place. They rarely did. Nevertheless, he was ready. And he waited.

The middle-aged man from Amman, short and stocky, always looked like he needed a shave. He called himself Namdar, but his real name was unknown to anyone outside Jordan. Not even his European associate knew—especially him. Namdar assumed, quite correctly, that Stephen Hecht was also a made-up name. As the sound of the crowd grew louder, Namdar passed along the rail tracks and approached a location on the fence. He too had chosen this spot the day before, just after learning the altered route the motorcade would take. Had anyone seen him, they would have taken him for a railroad worker or perhaps the sort of man Americans called a hobo, men so commonly seen in rail yards and along the tracks. He was dressed in old, gray, shabby clothes, and carried with him a long, thin, beat-up cardboard box. Inside the box was a rifle, exactly like the one now resting at the ready beneath the window on the sixth floor of the building across the street, down past the embankment lined with spectators, beyond the gentle bend in the road separating him from his associate; a spot he was certain would slow the speed of the car, making his task a simple one. Like the Czech had done, the Jordanian assembled the contents of his box quickly, then he held the loaded weapon against his leg, hidden under his long coat, and he too waited.

There was a third man, another eastern European, waiting on the curb just where the street began its slow turn toward the upcoming highway underpass. Although he was the third member of a team, Daniel Ondnok was unknown to his teammates. Neither his compatriot on the sixth floor nor his Jordanian accomplice peering down from above the grassy knoll were aware of Ondnok's presence. Unlike them, he had no rifle, yet his role in this plan might be the most dangerous and his risk the greatest. For nearly a half hour he had wandered among the crowd as they gathered in the plaza. He was a young man, clean-cut, short-haired, wearing a simple blue suit, white shirt, and a skinny, navy-blue tie. In his jacket pocket he held an Italian pistol packed with nine rounds. Unlikely as it was that the man in the window and the one behind the grassy knoll would both miss their target, if they did, the Slovakian would finish the job up close. He prayed the night before and once again standing in the plaza. If things went just as planned, he would actually do nothing, earn a great deal of money, and go on his way unseen. If, however, it went badly, he would do his job. No doubt he would be killed, but he would die certain his family would be well-provided for. He asked Jesus the son and God the father for victory and a good aim for his comrades.

When the Presidential motorcade rolled into Dealey Plaza, Lee Harvey Oswald was still eating, alone in the lunch room, nowhere near the window on the sixth floor of the Texas School Book Depository Building. He had no idea how badly the cards were stacked against him. As the President's open car approached the plaza, it slowed, just as the Jordanian knew it would. At that moment the Czech fired the first shot from the open window six floors above. The bullet struck the second son of Joseph P. Kennedy in the upper back, just below the neck.

Ripping through his chest, it exited his throat and tumbled in the air at more than five hundred miles per hour, smashing into the Governor of Texas who was riding in the front seat. Startled by the sound, Governor Connelly had quickly turned around to look behind him. The bullet hit his wrist. Kennedy was already in shock. Instinctively, he tried to raise his hands to his face. His upper body tipped forward, propelled by the force of the bullet's blow to his back.

The assassin Gambrinus had shot many people—men, women, even children—so he knew the hit was not fatal. In the quickest fraction of a second, angry with himself and thoroughly dissatisfied with the accuracy of his weapon, he squeezed off a second shot. It missed everything. Harmlessly, the bullet struck a road sign, then careened against a curb and rolled to a stop nearly all the way to the highway underpass, where it would be found later. In the instant following the second shot, the President's driver realized they were under attack. He pushed down hard on the accelerator. Trees now blocked the shooter's view. There was no chance a third shot from the sixth-floor window could accomplish anything. He had failed. "Shit!" he mumbled in his native tongue. Nevertheless, acting as he had been instructed to, he wiped the rifle clean of his fingerprints, laid it down, and left the building. Following his escape route he would drive a 1959 model Chevrolet, by himself, to Vancouver, British Columbia. He made his report along the way. A week later he flew to Japan, changed planes in Tokyo, and then went on to Rome. While using the restroom at the airport in Rome, he was assaulted by three knife-wielding teenagers. After taking his wallet and passport, the young thieves cut his throat. Josef Gambrinus bled to death in a toilet stall.

Even before the Czech's first shot, the Jordanian had the President of the United States directly in his scope. As the first shot hit the President from behind, Namdar pulled the trigger and let loose the bullet that killed John F. Kennedy. The shot struck straight into his head. It drove him backward, tearing a piece from his skull, scattering portions of his brain on the back of the limousine, on the seat next to him, and on his frightened wife.

Less than ten seconds later, Namdar had dismantled the rifle, loaded it back into his box, and was gone. According to plan, he drove his 1962 Buick slowly to Los Angeles. He made many stops along the way, leaving pieces of his weapon scattered, many miles apart, in the desert and sagebrush from west Texas to California. He made his report before staying with friends in Los Angeles, people who knew nothing of his activities. For six weeks he waited, celebrating the coming of the new year 1964 before flying to Montreal and then on to Athens. As prearranged, he booked passage on a ship from Greece to Egypt. Finally, in the first week of February, he made it home to his well-earned, comfortable retirement. His most lucrative job would also be his last. Two weeks later, on a busy street in Amman, he was hit by a truck and killed. All who saw it said it was an unfortunate accident. Witnesses, people who waited with him on the sidewalk at the intersection, said he seemed to jump in front of the truck. No one noticed or remembered the man who pushed Namdar from behind.

The third man, Ondnok, had watched it all, only a few yards away from the target. He heard all three shots. Of course, he enjoyed the advantage of knowing when they would come. The panic of the crowd did not disturb him. He too had seen many men shot with a high-powered rifle. The blow that struck the American President in the skull had clearly done the job. As the limousine sped away, Ondnok turned and walked in the other direction. He never drew his pistol. He never did anything. He knew a dead man when he saw one. His prayers had been answered.

He earned more money on November 22, 1963 than for any job he ever did. And he did nothing. His risk had more than justified his price. Like the others, he followed his prearranged escape plan. He met a small private plane at an airport south of Dallas. Posing as a West German businessman, an anti-Communist looking to buy arms for his Eastern brothers, he had chartered the plane two days earlier. His destination was New Orleans. Once there, he made his report. After three days and three memorable nights in the French Quarter, he took a commercial flight to Mexico City. There he made a connection to Havana before finally returning to his family in a small farming village in Slovakia.

Less than a month later, the day before Christmas 1963, to be exact, the barn in which he was working burned to the ground. Trapped, unable to escape, he perished in the blaze. To save his family added grief, no autopsy on the charred remains was performed. The small bullet hole in the back of the farmer's head was never discovered.

Two days after the assassination, as contracted for, Lee Harvey Oswald was shot dead. His shouted pronouncement to the press, his plea of innocence, was soon forgotten. As he was gunned down, Oswald was surrounded by Dallas police officers. He was still inside Dallas Police Headquarters, handcuffed and in custody, when it happened. A man simply walked up to Oswald with a drawn handgun and fired point-blank at his midsection. The whole world saw it live on television.

The men's room killing in Rome was local news for a day or two. The accident in Amman was not even reported. The tragedy in Slovakia also went unnoticed by the world at large. It was, however, the final detail. Within ninety days of the death of John F. Kennedy, the men who did the deed, as well as the man who stood falsely accused, were all dead themselves. Their killers had been retained professionally. They had no knowledge of who their victims were or what they might have done. Why they had been hired to kill someone, in a restroom, on a busy street, or in a rural barn, would have been an impolite question. They knew only how much they were to be paid. Only one person, the man responsible for all this, knew the truth. Only Frederick Lacey knew. He wrote extensively, passionately, angrily, about it in his private journal: The Lacey Confession.

ABOUT THE AUTHOR

Born and raised in New York City, Richard Greener studied American history, international relations, and law. He is a retired broadcast industry executive, and currently resides in Georgia with his wife of thirty-eight years.